The Sleepy Hollow Incident

Book Four

PD Alleva

Chamber Door Publishing, LLC

DISCLAIMER: This is a work of fiction. Unless otherwise indicated, all the names, characters, businesses, places, events and incidents in this book are either a product of the author's imagination or used in a fictitious manner. Any resemblance to actual persons, living or dead, or actual events is purely coincidental.

Chamber Door Publishing
Delray Beach, Fl

ISBN(s):
eBook: 979-8-9938039-5-1
Paperback: 979-8-9938039-6-8
Hardback: 979-8-9938039-7-5

Cover: Cherie Foxley
Editor: Chamber Door Publishing
Interior design: Chamber Door Publishing

Printed in the USA

"Love is not a victory march.

It's a cold and it's a broken Hallelujah."

Leonard Cohen (*Hallelujah*)

Part VII

Excerpt from *The Demon and Sleepy Hollow* by the Original Knickerbocker Dated 1856.

The Underground Tunnels

As I mentioned previously, the sacred ground surrounding the statue of Major John Andre is the same area where Olga's coven called home. The grounds also served as the staging point for our journey to Mr. Sam J. Curad.

The underground tunnel was discovered no less, by a boy who had been indulging in a game of hide and seek. This boy-Harold Lovelace-had hidden in a small alcove in the woods not more than fifty feet from Major John Andre's statue. It should be easy to discover, for any trained eye can identify its dark foreboding.

If you have never truly felt pure evil, you will undoubtedly understand the sensation when staring into the cavern. It begins like a whisper when traveling south from the sacred ground into the woods where the cavern is located. Like a twinge in your spine that keeps tightening with the uncanny sensation that something is wrong and to go back the way you came. But we scoff at such occurrences, don't we? Retreating to the safety of hope with a belief that all is right, reasonable, and fine. However, the closer we come to the cavern, the stronger the sensation of evil pricks the skin, raising the hairs across our arms like a warning sign of the hell that is to come.

It was in this cavern that we discovered the entrance to the underground tunnels.

There are many tunnels beneath the Hollow. Revolutionaries used them to provide supplies to our forces on the Hudson. An effort to thwart the eyes of the surrounding British Army. The tunnels are how the demon could move among us unseen. There are many entrances and exits throughout the Hollow, and we have done our best to seal them off to contain whatever evil continues to live there.

Evil is like a stain that cannot be removed. Once it stakes its claim, its essence coats the ground and the air we breathe with a noxious vibration that infects the cells and the minds of those who live within its confines. I fear that should the evil persist for too long, it shall pass from one generation to the next, strengthening with every new age. But know this, dear reader, evil's plan is to convince the people that it does not exist. We must accept the dark heart of humanity and the evil in our universe. For once we remove evil from our consciousness, evil shall have its way.

Carver woke up with a jolt. He'd fallen asleep while reading at the kitchen table. His arms were draped across the book, his head buried in it. He'd been dreaming about John Hardwood. In the dream, John was surrounded by darkness, living in a tiny room made of stone and stained with years of blood and sacrifice. The poor boy had become lost within his own mind, relegated to the simple instincts of a brutal existence.

Carver watched him in the dream, eating the raw flesh of a lamb, an offering from his captor. The boy was crouched in the corner of his cell, embedded in the thick blackness of a forever night with only the sliver of the moon to cast a shallow silvery glow. He bit into the flesh like a beast. The meat was soft and juiced with blood across his teeth when he noticed Carver was in the cell with him. John paused his chewing, assessing the detective as if he were some phantom come to claim his soul.

"John," said Carver, "I'm so sorry, John." His voice, like an echo in a cave, reverberated back to his ears.

John bit into the flesh, cautiously and slow like a child caught in shame. His beady eyes stared lost into the darkness as if some thought existed that continuously nagged at his conscience. He tore off a shred of flesh from the bone, dripping blood across his chin. Carver looked over the boy's cell, to the window where he could see the Hollow. It looked like he'd gone back in time, and in the dream, he remembered the book. 1856 is when it was written and he was certain he was seeing Sleepy Hollow as it was back then, but this was different. In the dream, the Sleepy Hollow of days past was burning. He could see houses and forests drenched in fire. He stepped to the window, his eyes wide, watching his city burn.

"It's in the soil," said John. Carver turned slowly to him. John held the bone close to his jaw. Blood stained his cheeks and lips as he stared into the dark folds of the cell. "Evil exists beneath the ground." And then he snickered. Snickered like a loon who'd lost all rational thought, wrestling with the demons in his head. "Won't be long now," he said then bit into the flesh, chomping the soft meat between his teeth then swallowing. "Nope. It won't be long at all."

Footsteps outside the cell now. The boy cringed and then cowered in the shadows in the corner. He hissed at the door.

"Come, John," said the person outside the cell. "It's time to take your medicine."

Carver was looking at the door. There was no one there, although he could hear the voice. Heard John too, whining in his throat, petrified like an abused dog. "Turn him away," whined John. "Turn, turn, turn away." Carver noticed he was wringing the bone like a dirty wet rag. "Away. Turn him away." Then his voice changed-rickety, breathy and sinister. "The ground is evil!" He shot his stare to Carver, and Carver's bones cringed. "They're going to cut off your head."

Footsteps were coming closer.

"Cut off your head. Cut off your head."

He dropped the bone and started punching his temples.

"Cut off your head. Cut off your head."

Footsteps shuffled outside the door.

"Cut off your head. Cut off your head."

The footsteps stopped, and John jumped with a jolt. He looked at Carver, his jaw grinding, his eyes wide, his nose curled in a snarl when he said, "I need hearts for the master," then jumped at Carver with a roar when Carver snapped out of his dream and awakened in his kitchen, the dream fading from conscious thought although the disturbed sensation clung to his bones and stabbed his heart.

Carver rubbed the sleep from his eyes. The kitchen was dark; day had yet to break. He looked at the clock-3:33-then flipped the light switch on the wall by the table. Nothing; the electricity was still out. His candle had gone out too. Carver snatched the lighter off the table then went to light the candle when he stopped. Something flickered in the corner of his eye. Silence. Cold, subtle quiet in the coming dawn. Thought he saw the comingling of a white wisp in the living room. Carver put the lighter on the table, listening to the subtle creaks from his house, his stomach twisted into a knot.

Again, the wisp, but now he could see it floating in his living room. Carver got up quietly, alert and oriented to the scene.

"Sheila?" he whispered.

He stepped into the living room. The wisp was near the window. Carver watched it drift and then vanish. Outside, the Hollow was draped in darkness, but even more apparent than the darkness was the fog, drifting off the ground like specters. A thin fog, but Carver knew this was the beginning of something more sinister to come. Carver scanned his neighborhood and noticed a parked car across the street, two houses down.

The hair on his arms stood at attention. The car disturbed him. Its presence tightened the knot in his stomach when a sudden breeze glided through his house from the kitchen, snapping Carver's attention. He investigated the kitchen. Nothing but darkness looked back. He turned back to the car, certain there was someone in the car. Now that breeze again, and Carver walked back into the kitchen where his jaw dropped from seeing the pages in the book flipping on their own.

His heart hammered in his chest when the breeze dissipated, and the pages drifted then fell into place. Carver read the title, illuminated by the silvery glow from the moon outside his kitchen window: The Underground Tunnels. Carver swallowed his breath then sat down to read. Reading by the light of the moon because he refused to light his candle. Read and used what he knew about today's Sleepy Hollow to locate the source of the cavern.

He knew exactly where it was. It was the same cavern where he discovered the body in Patriot's Park.

John's eyelids snapped open with the onslaught of a scream that curdled his blood and cringed his bones. The scream echoed across the dungeon, bouncing off the stone walls. It seemed like it would last forever.

He felt like run-over dog shit. As if every bone in his body was bruised or broken. Felt like his organs were failing him, his heart finding it difficult to pump blood through his veins. The same blood that sifted through his veins like poison. John felt weak and depleted. With his skin on fire, sweating thick bullets across his forehead as he lay in his cell, his eyes rolled across the scene below where his vampire had been joined by four others. A tall man dressed in all black-the man looked ancient and carried an energy filled with the most nefarious intentions imaginable-and who John assumed were teenagers or college aged-one woman and two men. He recognized none of them except his vampire, who stood across the dungeon from where John was, watching the scene in the center of the room.

Beneath John and close to the stone slab was the man in black. In front of the man in black existed a strange scene and the cause of the screams. John saw a man being squeezed, compacted like garbage, crouched inside what John assumed was a large metal or iron hoop or frame with a central hinge and various spikes attached to the inside. The man was stuffed inside the hoop, screaming bloody murder. His knees were on the ground inside a metal circle on the floor where the larger hoop he was crouched inside of was attached. His body, legs and arms were being squeezed inside the hoop that circled around his shoulders. The man in black was tightening the hinge, compressing the victim's body.

John could see that the spikes were ripping into his shoulders and that his body was contorting, compacting from the heavy strength of the device. His screams continued, and the man in black laughed, as did all who were below John. Laughed and twisted that hinge even more when John heard a crack as if the victim's chest had compacted then snapped like a twig. A bright grey hue coated the dungeon from the three open doorways. Beyond the doors looked like a cave.

"My master," said the vampire. "The astral plane..." He swallowed his breath. "I can feel it in my veins."

To which the man in black took it upon himself to twist that hinge faster, his eyes mad as blood coughed over the victim's chin. His breath wheezed through his throat. His bones cracked and popped. John was certain his stomach muscles were crushed into oblivion. The man in black stood tall, removing a long blade from his cane and then decapitated the poor suffering victim. Blood rained from the neck, soaking the man in black. The head rolled across the floor.

14

The astral plane swelled with a growl behind it, and a horde of fog-drenched apparitions spewed from the doorways. The man in black stood tall, basking in the glory of the apparitions. They flitted through him and around him.

"My ghost demons. Our time has come." The fog raced across the dungeon like a hurricane wind that tore out of the room. "Go and take up arms," said the man in black. "Tonight, we stake our claim on this world." The wind settled with the exit of the ghost demons.

"It's working," said the vampire, his eyes fixed on the man in black as if he were a god. "Everything you said would happen comes true on this night." He looked at the bright glow. "It's magnificent."

"Soon, Wren, the astral plane will be upon us, and Baphomet with it."

Quiet now. John scanned across the victims still chained to the wall. The man in black turned to the three young ones standing with him. He gestured to the latest victim. "Place him on the slab and take out his heart." He looked at his victim. "That heart is filled with fear. Offer it to the fire."

"Who shall be next, my master?" asked Wren as the three minions or whoever the hell they are went to work, removing the victim from the hoop.

The man in black gripped the red cane leaning against the slab then scanned across the people secured to the dungeon wall.

He locked in on one then stepped towards her when John noticed how she groaned beneath her gag. She started crying.

"This one," said the man in black, staring at the crying, defenseless victim. "Bring me the rack, Wren." He stomped his cane against the floor twice. "This one deserves a special brand of torture." He turned to Wren. "Let us tear her limbs off."

The three minions dragged the dead body across the slab.

"As you wish, my master," said Wren. He walked to the opposite side of the dungeon, obviously on his way to find the rack.

The girl was crying, with whimpers and howls in her throat. The man in black turned to the slab when the female minion carved into the man's broken chest. Blood raced across the body to the slab where John watched it become absorbed by the stone. One of the men reached into the chest and pulled out the heart, handing it to the second male minion who tossed the heart into the fire. John watched it crackle and burn, his eyes drifting. Drifting to the man in black. A small smile crept into the corner of his mouth.

"Good morning, John," he said when he cocked his head to the right. "So glad you can join us."

228

Now, Carver closed his front door and immediately heard a faint buzz. He held his key in the deadbolt, the book in his free hand, listening. The buzz was dull but constant, annoying more than anything. It made his stomach rumble, culminating in a dull headache.

Carver twisted his key then turned around. The slivered moon hung in the nighttime sky where clouds like the wisp he'd seen in his living room flitted past the crescent glow. An icy breeze nipped at his skin and bones. His street was barren, dark and quiet, the fog lifting off the cold frozen ground. Keys in his right hand, book in the left, he took in the scene with his senses on high alert when a light turned on in the car he'd seen earlier. Carver walked to his car, watching Detective Reilly step out of the driver's seat from the car across the street. Detective Hollister stepped out of the passenger seat.

"Now that's... odd." It's not like he forgot that he's supposed to drive upstate to question Jerry Hardwood, but he had no plans to follow the captain's order. Not with everything coming to a head and Carver was certain current circumstances were indeed coming to a head, and that right soon.

"Carver," called Reilly. "Ready to go? We've got a long drive."

Carver noticed he closed his door, as did Hollister, and now they were walking over.

"You drive," said Hollister, gesturing to Carver's car.

Carver just about froze, watching the two detectives traverse the street, passing through the fog with bright beaming eyes that gleamed in the moonlight. He looked at the book in his hand and then back to the detectives. He shook his head. "I'm not going. The last thing I need right now is a six-hour drive."

"Captain said you need to go. It's an order."

Carver eyeballed them, standing not more than five feet from where he stood. He looked at their car. "You've been waiting all night?"

Reilly looked back at his car and then returned his stare to Carver. "Been out most of the night scouring the town." He smiled. "Figured we could catch a few winks before the long drive."

Carver looked from Reilly to Hollister. "Well, sorry to disappoint you, but you'll be taking that drive without me." He paused, assessing their stoic stares. "I'm putting myself officially on leave, gentlemen. Gonna visit my nephew in Florida."

Reilly gave a smug grin and then gestured to Carver's hand. "What do you have there?" He looked at Carver. "Bit of light reading on your way to Florida?"

Carver knew what this was; his instincts were in overdrive. He looked from one detective to the other. This was a hit. Without a doubt, they came here to kill him and judging by the way they were looking at the book, they came to find the book too. He reached for his holstered weapon, but Reilly reached him first.

"Nah, nah, nah. Not going to happen, Detective." Reilly had his hand on Carvers and Hollister already had his weapon drawn. Reilly took Carver's revolver from the holster. "You know what this is." He wedged the gun into his waistband. "We're just gonna take a little ride." He took the keys from Carver's hand and gestured to the car. "Get in the back."

Hollister kept his gun trained on Carver as he stepped around the car to the back door where he entered and sat.

"Go on, Detective," said Reilly. "Don't worry. I promise it'll be painless. Just a quick bullet in the back of the head. The light will go out, and that'll be the end. The end comes for all of us. It comes for you too."

Carver stood by the car door.

"Open the door, Stephen… and get in."

A moment's hesitation followed before Carver opened the door. He took his seat with the book on his lap. Looked over at Hollister when Reilly sat in the front seat and started the engine. There was a red ring around Hollister's irises. He grinned and cocked his gun.

"Master's been waiting for you," said Reilly, staring at Carver through the rearview. His eyes carried the same red ring. "He's had his eye on you for a long time."

"Well," said Carver. "Let's not keep him waiting."

Reilly laughed and cocked his brow. "Indeed," he said, "Indeed."

229

"There's got to be a way," Marc whispered to himself while standing outside the blonde woman's crypt. "There's more to the story. Another side of the coin." He shook his head. "There has to be." His voice caught in his throat.

Things were making sense to Marc. Things that didn't just happen the way he thought they did. They were manipulated into existence. Manipulated by the man in black. He's always been with him, in the shadows, pulling on the strings on Marc's heart, driving him to insanity by destroying everything he ever loved. Lori. His mother. His father. Everything he'd ever known or cared for. Desecrated by the man in black with the sole purpose to drive Marc into his embrace, desperate for love and a happy ever after. All so the man in black can have his tirade over humanity. Marc's the pawn in a game that was larger than himself, and he played right into his hands.

The owl hissed above him. Marc looked at it perched on top of the mausoleum, hissing as if it wanted to rip his eyes from his skull.

"There has to be a way!" he screamed at the owl that lifted off the mausoleum, flying across the cemetery. He watched it glide to the crypt where the witch and her coven were where it landed on the cherub before it hissed in Marc's direction, its wings spread wide with its head craned forward, screeching at Marc before standing tall with its wings wrapped around itself. Staring at Marc, who stood frozen beside the mausoleum. He looked at the crypt door, and his mouth turned arid like the desert. His skin crawling, he pursed his lips and swallowed his breath down his gullet.

Marc knew what awaited him inside the crypt. More torture by the nefarious witch and a hell he wished to avoid. He looked up at the owl, his eyes roaming over the cherub as he did so, and he was certain he saw the cherub smile. The owl looked directly into his eyes. Marc shook his head. "I don't think so. There's nothing in there but torture. There's got to be another way."

"But there is no other way."

Marc snapped around to the voice over his shoulder. The blonde woman stood behind him.

"You must confront the past to put right what you've done. There is no other way to move forward other than understanding what has already happened. The secrets of the past reveal the hope for the future."

Marc shook his head. "But I've been there already. There's nothing but torture and suffering."

Now she shook her head. "None of that is true, Marc. You see what you take with you." She looked at the crypt. "Travel beyond the barrier," she said, training her eyes back on Marc. "Beyond the blue hue and through the forest. It is there that you will find hell and confront the temptation of your soul. This is the only way to save Lori. To save us all."

"I can't," he hollered, turning away from her gaze. "I just can't."

"Then all is lost and Holer will have his way."

He looked at the crypt and the owl in waiting, too ashamed to allow her to see how terrified he was.

"You are different than the others," she said. "That much is true. Perhaps your heart is bleeding for retribution, tired of the wrath existing within that heart, but until the past is confronted, there will be no deliverance."

Marc whispered, "Got to be another way," as he closed his eyes.

"But there isn't," she said, her voice an echo, reverberating in his brain. "There is no other way."

Wind rippled through the cemetery, tossing dead leaves across frozen ground. Marc turned to where she had been standing to find she was no longer there. He looked at the mausoleum; certain she had returned to its embrace. The owl screeched, and he turned to it, watching as it hissed and then jumped off the cherub, flying into the western woods.

230

Logan woke up in Father McKenzie's rectory. The wintry morning wrapped around him with a chill that rippled across his skin. He closed his eyes to ward off the dull headache between his temples, listening to a quiet, consistent buzz existing beneath the veneer of morning. He pinched the bridge of his nose, then draped his legs over the cot he had slept in and blew his breath across his lips. So cold in the rectory his breath came out as vapor. His arm went to his stomach when the pain arrived, like a stabbing in his gut. He felt weak and depleted. Sick, with his stomach rumbling his cells into a nauseating frenzy. Logan looked around the rectory, searching for Father McKenzie.

The rectory was quiet; not a soul stirred. He could hear a car pass every so often, but that damn buzzing wouldn't relent. Logan stood up and stepped to the window where light-grey fog stained the ground and dark clouds consumed the sky, bathing the Hollow in a dark veil. He could see the faintest hint of the sun beginning its ascent, understanding that not even the sun could penetrate the dark shadow overtaking the Hollow.

Logan stretched his eyelids and shook his head and then turned around.

"Father McKenzie?" he called, but his voice died in his throat. He pursed his lips and cleared his throat. "Father McKenzie?" He walked through the rectory towards the church.

Still that buzzing. He'd heard it before. The dull but constant buzz. Normally it subsided after a minute or two, but this seemed eternal, refusing to let go. He opened the door to the church, thinking about his father.

Last night, they tried to call Detective Carver. Tried to call Logan's father too but received no answer from either. At least he spent the night in a church and not out somewhere drinking it up and toking a few joints, although explaining why he was in a church would more than likely throw up a few red flags for his old man.

"Father McKenzie?" he called again, entering the church. It was also barren, with not a soul in attendance and no Father McKenzie. *Well, where is he?*

Logan walked across the church, his footsteps echoing with a clomp across the wooden floor, eyeballing the stained-glass windows, attempting to see outside when he came to the front door and opened it with an icy blast of air across his skin.

"Father McKenzie," he called and stepped outside onto the steps, scanning across Patriots Park and the fog lifting off the ground, saturating the park in shadowy wisps of foreboding. The park was empty, and there were no cars on the street. No people walking as if the Hollow had become devoid of life. Nevertheless, the buzzing existed, constant as if it originated from the center of his brain. Logan's brow pinched, the sound seemed louder outside.

His solar plexus rumbled and contracted with a squeeze filled with pain, leaving a sour taste on his dry tongue.

He took the steps down to the sidewalk; his attention focused on the cavern where they found the dead body. As he focused on it, he could swear the cavern was the source of the buzz. Sounded like a million dull screams had become one, refusing to die. Noticed the air was stained with a gray color that turned everything he saw into a blue-gray film.

Thoughts flitted through his brain. Thoughts that led him to conclusions he refused to accept. That everyone in the Hollow had died while he was sleeping, and he was now in hell. Where was Father McKenzie after all? And why was nobody on the street? He looked up at the dark clouds hovering like a shell, maintaining the Hollow under its dark veil.

"Logan, what are you doing outside?"

Logan snapped around to see Father McKenzie walking towards him from the opposite direction on the sidewalk.

"It's best to stay inside." The priest put his hand on Logan's shoulder.

"Sorry, Father. I was looking for you. Any word from Detective Carver or my dad?"

The priest shook his head. "Not yet, Mr. Reeves, but I'm certain we'll hear from them today. Come," he said, looking around. "Let's get back inside."

Logan followed dutifully, scurrying up the steps to the front door when he turned around. The priest was still on the sidewalk. Staring into the cavern.

.

231

Henry knocked on Elena's motel room door. His SUV was the only car in the small twelve-spot parking lot when he pulled in, which didn't surprise him in the least. When he first pulled up, he thought he had the wrong location. The place looked abandoned, run-down and faded. There were only six rooms, all facing the street, with the woods on the other side.

He knocked again. "Mrs. Francon? It's Henry. Are you in there?" He waited, stuffing his hands in his jacket pockets, and turned around. The motel sat on a corner of an otherwise barren street. The woods looked dead in the morning twilight with the fog-drenched trees and their bare limbs. He looked through the woods, as far as his eyes could see, and tilted his head. In the distance, he could see the faintest silhouette of a house. Henry wondered if that was the same house Detective Carver had warned him about. He'd be surprised if it were. From the looks of it, it didn't seem like anyone could live in such a place. Chills crawled across his skin, constricting his stomach.

When Henry woke up this morning, there was a pit burning in his stomach and he had a dull headache, aided, no doubt, by the constant buzzing that refused to relent from between his ears. He felt sick and wondered if he was coming down with something. Henry sniffled, turning back to the door and about to pound on it when he heard the chain lock come undone and the doorknob twisted, opening the door.

Elena craned her head, looking beyond Henry.

"Good morning," said Henry. "I would have called, but..." His voice trailed off, staring at Elena.

She seemed to have aged a hundred years since yesterday. Her hair sat on top of her head in a blue-gray mop. Her skin featured prominent wrinkles and crepe skin from her forehead down to her neck, with blotches and liver spots stained across her face. Her eyes were red-rimmed, her eyeballs dry with the slightest hint of yellow across the sclera. Somehow, she looked shorter and thinner. Henry wondered if he was looking at the same person, thinking that he got the room wrong.

She looked up at him, her beady eyes staring through his soul. Henry cleared his throat.

"Come inside," she said, gesturing to the room, and walked away.

She sat on the bed while Henry walked into the room and closed the door behind him. The overhead light cast a dull yellow glow across the cheap room. The carpet looked decades old. The yellow paint was peeling in the corners. Other than the bed, there was a chest of drawers on the opposite side of the room with a mirror above it. Two end tables sat beside the bed, and an old wooden table with two small chairs sat by the window. Henry sat in one of the two chairs then informed Elena about the conversation with Carver and what he and Lori had discussed afterward.

"She's hiding something about this Marc guy, and I think you're right. He's a part of these murders, and if we're not careful, he'll drag Lori down with him."

Elena shook her head. "We need to get her out of here today," she said, then looked Henry dead in the eye. "By nightfall."

"But…"

"No ifs, ands, or buts about it," she cut him off. Henry had thought he had until tomorrow morning.

Henry gritted his teeth, looking out the window, thinking.

"Where is she?" Elena interjected.

"Last I knew, the hotel."

"Did you see her this morning?"

He shook his head. "No. I came here right away." He paused. "Wanted to get a jump-start on a plan for the day."

"Well, you have your plan now." Elena sat up. "Do what you have to do. Convince her or just put her in handcuffs and force her into the car. Either way, I don't care." She looked out the window, and Henry could have sworn she saw something in the woods; her eyes grew wide, frightened by whatever captivated the woods. "By nightfall," she said, returning her gaze to Henry. "We need to be on the road."

Carver watched the tree line while the car sped across the winding road that circled a small pond in the western woods. He was familiar with the spot. Carver had spent more than a few occasions walking the nature trail over the last thirty years. He thought it was ironic that this particular trail was the first he'd walked when he moved to Sleepy Hollow. Ironic that if he doesn't get out of his current situation, it will also be his last.

The sun was coming up, and with it, the fog had grown thick. With the overcast sky, it seemed as if the Hollow had been carved out of existence and transported to another world where darkness reigned and the nefarious ran the show. Although that's not what held Carver's attention. The buzz continuously assaulted his instincts. It made him feel sick, nauseous and drawn. He did everything in his power not to lose focus. His fingers crept towards his belt, where his one-inch blade was sheathed and attached to the buckle, hoping Hollister didn't notice.

Carver played out his next move repeatedly in his head.

Grab the gun and stab Hollister. He hoped he could get to Hollister's jugular before the gun went off. Hoped he could live to see the rest of the day. He flipped the button on the sheath. Cautiously, he slipped the blade out, concealing it inside his palm. Hollister had his gun trained on Carver, but he was staring through the windshield. So quiet in the car, just the hum of the tires on the road and that damnable buzz between his ears. Reilly looked at him in the rearview. A conniving grin on his lips.

"So, how much longer?" asked Carver. "I've got to take a piss."

"You can't be that stupid," said Hollister. He tapped the book. "This is all we came for. You're just a loose end that needs tying up."

Carver nodded. "Makes sense. No one likes loose ends."

They both looked at him suspiciously.

"So, tell me something because I really just have to know. Since you guys are all from some netherworld of hell, what's it like? I mean, are the taxes too high or something, and that's why you want your own world?" He laughed. Laughed out loud.

"You'll find out," said Reilly. "After we put a bullet in your head, detective, we'll carve out your heart and feed it to the master. Then you'll know exactly what our world is like." He grinned again, and Carver saw a gleam in his red irises.

He was goading them, trying to get Hollister to raise his gun. Carver hoped he was fast enough, but then again, what did it matter? If he's about to meet his fate, the least he could do is take one of these fuckers with him.

"Well, well, Detective Reilly. I definitely expected you to be the asshole in this little macabre of horror, but this guy..." He reached his left thumb in Hollister's direction. "He couldn't find his dick in a whore to save his life."

Hollister slammed the butt of his revolver across Carver's nose. His head snapped back, and pain tore through his skull. He tasted blood on his lips when Hollister pressed the revolver to Carver's temple.

"Shut the fuck up," Hollister ordered when Carver pulled his head back. His left hand pushed the gun away as his right hand came up with the blade that sank into Hollister's windpipe just below his chin.

The gun went off, tearing a hole in Reilly's head with an immediate splatter of blood and brain matter across the windshield. Carver saw two things at that moment. The first were Hollister's eyes. They seemed to bulge from the sockets as smoke slithered out of his mouth. The same smoke that tore out of Reilly. He saw eyes in that smoke that shifted into two fang-riddled mouths caught in a scream that screeched through the car, piercing Carver's ears. The second was the car that hopped a curb and propelled into the woods where it crashed into a thick oak tree, bounced off and tumbled down a hill towards the pond.

The scene was in slow motion. Carver was tossed around the inside of the car, crashing into seats and shattering windows. Crashing into the dead Hollister until the car stopped, upside down in the woods.

He felt blood on his forehead. His body felt broken. He saw red just before the light went out.

Lori slung her backpack over her shoulder before opening the door. She looked through the peephole, making sure no one was outside her room. She licked her dry lips before opening the door, looking both ways and then at Henry's room when she stepped into the hall, then padded down the hallway towards the front desk.

Three o'clock was a long way away, but Lori wanted to make herself scarce before then, knowing that Henry would be over her shoulder every second of the day if she didn't. She was certain he was communicating everything she did to Elena. Lori still couldn't believe Elena had followed her all the way to the Hollow. Couldn't believe she paid Henry a million dollars to bring Lori home. The woman was relentless and gave new meaning to the term narcissist.

All Lori wanted to do was get away from her. Elena should be talking to insurance companies and finding new housing rather than hunting down her adult daughter. The intrusion was nauseating. Nauseating, like the constant buzz between Lori's ears. She woke up with it. Woke up with a headache too but scoffed both off to the weather, which was crawling beneath freezing with every passing second.

Lori passed the reception desk, noticing how thin the crowd was. Only a few people sat quietly, and the receptionist-some young woman named Heather-waved at Lori on her way out the door. "Have a beautiful day," she said. Lori kept moving, offering a thank you on her way into the fog-drenched day. The cab she had called from her room was waiting.

Lori wasn't certain where to go, but she knew she wasn't staying at the hotel until three o'clock. The thought did enter her mind to go back to Marc's apartment, but that thought was quickly dismissed when Mrs. Leiter rang through her mind. Her only other options were to walk through town or go to the library. Or both. Anything to pass the time.

She pulled out Marc's notebook when the cab pulled away, staring at the cover and the name written in red: Holer. She eyed the cabbie in the rearview mirror, then stuffed the notebook into her bag and sat back.

Watching the fog overtake the Hollow as the cab drove into the thicket.

Henry was sitting in his parked car, watching Lori exit the hotel and enter a cab. He waited for them to drive before he followed, maintaining a safe distance, although what did it matter? The fog was thick and grew thicker by the second. It was difficult to see anything beyond the headlights.

"By nightfall," he repeated Elena's order, rolling his tongue inside his cheek. "This is going to be difficult."

Other than putting Lori in handcuffs, he had little faith in his ability to coax Lori away from the Hollow. Although, considering his stomach kept roiling with anxiety and he had a dull headache courtesy of that damn buzzing between his ears, the idea of using handcuffs was increasingly likely. He'd gotten himself into something he wasn't certain he was ready for. It seemed trivial and easy at the time, but things changed once they arrived in the Hollow. Some sense of dread that Henry couldn't shake, and it kept coming, like a sign slapping him in the face to get out of the Hollow and never look back.

But that million dollars had sat in the center of his brain until this morning when he woke up with the nightmare still behind his eyes. In his dream, Lori was stabbed to death by a nameless, faceless person. Her bloodied body was still alive when she reached her hand to him. "They're gonna kill you too," she'd said, blood pooling out of her mouth as she garbled her words. He woke up with a sense of dread, and all he could think about was Lori. He feared for her safety. Feared for her life.

Henry was someone who believed in karma, and that life happened for him, not to him. So, he rationalized there was a purpose for him to be in the Hollow.

All indications pointed to one conclusion.

To help Lori Fracon.

Wren wheeled the rack in front of the stone slab and used his foot to press down on the wooden pedal to lock it in place. The rack is a mechanical device made of old wood. The contraption was the same height as the slab and comprised a crank and turning wheel with two ropes attached to the wheel. Wren had already placed the second wheel on the opposite side of the slab. He addressed Andrew and Sarah.

"Our beloved Cheryl, please."

"As you wish," said Sarah.

Wren breathed in the putrid stench lifting off the bodies of the dead, all disposed of like garbage in the dungeon's corner. The master stood in front of the entrances to his beloved cave, leaning on his cane. The astral plane swelled into the chamber, casting an auburn glow that stained the air, bathing everyone in a blood red sheen. Wren thought it was the perfect complement to the growing heat in the cave. Andrew and Sarah released Cheryl from her restraints, and she fell into their arms, limp and weary.

"No worries," said Wren. "She'll be awake soon enough." He paused before saying, "Lay her down."

Wren stepped aside, allowing Andrew and Sarah to drape Cheryl across the slab, his hands on his hips. He looked around the dungeon, assessing. After Cheryl, there was Nikita and Liam to torture. Their blood and sacrifice were necessary to open the astral plane and bring the master to full strength. By nightfall, the master will be at full strength, capable of unleashing hell upon the Hollow, sending his ghost demons to every man, woman, and child to take over their minds and allow his army to rise.

Then Baphomet will come once the celestial landscape has locked into place.

Wren gestured to Cheryl. "Bind her wrists and ankles." He gestured to the racks, one by Cheryl's feet, the other by her head. Wren gestured for Hal to assist them. He then looked at Ian and grinned. He hoped the master would allow him to keep Ian as a pet. His request depended on the astral plane. Should enough blood be spilled before three this afternoon, and the cave is opened, he may just receive his wish. He'll know soon enough. The time was ticking towards the hour when the Master would need to retreat and regenerate for the final hour of his victory.

The ghost demons tied off the wrists and ankles. Cheryl's arms were stretched above her head. Wren noticed she was still unconscious; her head lolled to the side. He looked at the ghost demons and said, "One for each crank. Sarah at the feet. Hal… you take the arms." He turned to the man in black. "My master, we are ready for the next sacrifice."

The master turned on his heels, his cane kneading into the stone floor. It seemed as if the air followed him, like a chemtrail off his shoulders. His eyes lit up when he saw Cheryl on the slab. Wren took in the master's features. His skin was turning dark, like burnt ash, and Wren could see the faintest outline of curled horns on his forehead as if they were ripping through the host's forehead, forcing themselves through his cracked and bleeding skull. The master's true form was manifesting, and once the final ceremony is concluded, his transformation will be complete and the host's body desecrated, his soul banished to the astral plane for eternity. The master looked at Wren. "Proceed," he said.

Without a pause, Hal and Sarah started turning the cranks on their respective racks. The rope pulled tight, stretching Cheryl's arms and legs, pulling the bones to where the crank resisted, her limbs stretched as far as her bones would allow.

Wren looked at the ropes, running his tongue inside his mouth. The ropes were as tight as they could go. He craned his head to look at Cheryl, still unconscious. He turned to Hal and Sarah. "Let's wake her up," he said with a cock of his brow.

Both Hal and Sarah pushed on the crank, forcing it around. When Cheryl's limbs stretched and her bones crackled and popped, the dislocation of her limbs shot Cheryl's eyes open with an immediate wail from her throat. The ghost demons stopped abruptly, pausing to take in Cheryl's scream.

Wren shook his head. "Continue," he ordered. His voice boomed across the chamber.

Cheryl's breath huffed in her throat. "Wait… no… please." Her eyes wide when Hal and Sarah forced those resistant cranks over, and the most god-awful pop erupted when Cheryl's legs dislocated from her hips with what can only be described as a wet sloshing pop that ignited another scream from Cheryl. She was crying now. Whining in her throat.

"Please," she said when her mouth tore open with another scream when Sarah rolled that crank over again, her legs stretching to inhuman length. Her breath stuttered in her chest. Wren watched her eyes bulge from their sockets with another pull of the crank. Wren looked at the master, his eyes wide, his mouth open, seething and drooling. Wren could see the formation of fangs in his mouth, tearing the host's gums open, pooling blood in his mouth. Whimpers from Cheryl now, followed by a wail when another pull of the crank snapped the right arm from her shoulder. Cheryl was crying, wailing and hollering.

Her screams reached a fever pitch, her tongue jutting from her mouth with that scream from her raging throat. Hal and Sarah, their faces contorted, constricted, pushed on the crank, forcing it to turn over. Wails and cries. Whimpers and bloodcurdling screams tore off Cheryl's lips in an endless stream of agony. Her skin ripped at the joints, her skin and bones separating as blood rained across the slab and the ghost demons gritted their teeth with the final push of the crank that severed her limbs with a wet squishing pop and an immediate gush of blood like a waterfall that sprouted from her severed limbs. The arms and legs, still tied to the wheel, dropped to the floor, dripping with blood.

The screams were no more. Cheryl garbled in her own blood, gargling before falling dead.

Wren looked at the master. Auburn smoke wrapped around him from the astral plane that glowed brightly in the chamber. Wren could see what looked like snakes in the water inside the ether. Slithering, frenzied slivers raged inside it. Heard the rickety snap of jaws followed by a loud boom as if some giant had awakened. And then the eyes gleamed in the ether. Cat-like and emerald green. They looked at Wren, and his heart constricted. It felt like evil, pure evil, had gripped his heart. Wind howled from the cave, ripping into the dungeon and swirling around the master.

Wren could see his demon form taking shape. The horns, so smooth, extended from his forehead and curled to the side of his head. His eyes red and beaming, his skin ashen gray, with teeth all jagged. The master's arms were outstretched, welcoming the Xibalba energy into his embrace. Wren-in awe and basking in the moment-turned to Cheryl and the river of blood pouring from her limbs. Watched as the stone absorbed the blood.

"My master," called Wren over the wind. "It's working," he hollered, his head swiveling from left to right. "It's working." He grinned while watching the wind sweep Cheryl's blood across the chamber. Wren could feel it across his skin. On his lips. He closed his eyes and lapped his tongue across his mouth.

John rolled over onto his back. His cage scurried, but just a bit. His eyes were closed; unaware his skin was covered in blood. Knowing the wind whipped across his skin but unaware of the wind itself, his breath labored in his chest, struggling to take a full breath. His skin covered in sweat, his hand reached to his chest, instinctively covering his thundering heart. With blood on his lips, he pulled those lips into his mouth and ran his tongue across them.

John's head trembled as his eyelids drifted open and his eyeballs rolled behind those lazy slits when, for the briefest moment, John left the prison of his mind, anchoring in a reality that was no more and no less than hopeless. The wind howled in his ears, closing his eyes and returning him to the very prison he accepted as the true reality of his situation.

He saw memories that weren't his, and some that were. Like drifting above the scene that seemed as if it were underwater, rippling across time to the next memory. Grandpa Claude being beaten to death. His mother's skull blown across the bedroom. His father's arrest and his sister's murder. So much blood was spilled. He saw himself bathing in their blood, with catlike eyes that revealed the suffering his heart had endured.

Now he hears music. He's at a party, and people are dressed so strangely. Top hats and canes were worn by men in suits and ladies with fashionable hats wearing dresses that looked like doilies with long strings of pearls around their necks. John sees himself in the house-the mansion in the western woods-walking among the guests. A specter moving among them unseen. The energy is nefarious, with a buzz beneath the surface. John looked down at his feet, to the floor when the buzz became even more prominent.

His attention was taken when the door burst open, and three men dropped a woman to the floor.

The woman is clearly crying, whimpering on all fours over a pentagram drawn in blood on the floor when one of the men says, "Another heart for the master." His grin is demonic. His emerald eyes sparkle in the candlelight.

"Another descendant of the coven," says a man who looks so familiar to John, although he can't place him. "You've done well, Detective."

John looks over every face in the room. It seems to him as if everything paused, although he can feel the energy beneath his feet. It's thick and pushing against the floorboards with a red glow as if the light is seething to devour this woman. She looks up and locks eyes with John.

"Please," she says. "Help me."

John's brow furrows, staring at the woman who, he now sees, is the spitting image of his mother.

"Come," says the man John can't place. "Let us dance in her blood tonight."

John feels the men approaching. "Wait," he says, but they don't hear him. Instead, they beat the woman with their canes. Both men and women take their turns, and John can see the demon in all their eyes when they slash and beat her down. The onslaught is never-ending. The woman's head was cracked and bleeding in various places. Her arms were broken, as were her legs, and all the while that red glow beamed from beneath the floor with a buzz John could feel between his ears.

"The power is immense," one man says. "I can feel it in my bones."

John looked down at the woman, all covered in blood and dead on the floor. Her eyes were still open and locked on John.

"It's the house," says the one John can't recognize. "It brings power to every part of my heart."

His words follow John. He's staring into the dead woman's eyes when he feels himself moving, spiraling as if he's being drawn into the vortex of her dead black eyes.

237

Lori had a feeling she was being followed. The sensation crawled across her skin, manifesting awareness with a tremble in her heart. She had seen no one following her, but the instinct was there, buzzing in her brain with a thick paranoia.

She had the cab driver drop her off at the library. Lori noticed the fog was thicker in the center of town, draping the Hollow in a perpetual gothic landscape where evil exists inside every atom consuming the town. The drive over felt like she was driving into clouds that led to hell, and that damn buzzing between her ears refused to relent. No matter what she did to shake it, the dulled whistle remained. The noise tightened her stomach with a nauseous rumble.

Lori paid the cab driver and stepped into the parking lot that shared a border with Patriots Park. She slung her backpack over her shoulder. The cold nipped at her skin. Her nose riddled with a nasal drip that she sniffled back. The park caught her attention when she closed the cab door. The buzzing seemed louder, as if the source of the buzz existed inside the park. The fog seemed to thicken in the sunlight, turning the Hollow into a gray hue. The church across the park was draped in a cloud of gray that seemed to devour the sacred house of God. She watched the cab pull away from the library only to disappear into the fog when she noticed how quiet the Hollow had become. No cars on the street. No people walking up and down the strip.

It's like a ghost town.

And the park was calling her to it. She felt a pull in her gut as if the park was pulling a string on her thoughts. Lori fixed her beanie over her ears, then crossed her arms over her chest and stepped towards the park. The parking lot sat on top of a hill with the park below it. She stepped to the wall separating the park from the library when the buzzing increased in volume. Lori squinted, her eyes closed, attempting to ward off the unrelenting noise that churned acid into the back of her throat. She felt sick, as if she could puke. Her lips trembled when she opened her eyes.

Lori remembered what she had seen on the news the other day and how this same park had housed the dead. She surveyed the landscape and the cavern in the park's center. The same cavern where the body was discovered. Noticed how the fog drifted then, gliding across the park and then spiraling, curling into itself towards the cavern where the buzz was coming from. The buzz seemed to amplify the longer she stared into the cavern.

It's like it's alive, she thought. *As if the dead are rising.*

If she hadn't known any better, she would have believed there were eyes in the fog. Eyes that were watching her with bated breath. The sensation was difficult to resist. Like an addiction, she had to force herself to move her feet and walk away from the buzzing vibration in her bones. With her hands in the crooks of her arms, she walked around to the front of the library, but the door was locked.

Her eyes narrowed, looking through the door's glass. The lights were off in the library, which looked cold and dark. She studied the hours stenciled into the glass and noticed the time was well after the doors should have been unlocked.

"What now?" She shook her head. "Shit."

The cab was gone, and walking back to the hotel was out of the question. Lori walked to the sidewalk and looked both ways. No cars. No people. Just the fog and that buzzing. She could go left and pass the park and head into Sleepy Hollow. Find a place to sit for a while until her meeting. Or go right and head into Tarrytown. She chose Tarrytown.

Lori wanted to avoid the park if she could.

He heard a dull buzz outside the cemetery. It seemed to circle the perimeter as if the buzzing longed for entrance and a visit with the dead. The wind rippled outside the cemetery as if in cahoots with the buzz, rolling like a monster of energy that consumed the western woods.

Marc's heart constricted. His scar burned across his skull, itching mad with fever as he licked his bleeding cracked lips and scratched at the chapped cracks across his thumb, unaware his hand was bleeding. Marc's attention was on his insides and what felt like poison in his veins depleting his strength and destroying his cells. He felt like he was dying, albeit a slow death. The poison rotting every atom in his body.

Felt weak, as if the cemetery was pulling on his core, dragging him down into a dark cauldron of death. Cold sweat dripped off his brow despite the freezing essence across the cemetery.

His mind raced with the memory of what he'd seen in the dungeon. Seemed like a dream now, but he knew that wasn't true. He tortured those people. The memories were thick, unrelenting with guilt. Cuts across bodies dripping with blood. Knives slashing into skin, filleting the flesh off the bone.

"Jennifer," he muttered when his stomach pinched with pain as if a knife pierced his abdomen. Marc hunched over and puked a river of blood. His eyes were wet with tears as the sweat dripped off his brow in thick bullets. Trembling, he stood up and trolled across the cemetery, his arms across his chest. Felt blood and vomit on his chin as he stared through wet narrow slits.

"The crypt," he said, the words trembling over his lips as his eyes rolled beneath his eyelids. Felt like he was under attack. Thoughts raced across his mind. An onslaught of negativity rushed at him a million miles an hour. The sensation bore down on him, constricting his heart, tearing at his skin.

Marc rushed to the crypt's door, slamming his shoulder into it. Paranoid, hungry and filled with fear, he slammed into the door again.

"Got to get in," he hollered, slamming his fist against the door, angry and determined. His thoughts hit a panic; he had to wipe them clear. Had to get into the crypt. The place he knew he could find a reprieve. With another slam of his shoulder, the door flew open with Marc landing inside with a thud.

The buzzing ceased. The air was clean. He took a giant breath, then coughed something awful, hunched over on all fours when he threw up again, releasing a river of noxious gas and vomit as if he just expelled the rot of death. Thought he heard something scurry somewhere deep inside the darkness of the crypt. Like a hurried anxiety filled with fear.

Marc stretched his eyelids and wiped his mouth, looking, seeking. The air was warmer here. He looked through the open door to the cold and windy cemetery. Seemed like he was looking at a television screen. His attention was taken by a snap in the dark. He grunted in his throat and slowly stood up.

"Hello," he called, his voice echoing in the crypt. He stepped closer, further into the crypt. Noticed he felt better already as he gasped and ran his hand over his face and stood still. His head craned to the left than the right, staring, assessing. Noticed the subtle wind tearing through the crypt as he walked into the thick blackness, allowing it to consume him.

Heard a squelched scream as if someone was hiding from him. Hiding in the darkness. Marc stopped in his tracks, craning his head for a chance to see.

"Hello," he hollered, his voice reverberating back to his ears. He thought he heard more scurries and a squeal.

"They're afraid of you."

The voice was on his right. Marc shot his head toward the voice. In the darkness, crouched against the crypt wall, he could see a silhouette. The person was draped in an old dark cloak; the hood hiding their features. He looked back into the depths of blackness in front of him.

"Why? They have no reason to be afraid."

The silhouette said nothing in response. Marc noticed the stick in the person's hand, writing in the dirt.

The person stopped writing and paused. "You must enter." The voice was soft, with a weight of childishness. "Show them there is nothing to fear."

"What's in there?" asked Marc. He turned to the silhouette.

Noticed the person paused. "Truth," they said, then went back to writing in the dirt. "We all must face our truth. Why would you be different?"

Marc ran his tongue inside his mouth. "But why are they afraid of me?"

"Because of the past." The silhouette lifted its head. "And the suffering you've brought."

Marc scoffed at the notion. "Suffering that I brought?" He shook his head, and the memories raced through his thoughts.

"See, you already know it is true." A pause, then, "The time for the truth has come. You must enter."

Marc looked at the silhouette, then turned to the darkness. He stepped in, with an immediate shriek from within. He walked, noticing white wisps racing across the ground. Walked for what felt like an eternity until he saw what looked like a reflective surface glimmering in the darkness. His footsteps echoed in the crypt. Seemed like every step took a century to complete as he stepped to the reflection. His eyes narrowed, his head moving from left to right, staring at his reflection. Staring at himself.

Staring into the eyes of the man in black.

Henry hung up the phone then stretched his coat collar across his throat. The temperature seemed to drop hour by hour. He rubbed his hands together before hugging himself when he turned to the street.

He had followed Lori to the library, taking a left right before the library and parked until he saw Lori cross the street, walking into town. He waited a few minutes to give her enough space before he left his car and followed her, grateful for the camouflage the fog provided. Considering Sleepy Hollow had become a ghost town in the short time since he arrived, Lori would have spotted him if it weren't for the fog.

Henry wondered if the town had been put on alert with a stay-at-home order. He hadn't watched the news this morning, but it seemed right to put the Hollow on lockdown. After following Lori down Broadway, he discovered the payphone and decided it was a good time to give Elena an update on Lori's whereabouts.

"She's trying to find him," Elena had said. "Be certain she doesn't."

"Of course," Henry had said before hanging up. He didn't need a long conversation with Elena. He needed to keep tabs on Lori. Henry started his trek down Broadway, into the fog-drenched sidewalk, noticing every business was closed. No lights were on. No employees and no pedestrians. Only the fog and that damn buzzing between his ears that tumbled nefarious thoughts over in his mind, churning his stomach with a noxious boil. He felt sick and depleted. His eyes dry and tired, he felt drawn and weary.

Henry came to the end of the street and assessed his position, looking up and down and all around.

He didn't see Lori anywhere.

Carver's eyes slowly rolled open. He tasted blood on his lips when the scene came into focus.

Carver stretched his eyelids. He was on top of Hollister. The dead and bloodied Hollister with Carver's knife still wedged in his throat. Carver noticed he too was covered in the man's blood. Noticed the car was upside down and Reilly's body was slumped over with the back of his head blown to smithereens. His brain bled with a drip that landed on the roof. The windshield was painted red with blood and tiny bits of Reilly's skull.

Carver's right leg was wedged under him; he moved it into the rightful position when pain raced to his brain with a squeal across his lips. With his hands over his leg, he assessed the damage and the three-inch gash on his thigh that cut across his jeans. His head felt weary, his stomach nauseous. He looked around, assessing his location, remembering they were driving around the lake when Carver lashed out. The surrounding trees confirmed he was still in the same location.

Carver then gathered all the weapons he could- Hollister's, Reilly's, and his own, along with the book. The book they had come to find. He kicked the window out and crawled into the woods on his hands and knees before standing tall with a hitch in his step from the gash in his leg. He leaned against the car and took a deep breath.

His head hurt something awful and felt like someone had stabbed his skull with a knife. When he wiped his forehead, his fingers came away with blood.

"Gotta get back to the Hollow," he whispered, his voice weak. "Got to get into the cavern."

Carver surveyed his surroundings, assessing his location and how long it would take to make the trek back to the Hollow, understanding he was about ten miles away.

"Ten fuckin miles," he said. It seemed like a million miles away. He checked his watch. "Just after twelve." He looked up at the sun, but there was no sun. The sky was overcast, and the fog clung to the ground. Carver gripped the book against his chest and walked up the incline to the street then looked toward the Hollow.

It looked like the fog, and the clouds had overtaken the Hollow. It looked ominous, as if he was walking into a dimension where hell existed. Carver shook his head before taking the first step forward, beginning the long trek back into hell.

At the same time Detective Carver was walking back to the Hollow, Lori was hoping to find a reprieve from the cold. A place where she could wait out the afternoon hours before three o'clock and warm her fingers around a hot cup of coffee.

The problem she was facing was that all the shops were closed. Lori never watched the news this morning, and she cursed herself for not reviewing the local newscast before leaving the hotel. There must be a stay-at-home order in place, which would explain why all the shops were closed, and no one was outside. She felt like a fool for being alone in the Hollow. The sensation was eerie, to say the least, leaving Lori with a decision she did not want to make. Where to go? She could huff it back to the hotel and wait it out, which seemed like the best option available. She thought about going to Marc's apartment, but Mrs. Leiter's memory took that option off the table. The woman was insane. Probably made one too many cappuccinos for her husband and snapped. Granted, Lori wanted to avoid Mrs. Leiter.

Or she could wait it out at the proposed meeting spot until three o'clock. The bench Marc was referring to in his letter was down by the water next to the tennis courts Marc and Lori used to frequent before the accident. They spent many hours sitting on that bench after a tennis game. So many conversations had happened there. They talked about the future. About marriage and children, and how they wanted to spend their retirement. So many deep conversations, and over time they considered the bench a part of their relationship. Marc had even carved their names into the wood.

The wind whistled across the street, snapping Lori's attention. The bitter breeze nipped at her bones as a soda can rattled across the sidewalk to a storm drain where it clanked to a stop. Lori narrowed her eyes in the wind, looking into the street.

"It's freezing," her jaw chattered, hugging herself tight, concluding that spending three hours by the water in the freezing cold wasn't a good idea either. She's either going to call a cab to take her back to the hotel or...

Tap, tap, tap on a window.

Lori spun around.

The door to the tearoom opened with a jangle of bells. At first, she couldn't see who was opening the door; the glass was stained with a reflection of clouds and fog. And Lori too. The reflection wavered as the door opened where a short, heavyset, middle-aged woman looked at Lori through a pair of thick glasses. Her hair was thick and gray and done up perfectly. She wore a black dress and a gray winter coat. She hugged herself while standing in the doorway.

"You do know there's a stay-at-home order in place," she said and gestured to the street. "It's why everything's closed."

"I kinda figured that out already. I should have watched the news this morning. I..."

The lady cut her off. "And you're aware there's a group of Satan worshipers killing people, right?" She shook her head. "It's not safe for you to be outside."

Lori paused, staring at the woman who was looking both ways down the street. "I just need a place to stay for an hour or two," said Lori. "I have a meeting at three." She paused, watching the lady whose stare was fixed on the street. "May I come in, please?"

The woman's eyes narrowed, staring at Lori. "You should go home."

"I'm staying at the hotel," Lori blurted as if it were an excuse to be outside. "I'm only in town for this meeting," she added when the wind kicked up another notch. "Please?" Her voice was soft, desperate.

"Well, I can't leave you on the street." She chewed her bottom lip, thinking. "If it's only an hour or two... I think that's fine." She stepped back into the shop. "Come in."

Lori caught the door before it closed, watching the lady troll across the room to the back. Lori looked back at the street and the thickening fog. She couldn't see the end of the street because the fog was so thick.

"Come in, my dear, and close the door. You're letting the heat out."

Lori stepped into the tearoom and closed the door behind her when an icy chill ran through her bones. Her breath frosted across her lips. It was colder in the tearoom than it was outside.

One true revelation. Just one, and the truth cuts like a knife to the heart. The reflection stared back at Marc. The man in black gazed into his eyes. Marc looked over his shoulder, but he was not there. He was in the mirror though, his features changing the longer Marc stared. Like the flip effect from a lenticular print, when Marc moved his head to the right, he saw the man in black. To the left, he saw himself, and when he looked straight ahead, a third, entirely different perspective took shape.

The demon had horns as smooth as raven claws that curled around his ears from the forehead. His teeth were all jagged. His skin the color of burnt ash, with thick violet-colored veins that spider-webbed from his cheeks around his eyes to his forehead. His fingers looked like talons ready to scrape Marc's eyes out of his head. His demon eyes, like those of a cat, yellow and red, glared at Marc as if he could devour him with those eyes.

Marc looked over the edges of the reflection, trying to find a way in. Now the sound, like a hammer against stone, raged from somewhere in the darkness. Constant and relentless, it chimed and reverberated across the crypt like a call signaling the war had begun. He pounded on the mirror. The demon did the same; the glass splintered with every punch from his fist. Cracking until it shattered into tiny little pieces that fell away into the dark pitch of the crypt, leaving Marc standing eye to eye with the demon.

The demon craned his head and stepped to the side, gesturing for Marc to enter.

"Come," said the demon. "We have such splendid things to show you."

Marc looked around, assessing the darkness as he stepped forward. Heard scuttling across the ground, like a million rats scurried into dark corners. That chink, chink, chink repeating in his ears.

"What is this?" The words flew off Marc's lips, confused and alarmed.

The demon answered, "The moment of our union. Polar opposites cut from the same cloth."

Marc turned to the demon. He seemed to hide, cast in shadow and embedded in darkness. Marc noticed his tongue across his bottom lip when his scar itched. He turned back to the black pitch in front of him.

"Our union could not be without attraction. Two souls born under the same sign. One born from light. The other from darkness. It is suffering that brings the light into the darkness. The darkness that consumes the light. Innocence… is evil's addiction."

In the distance, he could see fire and smoke. Could see the light that illuminates the universe, shedding its glow across solar systems that burst into supernovas then surged into space seeking distant homes to sow.

"Connected we are, Marc. It is that heart I feed on. It makes me strong. Powerful. The light is always attracted to the darkness just as the darkness is attracted to the light it seeks to destroy."

His voice dropped like an anvil off his lips, revealing the prominent sound of iron against steel. Marc's eyes narrowed, placing his thumbs to his temples to ward off the pain inching across his brain.

"What is that sound?" Marc whispered.

"My army is assembling to advance our desire across humanity." And he laughed, guttural and rickety. "And we have you to thank for it."

Marc shot his stare over to the demon. "I have no play in this. This… this is futile. I would have never…"

"Lies!" screamed the demon. "These are lies. You knew Marc. You've always known. You were just too weak to stop it. Always crying. Always pouting. Always looking to me to help you through it all."

Marc studied the demon, his thoughts clicking into place. "It was you," he said. "You're the man in black. It was you the whole time. Manipulating me. Manipulating Lori too."

"No, Marc." The demon shook his head. "It was you."

Now he could hear chains rattling around him. Heard groans and wails. Marc snapped to the sounds. He was no longer in the darkness. Now he was somewhere deep in the depths of Hades, gazing into the distance as far as his eyes could see. Mountains spit fire in the distance. Wind like a hurricane rushed from those mountains. The ground was like burnt earth as the groaning escalated. Mad, frenzied groaning erupted from the ground where the dead rose.

Marc turned to the demon. "What is this?"

"The turning of the wheel." He gestured to the dead rising. "The souls of those who've suffered by your hand." He turned to Marc. "It appears they want to tear your soul apart."

243

"You can stay here forever, if you'd like," said the old lady from the tearoom. "We could use a good girl like you."

She carried two mugs filled with tea to the table where Lori sat. Her thick hips swayed as she walked. Lori watched her from over her shoulder. Steam rose from both mugs, lifting in front of the old woman's face, but Lori could still see her eyes behind her glasses. Those beady eyes with pupils like pinholes carried depths that reached back a thousand years. She set the mugs down on the table and took her seat.

"Thank you," said Lori. "But I may only be in town for a few days." She eyed the old lady as she sat then shifted her thick frame towards the table.

The old lady paused, staring at Lori. "Does that depend on your meeting today?"

"Something like that." Lori took to steeping her tea bag into the steaming water, attempting to avoid the woman's heavy gaze by keeping her eyes down. She could feel the woman's eyes staring her down. Lori looked up briefly, and her heart skipped a beat. The woman's stare was piercing. "Have you been at the tearoom long?"

A small smile curled at the corner of the old lady's mouth. "My lady, let's just say that I've always been here."

Lori paused before she said, "Well, that's certainly a long time," attempting to placate the old woman with some light humor.

Now the woman laughed out loud. "Indeed," she said. "A very long time." She took a long pause to stare at Lori a little longer than was comfortable. Tension filled the pause, thick enough to be cut with a knife. She gestured to the second floor. "I grew up here. In the apartment upstairs."

Lori sipped her tea, welcoming the warmth to her bones, and yet she shivered when the tea made its way to her stomach. Her teeth chattered.

Another laugh from the old lady. "You really are cold." She took a pack of cigarettes from her coat pocket. "I can put the heat up if you'd like?"

Lori put her cup down and shook her head. "No need. The tea is helping."

"Excellent." She lit her cigarette with a lighter she retrieved from her pocket. The smoke billowed from her mouth as she studied Lori.

"It's a shame about all these murders." Lori took another sip from her mug. She couldn't stand the old lady's gaze or the tension building between spoken words. The silence was maddening, and she needed some conversation, but what was she going to talk about other than the murders?

"Where are you from?" she asked. Lori wasn't sure if she was ignoring the topic or finding a way to connect some dots Lori was unaware of.

"Long Island," Lori said. "But I've lived in the Hollow for a few years now… until recently." Her voice died with her last words.

"Oh?" She took another drag off her cigarette, the cherry burning red as she did so. The smoke wavered around the old lady, dousing her in a cloud of smoke. She craned her head, assessing. "It appears we have a lovers' spat on our hands?" Her eyes narrowed. "Or am I wrong? Is he the reason you left the Hollow? Broke your heart now, didn't he?"

Lori said nothing, surprised that the old lady had picked up on her heartache.

"Is that who your meeting is with today?"

Lori raised her eyes to the old lady, cursing herself for allowing her emotions to bubble up in her stare. She nodded. "I'm hoping we can talk things out."

The lady smiled, her cigarette dangling between her fingers. "Well, I hope you can get everything in order. Perhaps then I'll see the two of you more often." She smiled; her parted lips revealed a row of stained and rotten teeth.

"That would be nice." Lori sat back in her seat. Whether to get away from the smoke or to break the connection the old lady's eyes were holding, she didn't know, but she needed a little space to breathe.

"Wait," said the old lady. She almost jumped out of her chair. "I have the best idea." She smashed her cigarette into the thin tin ashtray on the table.

Lori watched her do so. "What would that be?" Her heart hammered in her chest. The old lady, for whatever reason, created a thread of trepidation that coursed through Lori's veins. She cleared her throat.

"A palm reading, my dear." She reached her hands across the table. "I've read palms since I was a child. I'm very good at it. Perhaps we can determine the fate of your lost love before three o'clock."

"I..." Her 'I' hung in the air. "Don't know about that. Is it an accurate practice?" She wasn't certain about palm readings, but what she was certain about was the fact that she didn't want the old lady touching her skin. Her hands were calloused, yellow, and rough, and her fingernails looked like they died last year, all cracked and jagged and black and bitten down to nothing.

"As accurate as they come," said the old lady.

Lori looked away from her hands. "I don't know. I..."

"Afraid of what we might find?"

Lori paused, staring at the old lady. "I just don't know if I want to know right now."

The old lady looked at Lori skeptically and disappointed. "Of course you do," she said. "Either you'll be beaming with a suitable answer for your meeting, or you'll know what to expect and it won't be such a letdown. This I can guarantee."

Lori shook her head. "How can you guarantee such a thing?"

"My lady, I've never been wrong."

The dead rose from the bowels of the earth, reeking of death and rot, with groans vibrating in their throats, growls hell-bent on revenge. Marc watched with wide eyes as their arms ripped out of the dirt then clawed their way to their feet. His heart jumped in his chest, frantic with nowhere to run. They came from all directions-in front, on the sides, and behind.

He almost jumped out of his skin when a hand gripped his ankle. His scream died in his chest, and who knew the dead would be so quick? They surrounded him as if they could vanish and materialize a second later closer to where he stood. The dead hand on his ankle used him for leverage and lifted itself out of the ground.

Marc watched with bated breath as the dead surrounded him. It seemed like a sea of dead people stood before him, their bodies rotten and foul with skin as dark as the dirt they crawled from. Every thought in his head told him to run. Run and hide and wait until dawn, but his feet refused to follow his command. His skin crawled as if a thousand bugs flitted beneath his skin as his scar dripped blood across his eye, cascading across his nose then dripping into his mouth.

The dead continued to rise. All he could hear was the earth ripping and tearing. The one who grabbed his ankle stepped out of the earth and continued to rise. To rise above Marc. He craned his head back to take in the tall stature reaching close to seven feet tall hovering over him with closed eyes. Marc noticed the headdress over the man's head, in awe of this dead zombie who just tore out of the earth, aware that the dead advanced their position.

His eyes darted around him, looking for...

The demon walked among the dead. He weaved in and around them, disappearing and then reappearing a moment later.

The tall dead figure snapped its head back and stretched its jaw with a creak and a scream as if it hurt to move. The sound of his scream echoed in Marc's bones, shuddering down his spine. Unrelenting, the scream continued, and Marc's hands went to his ears.

"What do they want?" Marc hollered at the top of his lungs when the screeching stopped, and all became quiet. All except for Marc's ragged, heavy breathing. He gazed at the dead standing in front of him, waiting, their chests and shoulders heaving up and down as if waiting for some command to satiate their bloodlust.

"Simple," said the demon. "You must pay for what you've done." He reached his hand out, snapping his talon into a fist. "To pull out the fear... the suffering and death you've imposed."

Marc shook his head, taking steps backward. "No," he said, looking at them, searching the eyes of the dead. "I don't know who these people are. I have nothing to do with how they died."

The big chief stepped in front of the dead, his long legs hovering above Marc's head. He seemed to grow taller the longer Marc watched him.

"Maybe not," the chief said, his voice thick, guttural. "But we certainly know you." He stomped his foot on the earth, and the ground trembled like a seismic earthquake. The ground shook violently. Marc shuffled on his feet when all the dead screamed an ear-piercing howl. Their jaws hung open, their teeth rotten and black like ink. Their eyes lit with a silvery glow.

The ground opened in front of him. Fire crackled inside the opening as smoke billowed from the fissure, accompanied by a white glow, and Marc dropped onto his ass.

Marc was mesmerized by the light. Mesmerized by the dead advancing towards him, led by the chief, who plunged his fist into Marc's heart.

"It is time," the dead man said, "for you to know the hell we've been living."

Marc's body shuddered, staring wide-eyed at the dead eyes of the chief. His scream, still in the back of his throat, tore out of his throat the moment the chief squeezed.

245

The fog seemed to thicken with every hour that ticked closer to dusk.

Henry lost Lori. He couldn't find her anywhere. He knocked on shop and restaurant doors, but everything was closed. The Hollow had become a ghost town. The streetlights were still working, the same as the crossing signals and lampposts, but there were no cars on the street and no one walking on the sidewalk. Other than Elena, Henry realized he hadn't seen another human face since he woke up this morning. Now he was questioning himself about following Lori earlier. Did he really see her get into the cab? Or was he living in a dream? Maybe he was still sleeping, comfortable in his bed.

The day seemed like a dream with its fog-drenched atmosphere. Even the unrelenting buzz between his ears could be attributed to a dream state. Such noises typically dissipated after a few seconds, but this was constant, as if the buzzing had become a permanent fixture in his mind. It made him feel sick, drawn, and weary, tapping his mental capacity and physical strength. He felt weak, his legs aching as he walked across Broadway in search of Lori.

Confusion wrapped around him like a blanket. He didn't know whether he should zig or zag. *Where the hell did she go?* It's like

71

she disappeared, swallowed by the Hollow. He tried to think about his next move and where he could post up. Everything was closed, and the temperature was dropping by the second. Freezing cold is how Henry referred to the temp.

He felt like a failure. Failed in his one and only task to keep Lori safe.

His anger fueled his outburst, and he called Lori's name into the barren street. The buzzing twisted his mind into rage. Now he was huffing it back to the library on the off chance that Lori would return to seek entrance. There was a reason she had come back to the Hollow.

To find Marc, obviously, but to find Marc where?

Perhaps Lori knew something that Henry did not? Maybe she had a plan she never shared with him because why would she? Knowing that Henry was being paid for his service would be a cause for not sharing information with him. What a fool he had been, taking money when there were lives on the line. Namely, Lori's life. Not a stranger but someone he had spent time with. Someone he appreciated for their sincerity and kindness. One of the good people in the world.

But bad things happen to good people, and the fact that she disappeared was troubling. Henry arrived at the corner of Broadway and Wiley, examining the library and the park next to it. He noticed the fog was thicker in the park. Hell, he could barely see the entrance it was so thick, and hiding within that fog was that damn buzz. It seemed stronger the closer he came to the park.

He ran his tongue across his bottom lip, thinking when the thought hit him and he turned towards Wiley, looking down the street that sloped all the way to the Hudson River.

According to Elena, Marc lived in an apartment off Wiley. Henry could see the building now, drenched in fog and overcast clouds that hovered over the roof as if staking an ominous claim to the building.

There weren't many options available. Perhaps he lost Lori in the fog, and she went to Marc's apartment? The notion made the most sense, because where could she have gone if not to his apartment? The shops and restaurants were all closed, so either she's walking in the freezing cold, or she found refuge somewhere. Where else could she be but Marc's apartment?

Henry stuffed his hands into his coat pockets. His head bent into the wind as he walked down the street, thinking about how he'll gain entrance to the building.

When all else fails, he thought, *try knocking on the front door.*

"Your hands, please." The old lady held her hands out, gazing into Lori's eyes.

Lori watched as those thick mittens unfolded in front of her. The hands looked like she'd been gardening. What looked like dirt stained her palms to her sausage-sized fingers. She could see dirt underneath the chipped and worn fingernails. The worst part of it was the smell. After she uncurled those fingers, a stench floated into Lori's nostrils, and she could have sworn she smelled death, like rot and decay she could taste on her tongue. The old lady shifted in her seat when Lori raised her eyes. There was a grin on the old lady's face as if she was aware of something that hadn't dawned on Lori.

The silence between them was maddening. Lori didn't want to touch her hands. Thought she'd come away with some strange skin virus. Her stomach rumbled, shaking her innards. Her heart constricted as if it slowed in an effort to thicken the blood in her veins and weigh her down. Lori's instincts were telling her to run, but to run where? The old lady was gracious enough to allow Lori to wait out the storm before her meeting.

Am I being rude?

Reluctantly, she brought her hands across the table with immediate regret. "I guess if it's just for fun, it's fine."

The old lady's grin spread wide across her lips. Her eyes seemed to sparkle when she gripped Lori's hands.

"No worries, my lady. I am very efficient."

Lori had no response other than to swallow her breath, watching as the old lady dipped her head down, scanning Lori's palms. Her eyes sparkled with that grin still plastered across her face. Her head moved like a snake, studying the lines in Lori's palms. She pulled Lori's right arm closer. Lori stretched across the table. The old lady ran her fingers across Lori's palm, the sensation tingling her skin.

"Love," the old lady said, "travels across time and space. From one life to the next, our souls seek those we share a connection with." She dipped her pointer finger into Lori's palm, dragging the thick digit across Lori's love line, her jagged nail scraping Lori's skin. The sensation caused her heart to contract. "Now we come to fate. Love and fate sometimes connect, driving inevitable through the heart of passion." She ran her tongue across her bottom lip. "Sometimes it is the desecration of that love that reveals purpose, driving the individual towards the very fate that love tried to spoil." She lifted Lori's hand off the table, closer to her eyes, as if she were looking at a piece of paper. Her eyes widened then, staring at the palm as if she'd discovered some hidden anomaly. "Yes, there it is. Fate and love intersect. But what is the outcome? What is the fate of this love?" She ran her thumb across the palm. Her head slowly craned to the right, staring, assessing as her tongue lapped across her mouth, her fingers kneading into Lori's palm.

"You're-hurting-me," Lori muttered, her arm stretched across the table at an odd angle, her hand thudding and pumping with pain from the old lady's thumbs.

She ignored Lori's statement; her attention held deep inside Lori's palm.

"Ahh, there it is."

Lori felt the pressure release across her hand all the way to her elbow.

"Fate and love..." Her voice trailed off, releasing Lori's hand then easing back into the chair. "You are indeed the one."

Lori cradled her hand close to her stomach. Her eyes narrowed at the old lady's statement. "What does that mean?"

"In time, my dear. All in time." She looked at the palm. "Your meeting will bear fruit," she said, standing up. "But such fruit often rots on the vine. Be careful in the aftermath of your meeting. What you choose to do after may have dire consequences for both you and your love."

Lori sat back in her chair, looking up at the old lady who touched her fingers to her temples, closing her eyes. She looked worn and weary, troubled yet relieved.

Lori wasn't certain what to say, so she said the only thing that came to mind. "Are you okay?"

The old lady nodded, opening her eyes. She touched Lori's chin. "Excuse me, my dear. I must attend to something." She gestured to the tea. "Enjoy your tea before your meeting."

And with that, she shuffled behind the counter to the back of the tearoom. Lori watched her go, the old lady's hips swaying back and forth. Lori didn't know if the old lady was elated or was holding the weight of the world on her shoulders.

Either or could be the case.

Henry stepped into the small foyer of Marc's apartment building. He scanned the names of the occupants, located Marc's apartment and pushed the buzzer next to his name.

He waited.

Nothing.

"C'mon," he whined, shaking his head. *Even if for some odd reason he is home, what do I say? I was hired to follow your ex-girlfriend around the Hollow to make sure she doesn't find you.*

Yeah, because that'll go over well.

He pushed the buzzer again, not knowing why he was doing it. Probably to cross Marc's apartment off his list of possibilities regarding Lori's whereabouts. The fact that he couldn't locate her was troubling.

No response from the buzzer.

Now what?

Not that he didn't enjoy the quick reprieve the foyer provided from the icy chill on the outside, but he knew he couldn't stay in this spot all day. Eventually someone will notice him, and considering all that was happening in the Hollow such an occurrence wouldn't bode well with the local police. Plus, Captain Flannery was someone Henry was hoping not to cross paths with again. Although Carver was a detective Henry respected, Flannery left much to be desired. And questioned, too. When Henry met with Flannery his instincts became flustered. Confused because he was a police officer, but Flannery's intentions were clearly in question. He didn't trust him at all.

He pushed the buzzer again. Third time's a charm, isn't it? Again, there was no response, and Henry turned to the front door, looking out onto the street, thinking. Looked left and then right. The street was barren, covered in fog and cold. Deathly quiet except for the dull buzz between his ears. He leaned his head into the glass, fogging it up with his breath, looking for a better view of Wiley Road, hoping to see Lori walking on the street. Hoping she would arrive at Marc's apartment, too.

Again, nothing.

Maybe call Elena? Maybe she would know likely places Lori would have gone.

He resolved to push that buzzer one more time. Even thought about pushing every buzzer for every door in the building, hoping someone might have seen Marc or Lori. Someone who would let him in. He could break into Marc's apartment and wait while figuring out where the hell Lori could have gone.

He turned back to the buzzer and jumped back, startled.

There was an old lady standing outside the door.

248

Carver stopped to catch his breath. His head felt like it had been hit with a sledgehammer, and every bone in his body felt bruised and broken. His legs ached with every step forward, and his arms felt like jelly, cradling the book close to his chest during his walk.

He wanted to sit down. Hell, he wanted to lie down and sleep for a week. He'd never been so tired, and he was still so far away. Carver leaned against a tree, gasping and then inhaling a deep breath. His shaking hand reached into his coat pocket, instinctively reaching for a toothpick. The pocket was empty; his hand fell limp inside it as he leaned his head back and closed his eyes. Took a deep inhale into his nose, certain his box of toothpicks was scattered across the crashed car.

Out of all that's happened over the last six months, the only thing he could think about right now was those damn toothpicks. Carver cursed himself for his lack of empathy.

After he followed the lake into the western woods, he trampled up an incline that brought him up a hill looking over the Hollow. From his vantage point, the cemetery was on his right and the Tappan Zee Bridge on his left with the Hollow in between. The problem was with the fog. It seemed to thicken with every hour that passed closer to dusk. He looked up at the overcast sky where dark clouds hovered over the Hollow, dousing his town in a forever night while destroying the sun's ability to shed light on the darkness.

Carver pictured what the earth would look like shrouded in the same darkness, forever doomed and cast in hell. He looked down at the book in his hands.

The book he came close to losing his life over. The same book that held the answers to defeating the demon. He'd yet to read that chapter, and considering where the day was going, he was certain he'd never read it.

Then why the hell do you still have it?

It wasn't like he was going to cop a squat and start reading here in the woods. He was growing frustrated, and that damn buzzing between his ears wasn't helping to calm his nerves. What he knew was that *they* had wanted it, which means everything McKenzie said about the book was true. The answers are in the book.

Carver gripped the book close to his chest then stepped forward to the end of the incline and looked down over the Hollow. He could see the outline of McKenzie's church, the cross standing tall on the roof although the fog drifted across it, ominous and foreboding.

He prayed McKenzie was down there. Prayed the priest could help him. Carver knew the demon's tirade would either end tonight or become a success. Either way, he was running out of time. He needed to get into the cavern in the park and find his way to the demon.

Most of all, he prayed that Father McKenzie would have the will and the strength to help him.

After all that has happened, the number of people he could trust was small and dwindling by the second. He wondered how many of his fellow officers, how many members of his own team were compromised.

Get to the church, he thought while nodding. "That's sacred ground," he said out loud. "They can't enter through its doors. Which means anyone who enters is someone I can trust."

He heard a branch snap behind him. Carver spun around, staring into the woods. He couldn't see more than thirty feet in front of him, the fog was so thick, but he saw nothing. No animals and no people.

"Sheila?" he whisper-hollered, moving his head, scouring the woods through the fog.

Nothing. No response. Carver pursed his lips and swallowed. His breath hushed across his lips like vapor. Still nothing, but he could feel the ominous energy in the woods. His innards roiled in his stomach. Carver winced through the pain before turning around.

Broken, Carver began his trek down the hill into the Hollow.

Logan wedged a small wooden crucifix into a flowerpot filled with dirt. Father McKenzie blessed the cross before Logan placed the small pot on the windowsill.

They successfully added new crosses with blessings from McKenzie by every window and door in the church and the rectory. According to McKenzie, they needed all the protection they could find before dusk arrived. So far, they haven't received a single return phone call. Not from Detective Carver and certainly not from Logan's father. Logan had called home several times since this morning, and all the phone did was ring and then ring some more. He kept trying until the phone lost its signal, which corresponded with the loss of power.

The fact that his father wasn't picking up was troubling, to say the least. He wanted to run home to check on his father, but McKenzie refused his request. The church was now the safest place in the Hollow, and he would be damned before he allowed a child in his care to venture into the unknown. If there weren't ghosts and demons scattered across the Hollow, Logan was well aware Father McKenzie could be charged with kidnapping. Either way, and no matter what was going on, Logan knew his father would have some choice words with the priest once this was all over.

At least he's a priest, thought Logan, who figured his old man would be a little less confident with murdering one of God's servants, which offered little if any reprieve for Father McKenzie.

"That's it…" said McKenzie, "for now at least."

Logan looked up at Father McKenzie. "The buzz is getting louder. What does that mean, Father?"

He was right too. The buzz was coming from the cavern; he was certain of it. It sounded like every dead person in the Hollow was calling the Ohm with an unrelenting hum from their throats. At this rate, if the buzz continues to grow, Logan feared it might turn into a sonic boom. And then what? Two worlds collide where one swallows the other?

Logan waited for McKenzie to answer. The priest paused. He seemed as if he didn't want to answer.

"Father?" Logan swallowed the lump that had grown in his throat.

"I hope the faithful find their way to us," said McKenzie, completely ignoring Logan's question. Father McKenzie had tried to get the word out to come to the church through his normal channels of parishioners but came up empty. No one answered their phones, and now that the phone lines were down and the power was out, they were both uniquely aware that everyone in the Hollow might meet with a dire fate. Logan hoped they would come to the church too. McKenzie looked through the window. It was dark outside already, though the sun had yet to set.

McKenzie rolled his tongue inside his mouth. "We should return to the confines of the church." He looked at Logan. "In case anyone seeks refuge." He put his hand on Logan's shoulder. Logan could never be certain, but he believed the priest was struggling with what he was about to say, staring at Logan with empathy in his eyes. Fear was plastered across the priest's face. "I was hoping Carver would have made it." He looked out the window again.

"We don't know that yet, Father. He may be on his way."

McKenzie nodded while gritting his teeth. "Perhaps. I pray he is safe." He turned to Logan. "But… just in case." He closed his eyes, as if praying for permission to say what he needed to.

"What is it, Father?"

The priest opened his eyes. "In case…" He cleared his throat. "In case there's no one left… I need to tell you how to defeat the demon." He paused before sucking his lips into his mouth and nodding. "Come with me. We will talk in the church." He walked to the door.

Logan stopped him when he asked, "I thought Carver had the book?"

McKenzie stopped in his tracks and turned around. "He does, but I only gave it to him so he could see that it was real. If I had just told him what to do, he would have thought of me as a loon and would have never believed me. He had to see the book. Had to read its chapters and see the nuances and similarities. Adults are always skeptical. They believe only what they see with their own eyes. Blinded by what they've been told was real." He gestured to

Logan. "Children, however, still hold magical beliefs." He paused to collect himself. "I spent my adult life reading that book." He nodded then locked eyes with Logan. "I believe it is time for me to share the story with someone who believes in what is going on in the Hollow." He nodded, swallowing his breath. "It may be the only thing that can save us. Come," he said. "Follow me."

McKenzie walked into the church, leaving Logan alone. Logan turned to the window, listening to the buzz growing from the cavern. His eyes narrowed. He could have sworn he'd seen something in the fog. A standing apparition. A specter, watching him with bated breath, anticipating his next move. The presence was different from the fog. It seemed out of place, as if it were watching for its own amusement. An image of a white lotus burned in his mind's eye.

He wasn't certain-it could just be the fog-but he thought the apparition was drenched in all white, like white marble stone.

250

Marc's heart constricted when the chief's hand squeezed. He breathed in the largest inhale he'd ever taken. Pain tore out of his heart, squeezing every vein in his body. His scream caught in his lungs and came out like a squeal, gasping for breath. His vision blurred in the periphery; darkness shrouded his line of sight until the cemetery turned to the size of a pin.

He could hear his own struggling breath. Difficult to breathe, as the darkness wrapped around him like a cloud that overtook the pinhole and then he was bathed in blackness where silence waited. Everywhere he turned, darkness greeted him. Now, there was a cackle followed by a crack of thunder. It felt like he was spiraling, falling, plummeting in some ethereal, celestial space. Then cold wrapped around him. His arms shook. So cold. So, so cold. Shivering, and it was so dark he didn't know if his eyes were open or closed.

Now a light. A light in the woods. He's in the woods. No, he's staring into the woods. The scene wavered as if it were underwater. He saw a child's birth and his heart ached. Saw a chief standing over the mother. Saw the light-a beautiful bright white light-surrounding the baby wrapped in cloth. The scene then wavered as if someone had dropped a stone in water. Now he sees that the child has grown. He's a warrior. A warrior with wisdom far beyond his age. He sees how the child does great things. He's a confidant, a seer and a medicine man all wrapped in one. His heart is pure. He stands on his own, and those around him look up to him. He sees the girl with him. Now they're older, hoping to start a family of their own. She loves him for his heart and not for the magical things he does. His heart glows with pure white light.

He's a leader, destined to be the elder of his tribe. His wife looks at him with adoration, but he doesn't see her anymore. His attention has been taken. He sees a cave in the woods, and he's intrigued by it. There's an energy he's never felt before. The energy is both exciting and calm at the same time. His wife calls his name, but he doesn't hear her. She's calling him back to her. Calling him because she's afraid. Afraid of the cave and the unknown.

He doesn't hear her plea. Instead, he walks into the cave.

That ripple now, and Marc's heart is squeezed even more. Feels like his heart is about to explode. When the ripple calms, he sees wolves eating. Eating the flesh of humans. He sees the mother who gave birth to the child. Sees how the wolves bite down across her throat. He hears screams, eternal screams that echo into the heavens with no recourse for help. Every bite he feels. Every ounce of fear, he swallows.

His tribe turns on him, and he feels every inch of their knives in his flesh. Even more, he feels their fury, their rage and hate, and he swallows it down. He sees the darkness then, knowing he's inside the cave. Knows he's in the cave because his friend comes to him. The one that gave him the power. He wishes for redemption, and the master grants his wish.

Marc snaps his eyes shut. He can't see anymore. Doesn't want to see. He's freezing, shivering, but the vision refuses to relent when the chief's hand squeezes as if his desire is to empty the heart of all the blood in it. Hard to breathe now. Feels like he's dying.

Now he sees a man taking a long journey. The voice had been calling him, telling him it was time. He arrives in the Hollow. Arrives at his new home where the voice calls to him in the night, but even more than the voice, his attention finds her. She is so sweet, he's immediately smitten, transfixed with her grace and beauty. It feels like he's known her all his life. She tells him she loves him, and he tries, so desperately tries, to fight off the voices, but they're unrelenting. They are forever. Despite her warning, he goes down into the basement, but he doesn't stop there. He keeps traveling into the dark where the voice is coming from. He desires power. Power over those who wish him harm. Control over those who try to take from him.

He can feel the thick energy in the cave. It brings elation to his heart with a power he cannot understand. He travels so far into the darkness he believes he's crossed a line into the unknown. In the darkness he sees him, the carrier of the voice, the harbinger of death who promises all his desires. Sees himself then with the demon in his eyes. She tries to leave, but he refuses her request. He's so scared, so frightened that he'll never see her again.

But the demon gives you want you want. Now she's inhuman. At least to him. She has trouble with her thoughts. Trouble with the most mundane tasks. The demon puts her out of her misery. He knows it's the demon, but it looks like she's the one who slit her wrists. He knows she'd never hurt herself. It's his voice. His damn voice whispering relentlessly in her ear that drove her to the brink.

He buries her in a funeral pyre. His tirade has just begun. The demon has taken his heart, his love, his purity. He's changing. He can feel it. Every day he feels less like himself. Evil deeds bring evil blood. The witches find him then. They're everywhere in the house and they listen. They listen to him when his voice is the demons.

Now the ripple blurs the scene, but he can hear the screams and torture. He can feel the resolve of men and women. Can taste their blood on his tongue and smell it in his nostrils.

The chief then squeezes with an iron grip, and Marc exhales his final breath with a sigh.

The lady behind the glass door introduced herself as Mrs. Leiter, the owner of the building and Marc's landlord. Henry introduced himself as a friend of Marc's girlfriend, Lori, and asked if she'd seen either of them recently, to which Mrs. Leiter provided a resounding, "No," to Henry's utter dismay.

Another door closed. Where is she?

Henry turned and looked out the front door, hoping to see Lori. He could feel Mrs. Leiter behind him. He could feel her beady eyes roaming over him, assessing his intentions. His bones felt heavy under her unrelenting gaze. Seemed like her stare could cut his heart out. An uneasy sensation crept over him, and he noticed the slightest tremble in his right hand. Shaky, his stomach twisted his innards into a ball of anxiety and uncertainty.

He felt the heat against his back when she opened the door to the foyer.

"So cold," she said. "So, so cold." Her voice was like a rickety drone. Henry turned around. She held the door open. "Best to stay with us and wait out the storm."

"Is it supposed to snow?" asked Henry. "I didn't see anything about a storm coming. I thought the streets were barren because of a stay-at-home order?"

"And the storm too," she said, bobbing her head ever so slightly. "Yes, the storm." She looked up to the heavens. "The storm that washes away the past." She paused, her eyes roaming from his toes all the way to his eyes. "You would be served best inside," she said. "Warm those hands for a bit."

He didn't like that stare. The old lady was creepy, to say the least. "Mrs. Leiter, is it okay if I use your phone?"

"Of course, child. Come with me."

Henry grabbed the door, and Mrs. Leiter shuffled into her apartment and disappeared. Henry paused before stepping through the door into the foyer, allowing the door behind him to close. It was so quiet in the foyer. He didn't hear a thing. Not from any of the apartments. No televisions on, and no tenants talking. Just profound quiet.

He peeked into Mrs. Leiter's apartment. The old lady was shuffling from one end of the living room to the other, picking things up and straightening the pillows on her couch. Henry pursed his lips and swallowed. He looked through the glass door to the street and then back to Mrs. Leiter's apartment.

"Come, child," she said from somewhere deep inside the apartment. Henry didn't see her. The voice seemed to come from all directions. "You're letting the heat out."

Henry wasn't certain, but he thought he heard the old lady laugh under her breath. He looked over the door and the entrance, hesitating.

"Yesss, child, come in, and we'll get you alllll fixed up."

Henry took one last look over his shoulder, then, reluctantly, stepped in and closed the door.

252

Marc's redemption begins in a hell disguised as a waiting room. He spends years, no, decades, a century waiting in a room with no doors, but there are windows. Windows he can't open.

He stares through the window, his eyes twitching, and the scenes outside make his brain squirm. Endless screams are carried to his ears. Screams brought through torture.

Marc can't help but stare at the scene outside his window. It's as if there's a subconscious command he must adhere to. He must watch. Watch what is happening outside. Marc steps closer to the window with his arms wrapped around his torso. He sees red sand-or is the sand stained with blood-as far as his eyes can see. There's a mountain spewing fire in the distance. It looks like it's miles away. Sees what looks like living gargoyles-hundreds of them-facilitating the scene. There are trees everywhere, as if he's staring at the western woods in the Hollow, but these trees are all charred and dead with bare limbs and trunks that bleed. The scene is dark, as if in a perpetual state of night where a blood-red moon casts a crimson film that stains the air.

He sees two lines of humans, standing and waiting. The lines begin somewhere out of his line of sight and stretch to the scene unfolding in the center of the woods where there is a witch with black hair. She hands the person in front of her a knife and whispers in their ear. There are many witches scattered around the center of the woods. They're chanting, but their chants are muffled, touching his ears as incoherent jibbers. Walking among the witches, weaving between them like a snake slithering around its prey, is a demon with thick horns that curl around its ears.

He snickers when the woman who was handed the knife turns around. Her eyes find Marc, who notices the demon laughing as she does so. With a sudden flick of her wrist, she slits her wrist then drags the knife down the vein to her elbow, releasing a river of blood. Marc can feel the cut across her wrist. Can feel it on his own wrist, and when he looks down, he sees the gash is there too, bleeding down his arm. He looks back at the woman. She does the same to her other wrist and then laughs when she raises her arms for Marc to see. The same gash is on Marc's other wrist, too.

It's the heart that's devoured. All the love inside those hearts is devoured through the infliction of pain. He sees how long the line is for those waiting for their torture, standing at attention. Like moths to the flame, they stand and wait, wide-eyed and unrelenting. He sees their eyes are all black. No irises or pupils. No sclera, just jet metallic black. He sees their skin melt off their bones, dripping in clumps to the red sand-covered ground. The same skin regenerates and then melts again. The process is endless-a constant recycling pattern.

As they wait for their turn with the knife.

Now he hears footsteps. Big booming footsteps that shake the foundation of the room he is in. The walls shake and the ground rumbles, and he sees a shadow darken his room. The footsteps continue, and he sees a giant hand reach down from above and swipe across the human lines, gathering a horde of humans in an iron grip.

He hears screams rage across the landscape and then sees the legs that belong to that hand-thick, muscular and stained red-stretch across the woods. He sees the back of this gigantic devil as it steps into the woods and turns to him. Its eyes are catlike, emerald green with yellow sclera. The massive devil is eating, gnawing on the humans it swept off the ground.

I need hearts for the master.

His teeth are razor sharp. They cut through the bones of the tortured, tearing them apart. Marc can see severed limbs, innards, and blood dripping across the devil's chin as their screams and shrieks echo in Marc's ears. He feels every tear of flesh, and every razor-sharp tooth rips into his bones.

Marc doesn't realize it, but he's crying. His tears burn across his skin as his lips quiver. "I'm so sorry."

Now the devil dips his chin to his chest, staring Marc down. He's paralyzed by the devil's stare until another shriek erupts from the line of humans. His eyes snap to the scene where another human sinks the knife into his chest and then drags the blade across his flesh, carving a circle around his heart. Blood cascades from the wound down his torso. He pulls his flesh off the bone and then saws across the chest bone.

Marc looks into the eyes of this man, his hand on his own chest where he feels that knife drag across his skin. He's staring directly at Marc when he reaches into his chest and pulls out his heart. The organ is slick and thick in his blood-soaked hands. The organ continues to beat as he dips his lips to it and takes a large bite from the organ, and the witch laughs-a bellowing cackle that rages across the firmament. After the heart is consumed, the man walks back to the end of the line to repeat his offering.

Marc closes his eyes; his face pinched in suffering. His heart is suffering from the torture they endure.

"So many," he whispers as he raises his head, opening his eyes. "This is all my fault."

Now, the next human steps up to take the knife. She hesitates with her head down that slowly lifts, revealing black eyes and Lori's face. Although she's not just Lori, she is also the women from his visions. The Indian wife and the girlfriend who slit her wrists. He can see all three faces wavering back and forth as she stares at Marc.

He's shaking his head. "No, Lori, please." He places his hand on the wall. "Don't do it, Lori. Run, Lori. Run for your life!"

The devil then dips his head down. He's so big his head is right beside Lori. He's looking at her and then grins as Lori drops the knife and looks directly at Marc. The devil's hand rips towards her and snatches her in his palm.

Marc's slamming on the wall now, rattling the windows. "No!" he screams, his head shaking. "Leave her alone. She doesn't belong to you. None of them do." He's hitting the wall so hard the bones in his hands shatter, but the glass wall shatters too. Shatters all around him, and he runs. Runs towards the devil holding Lori. The witch slams a red cane against the ground, and the humans standing in line all grip Marc, stopping him from moving forward. Before he knows it, there are a hundred hands on him, keeping him from Lori.

"Get away from her," he commands the devil. The hands are all over him, tearing him limb from limb. Their fingers, like talons, nip into his skin, ripping at his bones that they tear away from his flesh.

Marc's screaming now, but he can still see Lori. Sees how the devil drops her in his mouth and chomps down on her bones. Marc can hear his teeth rip into her flesh, gnawing on her skull that he swallows down, eliciting a bloodcurdling scream from Marc's throat that ends with a whining screech as the hands rip into his torso and pain races to every part of his body. He can taste blood on his tongue and lips. The hands rip and tear chunks of meat off his bones as he continues to wail.

There's so many of them. So many people. So many arms with hands that tear into his flesh. He feels those hands pulling at his lips, ripping his scalp off as blood gushes across his face.

"Please, God," he screams to the firmament. "Help ME!"

The hands and arms and bodies come over him.

"No God," the devil says. "Baphomet."

And he grins. His evil smile is the last thing Marc sees before those humans devour him, escorting him with a return to the darkness.

"Little Nikita," said the man in black, standing in front of his last sacrifice. He kneaded his cane into the stone floor. He looked so beautiful to Wren with his horns and razor-sharp incisors. His ashen skin and thick shoulders. The master looked as if his true form was tearing out of the host's body, ripping it to shreds. Nikita spilled tears filled with fear across her gag. The master dipped his finger to her cheek, cascading the digit to her jaw. "Such sweet innocence. Your blood is the final stroke required." He looked up to the ceiling as if addressing some god of his own understanding. "Baphomet will then grace me with the powers of Xibalba, and the witch's spell will come undone."

The master rolled his tongue inside his mouth, training his eyes on the tearful, whining Nikita. He clucked his tongue and turned around. "Strap her to the stone," he instructed, causing an immediate wail from Nikita. The master looked at Wren while Sarah and Hal went to work, unstrapping Nikita's chains. He craned his head, turning to Wren's prize, Ian. His stare then floated to Wren when he slipped the hidden blade from his cane.

"You desire power?" asked the man in black.

Wren looked at the knife in the master's hand. Sarah and Hal brought Nikita to the slab, and Wren raised his eyes to the master.

"Yes, my master." Wren trembled with excitement. "With all the hate in my heart."

"Prove yourself, Wren." The master offered him the knife then turned to Ian. "Take his head."

"As you wish, my master." Wren stepped in front of Ian. "I live to follow your command."

The master looked over at Nikita. "Lay her on her front," he instructed, turning back to Wren and Ian. The deformed Ian, with his one eye and one ear and no nose. His face all bruised and bloodied, staring at the knife in Wren's hand with his one good eye.

"Do it," said the master. "Now, Wren."

Wren stepped up and gripped Ian's head with his left hand, gripping his hair tight. He cut into Ian's neck and started sawing across his bones with an immediate gush of blood that rained across his shoulders. Ian's head jutted from side to side, but Wren was strong, holding it in place to continue to saw through bones and cartilage while Ian's hollers belted from his throat across his gag. He kept sawing, sawing through flesh and bone. Wren's eyes were wide, mad and filled with hate. He had to force the knife through Ian's windpipe and spine. His scream whistled from the sawed throat. Cut off with the next pull of the blade. Ian's head flopped to the left when Wren severed the spine as a river of blood gushed across his body, spurting across Wren from the severed neck, rising into the air like a fountain. Wren continued sawing, the head just about severed as he filleted the last strip of skin and Ian's head came off in Wren's hand.

Nikita screamed something awful, staring at Ian's severed head. She squirmed up the slab as if she could run away, but the restraints held firm and she flopped back down, kicking and screaming and wriggling against the stone. The ghost demons looked on as Wren raised Ian's severed head to the master.

"Am I worthy, my master?"

The master looked from Ian's head to Wren and bowed. "Indeed," he said. "A most loyal subject." He surveyed the dungeon, his stare tracing over the ceiling before training his stare on Wren. "Place it outside," he said. "For all who come to see."

Wren bowed. "As you wish." He offered the knife to the master, who took it. Wren looked up to the cage where John was as he walked out of the dungeon to take the stairs to the first floor.

The master returned the blade to the cane, then regarded Nikita, lying on her front with her wrists and ankles bound. She was whimpering, crying under her breath.

"You're an angel, Nikita," said the master. He looked at his ghost demons and smiled. "Let's give her some wings."

Marc felt himself moving. He saw the outline of hands. Weary hands, the color of moonlight, carried him from the darkness. His body hurt. Every inch of him felt twisted and mangled as if he'd been churning in a meat grinder. He could feel cuts across his skin, his face, his body, arms, and legs.

His soul was crushed. His heart shattered, bleeding into his innards. Half a millennium of torture rested in his bones, pumping noxious venom into his veins. The sensation of guilt poisoned his mind. He thought about Lori, and his heart ached. What he'd seen and what he'd experienced were as real as the morning sun. The revelation struck him then. Those tortures belonged to him. All the death, the heartache, and suffering were all his doing.

Aided along by the man in black.

He felt himself drift down where his feet landed softly on the earth. He looked around in the darkness, turning in time to see those hands disappear.

"Please," he pleaded. "Don't go."

He felt an ache in his shattered heart as if the organ had splintered into a million pieces. He didn't know if he could move on knowing that everything that had happened was his fault. Sure, the man in black may be a manipulative son of a bitch, but it was Marc's intrigue that sent him into that cave. His addiction to the darkness, to tragedy and defiance. To love, brought the sickness that has done nothing but taint his blood.

Evil deeds bring evil blood.

He should have accepted death. He should have accepted what happened in the car accident, but he refused to allow time to take its toll, too scared to face the truth within himself. The truth that he refused to play by the rules and what he had was never enough. Always wanting more. Always wanting things to play out his way, and in turn, people lost their souls.

He, Marc Saduj, was the harbinger of death. Marc allowed himself to be manipulated. He opened the door and invited the devil in. His life. His heart, and those who were closest to him, who he loved the most, had all met with a dire fate.

He heard a screech and a hiss in the darkness. He looked up and all around, noticing the subtle blinking of stars overhead when an icy wind raged across his back and the cemetery wavered around him, coming into view the longer he stood. Marc was staring at the stars, then the edges of branches and tree limbs, then down the trunk to the grass, the frozen grass in the cemetery where tombstones and mausoleums sat like ancient structures dying on the vine.

"Did they show you the truth?"

Marc snapped around to see the blonde woman standing beside her crypt. He tilted his head, assessing her. "I saw you in my vision," he said. "You were the one who cast the demon out. It was you who defeated him."

"And it was you who released him," she said, staring Marc down. "Just like you have before."

Marc stepped closer. "How did you do it?"

She smiled at him. "It was a moment of weakness on his part. We got lucky."

Marc shook his head. "That's not true. It can't be."

She looked at the stars. "Oh, it is. Believe me, we were lucky in our endeavor." She trained her stare on Marc. "As unfortunate as that may sound to you." She turned away again. "It is the truth."

Marc stepped closer. "What do I do? I have to make this right."

"And risk your very soul and the soul of your beloved." She shook her head. "I don't believe you're capable."

"Try me."

"And there we have it. Marc doesn't like the situation, so Marc needs to change it to his benefit." Marc furrowed his brow, staring at her as if she were insane. "Maybe it is time for the man in black to have his way. Maybe it's inevitable for humanity to lose itself. Perhaps that's been the plan all along. What other species rip and claw at each other for personal gain? Even devils don't turn on each other. They have a single purpose, and they all pursue that purpose. We..." She shook her head. "All we do is destroy each other."

"Then that is our doing," he said. "We don't need another species to do it for us."

Her stare cut through his bones. If looks could kill, hers would have.

"Please," Marc said. "Help me."

"Can the love in your heart outweigh your insatiable appetite for more? Your history would say no. You'll fold when the time to act comes."

Marc shook his head. "Not this time."

He could feel her heart stiffen in her chest.

"Please," he said.

She closed her eyes in contemplation and breathed deeply before opening her eyes to Marc. "There are a few things you need to be aware of."

"Okay. What are they?"

She started walking, and Marc followed. "When you released the demon, you broke my spell and cast him back into the Hollow. He's using your body to do his bidding, but once enough blood is spilled, he'll be granted his powers back." She stopped briefly to look at Marc. "Once that is done, the spells and magic within the Hollow will be lost, and the demon will take his true form and spill his tirade into the world. He's very close to accomplishing this task. In fact..." She looked around the cemetery, listening to the heavy growing buzz thickening across the cemetery's perimeter. "I believe he may be one death away from completing this task."

"What then? There's got to be a way."

She paused, thinking, gnawing on her bottom lip. "Lori," she said.

"What about her?"

"You love her, don't you?"

"Of course," Marc breathed. "She's the light of my life."

She gave a quick nod, her stare burrowing into Marc's soul. "The demon thrives off the love you have for each other. He feeds off the destruction of that love, taking you away from what is most important to you. He always has. No matter what life you live, Lori has always been with you. Only love can kill the demon, but you're weak, Marc. Lovesick and desperate, and in every life, it has been you who desecrated that heart of hers. Yours too, and the demon loves it. He feeds off the pain and suffering brought by the desecration. He gathers strength from it. You and Lori, your souls are connected from one life to the next. It is that connection the demon devours. It is his gateway to manifesting his darkest desires." She paused, allowing her words to sink in. "She should have killed you when this all first started. When you were taken by the demon all those years ago, but she couldn't because she loved you too much. Little did she know that driving that knife into your heart was the greatest show of love she could give. It would have broken your connection to the demon and allowed you to find peace."

"So, it's the connection between me and Lori that matters most?"

"Correct, Mr. Saduj. The heart connection you share with Lori is the demon's greatest asset. The destruction of that heart feeds his wrath. When we confronted the demon, you had already murdered Lori's spirit. All we could do after was cast the demon out and banish him here." She looked up and around and across the cemetery. "The problem for the demon at that time is that Lori was already dead. He needs her to complete his ritual."

Marc's eyes narrowed. "So, if Lori isn't in the Hollow, he can't complete this ritual?"

"Correct again. Make sure Lori does not stay in the Hollow." She looked up at the stars. "At three am, the celestial portal will open where Baphomet and the demon's minions will connect with our world and unleash their army across the globe. If she's not in the Hollow, the demon's window will close, and so will his ability to rule over humanity."

"And if Lori refuses to leave?"

"Simple, Mr. Saduj." She looked over to the crypt with the cherub on top of it. The same crypt where Marc had married the man in black. "Enter through its doors," she said, looking back at Marc. "Take a journey through hell, and when you're finished, your death is required."

The master leaned his cane against the slab. So gentle and calculating, he craned his head to look at Nikita, whose dark hair was pulled over her face. She was crying. Subtle continuous whines escaped across her lips. He crouched down and dragged his finger across her hair to reveal her crying eyes.

She was trembling from head to toe, her arms and legs secured to the rack that had claimed Cheryl's life. Her face was all blotchy and flushed, emaciated, her cheeks sunken, her eyes bulging from their sockets. The master craned his head, assessing Nikita, devouring the fear dripping off her essence.

"Pleeeaaase," she said, "don't hurt me."

Wren could only imagine the thoughts that flitted through Nikita's head, staring at the master in his mostly demonic form. He looked like two people in one body. His demon form was tearing through the host. The horns had torn the skin across the forehead, which was now all cracked and bleeding. The host's skin looked like purple spiderwebs had cracked around those horns. The master's nose, thick like a bull, tore away from Marc's button nose. And the teeth, his teeth, tore out of the host's gums, replacing the host's teeth, but there were still traces of the host. The shape of his face, and the blue pupils, although reduced to the size of a pin, were still there. The master stared for a long while, basking in the glory of his moment.

"No, no," he said. "You don't understand your importance." He looked up at the ceiling. "How right your death will be. How simply beautiful." He looked at Nikita. "How essential. Of all the deaths in the universe, yours will prove the most beneficial. You'll be celebrated in the bowels of hell for eternity." He stood tall. "They will tell the tale of Nikita. The one who sacrificed her heart for the devil to rise." He looked at Wren. "The knife, please." His request brought a whining wail from Nikita's throat. Wren smiled when he handed the master the blade.

"As you wish, my master."

Nikita pulled on her restraints. Pulling with every fiber of strength she could gather. The master turned to Nikita when a squeak raged from over Wren's head. He looked up at the cage where John was and grinned, hoping the young man was watching, then trained his eyes back on the master. The ghost demons stood at attention, surrounding the master. Their eyes wide in anticipation. Nikita kept pulling, and Wren could see that the ropes scraped her wrists and ankles, drawing blood that the stone swallowed.

The master stood over Nikita. "As I said before, Nikita… you're an angel." He pressed his hand against her back, ceasing her tirade to set herself free. Wren looked at his master, in awe over how his touch brought calm to Nikita. She ceased flailing. Stopped crying. "And all angels need to earn their wings." He dipped the blade into her back, mere centimeters away from her spine. Nikita's body tensed when the knife entered, her head shaking, her jaw clenched. Her mouth gaped open, but no scream came. No sound. No whines or whimpers. The master sliced down the ribcage, severing Nikita's ribs from her spine. Blood oozed from the wound, cascading across the stone where it was absorbed.

A thick guttural whine tore out of Nikita's throat. Wren was surprised she held out so long, but now those hollers, guffaws, and cries wailed from her lungs. The master did the same to the left side of her ribcage; the blade serrating her skin and bone, opening two thick gashes down the length of her spine. The blood loss was significant, raining across the slab, and all Nikita could do was take it, screaming bloody hell with a whining cry. The master's hands were stained with her blood. He placed the knife on the stone when Nikita belted out a high-pitched holler and wail. She was crying an endless stream of tears.

The master dipped his hands into the gashes across her spine. Nikita sucked in those tears with a strangled inhale as if all the oxygen in her lungs had suddenly evaporated. Her eyes bulged from their sockets when the master pulled her lungs through the gashes, his hands tight, clenched around the organs that he dragged out of Nikita's back, pulling those lungs through the slits then spread them like angel's wings across Nikita's blood stained back.

Nikita's head and shoulders jumped up and down, her mouth gaping open and closed attempting to bring air into her

110

body. Her eyes, stiff and wide, jumped from one side of her head to the other. Her head was shaking, whipping rapidly back and forth.

Wren's eyes widened at the glow from the astral plane. Nikita's blood spilled from the open wounds across the stone. The glow brightened across the dungeon in various changing colors. Violet faded to indigo. Indigo to blue then green. Yellow transformed to orange then to red, bathing the dungeon in a blood-red light when the master dipped his hands back into the cuts across Nikita's back. His nose curled when a snarl escaped his throat, and he pulled out Nikita's beating heart.

Now wind swirled from the cave into the dungeon, wrapping around the master. Wren looked at Nikita, dead on the slab, and saw how her blood was absorbed by the stone. Looked up and all around the dungeon, to the whirling wind breathing against his brow. To his prize, Ian, with his severed head, and then to the doorways and beyond to the master's cave. The master dropped Nikita's beating heart into the firepit, and the fire roared with flames that licked the air, devouring the organ.

The wind erupted in a frenzy, howling across the dungeon. He saw the master then. Saw how the wind wrapped around him. Saw how his demon self grew strong as if the wind filled his skin like filling a balloon. Wren watched, mesmerized, as the host body seemed to shrink into the demon form. The master was no longer a specter. He had become flesh and bone.

The master turned to Wren. His demon eyes glowed red when the lights went out, dousing the chamber in darkness. Silence then as Wren stared into the red beaming eyes of his master. Now he could hear breathing. Thick, guttural breathing erupted from the cave. Wren felt heat on his legs and the scent of sulfur in his nostrils. Heard a snap as if someone cracked their fingers, and the candles across the walls all came to life.

Wren looked up and all around. He noticed Nikita was no longer on the slab and Ian's body was gone too. In their place were skeletal remains that turned to dust with the next brush of wind. The ghost demons were on their knees as if praying to the astral plane. The cave. Wren noticed it was all black except for the pale smoke rolling from the entrances into the dungeon. He looked down at his feet, but the smoke wrapped around him, and he could no longer see the floor.

The dungeon rumbled like an earthquake, and Wren snapped his focus to the entrances to the cave. A crack of lightning followed by thunder sent shockwaves across the dungeon. Wren put his hand on the wall to steady his feet, thinking they were about to plummet into the earth. The dungeon shook violently.

"We have done it, Wren," said the master. "It is... accomplished."

The entire back wall, entrances and all, cracked into a million pieces that were drawn into the blackness of the cave then vanished. The sensation was immense, profoundly surging into Wren's heart. So far away it seemed as if it were in another universe, the black sun existed swirling in the thick pitch of darkness in the cave. Wren's jaw dropped, in awe of its power, then fell to his knees.

The master stepped to the opening with his cane in hand. He looked so beautiful in his demon form. Wren could barely see the host inside the demon as he reached his hand to the opening of the cave where the breathing was coming from. Guttural anticipatory breathing, like a bull's breath hushed out of the black sun across the master.

The spell was now gone. Wren felt it dissipate when Nikita's heart joined the fire. Now that the master has gained his supernatural strength, the door between our two worlds can be opened.

"Soon," said the master to the cave. "Our planets will align, and I'll lead you all into the glory of our union."

Now Wren saw eyes inside the cave. So far away, he first believed they were stars. One by one, those eyes were revealed, reaching from the vastness of the ethereal darkness. The master's minions waited for the cosmic door to open.

Not long now, thought Wren. *Just a few more hurdles to overcome.*

He heard a rickety growl come from the cave and saw two large emerald eyes staring at the master.

"My Baphomet," said the master. "We have a special soul chosen... just for you."

The master grinned.

"Oh," said the master. "I have no doubt she will come... all too eager, she will definitely come."

Lori felt a hot breath brush across the nape of her neck. She recoiled and snapped her head around.

There was nothing behind her, but the sensation tore down her spine. Lori swallowed her breath with a gasp, listening to the buzz between her ears disrupting the thick quiet in the tearoom. She looked outside, where the fog grew dense, billowing across the windows. It appeared the fog grew thicker with the increasing volume of the buzz, as if the two were connected, cooperating to bring confusion to the brain.

She looked at her empty teacup and wondered how long she'd been in the tearoom. It felt like minutes had passed since she first entered through its doors, but she knew that couldn't be true. And where was the old lady? Where had she gone? Lori examined the tearoom, listening for a sign from the old lady. Her inquiry yielded zero results.

"Hello," Lori called. "Miss..." She forgot the old lady's name. Did she say what her name was? Lori couldn't remember.

Maybe she went upstairs to her home?

Lori took her teacup and stood up. Walking to the counter, she set her empty mug down and looked through the oval window on the door leading to the kitchen. She saw nobody in the kitchen. It was as barren as the tearoom. She looked up at the clock over the kitchen door. Two-thirty. She had half an hour before her meeting with Marc. Plenty of time to head out and be on time for the meeting, maybe even a few minutes early.

She felt rude leaving without providing a thank you to the lady who provided a few hours of warmth and comfort, even if the palm reading was strange and off-putting. Common courtesy and gratitude are hallmarks of good moral character. So, she entered through the kitchen door.

"Hello?" She wrapped her arms around her chest. "Are you here? I have to go to my meeting, and I just wanted to say thank you."

She felt foolish talking to nothing when she heard a gentle thud and snapped her attention to the office door in the back of the kitchen where the door was ajar. Closing and opening with the breath of the wind. Lori craned her head to get a better look into the office but couldn't see anything beyond the one-inch opening.

Lori took slow, cautious steps to the office door. "Hello, Misses..." Her hand on the door, she pushed it open. "I just wanted to..."

Lori's jaw dropped. The walls were littered with newspaper clippings. Most were about the recent murders, and some were so old the papers were yellow and frayed at the edges. An inverted pentagram was written in red ink in the center of all those articles. Beneath the pentagram, the words *Initium Novum* were written in what Lori assumed was fresh paint. The edges of the letters cascaded down the wall. Intrigued, she stepped into the office, scanning the articles.

She read headlines like **Murders in Sleepy Hollow**, **Detective Carver Thrown Off The Case**, and **Hearts Missing In The Hollow**, before her stare stopped at one article that twisted confusion into her brain.

Car Accident In The Adirondacks.

Her eyes narrowed. She stepped closer to the article where she saw a picture of Marc's overturned car on the highway. She read through the first paragraph that detailed the accident when she saw the article next to it, the one from The Sleepy Hollow Gazette. The author was Marc Saduj. His picture was next to the article with a red circle around it. The title of the article read: **The Sleepy Hollow Nightlife.** Lori shook her head and felt her skin crawl. Her stomach twisted, noxious and sickly.

The revelation was disturbing. Who was this old lady? She scanned across the walls, reading headlines and noticing the articles became older with every passing article. One was so old it was tattered and the print was faded, but the headline could still be read along with the date and the picture, although grainy, dark, and faded, could still be made out. The picture revealed a mansion in the woods. The date was from the 1920s, although the exact year was faded to nothing.

The headline read: **Hardwood Realty Given Dominion Over Death Mansion.**

Lori scanned the article, which was difficult to manage considering the faded text. She read words like murders, spells, and possession. The ground is sour, evil, and cursed.

She read aloud, "Horatio Hardwood the Third of the newly formed Hardwood Realty stated in his interview, 'The ground in the western woods has notoriously been haunted. We believe the mansion is the heart of the evil existing in the Hollow and the cause of the recent murders. The original owner, Sam J. Curad, by all historical accounts, was a cult leader and Satan worshipper. We believe he placed a curse on the property, which was reopened five years ago by philanthropist Fredek Francon and overseen by Mr. Francon's employee, Brent Lockwood.'"

Lori's heart paused a few beats. Her eyes were lost in confusion. The revelation struck hard. She looked back at the article just to be certain she had read those names right and they weren't a figment of her imagination. She read it over again, and then again, and again. There was no doubt she read the names right.

Lori looked over her shoulder into the kitchen. The buzzing grew louder in her ears. She stepped into the barren kitchen, then looked back into the office before making her way into the tearoom where she slung her backpack across her shoulders and then paused, looking around the tearoom completely aware she was alone. She wondered whether the old lady was even real.

Her hands were trembling when she opened the front door and walked out into the Hollow. Into the fog, with the growing buzz.

Lori walked towards her destination. Her thoughts continuously looped back to the article and the names that were revealed.

Fredek Francon was her father's cousin, and Lockwood was the maiden name of Marc's mother.

The revelation was deeply disturbing.

257

The hidden door creaked open, revealing darkness as black as the foulest witch. John's breath hitched in his throat, his eyes adjusting to the dark when a fierce wind nipped across the nape of his neck. He looked over his shoulder, staring down the long hallway to the living room where he could see the front doors were open, creaking under the heavy gale.

Now he heard whispers coming from down below, and he turned back to the darkness. He could see the first step down into the basement-the dungeon, John thought-as his eyes adjusted. Heard the crackle from the fire down below where the whispers were, and he took the first step down with his hand on the wall to steady himself. There was no railing to hold on to.

Three men stood at the bottom of the basement. One was dressed in a suit, and one, who was clearly a priest, donned a red robe. The third wore what John assumed was an old police uniform. He was holding a candelabra.

"The place is evil," said the man in the suit. He noticed they were looking at what John assumed were entrances to another room. "The witch put a spell on the room. That's why we can't enter. The chamber is sealed."

The officer responded. "But the evil wants to live. It infected these people's minds." He looked up, clucking his tongue. "I've known Brent Lockwood for a long time, way before he was in charge of the house." He looked at the man in the suit. "The house changed him."

The others shared concerned stares. The priest said, "Then the book is real, which means the story is true."

"Of course it's true. I told you my grandfather was a young man when the demon and Sam Curad arrived at the Hollow. He passed the story to me." The man in the suit stepped forward, closer to the entrances bathed in darkness.

"Don't get too close," said the officer. "It'll send a shock through your system." He looked at the entrances. "That witch was very powerful. She definitely did not want these entrances opened."

"What do you think is in there?" asked the priest.

The suit answered, "According to the book, there's a portal to hell inside."

The officer shook his head. "We should burn this house to the ground."

But the one in the suit did not agree. "We do that, and we could very well unleash whatever evil exists in this house." He turned to his friends, revealing his face, and John's brow furrowed. He looked very familiar. "The witch's spell has held this long. We can only assume it will continue to hold."

The priest responded, "What're you thinking?"

"Fredek Francon has returned to his ventures in Manhattan. Considering his philanthropic efforts, what I assure you is that he wants nothing we've discovered to see the light of day. We can work with him to bury this story and all that has happened here if he agrees to relinquish his ownership of the home."

"What about his employee, Mr. Lockwood? He seemed to take a special interest in the house and may cause a problem if he goes to the press."

"Mr. Lockwood is a drunk," said the person in the suit. "He's already succumbed to the drink and will be eager to relinquish any claim he has to the house... I'll make certain of it."

"Then what do we do with the house?" asked the officer.

The man in the suit turned back to the entrances. "Simple," he said. "We leave it alone. Let it rot. My company can take control and leave it in probate for eternity so no one can ever open these doors again."

The priest said, "But the future? After we are all dead and buried, how can we be certain future generations will heed our warning?"

The officer looked from the suit to the priest when the suit answered. "There are only a few people who are aware of what went on here. We confide in all of them with our plan and create an organization whose sole purpose is to keep the house under wraps. It's in the middle of the woods and far away from the heart of the Hollow. After enough time, the house will fall into disrepair. Between my company and the organization, I believe we can be certain no one will ever open these doors again."

"And if we're wrong?" asked the officer.

"Then God help all the citizens in the Hollow." He looked over his shoulder, nodding, before turning back to his friends. "Come, gentlemen, I can already feel the evil in this place. We should take leave."

The others agreed, and the three men took the steps up. John was looking at the one in the suit as he ascended the stairs. He was the spitting image of his paternal grandfather, but he knew that couldn't be true because the man in the suit had a scar across his right eyebrow his grandfather never had, although they looked exactly alike. He'd seen a picture of his great-grandfather once. It was a black-and-white photo, and John didn't remember any scar on his face, although the picture was so grainy anything was possible. Horatio was his name. The three men passed John as if he were an apparition, a fly on the wall listening to their conversation.

He watched when they left the staircase, returning to the hall. Watched as they sealed the door, leaving John in the basement, casting him into darkness. He heard their footsteps echo across the ceiling, listened as they made their way out of the house when the most god-awful rickety groan erupted from behind the entrances. John snapped his head to it, staring into the dark depths those entrances held. He tilted his head. Could have sworn he saw something moving in the darkness. He could feel it in his veins, calling him to investigate. He stepped towards the entrances, his stare never relenting from the darkness.

Yes, he was certain there was something moving in the other room, in the place he knew was a dungeon.

There's a portal to hell in the basement.

He stepped directly in front, staring in when that rickety growl wavered from the left to the right across the three entrances. John reached his hand into the darkness, feeling the electrical current cascading across the black pitch. Felt it on his fingertips, raging into his bones, his veins and into his heart, calling him to enter.

John stepped in. Stepped inside the darkness.

Now he sees the Hollow, but not the Hollow as it is now but the Hollow from a long time ago. He's in a prison, eating animals raw.

"The hour draws near." The master kneaded his cane into the ground. Wren stood beneath the cage where he could hear the young John struggling through his nightmare. Grunts, labored breathing, and whines escaped from the cage, but Wren's focus was on the cave. It was hypnotic, staring into the dark depths of blackness and suffering was addictive. He could hear the wind inside the cave. Like a hollowed-out breath inhaling the Hollow. Wren knew the gateway had been opened and understood that hell existed beyond the barrier of the black sun. Once Baphomet takes his rightful place on this side of the door, hell will spill into the Hollow and unleash a tirade across humanity. Wren wished to venture forth, wanting to find a home in hell.

The master addressed his ghost demons. The three of them stood tall and waited for his order. The master looked beautiful in his demon form, although Wren was aware the ritual must be completed for his demon skin to become permanent, then the master can finally shed the skins from the past. The master has worn many skins before. He referred to them as vessels, allowing him to breathe the earthly air with a body that was configured to the planet's atmosphere. He'd been trapped in the body of Sam Curad for over a century after the witch cast the soul from the body and doomed the vessel to the cemetery's ether. Wren could see the new host beneath the veneer of the demon form.

"Go to the Hollow," the master ordered. "Gather the descendants of the Hollow and begin the rituals. Baphomet comes tonight." He looked at Wren, then continued. "Coax the others to the rituals to prepare for the army from Xibalba. They will need fresh bodies to occupy."

"As you wish," the ghost demons said, bowing to the master before taking leave with their new assignment when the master addressed Wren.

"The crystal bowl, Wren. It is time."

Wren bowed to the master. Now that the master has manifested his rightful body, the absinthe would do little to help him in his endeavor. The transformation liquid allowed the master to take occupancy of the body by taking over Marc's consciousness, but to continue forward, Marc's heart was required. The master required the vibrations from the bowl to align their bodies to the same frequency. Once Marc's heart aligns with the frequency, the master will devour his heart, absorbing his life force into the master's dark heart. And then Marc will cease to exist, doomed to live in hell for eternity.

Wren did as he was instructed and brought the crystal bowl to the dungeon where he placed it on a pedestal. "It is ready, my master."

He was staring into the cave when he turned his gaze to Wren.

"Just a few more hurdles to overcome," said Wren, offering the master the mallet, who stepped forward and gripped the thick wooden handle that looked tiny in the master's hand.

"When the sun sets on the Hollow, Wren, call me back from the astral plane. There are people I need to visit prior to tonight's ritual."

"Of course," said Wren. "Do you have expectations for the host?"

The master shook his head. "I expect him to act as we desire. He'll do his best to send Lori away."

"And if he is successful in his endeavor? What then?"

The master grinned from ear to ear. "Now *that* has been expected, but, in the end, it is love that will return her to our embrace. Such purity will always follow the longing of the heart." He held the mallet close to the bowl. Lifted his chin and breathed deeply when the wind spiraled around him with the force of a hurricane, reducing the master into the host body. His blood-red eyes gleamed. "I'll make certain of it."

The master paused while gazing at Wren. Wren seemed to shrink under the master's heavy gaze. "I have a gift for you, Wren. A most glorious gift for your undying loyalty."

Wren gritted his teeth, staring at the master in awed anticipation.

"Tonight, Wren, I open the doorway to Xibalba for you." The master pointed to the cave. "Once you draw me back to the host body, I grant you permission to walk the mile into the black sun."

Wren closed his eyes. Closed his eyes and bowed. "I am forever grateful for your mercy, my lord." He gazed upon his God. "You make all things new."

"My humble servant… I give you the gift of godhood."

The master rapped the mallet against the bowl, and Wren felt the vibration kneading into his heart.

259

A sudden searing pain gripped Marc's heart like a vise, dropping him to his knees. Outside the cemetery, the gong reverberated across the firmament.

The witch looked up and all around the cemetery when another gong echoed across the sky sending waves filled with vibration across the tombstones. Marc could feel the vibrations in his bones as he dropped onto his back, twisting and jerking while the pain in his heart squeezed the air from his lungs. His face pinched in pain, his hand shuddered over his heart as if he could reach in and yank the organ out of his chest. He rolled over onto his knees, attempting to bring air into his lungs, his eyes bulging from their sockets while the pain slithered from his heart, swelling into his veins like noxious venom tainting his blood.

"What is this?" He forced the words from his throat. "What's happening?"

Another gong and Marc dropped face first into the cold frozen earth, his hands crunching dead leaves as his mouth gaped open with a horrifying grunt. Lifting his head, he shuddered, pain racing from his heart as if some phantom wrapped its talons around the organ and squeezed with reckless abandon. Squeezing the organ dry.

The blonde witch kneeled beside him. "The demon has manifested its true form." Her voice was hurried with anxiety. "He's using the vibration to align your hearts. To bring you back into the host body through the heart." She shook her head. "This is an alignment vibration. It's meant to tether you to the host body."

The fourth gong gripped Marc's body, and he shot up to his knees. His bones felt like they could crack in half. Pain rushed to his brain.

"He's bringing you back to the Hollow," she said. "This is your chance."

Struggling to breathe, Marc looked at the blonde. Felt like he was sucking air through the thinnest straw in existence. Felt like his heart was splintering into a thousand pieces, gripped in the talon of vibration.

"Send her away," she said. "Make sure... whatever you do... send Lori out of the Hollow."

He managed a single nod when the fifth vibration wiped the scene away like an Etch-a-Sketch. The pain in his bones dwindled into oblivion, and he could now breathe. Breathe in the damp cold air in the tunnel he was walking in. Up ahead, he saw the end of the tunnel. It led to the park overlooking the Hudson River.

Henry tried for the tenth time to call Elena. His frustration was rising, aided no doubt by the consistent ringing and no pickup. Where could she be? It wasn't like the Hollow was open for business; everything was on lockdown. He hadn't seen a single person on the street. No cars on the roads either. Sleepy Hollow had become a literal ghost town. Looked like all the citizens up and left, abandoning their lives and homes.

"Come, child, have some tea."

Mrs. Leiter was a strange character. Henry didn't trust her. She had that exceptional creep factor that only old ladies have. More than a few times since he arrived, he caught her standing behind him, watching and listening. He could feel her eyes on him, and the sensation sent shivers up his spine. She kept going to check on her husband, but Henry started wondering if she even had a husband. He hadn't heard anyone or anything in the back room. Now she was in the kitchen, brewing some sort of tea that stunk up the apartment. The stench was nauseating, so no, Henry didn't want to sit down for teatime with Mrs. Leiter.

He hung up the phone for the last time, standing in the living room and looking through the window at Storm Street. From his view, he could see Wiley Road, listening to Mrs. Leiter stir her tea, the spoon rattling the mug as she did so. Henry craned his head to get a better look, hoping to see Lori walking through the fog, but the street was barren, the fog floating across the asphalt. The lights flickered overhead. Three flickers, then a pause, then two more flickers. Then dead, the apartment was thrown into a gray hue.

Henry turned to speak with Mrs. Leiter when he saw the framed picture on the side table where the phone was. He craned his head, staring at the picture. The very old picture. All grainy and faded, but he could see it. A woman with thick black hair wearing a black dress stood in front of a wall with a large, inverted pentagram written on it. The woman looked like she was melting into the wall. He picked up the frame, his eyes scrunched, staring around the woman's hips. There were words written beneath the pentagram on the wall behind her. The letters 'In' on the woman's right, and 'um' behind her on the left.

Initium Novum

He noticed Mrs. Leiter had ceased stirring; the apartment was drenched in quiet. Henry craned his head to investigate the kitchen. He didn't see her. He put the frame back on the table and stepped closer. The kitchen was tiny; only two people could fit at a time. There were two entrances to the kitchen. One from the living room and the other from the foyer that led to the front door. He noticed his tea was still steaming in the mug she'd placed on the tiny table stuffed in the kitchen corner by the window. He put his hand over his nose and mouth to ward off the stink steaming from that mug.

"Mrs. Leiter?" Henry whisper-called, hoping she didn't answer. He wanted to get and go and be as far away from this apartment as possible. He hasn't felt right since he stepped inside.

Standing there, as quiet as a mouse, he could hear the wind outside swirling up a storm. Heard the apartment building creak.

"Mrs. Leiter?" He called into the apartment. The situation was strange. Where did she go? She was right there in the kitchen and now, vanished without a trace. He looked at the front door, wanting to leave. Wanting to get the hell away from Mrs. Leiter and her strange and bewildered behavior. He stepped back into the living room, staring into the hall leading to the bedrooms and bathroom. Noticed the master bedroom door was ajar, creaking open and closed with a soft thud.

He tried again. "Mrs. Leiter?"

Henry jumped back when the door swung open, smacking against the bedroom wall. His heart tensed in his chest, staring into the bedroom where he could see the edge of a bed. Heard a groan coming from the room with the door open, inviting him in.

This is the point where a decision needs to be made. All he wanted to do was open the front door and continue his search for Lori, but the natural intrigue coursing through his veins was to check the room. He knew he couldn't live with himself if he left and later discovered something had happened to the old couple. Henry walked through the hall to the master bedroom and looked inside.

Mr. Leiter was the one groaning, lying in the bed with an IV in his arm, which wasn't the strange part. The strange part was what

132

was in the bag dripping into the IV. It looked like blood. The old man moaned, his mouth wide open as his eyes rolled to the back of his skull. Henry wasn't certain, but he believed the old man's face was changing in front of him. He looked like he was growing younger with every drip into his veins.

The other strange part was the cages lined up against the back wall and stacked on top of each other. Three cages with rats in them, squealing and scurrying. Henry's blood curdled, listening to those squeals. But there was no Mrs. Leiter. This is probably the strangest occurrence Henry had ever seen. A blood transfusion was the only rational explanation. Perhaps there's something wrong with his blood. Or he's losing blood from some other place in his body that Henry had yet to see because he had his covers pulled all the way to his chin with his arms draped outside the covers.

Henry didn't know what to say. He turned back to the hall, looking for Mrs. Leiter, then turned back to the old man when he saw a head bobbing past the window and he could swear it was Mrs. Leiter, although now she was dressed in a black robe.

He never heard her leave, although it was possible he was preoccupied with calling Elena and the old lady slipped out of the apartment without his knowledge. But the tea? She was swirling the spoon in the mug. He would swear by it. Up until the lights flickered. Henry stepped through the hall into the living room, watching Mrs. Leiter walk past the windows.

Is she coming back?

He went to the front door and opened it, looking through the glass door in the foyer as she walked by. She didn't even look at the door or the building. She just kept walking. Henry looked back into the apartment when he heard the old man groan with what Henry believed was elation followed by a laugh that ended with an exasperated sigh.

The old man's voice creaked when he said, "Agios O Baphomet," and a shiver squeezed Henry's spine. He immediately closed the door, then stepped through the foyer door and onto the street.

He turned to the left, in the direction Mrs. Leiter was walking. He couldn't see much; the fog was too thick, and now the buzz was back in full force, nipping in his inner ear with a constant barrage to his senses. Henry walked to the end of the road, looking for Mrs. Leiter, but she was gone. He couldn't see her anywhere, as if the fog had devoured the old lady, claiming her as its own.

Great. Now what?

He caught movement in his periphery and immediately looked in the same direction. Someone was walking down Wiley Road. He could see them within the wisps of fog that blanketed the scene, and Henry breathed a sigh of relief.

He finally found Lori.

Henry followed her cautiously.

"It's like a hierarchy," said the priest. "Relate it to the military, with generals, captains and soldiers and how orders are handed down. It's the same for them. Some demons are more powerful than others."

Logan listened to Father McKenzie, absorbing all the information the priest knew about the demon and Sleepy Hollow. The priest was relating all he'd learned and memorized from the book after decades of research and assessment. While he listened, Logan was piecing together his own research into the Hardwood family history, connecting the dots to the demon and the Hardwoods. They were in the church, sitting in the pews after having fortified the church grounds with the hope that the spell can keep the demon out.

"According to the book, for the demon to stake his claim on our world the host who brought the demon here was required to sacrifice what he loved the most to the devil Baphomet, allowing him to occupy her body like a vessel in this world. Once completed, the demon is granted dominion over the earth, allowed to infect every human with his cerebral venom. This is where the coven comes in. The evil coven and the witch Selena Vonder Dutch who attempted to mesmerize Mr. Curad with a trick of the mind and heart, finding love inside Selena's eyes."

The priest closed his eyes and sat forward, pinching the bridge of his nose. He looked old to Logan. Older than he had been yesterday as if the priest had aged half a century since the sun set on the Hollow. Logan could see how his hair seemed to turn grayer with every passing second. Logan looked around the church, waiting for him to continue. The buzz outside continued to heighten, and Logan didn't want to know what would happen once the buzz reached its pinnacle.

And his thoughts kept itching back to the presence he felt in the fog. His instincts were telling him that whatever it is, was still out there as if watching him to learn what his next play would be. He kept feeling breath on the nape of his neck and, in turn, he kept swatting at the area as if he could brush it off.

The priest sat forward, gaining his composure. He cleared his throat. "It was…" Cleared his throat again, his fist over his mouth before he continued. "It was believed by them that should Mr. Curad believe in his love for Selena, the sacrifice would take." He looked into Logan's eyes and shook his head. "Understand that Mr. Curad's heart had belonged to another. To a woman who met her fate by his own hand while he was in the throes of possession, so there could be no genuine sacrifice from him."

"The witch was willing to become possessed by this Baphomet?"

McKenzie's shoulders shot up along with his chin. "Dark hearts welcome evil." He shook his head. "They become consumed by it. Like an addiction. An affliction of the mind, body, and heart for which the only cure is to consume the light it so vehemently opposes." He paused to collect his thoughts. "Selena was more than willing to allow Baphomet into her heart."

"But it didn't work," said Logan. "Obviously, or we'd be having a much different conversation. What happened?"

"Baphomet rejected the sacrifice. Rejected Selena and banished her to the ether." He gazed at the stained-glass window as if looking outside. "Some nights," he said, turning his eyes back to Logan. "You can still hear her clawing across the cemetery, goading others to join her."

An icy chill ran down Logan's spine. The priest paused, and Logan swallowed his breath.

"In the book they arrived during the ceremony… or rather the botched possession and confronted the demon. It was the witch Olga who performed the spell, casting the soul of Sam Curad out and binding the demon's essence to the ether. She then placed a spell on the grounds where we are now." He looked towards the park. "And the cavern that leads to the house."

"But how did he break the spell? How was he able to leave the ether?"

"The book does not have that information, as unfortunate as it may be. It only tells the story and how the demon was defeated."

"Sounds like they got lucky." Logan's voice trailed off when the thought struck in the center of his brain. The information he received from the dark web told of spells and transformations. He didn't know if he was right, but it made sense that Selena's coven had returned to the mansion in the woods and used their own method of witchcraft to aid the demon.

"What my teachings have revealed within the church is that a demon cannot enter a human host without an invitation from the host." He cleared his throat. "I can only assume that he coaxed one of our citizens into his macabre. The demon is manipulative. He's the father of lies. Mixing truth with those lies, he catches people off guard, slithering doubt into their brains with the promise of redemption. A desperate man takes desperate measures, and it is there that evil takes hold."

The lights flickered. Flickered three times then paused, then flickered two more times. Logan looked up at the ceiling, waiting for the lights to turn back on, but they didn't. The church was now cast in a gray glow. Logan noticed the buzz increased in volume. He looked at McKenzie.

"Is it time, Father?"

McKenzie stood up, looking over the church. He went to the stained-glass window, looking through the glass to the park when Logan also stood, joining the priest by the window. The park was barren and looked all purple and red from the window.

McKenzie looked at his watch. "There is at least an hour before sunset," he said. "We have some time before then."

"Tell me, Father," said Logan. "What if the sacrifice is here in the Hollow? The book tells the story of the botched sacrifice, but that only happened because the other woman was already dead."

He shook his head. "If she is here in the Hollow, how do we defeat him if the possession holds?"

"It cannot be done. The demon must be cast out before that time."

Logan thought about that, chewing on his bottom lip. He turned to McKenzie. "But that'll only stop him for now, correct?"

"Correct."

Logan was shaking his head. "Then how do we stop this from ever happening again? How do we rightfully defeat this demon?"

There was a loud knock on the door, and Logan's heart jumped in his chest, snapping his attention to the front door. McKenzie stood behind him, he stepped around Logan to the door.

"You're not going to open that, are you?"

The priest studied the door and put his hand on it. He looked at Logan. "It'll be all right," he said. "They can't come in here."

Logan held his breath when the priest unlocked and then opened the door. That breath hitched in his throat when Detective Carver fell into McKenzie's arms, all bloodied and broken.

"My God," said McKenzie. He turned to Logan. "Water and towels," he instructed. "And the bandages too." He wrapped Carver's arm around his neck and walked him to a pew where he laid Carver down.

Logan noticed the book in Carver's arms.

"What happened, Detective? Who did this to you?"

Carver stretched his arm, pointing to the park. He never answered McKenzie. Instead, he said, "I need to get into the cavern." Logan darted towards the rectory to retrieve what McKenzie asked for, listening when Carver said, "It leads to the house."

Lori put her bag down then took a seat on the bench where Marc had said to meet him. The wooden slats were cold beneath her bottom. She hugged her arms around her torso, biting her lower lip, looking for him across the fog-drenched tennis courts and frozen field that stretched to the Hudson River fifty yards from where she sat.

The fog was so thick, she could barely see the river. Even the Tappan Zee Bridge was drenched in fog, barely noticeable in the overcast sky. If Lori didn't know any better, she would have thought the fog served as a kind of shell, a dome that hung over the Hollow, separating it from every other part of New York. From every other part of the world for that matter.

The wind blew across her skin, tightening her face as she sniffled, hoping Marc would arrive soon. She was hoping he wouldn't stand her up, but now that she was sitting here, waiting, she felt like a fool. Maybe he just wrote the letter to be cruel, knowing she would come and having no intention of attending. She'd never known Marc to be cruel, but who knows what changes he's endured since the accident. Could she blame him if he was cruel? Cruel to her, his fiancée? After all, it was her mother who wrote the letter that shattered his heart.

She wondered what time it was. When she was in the tearoom, the time was just after two thirty, so it had to be close to three by now, maybe even a few minutes after.

Lori looked over her shoulder, scanning the park when she realized how alone she was. The quiet was as thick as the fog.

Maybe this wasn't such a good idea. She swung back around, hoping to find him. *Maybe being alone is not the best decision when there are murders happening in the Hollow?*

She kept looking, searching, scanning. Nothing.

I don't think he's coming.

An icy chill raged off the surface of the Hudson River. She could feel its icy breath rattle her bones. Lori pulled her beanie over her ears when she remembered Marc's writing and looked down at the bench. He'd written it the weekend before they went to the cabin.

Lori and Marc. As you wish!

Marc wrote those words that day. He said they could come back decades from now with their grandchildren and show them the sign. The ink had faded a bit, but the words were prominently on display, surrounded by multiple displays of affection. She ran her fingers across the words and felt her heart crack as if a cavern had been opened in the organ and all her heartache came flooding out. She couldn't stop the tears from coming. She sniffled them back and wiped her eyes.

263

Marc stood in the park covered in fog, but he could see Lori. His heart dropped into his stomach the moment he laid eyes on her.

He didn't know if he had the strength to continue. He'd dreamed about this moment since leaving her in the hospital. Dreamed about wrapping her in his arms and never letting go. Kissing her once again as if it were the first kiss they'd ever shared.

His head was down, fixated on the frost-covered, fog-inducing ground but not seeing the ground. Memories as thick as the fog raced through his mind. Their meeting in the tearoom and how he was immediately smitten with her. How he looked her up in the phonebook and discovered she owned the antique shop and how he went there and bought an armoire-an item he had no need for, but he did have a need to see Lori. He couldn't get her out of his head since the tearoom. The mere thought of her occupied his every thought. It was love at first sight. At least for him it was as if he'd been struck with Cupid's arrow and his entire life came into focus. Came into focus because Lori had been the missing piece in his future, and once he laid eyes on her she brought his future into the light, and it was brilliant.

The laughter and the long talks filled with meaning. Her little quirks and trivial notions that now meant everything to him. How they cared for each other with an acceptance of each other's faults that they embraced with the vow that no one and nothing will hurt you while I'm with you. Lori's night terrors and Marc's depression and how those parts of themselves seemed to dissipate the longer they were together. So happy together.

He lifted his head, his jaw tight, gritting his teeth. A single tear fell from his bloodshot and burning eyeball. Felt like he had just swallowed a wallop of pain and suffering, all hollowed out inside.

He wanted to go to her and make everything right. Wanted to take her and get the hell out of Sleepy Hollow and never look back, but he knew he couldn't.

No matter where they went, the man in black would be there like he's always been there, waiting. So patiently waiting to douse their love in darkness. Their union, their light, their loving hearts as innocent as a child, drew the demon to them. A love so pure, there was no way the devil would allow it to breathe.

Whatever you do… send Lori out of the Hollow.

The witch's words erupted in the center of his brain as if she were talking to him from the netherworld. Marc gasped, then held in his pain, sucked it down his gullet and stuffed it inside a room in his heart where all his pain was kept. He swallowed it down and stepped forward.

Knowing the devil was listening.

He's not coming, is he?

She wondered if he'd written the letter. Maybe she was playing the part of the fool. It's been at least fifteen minutes since she arrived. How long does someone wait until they admit they've been played? She didn't know, and she also didn't want to leave. Part of her wanted to stay on the bench and die. Allow this moment to be her last, because how could she move on from this pain? She lost him once, and now she's losing him again.

Lori looked up when a sudden spear of sunlight warmed her face. She looked up at the fog and overcast sky, feeling the sun's heat penetrate the dark that had befallen the Hollow. Like a ray of sunshine in the middle of all the hurt. The sun hovered just above the horizon, slicing through the clouds and fog. It found Lori before the dark clouds rolled across the sky, returning the darkness. Returning the bitter cold. Lori looked at the ground, then turned around, and her heart dropped.

She stood up, observing that she was trembling, watching Marc traverse the field amid the fog. Her eyes were steadfast; she refused to take her eyes off him as if he could vanish like a specter the moment she turned her eyes away and never return. Her chest constricted; her entire body tensed. Before this meeting, Lori had rehearsed what she would say when she met him eye to eye, but now she couldn't think of one thought, her mind wiped clear, watching as he approached. He looked like an apparition in the fog, his feet crunching across the frozen grass and packed snow.

Her jaw dropped further with every step that brought him closer. He looked… different. Sickly. Emaciated wasn't the word. It looked like he hadn't eaten in the last six months. His face was sunken and pale, with thick black circles beneath his eyes. She could see his cheekbones he was so thin. His hair, disheveled and long, did little to hide the scar that ran from his head to his eye. His hands were all cracked and chapped and bleeding, as were his swollen and busted lips. His fingertips were swollen, the nails close to nonexistent. Lori noticed dried blood on every scar and chapped skin, including the scar across his eye that looked like it had happened yesterday, all swollen and red with dots of pus embedded into the scabbing skin. He looked like he was rotting to death from the inside out. Lori could feel her face turn into an expression of awe and fear. She held her hand over her mouth to stop the whining cry that wanted to escape her throat.

Now, there were tears in her eyes. Tears filled with sadness over what had happened to him.

His transformation sunk her heart into the depths of despair. He wore all black, which only emphasized his deathly pale complexion. He looked like a ghost. As if he'd died in the car accident only to return for this meeting after raising himself from the grave.

He stopped ten feet from where she stood. Her hand drifted from her mouth, her jaw trembling while tears streamed down her cheeks. She didn't know if she should run into his arms or take him to the hospital, and then there was the fear that slithered into her heart. The fear that he would refuse her embrace. His expression was tense, his teeth gritted, his jaw tight. He looked like he'd had a nervous breakdown, but when she stared into his eyes, she saw how scared he was, how absolutely frightened and filled with fear. And in the depths of his eyes, she could see how much he loved her, as if that love were the foundation for his suffering and the only reason to live. The sliver of light in the shroud of darkness.

She wondered what she should say, but Marc handled that himself.

Gritting his teeth, his nose curled in a sneer, Marc said, "What are you doing here, Lori? There's nothing left for you in the Hollow."

"That's... him?"

Henry had followed Lori to the park, concealing himself close to the restaurant that shared a border with the tennis courts. At first, he had no idea why Lori had come here. It made no sense, but his detective instincts knew there had to be a reason. He didn't expect he'd be seeing Marc. Didn't even know Lori had gotten in touch with him-or vice versa. Now that he was here, he felt like he was intruding on a private moment. *I am intruding on a private moment.*

A private moment with someone suspected of murder, and not just murder, but mass murder. There were too many bodies in the Hollow not to conclude that this was indeed a mass-murdering spree, which may have been sparked by the relationship he was currently witnessing. Henry studied Marc, although it was difficult to see him through the fog, but the man didn't look healthy. In fact, he looked like the murdering son of a bitch Detective Carver said he was.

It was difficult to hear what they were saying from where he stood, but it looked like they were arguing. Their body language said it all. Looked more like a standoff than a conversation between two former lovers.

Henry unlatched his holster. His trusted Glock 22 Gen 4 now ready in case he needed to intervene. If this meeting gets out of hand, he'll be prepared.

The conversation had stopped. Now Lori was taking something out of her backpack.

Henry's eyes squinted; certain he was looking at a blue notebook.

Lori held the notebook for Marc to see, but his stare was elsewhere as if he didn't want to look at her. As if he couldn't look at her.

"Do you remember this? You were writing this story when we were at the cabin." She could see he was clenching his jaw, gritting his teeth. He looked like he'd just swallowed poison. "Look, Marc," she hollered when he snapped his eyes to her. She shook the notebook. "Look!"

He locked eyes with her, and her heart tensed in her chest. So much pain. She could see the depths in his eyes, reaching into despair. He looked at the book.

"You wrote about the murders before they happened."

His gaze floated to her eyes. "And?"

She clenched her jaw, swallowing her own desolation. Lori closed her eyes. "Are you hurting these people, Marc?" Her jaw trembled, her lips quivered, opening her eyes to him. "Like what happened in your story?"

"I told you already. It's the demon killing those people."

"There is no demon, Marc. It's just part of the story. I…" Her voice trailed off, and she gritted her teeth then swallowed her breath. "I think it's best for you to hand yourself in. You're sick, Marc, and more people are going to suffer if you don't."

His stare was hypnotic. She noticed the tension in his face and shoulders slacken. He looked like he was about to laugh.

"Suffering," he said. The word flitted off his tongue as if it were soothing or something to scoff at. "Suffering comes to those who embrace the light. For it is through our suffering that we find the light."

She shook her head. "I know you don't believe that, Marc. You're hurting these people. You're killing people. Innocent people. This all needs to stop."

"Innocence..." he said, his voice guttural, born from the depth of heartache. "Is evil's addiction."

She saw red in his eyes. Saw hate and rage leap from his pupils and her jaw dropped, remembering how Gerrard had said the same before he attempted to rape her in her mother's home.

He stepped forward, and Lori cringed. Icy chills ran down her spine. Her flesh cringed at the sight of him, those dark red eyes beaming with rage. "There is nothing left for you in the Hollow. It is time for you to leave." He was gritting his teeth, and Lori thought he could reach out and strangle her. Her heart splintered, staring at him and how lost he was. How mad and filled with hate. "Your presence here is not wanted. Leave," he said, gesturing to the Hollow. "And burn that book. Light it up like a funeral pyre and say your goodbyes to love." Lori scanned him, her jaw hanging open with tears rolling down her face. He looked like he was struggling, acting mean to discard her.

Lori shook her head. "Please," she groaned. "Let me help you... You're sick. This isn't you, Marc. I know you, and you'd never hurt anyone but this..." She met his eyes with hers. "Something's gotten into you. I can feel it. Please..." She reached for his hand. "It can all end now. Just please come with me. Whatever it is you've done, I'll help you through it. I owe you that much." He didn't answer; instead, he cringed away from her touch. It looked like he was struggling with his thoughts. Struggling to maintain in the face of tragedy. "PLEASE!"

Her voice travelled across the field, echoing across the Hollow. Then quiet returned with the fading of her voice. Lori could hear her own ragged breathing, staring at Marc while he stared into the Hollow. He said nothing. He just stood there, staring at nothing, but he was thinking. He looked like he was wrestling with an internal catastrophe.

"You know what it is... Lori?" His voice was soft, the same voice she knew. "After all this. After all the suffering and heartache, it's always been me in the shadow, invisible to the world." He trained his eyes on her, and Lori's blood froze. "Well, I'm not invisible now, am I? Those people you so vehemently care for. Whose blood and suffering made me whole." His teeth gritted, seething his words across his lips. "Whose deaths gratified my hunger for pain. Those deaths are the only thing that has brought me peace." She could see the rage in his eyes. Those wide, blood-red eyes filled with tears. His face pinched in pain, suffering to force the words across his trembling lips. "I wonder," he said, "what kind of peace will your death bring?"

She stepped back, her head shaking.

"What wonderful gifts will your suffering offer?"

"I don't understand," she cried, wiping the tears from her eyes and nose. "What are you saying?"

He closed his eyes as if he himself were the one suffering. His jaw quivered to force the words out. "I'm saying... that if you stay in the Hollow..." He gnashed his quivering jaw. "I'll hurt you. With all the hate in my heart, I will make certain you feel all the suffering you've caused... all the pain you brought will be delivered upon you tenfold."

His words were like a punch in the gut. Lori breathed a ragged breath filled with tears. "Marc, please. Don't do this. I love you. I-I've always loved you. You're sick. Something cracked after the accident. This isn't you. Please let me help you. We can stop this together; just come with me. Please, come with me now." She closed her eyes, and the tears fell like a flood down her cheeks. When she opened them, he was still there, wrestling with his own mind.

His stare was stoic, but with tears that fell silently. "If I see you again... on this night or the next, that moment will be your last."

Her jaw dropped as a whine escaped her throat. She put her hand over her mouth.

"Now go," he said, gesturing to the Hollow. "And take that pathetic notion you call love with you."

Lori backed away from Marc. Henry had his hand on his service weapon, ready to arm himself should Marc reach for Lori with ill intent.

It didn't look like the conversation had gone in Lori's favor. Shit, it looked like the worst lovers' spat he'd ever witnessed. He wished he could have heard the conversation, relying on body language to fill in the gaps. It seemed as if the conversation had arrived at a standstill. He saw Marc's mouth move, and what he said to Lori caused her heart to drop. She gathered her bag and the notebook, stuffing the notebook back into the bag before slinging it over her shoulder and walking away. Henry could see she was crying, walking away from the courts and the park.

Henry turned back to Marc, but he was already gone, enveloped in the fog. He took the opportunity and went after Lori. She walked across the street, headed back towards Wiley Road. He was certain she was crying. He looked back at the park. Still no Marc, and the fog seemed to turn thicker. Turned back and hurried across the street.

She was walking through a store parking lot when he called her name, and she immediately turned in his direction. Her mouth hung open, and Henry wondered if she thought he was Marc, calling her back to him. He saw she was crying, tears dripping from her watery eyes.

He stepped closer to her. "I'm so.." She folded into his arms, and he took her in. "I'm so sorry, Lori." He held her tight. "Sorry for everything." He stayed there with her, allowing her to cry, to allow the pressure and heartache to dissipate.

She was trembling; every part of her was shaking like a leaf. "My God," Henry whined. He held her for another minute longer. "I think it's time we got out of the Hollow. Your mom was right; there's nothing here but heartache."

He held her and then held her some more. She seemed incapable of talking; the emotion overwhelmed her ability to speak. Henry walked her through the fog. Walked with her up Wiley Road while she shivered and shuddered and cried relentlessly. Henry walked her to his car, and Lori mindlessly took a seat.

Henry walked around and sat in the driver's seat, turning the key in the ignition. Lori was wringing her hands, her eyes watery as she stared through the windshield, her quivering lips sucked into her mouth.

And then she said without turning in his direction. "We need to call that detective."

Henry's brow furrowed. "He said something, didn't he? Something that convinced you he's the one committing all these murders?"

She looked at him. "I just need to talk to the detective."

Henry nodded. "Okay. Let's get back to the hotel, and I'll call him to come there." He looked at her, meeting her gaze with his. "And then you can tell me everything."

A simple nod was all Lori could manage before the tears came again.

268

The fog drifted in front of him like specters witnessing heartache. Marc had waited for Lori to leave, watching her cross the street when he returned to the bench and took a seat.

He looked at his own writing on the bench. Words that have come to mean everything and yet nothing at the same time. He struggled during the conversation. Struggled to find a way to force Lori to leave. He didn't want to admit that he was responsible for the murders, but he did, thinking it was the only way she would leave. He knew he was anyway. He may not have been the one who inflicted the torture and death on those people, but it was because of him that they met with an ill fate. Tortured by the man in black.

"Now what's your plan?" he whispered, shaking his head, because the devil always has a plan.

He hoped Lori was on her way out of the Hollow. Hoped that his threat was taken seriously, because at the moment that was all he had, all he could come up with to reveal how serious the situation had become. If she refused to leave because of her commitment to him, then he needed to sever that commitment. Desecrate it and douse it in darkness.

Marc could still see her face when he threatened her. The look in her eyes brought him to tears. He delivered the worst possible heartache any human could threaten another with.

He prayed she was leaving. Prayed he would never see her again. No matter what torture the man in black had ready for him, he would deal with it. Albeit with a smile. A smile because he would know Lori was safe. That she'd gotten away and made a life for herself somewhere where she could be happy, even if the love they shared no longer existed. Even if he wasn't with her and instead was reduced to a passing memory or a nostalgic thought that came every once in a blue moon. It was there that Marc would find peace within the suffering the man in black would certainly dole out.

Marc noticed a shift in the atmosphere, and he looked up to see the last remaining rays from the sun. The rays that touched his scars and warmed his skin.

The beams dissipated at the same moment they arrived, when the sun dipped below the horizon, clawing night across the Hollow.

He had only a second to take a single breath before he felt the gong vibrate in his heart, leading him back to hell.

Logan felt a shift in his gut as if the earth shifted out of orbit. Felt like he was slipping, grasping for the former reality and holding on for dear life while humanity unknowingly accepted a new transformation.

As if everything he knew had suddenly shifted into a new reality.

Detective Carver was in terrible shape. He talked about a car accident and possessed officers while Father McKenzie did his best to patch up his wounds. And he talked about the book. The book that was sitting on the pew in front of Logan.

"Everything is true," he'd said, which, to Logan, seemed like a hard truth to swallow for the detective. It made sense to Logan, considering most adults lost their imagination after high school and police officers were on top of that list, adapting their point of view to simple logic with no need for the notion of the supernatural.

The gash across Carver's forehead was concerning, and he'd lost a lot of blood. He said he needed to get into the cavern where the buzz was coming from. Said it led to the house in the woods, the house where Logan knew John was held captive. And then he passed out. Whether it was from the loss of blood or the exhaustion Logan wasn't certain, but Detective Carver kept weaving in and out of consciousness. His determination forced him to get up. His police instincts the driving force behind his resolve.

"No, no, detective. Stay where you are." McKenzie looked at Logan, and his stare said everything that was happening in the priest's brain. He looked as if he had lost all hope. "We need to bring him to the rectory." He looked scared to death. McKenzie swallowed his breath. "Come…" McKenzie wrapped Carver's arm around his neck and heaved him off the pew when a groan escaped Carver's throat. "Help me."

Logan met him on the other side of Carver, wrapping Carver's free arm around his neck, and together the three of them shuffled out of the pew into the aisle. Logan got a good look at Detective Carver. His head all bloodied and swollen, and when Logan touched his side, the man cringed as if his ribs were broken.

McKenzie stopped and looked at Logan, gesturing to the pew behind him. "Take the book," he said.

Logan shifted on his feet, then reached for the book, tucking it under his arm. He looked at Father McKenzie and nodded. Together they hauled Carver down the aisle, where the door to the rectory waited behind the stage where Father McKenzie provided his sermons.

"What do we do now, Father?" He looked at Carver, his head resting against Logan's shoulder, his breath coming out all ragged and labored. "I don't think he'll be much help to us tonight." Logan understood that the demon would need to be confronted. Aware the priest had said Detective Carver was a part of that

160

confrontation, but now that plan just flew out the window. He could see that the priest was wrestling with the current circumstances.

"I'll have to go myself," he said. "I don't see any other way."

They got as far as the stage when Detective Carver fell from their arms like dead weight. McKenzie and Logan caught him before he dropped like an anvil, guiding him to the floor where he rested against the stage steps.

"My lord," said McKenzie, hovering over Carver. Clearly, the detective had passed out. McKenzie crouched in front of him, his hand on Carver's forehead. He took Carver's hand and silently prayed when something flickered in Logan's peripheral.

His attention snapped to the stained-glass window. Carver groaned from the floor, but Logan never took his eyes off the window. Night had now arrived in the Hollow. He could see the dark stain on the other side of the glass.

"Father?" Logan said when he looked down at the priest while Carver's eyes rolled beneath his eyelids and McKenzie turned his attention to him. "The sun has fallen." He looked up and all around the church. "The battle has begun."

His heart skipped a few beats when the church doors groaned, the wood bending into the church.

"Yes," said Henry, followed by, "No," a second later. He was on the phone with the police station, calling for Detective Carver. Lori sat on the bed, wrestling with her own mind.

Henry had already called Elena with the information that they were leaving the Hollow after Lori speaks with Detective Carver, although that was not a requirement for Henry. He could always stay in the Hollow and inform Carver of his discovery-namely Marc's notebook that detailed all the murders-while Lori and Elena found comfort somewhere outside of the Hollow. Considering a threat had been made, it was best for Lori to be as far away as possible. She obviously just became the key to Carver's investigation and would need to be protected from here on out, and since Henry assumed Carver had his hands full, that meeting may not happen tonight.

"Just let him know I have the key to his investigation and to meet us at the hotel as soon as possible."

The dispatcher took his information, and Henry hung up. He turned to Lori. She was still trembling. Crying too. She looked up at Henry. "They'll want to take him in, right? They'll want to arrest him to stand trial and not just kill him, correct?"

"That'll be their primary goal." Henry knew how this went, and if Marc showed aggression towards the police, they'll shoot him dead right where he stood.

Lori nodded, sucking her lips into her mouth, wringing her hands across her lap.

"How are you holding up?" he asked. "Can I get you anything?"

Lori shook her head and then looked away as the tears fell like a freefall. "What if the detective doesn't come or call you back?"

"He will. It's his investigation, and he wants it solved as quickly as possible. I wouldn't be surprised if he's on his way here now."

Henry paused, thinking. "Why don't you pack all your belongings? That way we can get you to the motel right after then leave the Hollow."

Lor nodded.

"Okay," said Henry and paused. "I'll do the same, okay?"

Lori paused, staring at Henry.

"I'll be right across the hall, and I'll leave my door open. Anything happens, just yell and I'll be through that door in a heartbeat." He looked at her, nodding. "Is that okay?"

Lori looked at the door and then at Henry. "Whatever gets us out of here faster is all I care about. I can't stay here anymore."

"I know," said Henry. "Just get ready and I'll be back."

The doors stretched until they burst into the church. McKenzie shot his stare at Logan and then gestured to the book. "Take it and go," he said, staring at Logan with desperation and fear. "It all comes down to you now, Logan." He paused. "I'm sorry."

Now, a guttural laugh consumed the church, drawing the priest's attention before he snapped around to Logan. "Go!" he just about hollered. The laugh echoed across the church, bouncing off the walls before dying quickly as if the throat that laugh belonged to had been cut.

Logan took one last look at Carver and McKenzie and then scurried behind the stage where he waited in the shadows.

Father McKenzie turned to the shattered door. Logan could hear heavy breathing at the door. Father McKenzie made the sign of the cross over his forehead, his lips, his chin, and chest. "My lord… give me strength."

The lights flickered on, returning light to the church. Logan saw Detective Carver stir, his eyelids fluttering as if the light had found its way to his brain and was waking him up. Logan looked towards the door when the wind howled from the outside through the open doorway, sending the light into flickers that danced across the walls, rippling shadow across the church.

Father McKenzie stood strong in the center aisle, protecting his flock. Protecting Logan and Carver. The silence was maddening, the waiting. Logan looked down at the book in his arms. His breath hitched in his throat when the demon stepped into the church.

Logan's eyes grew wide. The demon's presence was thick with tension and seemed to arrive before the body. Logan pursed his lips and swallowed his stuttering breath. He saw the feet first, followed by the red cane the demon was holding. He was dressed all in black, from his shoes to his collar. The clothes seemed to be melted onto his skin, tight around his thick frame, accentuating his dark skin that looked like burnt ash. When he moved, it seemed as if the air rippled around him, following him as if obeying his command. His footsteps echoed across the floorboards that buckled from his heavy weight.

The demon's voice was guttural and goading and boomed across the church. "In him. With him. In the name of the Holy Spirit." His arms stretched to his sides, palms up, the cane dangling from his palm.

Father McKenzie stood with his jaw hanging open when the demon turned to him, and Logan would swear the surrounding air thundered with his movement. Logan saw a glint of red in the demon's eyes. His skin was cracked and bleeding. His horns tore out of his cracked forehead, the nose split at the nostrils, thick across his face. His lips were cracked and bleeding, and his teeth were jagged pebbles with incisors that looked like a vampire's fangs. It looked like there was one body beneath another, and the dominant larger body was ripping through the foundation. Logan noticed the demon's hands were in the shape of talons, with long bony fingers and sharp black nails.

"Be gone, demon. You are not allowed here," said Father McKenzie, holding his cross towards the demon.

McKenzie's declaration fell on deaf ears. The demon looked around the church. "So, this is what you've done to sacred ground." His eyes found the priest. "This is blasphemy, and it must be destroyed."

Father McKenzie waved his cross at the demon. "No, spawn of hell, you have no place here. Be gone from this night and cast yourself back into darkness."

"Sorry, Father, but we were here first. Now... where's the book? I see Detective Carver has found his way here." He looked from Carver to McKenzie. "I'll ask again, but then I'll do what must be done."

Logan held the book close to his chest and started looking around for a quick exit.

"There is no book here other than the lords," McKenzie hollered, waving his cross in front of him.

The demon shook his head, stepping closer to McKenzie, walking tirelessly towards the priest, who took steps back.

"A century of waiting, Father, but I'm sorry... I won't wait any longer." He gripped McKenzie's forehead, and the priest dropped to his knees, his head shaking. "Now, where's the book?"

Logan could see smoke rising from McKenzie's skull. Saw blood drip from his nose and eyes. White foam across his lips.

"One last chance, Father." He craned his head, staring at Father McKenzie. "Where's the book?"

McKenzie raised the cross in front of the demon's face, his hand trembling when the demon gripped the priest's hand and the most godawful shriek escaped McKenzie's throat as his hand melted in the demon's grip, the skin and bone gushing a river of blood and flesh across his arm.

"Very well, Father. I give you permission to die."

He released McKenzie's skull, and the body flopped to the ground. Logan turned away immediately. McKenzie's forehead had melted. The heated skull dripped off his forehead, exposing brain matter; the skin across his face melted and bleeding.

"Fuck!" Logan whisper-whined, watching as the demon approached Carver when the door next to Logan popped open and Logan's heart lurched in his chest. His first instinct was that someone was coming through the door, but only silence greeted him. He looked through the door of the rectory when an icy chill gripped his bones. He turned back to the church when he heard footsteps on the floorboards. There were three people entering the church. Two men and one woman. The demon was hovering over Detective Carver, assessing him. Father McKenzie's dead body lay in waiting.

The demon addressed the three people standing and waiting. "Take him to the house," he instructed. "Detective Carver will offer his heart for sacrifice."

The two men bowed before attending to Carver, and the woman stepped closer to the demon. "What do you wish for the church?"

The demon looked around, assessing before training his eyes on her. "Burn it," he said. "Let it rise into a funeral pyre where we can burn the dead with a fire that reaches into the zenith of Xibalba. But first, tear this place apart. Look for the book." He looked around the church. "I know it's here. I can feel it."

"And if it's not located?"

One of the men heaved Carver over his shoulder.

"Then it'll burn with the church."

"As you wish, my master." The girl bowed.

The demon took her chin between his talons. "I'll leave you to it," he said, and Logan could see the grin that spread across his charred and bloodied lips. "I have to meet with an old friend. Tend to your duties. Our victory comes tonight."

The one with Carver over his shoulder walked out the front door, and the other man and the woman looked at each other before beginning their search for the book that was in Logan's arms.

He slipped into the rectory and closed the door with a soft touch, locking it quietly, then backed away from the door. He knew they were coming through that door; it was only a matter of time.

Logan looked around the rectory when the wind howled outside as if calling him to it.

He heard footsteps outside the door and someone rummaging through drawers and turning over pews.

There wasn't any place for him to hide without being found. He had no choice but to follow this through. Logan pursed his lips and swallowed, turning the knob on the rectory door that led outside to the parking lot, and stepped outside quietly. He hid in the shadows, looking through the stained-glass windows where he could see the man and woman tearing the church apart when he felt something brush across the nape of his neck and he turned quickly with a stuttered whine that escaped his throat.

There was nothing behind him, but the wind rippled across his brow, turning his attention to the end of the church where he could see the white wisp comingling with the fog.

"I can't believe I'm doing this again."

Logan gripped the book close to his chest then scurried across the lawn, past the stained-glass windows to the end of the church where he stopped and looked around the corner, watching the wisp float around to the other side of the church. He followed again, breathing in the cold and bitter winter wind to the end of the wall and peeked around the corner at the park and the cavern with the buzz.

He watched as the one who had Detective Carver entered the cavern. Noticed the wisp then, traveling through the fog towards the same cavern.

Logan was shaking his head. "I really don't want to go in there," he said, although to whom he wasn't certain.

Now he heard footsteps, but not just one pair of feet but what sounded like hordes of them coming from all directions. The sound grew louder, like the running of bulls. Logan raced across the street into the park, scuttling across the grass to the cavern where the buzz was ear-piercing. He investigated the thick blackness that existed inside the cavern, and his heart lurched in his chest. He squeezed the book against his beating heart and looked around.

He saw what looked like torches on the street, coming from the east and the west, the north and the south. People were coming to the park. Who or how many Logan didn't want to stick around to discover. He looked back at the church and the busted doors and the two people tearing it apart. Heard the thunder of footsteps approaching on the streets.

Logan stepped into the cavern, allowing the darkness to envelope him like the dark hand of death.

Elena stuffed her last garment into her suitcase, her hands shaking the entire time. She turned around and surveyed the room, then went to the closet and took out her coat, draping it across the bed before retreating to the bathroom to collect her toiletries.

She had to admit she was impressed with Henry. Lori has always been a tough nut to crack, and when she gets an idea in her head all logic and reason fly out the window until she believes the idea has been satisfied, at least in her own mind. But the situation with Marc differed from the normal Lori Francon situation, and Elena had a large part to play in her daughter's current heartbreak.

The demon has always had an interest in Lori, the same as the entire Francon family. Their lineage was rooted in a more than a thousand-year history. Cursed! Elena had always said the Francon family was cursed, and after what had happened to her husband's cousin, Fredek and his daughter, Elena had proof positive that the curse was true. Those Francons are like magnets for the damned.

And her daughter was no exception. Elena always believed that if the Francon's could just get over themselves and allow the demon to have its day, they would have been spared centuries of heartache. It was like their wealth was the curse, always conforming to the whims of high society while their personal lives unraveled around them.

Don't they know it's better to placate the damned?

She took her hairdryer, makeup bag, and hairbrush off the sink, then gave one last look around before turning off the light and stepping back into the room. She walked around the bed and added the items to her luggage when something glinted in the corner of her eye, and she snapped her head to the window beside the door. Her heart was pounding against her chest.

Elena knew she was walking a fine line with the demon. Knew she needed to get the hell out of the Hollow as soon as possible. She tried to coax Henry to leave the hotel immediately during their phone call, but he was adamant about waiting for Detective Carver. Not that it mattered anyhow, once Lori is out of the Hollow the demon's plan will crumble. What happened to Marc Saduj after was not her concern either. More than likely, he'll be arrested for the murders and spend the rest of his days behind bars while the demon shifts his focus to another.

Elena understood she had an intricate role to play in the current situation, but she never realized the true weight of her involvement. She knew she was guilty, and that guilt led her to the Hollow. She couldn't allow her daughter to become a pawn of the devil.

She stepped to the window and noticed the fog drifting across the parking lot. It looked like it was coming from the western woods. Looked like it was coming straight for her.

She jumped when someone knocked on her door, and a high-pitched squeal escaped her throat. Her heart was beating like a drum. She looked back into the parking lot and saw no cars.

The lights went out, plunging the room into darkness. Elena's eyes flitted from one corner of the room to the other. The fog drifted beneath the door, flowing like a waterfall into the room. Elena watched as it billowed into the room. She stepped back, closer to the window.

"I've come for you, Elena."

She knew that voice. She'd heard it many times before. "I-I did what you asked. I wrote the letters. The rest was up to you."

The fog drifted towards her, rolling towards her feet.

"And now, Elena? Trying to take her away. Wanting to tell her everything to relinquish the guilt from your mind."

Her lips quivered, wringing her hands as she backed up against the window and the fog coiled around her like a snake, squeezing her bones when a groan escaped Elena's throat. The fog swirled in front of her eyes, revealing the demon's face, his shoulders, his body manifesting from the fog with his hand wrapped around her throat.

Elena gasped when his face was revealed. He looked like he was rotting, as if there were two bodies in one and the dominant body was tearing through the other. His breath stank of sulfur and blood.

"Allow me to relieve you of your guilt." He squeezed her throat with such strength she thought her windpipe was going to crush in his hand.

Elena struggled to breathe, her voice strangled in her throat.

"No need to be afraid. Death will welcome you with open arms." And he smiled. Grinned from ear to ear before plunging his talon into her chest, and Elena's scream belted across the room. Pain ripped from her chest to every bone in her body.

"Your heart, Elena."

He inched his talon down her chest bone, blood flooding down her torso. He raised her off her feet and brought her down onto the bed then growled when he dipped his face to hers. Staring into her eyes, his talon embedded in her chest.

"Your heart, Elena, I will personally devour."

The tunnel smelled of dank earth, sulfur and something Logan wasn't familiar with. Something noxious and foul, as if the ground had spoiled like rotten meat. He coughed across his dry throat, noticing the air was growing hotter the farther he traveled and the noise, the buzz that had overtaken the Hollow, grew louder. Logan was certain the source of the buzz was somewhere down here with him.

After he stepped into the cavern he was enveloped in a thick blackness and had to feel across the walls to find the opening that led to the tunnel he was in now, listening to the footsteps he believed belonged to the person who took Detective Carver. Logan used it for direction. Wherever they were taking Carver was where Logan wanted to be. Plus, he was certain they were taking him to the same place where John was.

The house in the western woods. The one place he was hoping to avoid above all others in the Hollow.

Logan clutched the book close to his chest, taking careful steps as he followed. The tunnel was dark, and his ability to see more than a few inches in front of his face was limited. He couldn't see his feet because it was so dark. He couldn't see the ground he was walking on, so he took each step with caution.

The demon's cane kept ringing in his head. Seeing it brought a sensation that rippled across his skin. It had some meaning he'd read about on the dark web, but for the life of him he couldn't locate the information in his brain. At least not now.

He hoped he'd remember it. He hoped to see his friend again. Logan didn't want to think about what John was enduring at this current moment. He just hoped he could get his friend out of harm's way.

He heard a splash like someone stepping into a puddle and stopped. Frozen in the dark. Gooseflesh rippled up his arms, the hair on his arms and the back of his neck erected across his skin. His heart contracted with a held breath in his throat.

Quiet except for the wind. The subtle groaning wind howled through the tunnel. Logan swallowed his breath and felt sweat on his forehead. He wasn't certain, but he believed something was following him.

The presence outside the church. He was sure of it.

Now the wisp materialized in front of his eyes, and he could hear the footsteps again. He didn't remember missing them, but now that he was looking at the wisp, he could hear the footsteps.

Another drip into the puddle, but the wisp floated forward towards the footsteps.

Logan stood for another minute longer, staring behind him. Waiting for someone or something to come barreling out of the darkness. The only thing that greeted him was the wind.

Now he heard more footsteps but not from up ahead but overhead. Sounded like thunder. Sounded like the entire town was walking up above.

Logan turned and looked behind him before turning around and following the wisp into the darkness.

274

The phone started ringing, startling Lori with a holler. She jumped off the bed as if she had been shocked by electricity. With her hand over her mouth, she stared at the phone ringing on the nightstand beside the bed.

Her blood curdled in her veins. Who could it be, calling her at this moment? Henry was right across the hall; he would have just come over. Maybe it was Detective Carver? Maybe he was here and the receptionist was ringing her room to tell her she had a visitor?

Lori stared at that phone hoping the ring would stop, but it didn't. It just kept ringing.

She looked around her room before walking over to the phone. She picked it up, slowly placing the receiver to her ear.

She cleared her throat. "H-Hello." Her voice trembled.

Lori listened to the voice on the other end of the line. Her eyes grew wider the longer she listened.

"There's a car waiting for you. Come over immediately. Alone."

It was her mother.

"Don't wait."

Her voice was different, as if she were gargling blood.

"It's time you knew the truth."

The voice went quiet as if Elena took a breath.

"All is not lost. The game has just changed."

Lori looked at the door.

"There's so many things I need to tell you."

Looked out the window at the fog that seemed to stare into her soul.

"If you don't come... he'll kill me. Come now, Lori. Please come now."

The icy wind rippled across the cemetery as Marc gagged on his own vomit. The taste of blood on his tongue brought a wave of nausea as if he'd swallowed a bucket of blood and it was sitting in his stomach like a lead bullet.

Every organ in his body was on fire. Heat flowed across his body to his neck, steaming off his skin. His flesh was wet with sweat, flushed and grimy as if a sheen of decaying moss stained his skin. Rotting. Marc was rotting, dying on the vine of life. He understood he was already dead. He gave his life to the demon to save Lori, not knowing that it was Lori the demon wanted all along and Marc was the method in his madness to secure his desire.

He'd unleashed hell upon the Hollow. Unleashed hell upon humanity and hell upon his beloved. What do they say about the path of good intentions?

It leads to hell.

Pain in his gut ripped through every inch of flesh and every bone, shuddering his limbs as his eyes drifted behind lazy eyelids. His breath tasted like sulfur, churning noxious fumes off his tongue. Marc could feel his wounds bleeding, his skin cracked and coarse, dried to the bone. The scar above his eye itched with mad fever.

He thought about the blonde woman's crypt with its regenerative powers, but it was a fleeting thought. A momentary lapse of reason. The last call from his ego, waiting with bated breath to be set free. But Marc knew he deserved neither life nor love, and happily ever after only happens in movies.

Instead, he rolled over, welcoming the anguish.

His heart hammered against his chest as he breathed a deep ragged, and labored breath. His mouth opened wide, suffocating on his own breath, trying to bring air into his lungs, but it felt as if those organs had shrunk to the size of pins, incapable of a full breath. His head felt like it was swelling like a balloon with the limited amount of oxygen to his brain. His heart beating like a drum between his ears.

His eyes were stiff and staring wide as he struggled to breathe.

Now something floated above him. A face in the thick blackness of the cemetery. Hovering over him, a light in the darkness. His skin crawled with gooseflesh, defenseless against whatever spirit had come for him.

Felt a hand over his heart, warm and comforting.

"Focus here," she said. "Focus on your heart. Everything else can go, but the heart is what matters."

His heart thundered against his chest as if the organ attempted to break free, twisting anguish to his brain.

"There you have it. There is where the journey continues."

Marc looked at the stars, focusing on his beating, raging heart.

"He's rotting. The demon is manifesting, taking over his life-force." Marc could hear this second voice, but he couldn't see who it came from. Like a voice drifting in the darkness, a phantom to his eyes. "It depletes the soul and the heart."

His heart squeezed in his chest. Marc gripped frozen grass as he wretched and stretched, attacked by his own heart.

"Squeezes everything pure from the organ before his descent into torment. There can be no love in hell, only anguish."

"Hold on," the other voice said. The one above him. "Focus on your heart. Your love for Lori. She's the reason why but also the way through."

Marc's head shook. His eyelids hung low over his eyes when he looked to his side.

And Jennifer offered him a smile.

276

The motel looked ancient and abandoned. Lori couldn't believe her mother had stayed in such an establishment. It looked like a brothel for local addicts and pimps. At first, she thought she was in the wrong place, but the driver assured her it wasn't wrong, and she was in the right place.

The police officer who drove her had said nothing during the drive. It was a simple process. She walked out of the hotel, and a police cruiser was waiting for her. At first, she thought Detective Carver had arrived, but when the back door opened, she looked inside to see an officer she'd never laid eyes on before. She asked if he was there for Lori Francon, and the officer turned to her and gave a single nod.

She wondered if she should go back and get Henry, but her mother had said to come alone. The voice was different, but she knew it was her mother. She felt it in her bones.

Now Lori sat in the cruiser, staring at the ominous motel. The officer said nothing, waiting for her to leave. She looked at the room number, the nine on the door. She could see there was a dull light on through the window. Lori swallowed her breath and exited the car, which pulled out of the small parking lot the moment she closed the door. Lori pulled her beanie over her ears and then hugged her arms around her torso. The motel stood like a stain on the night. She scanned the parking lot and surrounding area. The western woods stood across the street. The motel was located on a side street that Lori assumed at one time had been a major artery in the Hollow. She watched the police cruiser bank a quick right after the motel, disappearing into the fog.

The door opened to room number nine. With just a crack, it floated open and closed. Lori walked over, paused, then rapped her knuckles against the wooden door. The knock boomed like an echo across time.

"Mom?" she called, but Lori knew her mother would not answer. She craned her head, looking through the crack in the door, her stare looking up and all around, when she saw blood on the carpet beside the door under the window. A large swath of blood.

She pushed the door open slowly, revealing the bed with what looked like a body beneath the sheet, and Lori's heart sank. She stepped in, her feet squishing into the blood-soaked carpet, walking to the side of the bed where she looked down at the white sheet stained with blood.

"Mom?" Her voice died in her throat. Tears pricked in her eyes. She may have been at odds with her mother for most of her life, but this-dying a death like what Lori believed was under the sheet... no one deserves such a final act. She reached her trembling hand to the sheet and pulled it down, revealing her mother's battered face, and she jumped back with a startle. "Oh, my God. My god. Oh, my God!"

Elena was barely recognizable. Her face was caved in from the force of the crushing blows against her skull. If it weren't for the hair and body style, Lori could have convinced herself that this was not her mother but some other ill-fated woman. She dropped to her knees, weak and suffering, staring at her mother. She reached her shaking hand to the bloodied forehead and prayed silently for her mother's soul when the tears came full force, her heart splintering. "I'm so sorry. I didn't know... I didn't know."

Felt something shift in the corner over her shoulder, and the hairs on the nape of her neck cringed across her skin and every ounce of blood in her veins froze along with her heart. Then warmth, as if something were wrapping around her. Lori turned her head slowly around. Someone was sitting in a chair in the room's corner, just outside of the light, wrapped in darkness. Red eyes glowed bright in the darkness, and Lori was convinced one of her night terrors was in full bloom, the stress from everything she'd been through over the last week being the catalyst for terror.

Just like in her night terrors, those red beaming eyes found her. The silhouette then shifted in the seat.

"What do you think of my work? See how beautiful your mother is now, Lori? It's what you wanted, is it not? To bash her brains in? Now she lives like the others, *rotting* in my black heart."

The voice was distinct. She'd recognize it from a million miles away. The voice belonged to Marc.

"I never wanted this, Marc. Never." She turned to Elena. "Never," she whispered, listening as he stood up from the chair, the wood creaking under his weight. "No one deserves to die like this." She was crying, tears falling ceaselessly. "How could you do this?"

"Allow me to show you."

She heard him move, and Lori jumped up, springing to her feet as he walked into the light.

Her senses were assaulted by the sight in front of her. She couldn't wrap her head around what she was looking at. It looked like Marc's body was being ripped to shreds, as if something else was clawing out of his skin. He wore the same clothes she'd seen him in a few hours ago, but then they seemed loose across his emaciated frame where now, they fit like a glove, wrapped tight around the thick frame. And his features were different. So very different.

His skin was dark and gray and cracked along his face and head. Across his forehead, it looked like two horns were splintering through his skull as if this demon's form was shredding Marc's body from the inside out. There were cracks along his face, as if the skin were splitting, the body beneath the skin overwhelming Marc's flesh and bone. The eyes were the most telling. The red beamed angrily at Lori, but she could still see Marc's baby blues as if those pupils had dwindled to the size of pins within the red irises. He held a red cane in his right hand.

"What are you?" she breathed with her hand over her mouth.

"Do you believe the story now, Lori?" He craned his head. "If seeing is believing, what do you believe now?"

Lori snapped her attention to her mother. Thoughts flitted through her brain like a conveyor belt on high speed. Gerard. The basement. The night terrors. The money... all that damn Francon money. The accident and the red eyes that rocketed towards them the moment before the car spun off the highway. The murders and Marc. My poor, poor Marc.

What's happened to you?

"The deal he made," said this thing in front of her. He reached out with his talons, gesturing to her. "To bring your life back. Comes at a heavy cost."

Lori stood frozen and shivering from head to toe. She couldn't wrap her head around what her eyes were seeing.

"Do you see what I've done to your beloved?" He gestured to himself. "His body is my vessel for living in this world."

She shook her head. "No, that can't be true."

"It is Lori."

"Where is Marc? You. What have you done to him?"

The demon grinned. "Marc's heart dies tonight, Lori. His soul will burn for eternity, and for an eternity I shall feed on his heart, devouring the love he has for you." He tilted his head. "His gift to me so that you may breathe." He closed his eyes and clucked his tongue with a rickety laugh before training his eyes on Lori.

She shook her head. "That can't be true," she whined, her lips quivering. "That's impossible."

And he laughed even more. "But it is," he growled. "LOOK at me, Lori. Look at what your heart has done to the one you love. See the suffering only love can bring."

She felt weak, weighed down by heartache when the demon snatched her by the throat and raised her to eye level. "Do you wish to reciprocate?" he snarled. "Marc's heart dies tonight, Lori. What are you willing to do? Will you give him what he so willingly relinquished?"

She lost oxygen, her eyes bulging from their sockets, but all she could see were the red eyes from her nightmares. He tossed her to the ground, and Lori collapsed onto the carpet, shaking and crying.

The demon stood over her. "Your presence is required, Lori. Tonight, everything ends. How it ends will be up to you."

Lori held her hand over her throat, sucking air into her gullet. The demon shifted to the door then turned to Lori.

He gestured to the western woods. "Follow the path to the house in the western woods. Look for the candle in the window like a light in the blackest depths of despair. The candle that burns just for you."

A whining groan escaped her throat, holding her head in her hands and shaking, bobbing back and forth. "This can't be true. It can't. My God, Marc... what did you do?"

"Marc waits for you in the woods. He's given his eternal soul for your life. Will you keep him waiting? Allow him to serve in hell? Or will you make a show for redemption? The choice is yours."

One second, he was there, the next, gone. Thick billowing fog drifted across the parking lot towards the western woods.

The demon's voice boomed across the room.

"What will you do, Lori... to save the one who gave everything for you to live?"

Henry pulled the zipper on his luggage when the phone rang. Immediate relief washed over him, thinking it was the police station telling him an officer was on the way, or even better, Carver himself.

He picked it up on the second ring. "Henry here."

"Henry Clavell?" He was surprised by the voice. He'd heard it before.

"Correct. Who am I speaking with?"

"Captain Flannery."

Henry shot his head back. The last person he wanted to talk to was Captain Flannery. When Henry met him, the guy didn't sit right with him. He seemed corrupt and arrogant. The two worst traits for a police officer.

"Yes, thank you for calling me back. I was hoping to talk to Detective Carver."

Henry waited. Sounded like Flannery was preoccupied.

"We have not seen Detective Carver since yesterday," he said. "Since he talked to you and your friend."

Henry didn't know what to say. He was caught off guard.

"I'm sorry to hear that." A pause, then. "I hope he's okay."

Nothing in return.

Henry continued. "Anyway, I have information that may bear some fruit on all the murders, Captain. Can you meet me at my hotel?"

"No need," said Flannery. "In fact, I need you to come to the Sundown Motel up on Sixth."

That was a strange request, but his interest was piqued. That was the motel where Elena was staying.

"Is something wrong, Captain? A friend of mine is staying at that motel."

"Which is why I'm calling *you*."

"I don't understand. What happened?"

"I need you to come and identify the body we discovered not more than an hour ago. See if you can recognize who she is."

Part VIII

278

Excerpt from *The Demon and Sleepy Hollow* by the Original Knickerbocker Dated 1856.

The Spell and the Demon

What we discovered upon entering the demon's lair was not what we expected. I don't believe any human being could prepare themselves for what we endured.

There were seven of us who travelled through the tunnels that night. Six men and Olga, whose bravery and sacrifice must be brought center stage in this proceeding. If it weren't for Olga's quick wit and fearless effort, all would have been lost. The result of our aggression found only myself and a young boy leaving the very dungeon we so vehemently came to dissuade.

What I dare say now is a warning to those who come after us. A warning that should the beast rise once again may have dire consequences for those brave enough to confront evil in its purest form.

Hell exists beneath the Hollow, but this is no hell like the most educated of humanity have written about. What we discovered on that fateful night is that the hell we endure is one we contrive through our attachment to our own fears, treachery, and guilt. It comes from our own minds. Hell is a tenfold truth that shakes the very foundation of core beliefs. It is easy to give in to, and difficult to comprehend. The demon used our own minds against us, testing our psychological strength to the limit. Hallucinations. Mind control and manipulation, all born from the crux of truth with an ominous interpretation.

I can honestly say, as I sit here writing this page, that I have been to hell and damnation. It exists as if teetering across the universe. Lonely, cold and filled with hurt, with waves of unrelenting misery no creature should ever endure. If it weren't for two opposing factors, I would not be alive today. The first was Olga's quick wit, and the second was pure unadulterated luck.

The demon had possessed Mr. Curad, taking command of his body and his mind while his soul was banished to the same ether that manifested the hell we traveled upon. However, Olga's knowledge provided us with direction, for the demon cannot manifest fully in our world without permission from its superiors. How strange such things are, as if regulation and dominion over others far surpass humanity's need for the same and stretch to otherworldly beings. Furthermore, there must be connectivity between the two opposing forces. Such connectivity results from the pairing of frequencies, either aligned or opposite, depending on the desired result of the pairing from the demon's perspective. Thus, it was the aligned connection between Mr. Curad and the demon that first offered the demon dominion over him. However, for the demon's curse to manifest fully in our world, a second pairing was also required.

On that fateful night, we arrived to witness what can best be described as a botched pairing. The witch Selena offered herself to the demon's overlord, a god among demons, a devil known as Baphomet. A pairing that brought dire consequences to Selena and the demon. From what I have been able to garner, between my conversations with Chief Alo along with my own experience with the demon, is that only love can slay the demon, and it is that same love that is required to set the demon free from the human shackles that have allowed him to breathe in our atmosphere.

Selena's heart did not belong to Sam J. Curad, but the heart of another did. One who was already lost before the demon's ritual. This is where the luck portion of our victory took hold, because Selena was cast into the ether, doomed to live in a perpetual state of limbo within the western woods and the cemetery, leaving the demon to rot inside the body of Sam J. Curad. An existence that would have allowed continued hell to wreak havoc across the Hollow.

Olga provided the second bait of luck for us, binding the demon to the body of Sam J. Curad while relinquishing Sam's soul from the body. She used a binding spell, along with a spell that cast Sam's soul from the body, ultimately condemning the demon's essence into the cemetery, sentencing him to walk in eternal death.

However, we know that such a spell cannot hold forever. The spirit of Sam J. Curad will once again return to the Hollow. We can only hope the demon will not find a method to convince this risen spirit to hold court with him once again and bind his spirit back to the demons. Should such an occurrence take place, death will come to the Hollow.

And the following is how it can be defeated. All it requires is the sacrifice of a beautiful soul.

The tunnel proved more difficult to traverse than Logan had first expected. He'd already fallen three times while following the wisp across the darkness and towards the origin of the buzz.

He'd lost Detective Carver and his captor, relying on the wisp to bring him through when the ceiling started pounding, raining dirt across his head and shoulders.

People were walking up above, and how or why so many people took it upon themselves to congregate in the middle of winter in the middle of the night while murders plagued the Hollow's citizens was beyond him. Although Logan calculated the occurrence must have something to do with the coming ritual. He looked up at the ceiling, feeling more alone than he had ever been.

He hoped he could find Detective Carver. Hoped he could help John get out of whatever predicament the poor child was in, but hope is a four-letter word that means nothing more than can't do. Logan didn't believe in can't. There's nothing that can't be accomplished. His mother taught him that.

He heard shuffling and laughter up ahead. Someone was coming, and from the sound of it, more than a few people. He looked left and then right, unsure which way he should go. It didn't matter to Logan who it was; in his mind, every citizen in the Hollow was now compromised. He knew he couldn't and shouldn't trust anyone.

Except for Detective Carver and the wisp. The wisp that disappeared into the darkness on his immediate right.

His breath hitched in his throat, and he swallowed his breath with a gulp. His innards twisted in his gut, and the smell of sulfur and that damn buzzing manifested nausea into the back of his throat, but the sound of those approaching footsteps brought him into the darkness with the wisp. Logan squatted down, his back leaning against a cold stone.

Now he saw a light, but not just a light; it was a flame. A torch someone was holding, and they were coming out of the darkness towards him. With the light from the torch, Logan could see they were in another tunnel. The light stopped and paused. And as Logan's eyes adjusted to the light, he could see more clearly. He could see his friend's Chad and Michael step into the light. Their faces were contorted as if the torch's flames flickered shadows across their skin, causing their features to look distorted. Both boys looked like they were changing. As if some sinister creature had burrowed into their skin and was now boiling out of their flesh. Their red eyes gleamed in the darkness. Ten others joined the boys, all with the same distorted features.

"This way," said Chad. He was the one holding the torch. The others followed dutifully. "Master wants us to join the others in celebration. Some have taken occupancy in the park and at the

GM plant. We…" he said with a laugh behind his voice. "We get the honor of taking the cemetery."

Logan watched until they were no bigger than his thumbnail before getting up and stepping away from the wall. He looked down in the direction Chad and Michael had come from.

The wisp glided in that very direction.

Logan looked behind him and then returned his gaze to the wisp. He looked in the direction Chad and Michael had gone, then turned back to the wisp.

His feet sloshed through shallow water on his way to the tunnel. He stepped in, and the buzzing grew louder.

Logan took a deep, stuttered breath while staring into the darkness. His feet and legs hurt, and his arms were cramped from clutching the book so tight. His lungs burned with cold and heated breath.

He followed the wisp, thinking the entire time. Thinking about how he and John were going to kill the demon.

280

Henry Clavell stood at the edge of the motel parking lot, investigating the woods. He was certain Lori had entered the woods. Her footprints pointed in that direction, and Henry knew Marc's house was in the same location.

What the fuck happened at the motel? Did Marc murder Lori's mother? Is Lori on her way to confront him? Henry wasn't having it. It wasn't even an hour ago that she was ready to leave the Hollow and put all of this behind them, but now the rug had been pulled out from under him, and he was sinking. Sinking fast.

And he knew Flannery was looking to pin these murders on him. The guy was eerie, to say the least. Corrupt, Henry was certain, but what was Flannery's current angle? Henry couldn't piece it together, couldn't piece it together because something was missing. Some part of the story that Henry wasn't privy to, and the missing part meant everything.

Henry was scanning the woods, hoping to see Lori. The snow was coming down faster now. What started as a light flurry had just taken a turn into a potential blizzard.

Captain Flannery told him to wait outside, but Herny was thinking about climbing into his SUV and going back home to the Hamptons, although he knew he couldn't. He refused to allow Lori to face Marc alone.

Why didn't she just call the police? That part didn't make one iota of sense. She still can't be convinced that Marc's innocent, can she? *Impossible!* The man beat, bludgeoned, and mutilated Lori's mother. How could she convince herself he was innocent?

This made no sense.

He heard footsteps in the snow behind him. Henry turned towards the motel and the red and blue lights trolling across the parking lot, watching the person walking towards him. He was young-Henry put him in his late twenties or early thirties-and wearing a suit. Obviously, he wasn't trolling around the Hollow in a black and white.

The man stopped and took a long look at Henry. He seemed to investigate Henry's eyes.

"Agent Clavell?" His eyes squinted from the falling snow.

Henry nodded. "Yes, that's me." He wondered where the conversation was going.

The man looked suspicious, holding his coat over his throat. Henry wasn't certain, but he believed the officer was concerned about being overheard. He may have been turned in Henry's direction, but he was clearly focused on what was going on behind him at the motel and the investigation that was underway.

"You spoke to Detective Carver last night?"

"I did, yes."

He looked left and then right, as if listening to the investigation. He gripped his coat collar tighter, staring at Henry as if assessing him. His stare was stoic, although Henry could see there was a thread of anger coursing through the man's bones.

"And you are?" Henry had had enough with the strangeness in Sleepy Hollow. Getting to the point was all Henry cared about. Whatever the Sleepy Hollow Police Department had in store for him, he wanted to get it over with as fast as possible. He needed to get to Lori and stop her confrontation.

"Come with me," he said. "Captain wants you brought in for questioning."

Henry looked at the motel. He could see Captain Flannery inside the motel room, his back to the door, talking with a few officers. Henry didn't want to alert anyone to who had been murdered in the motel room. He didn't trust anyone in the Hollow, and he wasn't about to allow his knowledge to slip by him before he could find Lori. He needed to get out from under the watchful eye of Captain Flannery. From there, he could find his way to her. By hook or by crook, he'll find her.

Henry nodded. "Ok." He gestured to the parking lot. "Which car is yours?"

"This way."

The officer walked into the street to the Chevy Impala parked outside the parking lot. Henry noticed the officer looked at the motel twice. They stood by the car, and the officer's stare burrowed into Henry.

"It isn't locked." The officer opened the door then climbed into his car.

Henry followed, sitting in the passenger seat when the officer keyed into the ignition and started the car. Henry looked at the motel.

"I didn't catch your name." Henry turned to him.

"Detective Montgomery," he said. "I was on Carver's team."

"He's sealed his doom. Gave his heart to the demon, and the demon is feeding off the essence from that heart." The blonde witch turned to Jennifer. "His heart and soul are rotting. There is nothing we can do."

Marc's head was burning to the touch, sick with fever. He felt like his blood was on fire, poisoned and noxious.

"His heart lives in hell." The blonde turned to the night sky. "Burning for eternity. That is why he's rotting in the ether."

Jennifer patted the sweat off his forehead, and her touch cringed his bones, sending waves filled with agony coursing through his veins. His stomach wrenched as if his liver were attacking him. Felt dried out and weary, wanting nothing more than to give in to the pain. "I'm so sorry." Jennifer offered him a reassuring smile. She looked so different now. So different from before. He remembered the petrified and bleeding Jennifer. The one he carried into the blonde woman's crypt, but now she looked almost heavenly.

Marc's voice arrived stuttered and labored. "Why are you being so good to me?" She had suffered the most unimaginable fate and torture, and all because of him. Because he couldn't accept death when it came to claim the only love he'd ever known, yet she was here with him now.

She placed the back of her hand on his forehead. Her blue eyes gazed into his. "Because it wasn't your fault, Marc. These things you see. The things you hear and the ghosts who torment you." She shook her head. "They exist only because you manifest them through guilt." She smiled, a knowing, calming smile. "Once we give in, we understand the demons we first believed were tearing our soul apart are really just angels ridding us of our attachments on our way to bliss." She looked him dead in the eye. "You taught me that. Your kindness delivered me into peace, and you are forgiven."

"It is different for him," said the blonde. "He gave his heart freely. There can be no peace for the heart burning in hell."

Marc jolted upright when pain surged in his heart. Felt like his heart was on fire, being devoured by sharp incisors and clawed at with talons. Held breath. So hard to breathe.

"He is destined to rot for eternity."

His vision wavered, his heart hammering in his chest, and Marc could see his parents in the cemetery. They looked at him, then at each other, before holding hands and walking away.

He heard a gong reverberate in his bones, squeezing his heart with a pain that rippled to his brain.

"The demon has won this round. Now he can torment the soul through the heart he owns."

"What is to become of him?" Jennifer gestured to Marc. She took his hand and turned to the blonde, waiting for an answer.

"Olga," she hollered when Olga turned to her. "What will be his fate?"

Olga swallowed her breath. "Now that Baphomet's possession cannot come to fruition, the demon will walk the earth as Marc Saduj." She gestured to Marc. "He will be among the ghosts of the Hollow, his spirit hollowed out, fading slowly. Without a connection to the heart, he will be lost. This is an acceptable exchange for the demon. If he can't have all he desires, he shall find another to accommodate. There may be times when the demon sees fit to draw Marc back into the fold, but even then, there shall be suffering." She shook her head. "He agreed to the union. Now he gets what he deserves."

A fierce wind howled across the cemetery, surging pain through Marc's veins. His chest jumped and stretched as if the dark hand of death squeezed his heart. He clawed across the frozen ground with a scream in the back of his throat.

"We'll be listening to those screams for eternity."

Jen squeezed his shoulder, hoping she could provide comfort in his time of need.

"All that has transpired. All our spells and bravery have all been for nothing. The demon has finally had his day. Come," she said. "We should return to the astral plane." She looked around the cemetery. "There is nothing left for us to do."

"I can't leave him," Jennifer protested. "Not like this." She shook her head. "Not like this."

Olga went to speak when something caught her attention. Her head sprang up, looking over the cemetery. Her eyes flitted from left to right as the sky scorched with red lightning, howling winds and thunder that shook the earth.

"What is it?" asked Jennifer. "What's happening?"

Marc's heart wrenched in his chest, his legs stretched and trembled. His hands were shaking. Olga paced across the cemetery, and Marc coughed blood over his lips, his breathing labored yet frantic, lying on his side while his head trembled. Shaking, with his eyes rolling beneath his eyelids.

"What is it?" Jennifer hollered.

"My God," said Olga.

Marc peeled his eyes open, looking at the sky and the rolling clouds filled with fire slithering over the Hollow.

Jennifer was looking up too. "What does it mean?" she hollered when the wind kicked up a notch, spiraling across the cemetery.

Olga looked down at Jennifer and Marc, her head shaking. "Lori has not left the Hollow."

She saw the flame in the window, dancing in the darkness. The single candle burning just for her.

Lori made the trek to the dilapidated mansion in the western woods, accompanied by ghosts that wished her harm but had yet to receive the go-ahead from their master. The demon Holer wouldn't allow it. Lori knew she was important to the demon's cause, but exactly what he had in store for her she couldn't fathom.

She thought she felt Marc in the woods, begging for her to release him. Perhaps his soul called out for hope, knowing that she was his only hope.

Only love can slay the demon. She remembered Marc had said that the night he proposed, right before Lori's night terror in the restaurant.

She hoped he was right, because standing at the edge of the woods and staring at Marc's home brought a chill to her bones that she found unnatural. Snow blanketed the house, clamoring for a place to view the final catastrophe. The fog descended upon the house. Thick and slithering around the house like an ethereal guard, and that buzz sounded like a sonic boom on the verge of eruption. She could only assume the house was the source of the buzz. Lori could feel it vibrating in her bones. In her heart, twisting the organ with a profound hurt.

Lori felt hopeless too. For what could she do to help Marc other than give herself to the demon so that he might live? She was still attempting to wrap her head around what she'd seen. Marc's appearance in the park. Her mother's bloodied corpse, and the demon in the corner, pulling the strings and watching the scene unfold.

Some things are difficult to accept, especially when they betray the eyes and all she's come to know as truth. She had accepted that Marc was responsible for the murders, and she begged him to turn himself in, but she knew now that wasn't true. Marc was doing what he thought was best to keep Lori safe, even though his soul was on the line.

She didn't know that the story he wrote was the truth. A premonition of things to come.

The demon is real. Marc's demon is real. She wouldn't have believed it if she hadn't seen him for herself. The demon was right in that regard. Seeing is believing, and now that she knows the truth, there isn't anything or anyone on the planet that could stop her from entering the house.

The demon had always been with her, waiting in the shadows, manipulating the lives of everyone Lori knew. Her mother. Gerard. Her father too. The Francon family was cursed. And the curse was bursting at the seams, infecting everything she cared for. Infecting Marc too. She couldn't fathom what he was going through. The demon was ripping him apart, rotting him from the inside out, and Marc welcomed him with open arms. Welcomed the demon so that Lori could live.

It was time to even the score. She drew in a deep breath before she stepped into the clearing towards Marc's home. The moment she stepped in, she felt heavier, as if gravity worked differently here, and the buzz was more prominent. It caused distraction, confusion, and she could feel her atoms vibrating, wrenching a dull pain across the center of her brain.

Lori kept her eyes on the candle in the window, trekking across the snow-covered ground into the thick fog through the blizzard. The fog floated around her. It seemed to spiral, as if the fog purposely circled the house. The wind whistled across the property.

She walked to the front of the house and stopped cold in her tracks.

A severed head was staring at her from the front porch.

Lori couldn't be certain, but she believed she was on a path to hell.

283

Montgomery pulled the car over to the side of the road. They hadn't driven very far. A few minutes away from the hotel was all Henry could tell.

He killed the headlights, and Henry's heart stammered in his chest, looking through the windshield, the snow falling in sheets across the car inside the fog-drenched night. The buzz in his inner ear, he could feel it in his cells, vibrating every atom in his body.

Henry believed he was about to meet his death. Was this guy Montgomery going to kill him? Why else would he pull over on the side of the road with nothing but the western woods surrounding him? He eyed Montgomery out of the corner of his eye. The guy was looking through the windshield, thinking. Henry could see the cogs turning over in his brain.

"I don't believe this is the precinct." Henry turned towards Montgomery, his hand clenched in a fist at his hip. If this guy tries anything, he'll be ready. He'll at least make it a bit more difficult. Henry would never go down without a fight.

Montgomery then shifted and looked at Henry. "You're from Long Island, right?"

Henry nodded. "Correct."

"And you don't know anyone in the Hollow, correct?"

Again, Henry nodded.

"You came here to help a friend, from what I was told. A friend who has information about the murders?"

"Correct, Detective. A friend who I'd really like to see right now, so if we can get this over with, I'd be a lot happier."

Montgomery kept going. "And you and this friend of yours met with Detective Carver last night, correct?"

"Yes. Did something happen to Detective Carver?"

Montgomery turned to the windshield. "You see, that's where things take a dramatic turn." He turned to Henry. "Possibly not a good turn either."

"What do you mean?"

He paused to clear his throat. "You see, there's a few of us who saw some strange occurrences within our own department over the last twenty-four hours. People acting strange… not like themselves." He gestured toward the motel. "Captain Flannery especially." He paused, shifting his gaze to the windshield. "You see, what I know is that Detective Carver was supposed to take a trip this morning with two detectives. But Carver was supposed to check in with me this morning, and when he didn't, I went searching for him, and you know what I found?"

Henry shrugged, not sure where this was going.

"The detective's car is off the side of the road. Apparently due to some accident. The detectives who went with him are both dead, but Carver wasn't in the car."

"He survived? Do you know where he is now?"

"I do not, but I have an idea."

"Where?"

Montgomery turned in Henry's direction. "I assume the same place your friend may have gone to. I saw you looking into the woods. That's where the house is located."

"Shouldn't you be telling this information to your superior officer?" That would be Captain Flannery, Henry knew, but he wanted to see Montgomery's reaction.

"I don't believe Captain Flannery can be trusted. He seems to be throwing a wrench into the investigation, and he's doing it on purpose. I'm confident he sent those two detectives to murder Detective Carver. Plus, there's something different about him. I can't put my finger on it, but it's the same I've seen in many other people in the Hollow. There's an aggression behind the eyes that feels... off. Like its wrong or just plain evil." He studied Henry, assessing his eyes. "And then there's the hint of red in their eyes."

Henry's eyes narrowed. "What do you mean?"

"Just what I said. A hint of red in the pupils. They all have it; everyone who has the same change, there's a hint of red in their eyes. The captain has it too."

"So, what does that mean?"

He shook his head. "I honestly don't know, but here's what I do know. All this started after Carver went to the house in the woods. Now, everyone in the Hollow has lost their mind. Carver's missing and your friend is too, and Carver was adamant about this guy Marc's involvement, who just happens to be the ex-fiancé of your friend."

"Which means?"

"Which means, there's only a few people I can trust right now, and you're one of them."

Thank God!

Henry looked through the windshield, processing what Montgomery said. "What do we do now, Detective?"

Montgomery reached under his seat and came up with a nine-millimeter Beretta. Checked the clip and offered Henry the gun. "I'm sure you're carrying, but you may need more where we're going?"

Henry took the gun, wedging it between his belt buckle and stomach. "Where *are* we going?"

Montgomery turned on the headlights and put the car in drive. "Where else? To find Carver and your friend. To the house in the western woods." Henry nodded, relieved that not everyone in the Hollow had lost their mind. "After we pick up a few more people."

284

Carver could feel the heat before he tried to open his eyes. He had slept so peacefully, so soundly and so deeply that all his worries and concerns melted away like ice.

He saw his ex-wife and his children. They were on the Jersey shore when the kids were young, and he was still married. The scene was a memory he'd replay in his head every time life got a little too tough. It brought clarity of mind with the purpose of finding peace.

The memory followed him into wakefulness. His eyelids fluttered open, and the room came into view. He could hear squeaking as if something was moving above his head. His back was stiff, lying on a cold, hard surface. He heard the buzz as if it were arriving in thunderous waves, squeezing into his brain and scrambling his thoughts.

Carver's eyes rolled behind his eyelids. His head stung between his temples, and he lifted himself up with a grunt, swaying his legs over the cold hard surface. The buzz was more prominent here, sending waves of vibration rattling through his bones, causing confusion and lethargy. He felt so tired. So tired and distraught. It was difficult to collect his thoughts; his brain kept hitting a brick wall, the thoughts existing on the other side. Numb and sick, with his head floating and still that buzz refused to relent.

Now he heard frantic breathing, moans and groans. Carver held his head, wincing from the pain when his eyes shot open, and he realized where he was.

A dungeon.

There's a portal to hell in the basement.

His heart hitched in his chest, and he jumped off the stone slab, looking around, his head on a swivel. Felt like his head weighed a thousand pounds. He immediately felt evil in his bones, and what he saw could only be described as supernatural.

The dungeon was colossal, with walls and floors made of stone. Various torture devices-*do you know anything about medieval torture*-were scattered across the room. Shackles were secured to the walls, but there was no one in them. He saw bones on the floor, the stone slab he was lying on, and a firepit burning next to it, but what caught Carver's attention was the dark cave. That's where the buzz was coming from, and the fog too. It billowed into the room, bathing the dungeon in a faded grayish-blue hue.

The fog was everywhere, and Carver had to widen his eyes and shake his head to understand what he was seeing. It looked like the fog and the buzz were rushing away from the cave, as if they were meant to overflow into the Hollow. He could see the buzz vibrating inside the fog. It looked like he was staring at the vibrating strings on a guitar. The buzz affected the fog; he could see it taking form, slithering like snakes about to bite. Carver turned his shuddering head to the cave, his mouth hanging open with a gasp across his lips.

He could hear burning inside the cave and distant screams of torture and suffering. Electrical sparks raged inside the fog. Carver stared into the raging, mesmerizing electrical waves. Hypnotized by it. His eyes grew wider every second. He could see hell in those electrical waves. Devils and imps clucking their tongues with the memory of nefarious truths.

His attention was interrupted by another loud groan. He was surprised that it never manifested as a scream. He looked around, turning his focus to the cage swaying ever so slightly above his head.

"John?"

The boy was lying down in a cage hoisted close to the roof. He could see the boy was sweating, his skin saturated with sweat. There was blood coming from his nose that pooled around his mouth and chin. His breath struggled to release from his lungs, but it was John's eyes that turned Carver's blood cold. Carver shook his head, attempting to wipe the cobwebs from his brain, and took a good long look at John, confirming his eyes were open. Carver could see the fog reflected in John's black eyeballs. He looked demonic. Looked like he was struggling to breathe. He stepped closer when he saw the dead, skinless body hanging from the rafter close to John's cage. Fog drifted across the body, and Carver's blood turned hot.

"Sick... *fucks*." Another moan from John caught Carver's attention. He had to get the cage down and get John out of here. He scanned across the cage, following the rope secured to the wall behind the cage.

"Hold on, John. I'm coming."

Carver scurried over to the wall and started tugging on the rope, but it was tied taut and refused to relent. "Come on." Carver pulled and tugged, then looked around the room, finding a knife by the slab that he snatched off the floor, then hurried over to the rope and started sawing, trying to piece together why the hell John was here.

My son... Bang!

Carver flinched at the memory of Sheila's suicide. He looked at the rope, thinking. John plays an intimate role in this game of the macabre. Sheila was convinced of it. Convinced enough to take her own life. He remembered the wisp that had helped him discover the basement. Helped him when he was at Hardwood Realty too, and he knew she was with him last night, alerting him to the two detectives outside his home.

He wished she were here with him now.

Carver went to work on the rope, holding the rope above the location where he sawed when the hairs on the nape of his neck erected from the breeze that wrapped around him like a hot, nefarious breath. Over his shoulder came a rickety cackle from the devil. He craned his head slowly around and saw John's black eyes staring in his direction.

Heard John whisper, "Detective Carver... run!"

The front door creaked open like an invitation to come inside. The door swayed ever so slightly, gently thumping back and forth against the frame, leaving the door ajar. Lori stepped onto the porch, her head craned as she investigated the house.

She could see darkness beyond the door, stark blackness like a black hole, cold and ominous. Lori licked her lips, gnawing on her lower lip when she pushed the door open that creaked as it swayed against the back wall with a soft thud. Wind behind her ear, funneling into the house. She stepped in.

The mansion was vast, and Lori believed she was in a living room or a ballroom. The room was so big. A fireplace, cold and gray, was on the wall to her right where she could see a hall that led to more blackness. The house creaked in the wind. The foundation groaned beneath her feet.

"Okay," she whispered. "What now?"

As if on cue, she heard a creak on the floor above. She looked up, listening to the feet shuffling overhead. She knew the room with the candle was up there. Lori swallowed the lump in her throat, scanning across the house to the hallway that she stepped towards, all the while keeping her eyes on the ceiling and her ears open, listening to the creak with the buzz beneath it.

She stepped into the hallway to the stairs.

More footsteps and shuffling. More wind outside. The mansion groaned under its weight. She looked down the hall but couldn't see more than a few feet in front of her. Lori turned back to the staircase and took the stairs up, the steps creaking with every footstep. She climbed to the top then investigated the hall. More blackness and darkness greeted her.

Now she heard a rapping, as if something was tapping against a wall. She could also feel the icy wind slithering across the floor to her toes and legs. It was coming from the door on her immediate left, the one where the candle was burning. She was certain of it.

She turned the doorknob and inched the door open, stepping inside, her heart thundering and her hands trembling.

The door ripped away from her hand and slammed against the back wall, sending a shudder racing down Lori's spine.

The candle burned in the open window, and the buzz grew louder in the room. It nipped at her inner ear, annoying and relentless. She assessed the room but found no one. The only things she could see were paintings scattered across the room. Some were hung on the wall, but most were on the floor, leaning against the wall. A tattered mattress sat on the floor on her right.

And it was so quiet, like the quiet in outer space, deathly quiet with the buzz nipping in her ear like the moaning breath from a dying sun. Lori looked around, frustration boiling into rage.

"Well, you wanted me here. What should I do now?"

Nothing. No response, just the icy wind whistling through the open window. Lori went to the candle, scanning across the windowsill the candle sat on, hoping to find a letter or something to tell her what to do next, but there was nothing there. She gripped the candle, thinking she could use it to search the house.

A gawk ripped through her bones from the outside. Lori turned to see an owl swooping out of the fog and over the house. She could hear it land on the roof, hissing when Lori's eyes narrowed, staring into the fog.

She stepped closer to the window, her head craned, looking, scanning, when her heart constricted, her blood curdled, and her bones tensed. She could see ghosts and specters in the fog, with silvery eyes and mouths filled with incisors she knew could eat her heart out, floating in the fog around the house.

Lori stepped back from the window. The sight was terrifying. There seemed to be an army of ghosts outside the window. She stepped back again, her hand over her mouth, when the painting on the easel caught her attention.

She wasn't certain what she was looking at, but it looked like Lori in the painting. There was fog in her eyes and in her mouth and nose. Her ears too, as if this fog was entering her body, but that wasn't the only insidious part of the scene. Above Lori was the devil himself. And he had his claws wedged in her skull.

286

Carver snapped around on his heels when the buzz grew louder in his ears. He felt heavier, like his legs were filled with cement. His stomach rolled with nausea, but neither the heavier weight in his legs nor the nausea in his stomach was Carver's chief concern.

He saw eyes in the darkness inside the cave. Red beaming eyes he was certain were grinning over his presence.

"Detective Carver, how nice to see you again."

The demon stepped out of the darkness, and Carver's head snapped back. It was not Marc Saduj walking out of the cave. It was something else. The demon from Sleepy Hollow.

He'd read the book, but nothing could have prepared him for what he was looking at. Yes, he could see Marc Saduj, but it looked like this demon was wearing Marc's skin and the demon's body was ripping his flesh apart, splitting the skin so that the demon could rise. Carver's jaw hung open, staring at the abomination in front of him. The flesh was split across his face, revealing charcoal-covered skin beneath Marc's pale complexion, and there were horns tearing out of the skull. In his right hand he held a red cane.

"Do you like what I've done to Marc Saduj?" The demon grinned. He looked like he had two rows of teeth. One was Marc's, but the sharp pointed teeth and incisors belonged to the demon.

"His soul and consciousness may tear apart in the ether, but his heart will forever belong to me."

Carver tried to think. Tried to think of a weapon he could use. He reached for his gun, but it wasn't in his holster, and he had already lost his one-inch blade. He had only one weapon, the knife that was in his hand.

"My my, how frightened you look. How simply terrified." The demon craned his head. "What could possibly be scaring you right now, Detective?"

"Run, Detective Carver," John mumbled from his cage. It was like the boy wasn't psychologically present. As if he were playing out whatever nightmare besieged him. His black eyes were mesmerizing, polished to a fine shine. His breathing continued to be labored.

"Yes, detective..." A wild, bending growl escaped the demon's lips. Sounded like bending steel. The demon's eyes lit up with rage. "RUN!"

Carver's heart jumped in his chest. His entire body jumped. The demon stepped forward, stomping on the floor with a roar that pierced Carver's ears, sending noxious fumes across his face. His eyes flitted across the dungeon, looking for a place to run, when the demon stomped towards him, swinging his cane with lightning speed that crashed into Carver's temple.

It happened so fast, Carver could barely deflect the blow that crashed against his skull and dropped him to the floor. He had only one second to open his eyes before the demon swung again.

Carver raised his arm for protection, and the cane shattered his bone with a loud screech from Carver's throat. He cradled the arm close to his chest. The arm shook limply. Then came a third blow crashing across his skull. Pain ripped through his temples, and he felt blood on his forehead. Carver rolled over, attempting to get away, clawing across the ground with his one good arm, to the cave where the fog was billowing from.

A blow across his spine and Carver's head arched up, grunting in his throat. His body was so heavy, he felt like he was dragging a semi-truck across the floor. Every muscle in his body ached, throbbing with pain. He dragged himself another foot across the floor where he found feet.

Another blow rapped across his spine, and Carver lost feeling in his legs when the owner of those feet crouched in front of him, and Carver investigated the face of John's vampire. Wren offered him a smile, his eyes beaming with a white silvery glow.

He poked Carver's head with his long fingernail, dragging his nail across Carver's forehead, the nail burning across his skin while Carver grunted from the pain. Wren craned his head, glaring into Carver's eyes. "It really is remarkable, Detective. Once you accept all the fear and all the darkness in your heart, there comes deliverance."

He rolled Carver onto his back, and the detective flopped across the floor with the demon standing over him. He unsheathed a hidden blade from his cane.

"Give in," whispered Wren. "The master will lead you across the bowels of hell." He stood up, hovering over Carver. "Accept our gift of death, Detective. You have only your heart to lose."

Carver was defenseless. His spine paralyzed, his arm shattered, his face and head all bloodied and beaten. He coughed blood across his lips. He looked at John through swollen slits. *I'm so sorry, John.* He didn't know if he actually spoke those words or if he thought them, but the demonic stare across John's face was enough to bring a total loss of hope.

"We'll place your head up high, Detective. For all in the Hollow to see."

Carver returned to that day on the Jersey shore. It was the last image he wanted to take with him, but the pain he felt when the demon's blade sawed into his neck snapped his eyes open. He could feel it when the demon severed his spine. He was suffocating, drowning in his own blood when Wren gripped his hair and removed his head. But he could still see.

Instead of the Jersey shore, the last stain on Carver's memory was the demon's delightful grin.

287

John watched the vampire raise Carver's head to the demon. It looked like he was staring at the world through glass prisms. He wished he could unsee what he'd witnessed, but his eyes refused to close. His heart was racing a million miles an hour, and his body was shaking, trembling with rage.

They cut off his head. They cut off his head. They cut off his head.

The thoughts kept flitting through his brain. He could barely move a muscle. Pinned to the cage as if he'd been tied to it. He felt so heavy, heavy and lethargic.

"Where do you wish the head to be placed?" That was his vampire. All John could do was watch the scene unfolding in a wave of prisms, and he couldn't focus, the scene moving in front of him like waves in the ocean.

Why didn't you run?

"Our precious Ian," said the demon. "Needs some company."

"How medieval my master. Consider it done, my lord."

"Let us toss the detective's heart into the fire. He deserves an eternity of anguish."

"My pleasure."

Footsteps from above. John could hear shuffling. Sounded like someone was in the house, walking above their heads. Quiet in the dungeon now, except for the buzz.

"She is here, my lord." John watched as both the vampire and the demon looked at the ceiling. The cave across from him, where the buzz was coming from, echoed icy wind into the room through the fog.

The demon started nodding. "Let's lead her here, Wren." He turned to the vampire. "She'll have plenty to keep her company until the final hour. The astral plane is growing strong. Once the transformation has taken place, our dominion will spill into the earth, and we will rise victorious. The vibration will turn their minds into rage; the ghost demons will take the rest, and Baphomet will grant me dominion over the earth."

"You have done well, my lord. I bow to your wretchedness, but what if Baphomet refuses your offering?"

The demon paused. John noticed how he clenched the cane in his long talons. "The pairing is accurate, Wren. There is no reason for Baphomet not to take occupancy in the female vessel, but to provide comfort to you, my most loyal subject, allow me to relinquish your fear. As long as the heart of Marc Saduj beats in my chest, I shall walk this earth for eternity."

A smile curled across Wren's lips. "And together we shall bring our own brand of hell."

The demon laughed, thick and guttural. "Now, go, Wren. Prop Detective Carver's head for all to see. A warning to those wishing entrance into our abode. Hell has come to the Hollow. And his name is Marc Saduj."

John watched Wren leave the dungeon with Carver's severed head when the demon turned to him. His red, beaming eyes glowered at John.

The demon shook his head. "No concern's John. We have a special plan for you. A little payback for past deeds. You've seen them, yes? In your dreams. The sins of your ancestors will be delivered upon the next generation."

John gnashed his teeth, grinding his jaw, attempting to speak, but he couldn't bring the words to his lips although he noticed the buzz grew louder.

"Do you feel it, John?" The demon turned to the cave. "The vibration from Xibalba infects every atom in the Hollow. When dawn rises in the morning, the Hollow will belong to me." The demon kneaded his cane into the ground when he turned to John. He started walking towards the cage. "Come now, John. I have a special task for you."

Montgomery parked outside the Old Dutch Church of Sleepy Hollow, with the cemetery in its backyard. Henry noticed there were three cars in the parking lot with them.

"A church?" Henry turned to Montgomery. "I didn't realize this was the time to suddenly find religion."

Montgomery laughed. "Looks like we could use some religion right now." He got out of the car. Henry followed, stepping into the cold fog and the buzz. The snow had stopped, leaving in its wake an icy chill Henry could feel in his bones. His legs felt heavy. The air was strange, as if it were grinding, turning itself into something else. Something thick and difficult to traverse while the buzz saturated the center of his brain, holding there like an unrelenting sting. His stomach rolled with nausea.

He heard a commotion over his shoulder, and he turned to look. People were funneling into Sleepy Hollow Cemetery. He could see them through the wisps of fog that blanketed the street. Some held torches, while others were scattered across the cemetery, around headstones and mausoleums.

They looked like they were digging.

More commotion behind him. He turned around. Saw more citizens walking towards the Hudson, carrying torches, and some of them were chanting, but Henry couldn't make out what they were saying over the buzz in his ear. Sounded like *Agios O Baphomet.*

"See," said Montgomery. Henry turned to him. Montgomery looked like a man at the end of his rope, holding on for dear life. The fog flitted past him, rolling across his features and bathing the detective in a blue hue. "Something's off with them. It's like they're all possessed." He rolled his tongue inside his cheek. "We've seen it in people we know too."

Quiet then. Henry watched the people walking down the street. "Where do you think they're going?" He turned to Montgomery.

Montgomery shifted on his feet and cleared his throat. "I don't know for sure, but..." He gestured down the street towards the Hudson. "It seems they're congregating in the same places where we found all those bodies."

"Like they're getting ready for something," said Henry. "Preparing."

"For what is the problem?" Henry locked eyes with Montgomery.

"Is it me or do you feel... heavier? Like you're wearing cement boots."

Montgomery nodded. "And my insides are on fire, like something's changing inside."

Henry thought about that. Thought about the buzz and the sickly sensation in his stomach. In his cells. He could feel them vibrating as if he'd just consumed an ounce of psychedelic

232

mushrooms and his innards were buzzing in frantic vibrations across his flesh.

"Come on," said Montgomery. "They're waiting."

Henry waited another second before following Montgomery. He opened the church door and stepped inside. It was dark in the church and stuffy, but a candle had been lit, providing the only light. Henry saw three people in the church. A woman sitting on a pew in front of the stage, and two men. One of them stood by the candles. The other was staring through a stained-glass window, looking into the street and across the cemetery.

They were all wearing tactical gear. Bulletproof vests, goggles, and all three were armed to the eyeballs. They all turned when Henry walked in with Montgomery.

"Any word from Stephen?" asked Montgomery, walking towards the front of the church.

It was the woman who answered. "Nothing. We might as well assume he's dead."

"I won't make that assumption," said Montgomery, "not until we know for sure." He looked at the man by the window and gestured to the cemetery. "What's going on out there?"

The guy shook his head. "I have no idea, but it looks like they're digging." He stepped away from the window and joined the others, the same as the person who was standing by the candles. He gestured to Henry. "Is that him?"

Montgomery nodded when Henry stepped closer. "Yes. Special Agent Henry Clavell, meet Sleepy Hollow's finest detectives." He eyed each of them when he said their names. "Cindy Morgan. Theo McMaster and Tom McCoy." Theo was the one who had been by the window. "Also, the remaining members of Detective Carver's homicide team."

Henry looked from one to the other. They looked worn and tired. Angry and frustrated. "*Remaining* members?" Henry asked. "What happened to the others?"

To his question, they all shared glances filled with uncertainty. It was Montgomery who answered. "We believe they are compromised. Like just about every other citizen in the Hollow."

Theo said, "I caught my wife this morning trying to eat her arm."

Tom added, "My kids are acting strange too. They turned defiant out of nowhere, but it's more than your typical teenage rebellion. Something changed in them; some evil has infected them." His head was shaking. "They're just not the same people."

And Cindy said, "I live with my aging mother, and lately her ill health has taken a turn for the worse. Like the cancer took a dose of steroids."

Henry thought for a moment before asking. "Why?" He shrugged and received more than a few perplexed stares. "Why them and not the four of you?"

"Why not you?" asked Theo. Henry looked at him when Theo shrugged. "Your guess is as good as mine."

Montgomery turned to Henry. "Look, we know nothing about what's going on out there, but what we do know is that it's some pretty serious shit and it's gotten into everyone we know." He gestured to the street. "Look at it out there." His head shook. "It's like the entire town is possessed, and none of us know how to fix it." He paused, maybe to clear his head. That buzz turns the thoughts in your head all twisted and confused. He looked at his other officers. "What we know is that Detective Carver was adamant that the murders were happening at the house in the western woods." He gestured to Henry. "By your girlfriend's ex-fiancé, which means there's a connection to the house, Carver's disappearance and your friend, which makes you our new best friend. And since everyone we know seems to have undergone some insane transformation, there's very few we can trust."

Henry stepped closer. "What's your plan?"

Cindy answered, "Take down the house." She stood up from the pew. "That seems to be the source of all this carnage and change. It's time for us to do the right thing and take this fucker out." She looked around. "Maybe then all this shit will stop, and we can all go back to normal. At least, as normal as Sleepy Hollow can be."

Montgomery turned to Henry. "The question is, are you in or not?"

Henry paused while scanning everyone of them. He nodded. "Of course I'm in. Lori is in that house, and there's no way I'm allowing her to meet the same fate as the other victims. That son of a bitch murdered her mother in cold blood. There's no telling what he could be doing to her right now."

"That's what I like to hear," said Tom.

Henry addressed Montgomery. "Do you know how to get to the house?"

He nodded. "I do, but there's no clear path. We'll need to take a trek through the woods."

Henry nodded, his hand on his chin, thinking. He looked around the church, then at the window, listening to the people chanting and digging. He thought about the fog and the buzz and the murders and Lori and Marc Saduj and Elena's dead, bloodied corpse in the motel room. Theo checked his assault rifle when Henry had a thought.

He locked in on the rifle. "I think we should take additional weaponry."

The four of them stopped and looked at him.

"Like what?" asked Cindy.

He shrugged. "With all that's going on out there, maybe we need something a bit more spiritual to help us." He walked over to the bowl of holy water propped up on a pedestal and looked at the four detectives. "Does anyone have any water bottles?"

They were interrupted by a loud explosion.

Father McKenzie's church was on fire, courtesy of the ghost demons who were congregating in the park by the cavern. The boiler exploded, to a parade of cheers.

Hal and Andrew led the congregation in the park. They were preparing for the coming of Baphomet. A most glorious moment and one that will cement their hold on humanity. Sarah was currently with the master, but she will be headed to the river soon, leading the congregation in that location while the others were in the cemetery, digging up the bones of dead ancestors-the coven who provided protection until the demon could rise once again-preparing the dead for reliving in a town of ghosts.

Their orders were simple: burn the Hollow to the ground to make way for the new atmosphere where the ghost demons can thrive and regenerate. Sleepy Hollow was becoming ground zero for the death of humanity. Next on their list was to burn the library, followed by Broadway, then all the way down to the Hudson. Sarah and the others had their orders too. By dawn, the Hollow will be transformed into a literal hell on earth.

Andrew led the bonfire's creation they were setting up in the park. A fire to chant over and to ritualize around, aiding in the coming of Baphomet. Hal was gathering a flock to help burn the library when the ghost demons all went quiet. One of the coven's descendants had arrived. One who has played a crucial role in the master's resurgence.

Mrs. Leiter was dressed in a black robe. She looked at the burning church with delight.

"It has begun," she said, turning her head to the sky. "Agios O Baphomet. Tonight, we take back our pride."

Hal took Mrs. Leiter's hand. "It is splendid to see you, my lady. Come, we have a special place reserved just for you."

He led her over to where the bonfire was being set up.

"For you, Mrs. Leiter, we provide the north point of the star."

"Oh, to dream," she said. "I'm living a dream. My coven would be proud. They shine down on me tonight."

"Always, Mrs. Leiter. Always." He gestured to the park and all its inhabitants. "You are in good company," he said and bowed to her. "But I have a task to complete. Prepare yourself and bask in the glory of Baphomet. You've earned your right."

Mrs. Leiter said in that whining drone of a voice, "Dispense with the pleasantries, young man, and go… Burn it. Burn it all to the ground."

He heard the drips from the cave plummeting into a puddle by his feet. Logan had stopped to hide. He stopped several times during his journey. There were people walking through the tunnels. Multiple people and they were always in large groups. He heard footsteps overhead too. It sounded like an army marching across the Hollow.

Logan held his breath, watching the people walk past him. One held a torch, illuminating the path for the rest of the group of ten. He was hoping he would arrive soon. Things were getting strange down here in the cavern. His legs felt like they weighed a thousand pounds, and his thoughts kept racing, accumulating into no thought at all. He felt like something was sitting in the center of his brain and pulsing into every synapse, strangling his thoughts then sending them into oblivion.

His stomach rolled with nausea. Felt sick and depleted, as if gravity was pulling down on his core while he was hanging off a cliff, ready to plummet to his death. He waited for the torch to shrink to the size of a pea before stepping out of the darkness. Logan watched the flame fade into the distance when he turned around and his heart took a sudden jolt when he bumped into a black car that had no place being in the tunnel. He gazed over the car, perplexed and unnerved by its presence, with his jaw hanging open and his thoughts twisting in his brain. A second later he turned in the direction where the people had come from, and his heart took another jolt.

He stepped back while staring into the eyes of a woman.

"What are you doing?" she asked, her voice scolding. "We're needed at the river."

She took a good long look at Logan, gnashing his teeth, trying to put some thoughts together, a lie or a story, but his thoughts were grinding in his brain like his jaw was grinding his teeth. She had short red hair and green eyes with the slightest hint of red in the irises.

"You're... new." Her stare carried suspicion. She looked as if she were about to attack. "It gets better," she said. "It's difficult for us to adjust to the atmosphere, but that'll change soon." The book he was holding piqued her interest. Her eyes narrowed. "Is that the book the Lord is looking for?" She looked into his eyes, but all he could do was stand there, watching as a grin spread across her lips.

She stood staring at him, assessing and thinking. Logan couldn't say anything. His thoughts weren't connecting, but he could feel a change coming on, dancing in his cells, turning his blood on fire. He knew he was in trouble. Knew this woman could tear him apart right now, but he couldn't for the life of him snap out of the trance he was in. As if some dark hand of the devil had wrapped around him and was squeezing every ounce of life from his body.

240

"The master wants the book," she said. "Come with me. We'll bring it to him together." She took him by the wrist then led him into the dark tunnel.

"The master will reward you for this. You'll be a god among gods."

But Logan didn't want to be a god among gods. He wanted to help his friend send the demon back to hell, and this task was the only thought he could remember.

Lori opened a door on the second floor to find a staircase. She looked back into the hall before stepping in then climbed the stairs, holding the candle to light the way. She could hear the wind outside, howling and whistling across the house, creaking the foundation. And the buzz. The buzz in her ear brought confusion to her mind.

The staircase was narrow, with walls on both sides that were dark and musty. It smelled of mold and rot. Her candle cast a faint glow in the darkness as she took the steps up.

When she was outside the house, she remembered having seen the third floor. It looked like something out of a fairy tale. Round and tall with a peaked roof. She wondered what she would find in the room. So far, Lori hadn't seen a soul in the house. She wondered if Marc was here. Lori was still struggling to wrap her head around what she had seen. A demon in Marc's skin? How was that even possible? It defied logic and rational thought, but reality had flown through the window when the demon revealed himself.

She wanted to convince herself that what she'd seen had been a waking nightmare and that none of it was true. Wanted to believe that everything she'd learned resulted from an overactive imagination and a trauma response resulting from the accident and the break-up with Marc, but she knew that wasn't true either.

People were dead. Her mother too, and she couldn't fool herself into believing that Marc could transform himself so quickly. It's not like he's a magician and can throw out an optical illusion whenever he wants. No, the demon presented himself because he wanted Lori to believe and to know without a doubt that he was real, and he had Marc. Had his soul in the palm of his hand and all he had to do was squeeze and Marc would be no more.

She came to a door at the top of the stairs and pushed it open. First, she saw wisps of fog, but how the fog was in the house she wasn't certain. The room was bathed in black. Lori could hear her breath in her ears when she stepped further into the room and her foot crushed something hard on the floor. She could see something on the floor, and she stretched the candle further into the room when her breath hitched in her throat with a squeal.

There were dead people on the floor. Five of them. They were all women in various stages of decomposition. Someone had lined their bodies across a circle where she could see an inverted pentagram had been painted on the floor. Each woman had her heart torn from her chest. Fog floated off their bodies.

Lori held her hand over her mouth. "My God," she muttered.

Bang!

Lori jolted around to the door that was now closed. Someone or something was behind the door, sliding the lock into place. She went to it, banging on the door. Dust fell over her.

"Marc, is that you?" she called, slamming on the wooden door. "Marc!" she hollered, but her voice fell on deaf ears. She heard someone shuffling down the steps. Heard them close and lock the door in the hallway that led to the narrow staircase. She banged again, frantic and frightened. "Marc, please," she cried, her head leaning against the door. "I don't know what to do," she groaned. Tears rolled down her cheeks when all of life's hardships came flooding from her heart and her eyes, crying a desperate plea.

She breathed deeply, her chest rising and falling in quick, heavy swallows of breath. Lori sucked back her tears and raised her head off the door then turned around.

Turned around to the cold dark of the room with the dead bodies on the floor.

"What do you want from me?" she screamed into the night when on her left she heard a soft thud, and she looked in that direction. Heard it again. Lori swallowed the lump in her throat before taking slow steps in the same direction. The candle's flame illuminated her path to the hidden door that opened and closed with the wind.

Lori craned her head to the door, holding the candle in front of it. She licked her lips before opening the door then stretched the candle in.

Another staircase was in front of her. Small stone steps spiraled to the left and into more blackness. She noticed the buzz was even louder with the door open. Obviously, the sound was coming from downstairs.

They drove through the fog towards the western woods. Montgomery was driving with Theo in the passenger seat, and Henry squeezed between Cindy and Tom in the back. Everyone in the car was armed to the eyeballs, but Henry kept thinking their weapons were futile. Somehow, he knew they wouldn't have the impact they were all hoping for.

Something was wrong in the Hollow, and the fact that the small riverside town was burning was proof positive that something more sinister was at play. When they drove away from the church, they could see the fires in the Hollow. It looked like hell had erupted across Broadway, and the fire was spreading, aided no doubt by the winter winds that drove the fog across the Hollow.

They had passed the park on their way to the woods. The park where Henry knew a body had been found. Someone had set the church on fire, and the library was on fire too, wedging the park between two infernos. Through the fog, they could see a horde of people congregating in the park around a bonfire. It looked like they were chanting and praying. They were on the street too. Montgomery had slammed on his brakes when a family of three walked past the car like it wasn't even there.

"It's like they're possessed," said Cindy as she watched the family pass on their way to the park. "Did you see that little girl? Her stare gave me chills."

They heard another explosion towards the Hudson River.

"That's where the other body was found," said Theo. "At least, it was in the same direction."

"It doesn't matter," said Montgomery. "We've got to kill the source of all this confusion."

Montgomery theorized that once Marc Saduj was dead, everything in the Hollow would return to normal.

Henry looked out the window at the fog and the fires and the people acting all psychotic. He hoped Montgomery was accurate in his belief, because if he isn't, they may need to call the National Guard to stake a permanent claim on the Hollow. Although he didn't believe they could do anything about what was happening. Henry was a rational man, but everything he's seen over the last few hours made no rational sense.

Blood crawled across the ceiling in Elena's motel room. The buzz and the fog and the sickly sensation he couldn't for the life of him understand were doing to his insides. Lori and Marc and Carver's gone missing. Now the Hollow was burning, and its citizens were possessed. Henry may be a rational man, but he understood what was going on in the Hollow wasn't rational at all. He believed it was supernatural.

And nefarious, considering the carnage, chaos, and anarchy he witnessed on the drive to the woods.

Montgomery put the car in park and killed the engine. "We walk from here. It's about a half mile to the house."

Henry noticed the fog was thicker in the woods and the buzz was louder. He leaned forward, looking through the windshield. He couldn't see the house through the fog. Montgomery and the others climbed out of the car. Henry followed a second later.

"Weapons check," said Montgomery.

Henry was looking through the woods, listening to the buzz and closed his eyes. He noticed his hands were shaking. His stomach rolled, squeezing his innards. It felt like his atoms were on fire, vibrating with a profound struggle to churn over in his gut. He felt hot despite the frigid temperature and noticed how quiet it was in the woods, beyond the buzz in his ear. He looked over the Hollow. From his vantage point, he could see all the way to the Hudson if it weren't nighttime and there wasn't a fog blanketing the Hollow, but he could see the fires burning in the Hollow. It looked like a nuclear bomb had gone off. He turned to the officers and couldn't help the thought that passed through his brain. They looked like lambs charging into a slaughter.

The officers all called 'check' when they were done with their weapons, and Montgomery spoke up. "Okay, here's the plan. Once we get to the house, Theo and Tom, take the back of the house." He gestured to Henry and Cindy. "We'll take the front. Carver said there's a basement where he believed all the murders happened, so that's our play. Whatever you do, get to the basement and remember, shoot to kill. Everyone dies tonight. No mercy to anyone other than Henry's friend, Lori, and Detective Carver. Other than that, everyone goes. We'll deal with the repercussions later."

Cindy stepped up. "Are you sure this will work?"

"No. Next question." He looked around, studying their eyes. No one said another word. "Okay, let's go. Times wasting."

"Wait," said Henry when everyone stopped and turned to him. He swallowed his breath. "Listen, I know you all didn't agree with my holy water idea, but... it's possible that we're dealing with something that can test our limits."

They looked at him as if he were cockeyed.

"I don't mean physical limits either. I mean psychological." He gestured to the house. "Considering what's going on in the Hollow right now, there's got to be more to the reason behind it."

"What're you saying?" This was Theo; he leaned his rifle on his shoulder.

"I mean, keep your wits in check and don't trust your eyes but rely on your instincts. If something's telling you to get out of Dodge, listen to that impulse and don't question it."

Tom shook his head. "Is that it?"

Henry felt his heart sink. "Yeah... that's it."

"Good, let's go." Montgomery turned around and stepped into the woods. "Keep your ears and eyes open and follow my lead."

Henry watched them file behind Montgomery, entering the woods through the fog.

He'd never seen people so eager to die.

293

He could see the police entering the path through the woods towards the house. Wren watched them from the window on the second floor.

He couldn't help the grin that spread across his lips, knowing the master would invoke his will against them.

"Guns," he whispered, clucking his tongue. "Foolish." Their weaponry was no match for the hell they will undoubtedly experience, and Wren was itching to dole out some much-needed torture. He pictured slitting their throats and drinking from the fountain of blood that raced across their open throats.

The girl, Lori, was on her way to the dungeon. On her way to hell after Wren locked the door to the third floor as the master had instructed. "Let her see the folly of Marc's passion," he'd said. The murdered women on the third floor served a different purpose. They comprised the many women Marc had brought to the mansion over the last six months. He never asked what happened to them after he'd fallen asleep. That was in the beginning, when Marc had most of his faculties and the master was growing inside his heart. The women's sacrificed hearts were a signal to Xibalba that the master had awakened. The third floor was a beacon to Xibalba; the roof pointed directly to its constellation, providing additional power to the house.

The house that was ushering Xibalba into the Hollow. Wren licked his lips, thinking about what Lori would see once she arrived to greet the master. Once she passes the test, she'll meet hell on her own. A preliminary to Baphomet's arrival. Souring the heart with fear before Baphomet takes his rightful place in her heart. The master's meeting with Lori must take place alone, the master had told Wren, but that didn't mean Wren was kept in the dark. Not at all. He had his instructions. Namely, the police who were coming to the mansion. The master had said they would come. "They always come, Wren. Some men refuse to give in." Wren welcomed the challenge.

The buzz was doing what it was meant to do, changing the atmosphere in the Hollow so that the hordes from Xibalba could walk freely on the earth. Changing the chemical structure of the human body too, turning them into feeble weaklings easy to overpower. The fog escorted the master's ghost demons into unsuspecting humans to take control of their minds and bodies, and the fires were destroying the Hollow to make way for Xibalba structures to be erected on earth. By morning, the Hollow will be transformed, and the hounds of hell will spill across the earth. The last hurdle to overcome was spiraling towards them. All it took was a little possession.

Wren wrung his hands, thinking about it. The anticipation was maddening. Watching the police trek through the woods, he enjoyed his gift from Xibalba. The master granted him entrance to the astral portal in the dungeon. Once there, he witnessed hell in all its glory. They took his eyes and nipped at his heart, but Wren gave himself over willingly and in turn they granted him new eyes and immense strength.

According to the master, Xibalba was different for everyone. You experience all that you take with you. All your nefarious attachments. He wondered what Lori would see. And now that the police were inching closer to the house, he couldn't wait to see their response to Detective Carver's head.

294

The staircase seemed to spiral for an eternity. At first everything was black, cold and musty, but the further she descended, the less cold it was, as if the temperature were rising from below. She could hear a dull roar from a fire beneath the buzz raging in the center of her brain, crackling from the bottom of the stairs. She took another step and felt the heat across her skin. Sweat beaded across her forehead. Lori tossed her beanie off then took a deep gulp of heated breath.

The staircase spiraled and then spiraled again. It seemed like she was on a downward spiral that reflected her life's constant changes, never knowing what was around the next turn. She felt heavy too, like her legs were filled with cement. The constant buzz fluttered her eyelids, unrelenting in its purpose to grind the mind into oblivion.

Lori turned a corner and now she could see light down below. A grayish-blue hue vibrating within what she assumed was more fog slithering up the staircase to greet her. The color pulsed like a strobe light with waves caught in a low frequency, infecting the staircase with shadows that Lori thought looked like devils ready to strike. The shadows groaned, crawling across the stone walls of the narrow staircase. Lori stopped cold in her tracks, staring into the abyss of light. It looked like a light in the darkest depths of the ocean.

Stopped because she could see inside the lighted fog. It looked like…

Memories.

Lori's memories. From childhood and beyond. She saw herself in the throes of a waking nightmare with her parents around her, attempting comfort and logic to explain her distraught mental state. Saw the day she met Marc and the tragedy from the accident. It was hypnotizing. Hypnotizing and yet…

Beautiful.

Like witnessing the blossoming of nostalgia with a profound sensation of content.

"We turn out the light." The voice was inside her head. The demon's voice, the one from the motel, was thicker than Marc's voice. Guttural and gruff, Lori could feel it in her mind as if the demon was in her brain, having his way with her. "Before we turn out the light."

A warm rush of wind rifled up the staircase, subtle yet profound like a hushed exhale bending the candle's flame that extinguished in the next moment. Lori stared at the smoke lifting off the dead candle, rising to her nose, raising her eyes to the fog and the hue.

She understood she had arrived, but what will she see once she finds solid ground? The candle shook in her trembling hand. She didn't know. She didn't know if she had the strength to see this through. Lori had yet to fully understand what was happening in the Hollow or what had happened to Marc, and now she was thrown into an impossible situation, but she knew she had to go. Had to because that's what Marc would do. He would do it for her.

Was there hope in her heart? Love and admiration? Courage and resolve? Of course there was, but was it enough? How is a demon defeated? How are they expelled from the host if not through an exorcism? If you kill the body, what happens to the soul? What happens to the heart and all the love within it? Questions she wished she could answer because she was in the dark, riding a wave with a hope and a dream that she and Marc would see the dawn of a new day once the sun rises over the Hollow.

"Whatever happens," she whispered. "Whatever you see…" Her breath hitched in her throat like a lump of heartache. "Don't let go of the love in your heart. No matter what, they can't take that away from you."

She thought about Gerard.

"Innocence… is evil's addiction," he'd said.

The revelation struck hard. *They want…* me.

For what purpose Lori wasn't certain, but she knew in her heart it was true.

Lori took a deep breath, then bent down and placed the candle on the step behind her. She pulled off her coat and sweater and dropped them by the candle, then turned to the light in the staircase. Lori kept her hand on the wall to steady her feet as she made her way into the light and the fog.

With every step down, she could feel change coming.

It felt like pure rage determined to devour innocence.

295

Marc's eyes rolled beneath his fluttering eyelids. He felt like rot was inching its way up into his throat. His insides were twisting, as if he were being squeezed and wrung out dry. His heart constricted, twisting in his chest as if a dark hand was squeezing every pure emotion, every ounce of goodness from the organ.

He rolled over onto his front, his arms shaking. He felt so cold, shivering from head to toe when he coughed blood over his lips. Marc tried to push himself to his feet.

"Stay down," Jen told him. "There's nothing you can do. You just need to accept it."

But he wanted to get up. He had to get up. His ruse didn't work. Lori was still in the Hollow, and that fact drove his actions. He needed to see her. Needed to send her away. He dragged himself across the cold cemetery ground, staring at his hands and how the skin had turned gray. The cracks along his flesh spread to his forearm. His split lips burned across his mouth, stinging with pain. He was indeed rotting. He could feel the rot coming from his heart, infecting his blood.

He managed to lift himself to a seated position, his legs beneath him when the sky cracked with a thunderous boom that shook the cemetery.

"It comes," said Olga. "It comes for all of us."

Marc gazed through narrow wet slits to the sky above the cemetery and the rolling dark crimson clouds progressing towards them from the western woods. The clouds seemed to cover more than the sky, as if the overcast reached from the ground to the heavens like a wall of dark crimson overtaking the ethereal plane of the cemetery. He could see heads and bodies walking within the overcast. It looked like an army of devils marching through the clouds. Devils and ghosts and what he thought looked like gargoyles were in the clouds. So many of them.

Jen hollered to Olga, "What are they?"

His heart squeezed in his chest, trembling anguish coursing through his veins.

"The devils of Xibalba," said Olga. "Marching towards the Hollow." She paused when another thunderclap rolled across the cemetery with a sonic boom, shaking the ground. "Lori's test is now. It won't be long until hell overflows into the Hollow."

"What if she fails the test?" asked Jen.

Marc forced his head around to look at Olga, and Olga met his stare.

"She won't," said Olga.

"But we can hope."

Olga shook her head. "You don't understand. This isn't a test of bravery, nor is it a test as we think of it but as *they* think of it." She gestured to the rolling, thunderous clouds inching their way closer. "In order for her to fail…"

"She has to destroy my heart." Marc finished Olga's sentence.

"Exactly. She has to kill him."

296

Lori took the last step down into a sea of light and fog. The light pumped like strobe lights across the fog in blue and gray hues. Pumping vibrations into Lori's bones. She had thought she was walking into a basement, but what she saw looked... different.

The area was vast. It seemed like the universe existed beneath the Hollow because the light and fog and buzz went on as far as her eyes could see. She saw no walls, just fog and shuddering colors. The floor was covered in so much fog Lori couldn't see her feet. She studied the landscape. Oddly enough, on her right, a cave existed beyond the basement. Drenched in a pitch black that Lori believed was like a black hole. The darkness seemed to go on forever, culminating in what she couldn't believe. It looked like a black orb existed deep inside the cave. Its constant spin is where the buzz was coming from. The fog and light too, churning and releasing hell's wrath from the black orb. The temperature was hot, burning. Lori could feel sweat slicked across her face.

Now she could hear whispers, like the clucking of tongues, existing beneath the buzz. Incoherent whispers from forgotten languages spoken from nefarious tongues like chanting, repeating the same over and over. She could feel those voices echoing in her bones and sense the devils surrounding her. Lori could feel them in the shadows, wanting to be free. So many devils, Lori could feel their stares crawling across her skin.

"Come, Lori." The demon's voice slithered across the fog to her ears. "Just a little further. Come and see me, Lori."

She craned her head, searching through the fog when she stepped toward the demon's voice and the fog recoiled as if the fog carried intelligence, slithering like a snake to escort her to the demon. She stepped closer as the fog parted, opening a doorway into the cave that Lori stepped through.

She saw the demon then. Marc's demon with Marc's skin. He sat on a black throne made from rock with a red cane in his right hand. The ground rumbled beneath her. Lori turned to the floor. The ground consisted of large, cracked stones with blood boiling inside those cracks that flowed towards the demon's throne. She noticed the fog was gone, and the buzz too.

Lori looked up, scanning the cave. The ceiling was high above her head, the walls so far away. On her right, a hundred yards away, were three large doors. Fog slithered through the doors like a congregation of ghosts.

"Do you like my home, Lori?" The demon looked up when thunder crackled from above, rumbling in the cave, followed by howls and screams filled with torture. "It's been so long since I've seen it." He panned his head around, meeting Lori's gaze. "Beautiful, isn't it?" He closed his eyes as if savoring the screams and howls.

Lori could feel them in her bones, like constant raging moaning groans beneath the fold, beating thunderous vibrations to her heart. It was like a drug coursing through her veins, melting her inhibitions. Deleting fear. Lori turned to the demon and stared into his blood-red eyes.

"What is this?" She shook her head. "Your home?"

"The cave," he said. "A direct connection to the Hollow. Pockets like this exist across the universe. A place where I waited an eternity." He sat back on his throne. "Waiting for someone to come along. Waiting for my opposite to raise me from the depths of darkness. Waiting for this moment."

"Waiting for Marc," she shot back. "You played off his fears. You played off his heart. If he had known what you were going to do, he would have never agreed to it."

The demon grinned. "Still the love-starved fiend, Lori. Even now, you refuse to see that part of him. The darkness has existed within him since the dawn of his creation. His denial and shame brought him to me. All I did was piece him back together."

"No. It was love that brought him to you. He sacrificed himself for it."

Shadow floated across the demon's face, bathing him in darkness except for the red eyes. "He made his choice. Now it is time for you to do the same."

Lori paused, watching the demon as he rose from his throne. He took his cane and stepped towards Lori. Lori stepped back as the demon's feet pounded towards her and he unsheathed a sword from his cane.

He stopped walking and paused in front of her, holding the blade.

Lori's breath hitched in her throat while listening to the heavy breaths from the demon. He stood there, staring at her as if savoring the moment. His eyes, his red eyes, were hypnotic. It was all she could see. The two red eyes in the darkness.

"You wish for the nightmares to end, do you not?"

Lori swallowed her breath. "More than anything."

The demon closed his eyes. "Marc's heart beats in my chest." His eyes peeled open. "This can all be over so quickly, Lori. It was Marc who brought me to the Hollow. It was his heart that brought him to me." He raised his shoulders, standing tall above Lori. "And it is his heart you must destroy for this to end. You must deny him, Lori."

Lori looked from the blade to the demon. "I don't understand."

"Drive this blade into his heart and all that you see will no longer live in the Hollow." She looked at the blade again. "This is the only way to stop what is happening."

Lori shook her head. "No." She stepped back. "You're lying."

"But it is." The demon's voice hissed over his lips. "What do you choose, Lori? Hell has come to the Hollow. Has come to claim dominion over humanity and yet you choose not to relinquish it when the power is in your hands."

Her thoughts flitted through her brain. "This is a test. You want me to strike him down because then I'll be like you. Your test is a trick."

The demon stretched the blade towards her. "Many have sacrificed. What will you sacrifice tonight, Lori? Believe what you want, but what I say is true. The only way this ends is if you strike at the heart of causation." He slipped the blade into her hand. "Stab the heart and this can all be over."

He opened his shirt, revealing his chest. His chest with the white skin. Lori's brow furrowed, raising her gaze to the demon's face.

Marc looked back at Lori, but not the demon with Marc's face. The demon was no longer there; instead, she was staring at Marc, and not the emaciated Marc she'd seen in the park but the old Marc. The healthy, vibrant full of life Marc she had fallen in love with.

When he spoke, it was Marc's voice.

"It is the only way."

She looked into his baby blues. Saw his face, the gentle, caring stare that always melted her heart.

"Please, Lori."

The blade was heavy in her hands when memories as thick as thieves raced across her eyes. Her initial meeting with Marc. The tearoom and his apartment. The armoire and their first night together. As if she were living those memories fresh in her mind. Tennis. Passion. Writing. Drinking. The cabin. Everything about the cabin. White water rafting. Sipping beer by the water. Watching Marc in the sun. His gentle touch. His caring smile. His innocent eyes. A proposal by the lake.

Together forever. Forever and ever until the end of time. The accident and his sacrifice.

"LORI!" Marc's voice boomed around her, releasing her memories. "Do it now, Lori."

Her heart thundered in her chest. Lori shook her head, dropping the blade to the floor where it rattled to a stop. She backed away.

Staring into Marc's eyes. "I can't," she told him. "There's got to be another way."

Marc's mouth was open. She watched as a smile crept across his lips. Lori could hear her own heavy breathing shuddering into the room. Marc crouched down to pick up the blade, and when he emerged, the demon had returned.

"Thank you, Lori." The demon held the blade in his hands. "I knew I could count on you."

He replaced the blade into his cane when Lori sensed a change coming on. Sounded like a million bats had suddenly awakened and were racing towards the cave.

"What is that?" She stepped back. The sound was everywhere.

"Just the devils of Xibalba, rising in honor of Baphomet."

264

He craned his head to the ceiling. His voice boomed across the cave. "My lord, she now awaits your arrival."

Sounded like thunder suddenly ceased. Lori could feel the silence in her heart as if the world had been tossed across the universe. Felt it slipping. Slipping away.

The demon's eyes found her. "The ritual will now begin."

Lori's eyes squinted.

"John. Do what is necessary."

Lori felt a stab in her back. Pain rifled up her back to her brain as her hand gripped her kidney.

"The blood of the innocent bathes the stone."

Lori dropped to her knees. Dropped to her knees in the fog-drenched dungeon, where the fog vibrated under the weight of the heavy buzz. The pain was immense, and she saw blood on her trembling hand. The demon gripped her by the hair, and Lori belted out a scream, squirming in his grasp. Felt like he was shredding her hair from her skull.

"Come, Lori." The demon pulled her across the fog-covered ground to the stone slab in the center of the room where a young boy with black eyes and a knife in his hand dripped Lori's blood onto the stone. "Baphomet is waiting."

Heard the boy raise his voice. "Agios O Baphomet." Lori, kicking and screaming, clawed at the demon's hand when he slammed her onto the stone slab.

She hit it hard, and the world went out in a blink of darkness.

They were at the edge of the woods, investigating the clearing that led to the house.

The house was bathed in fog. Darkness clung to every window. The mansion was colossal, standing like a beacon to a dark world where pain and suffering existed tenfold within its confines. Henry scanned across the fog to the house, listening to the buzz. He was certain the buzz was coming from the house. It seemed to send vibrations that thickened the fog.

The house looked like death, a stain on the Hollow that refused to rub off. Staring at the house, it seemed as if the house had a life of its own and was calling them to its embrace. Henry looked at his fellow officers. Montgomery had ordered everyone to hold once they arrived at the clearing. He was looking through a pair of binoculars.

"Do you see anything?" This was Cindy, crouched down in the woods. She looked at Montgomery, waiting for an answer.

Montgomery scanned across the house and paused before removing the binoculars. "Nothing at all."

Theo added. "There's not a single light on. Are we sure this is the right place?" He was also looking through a pair of binoculars.

"How many abandoned mansions in the woods do you know about?"

"Good point."

"It's also obvious that's where this frigin buzz is coming from." He turned around and squatted against a tree. "Remember too, it's the basement we need to get to."

Henry gestured to the binoculars. "May I?"

Montgomery nodded and handed them over. "We go in two minutes. Whatever you do, try to maintain the element of surprise for as long as we can. If we can get into the basement before we're noticed, all the better."

Henry scanned across the mansion, focusing on the windows on the second floor and stopped. His eyes squinted. It looked like someone was watching them from the window, although he wasn't certain. All he could see was an outline.

"I think someone is on the second floor. It's hard to tell. I think he's wearing all black." He looked at the officers. "I think he's watching us."

"Where?" said Theo.

"Second window from the left."

A pause while Theo looked to confirm Henry's sighting. "I don't see anyone."

Henry looked again, but there was nothing there. No more outline, just a thick blackness. "Maybe he saw us and left, but I know what I saw." He looked at Montgomery. "We should assume the element of surprise is off the table."

Montgomery nodded. "We still go in stealth and quiet." He turned to his officers. "Keep your wits in check and watch your backs for any surprises. And shoot to kill."

Henry paused before taking another look through the binoculars. He scanned across the house again, then followed the fog to the front porch where he scanned across something that seemed out of the ordinary and locked in on it.

Someone had staked a thick rod into the frozen ground. On top of the rod was Detective Carver's head. Henry froze while looking at the dead detective, the fog racing across the severed head. How his eyes were open, the face stained with crimson streaks of blood with his jaw hanging open as if he was about to scream when the devil's blade swiped across his neck.

The scene was enough to boil his blood despite the icy chill that wrapped around him like a cold hand of revenge. Henry removed the binoculars. He turned to Montgomery and the team. He couldn't allow them to find Carver's head waiting for them. They needed to know now that their comrade was dead. Even worse, Lori was still in the house, alone, and if one of the officers gets startled over Carver's death, they may start shooting first, which could put Lori in danger.

"Let's go," said Montgomery. "Theo and Tom, skirt the perimeter and come around the back of the house. The three of us will fan out across the front yard and take the front door."

"Wait one second." The team paused collectively. Henry scanned everyone. He didn't know how to say it, so he just came out with it. "Detective Carver is dead." His voice caught in his throat.

Montgomery took a step forward, looking at Henry suspiciously. "How do you know?"

Henry gestured to the yard and offered him the binoculars. "About halfway across the yard."

"What?" Cindy balked.

Henry locked eyes with her when Montgomery took the binoculars. "They cut off his head."

"It is done," said Olga, her stare fixed on the bleeding firmament crawling towards the Hollow. "All that remains is for Baphomet to take possession." She turned her gaze to Marc and Jennifer. "We lost! Lost forever. We brought hell to humanity and now hell will have its way."

Marc struggled but managed to climb to his feet. His bones and muscles ached something awful. His bones were so dense they felt like they weighed a thousand pounds.

"But Lori still lives," said Jen. "Baphomet has not taken possession." She rose to her feet, pleading with Olga as if Olga could do something. "We have until that time. You said it. All is not lost until Baphomet takes possession."

The earth rumbled with thunder, trembling across the cemetery.

"There is no one to stop him. No method to thwart his power. They're like feeble lambs walking into a slaughter. Once Baphomet takes possession, he'll grant Holer dominion with all the power of Xibalba behind him. There is nothing more we can do."

Marc breathed hoarsely across his lips. Felt like his lungs were deteriorating, burning in his chest. "Yes, there is." His hands shook by his sides, his skin burned across his bones, his stomach rolled anguish to every bone in his body. Both Jen and Olga looked at him.

"What do you mean?"

He gazed into Olga's eyes. "I have to take my heart back." He could feel the thick beat of his heart thump against his chest, painful like a hand was squeezing the organ.

"How do you propose pulling off such a task?" Olga asked, scoffing at Marc's notion.

He craned his head around to the crypt with the cherub. The same crypt where he bonded with the man in black. The nefarious crypt that led to hell. Olga stepped forward.

"Will it work?" hollered Jen.

Olga turned to the two of them. "If he's strong enough to survive, there's a chance he may succeed. But look at him. He doesn't have an ounce of strength left."

"But there is no other way. I have to try. For Lori. For the Hollow. I owe it to them."

Olga studied Marc for a long minute. "Very well then. But know this, Marc Saduj, you will confront what you take with you."

"To help Lori, I would do anything."

"As you wish, Marc Saduj." Olga rolled her tongue across her lips. "As you wish."

The heat kept rising the closer Logan came to the house. He could feel sweat pouring across his brow as he grinded his teeth, following the girl on her heels. His insides were twisting anguish to every part of his body, and his vision kept wavering as if he were looking through water, gleaming prisms across his eyes that turned the fog into twisted memories.

His mother's passing. His father's brutality. John and the vampire. Father McKenzie dying horribly and Carver beaten to a bloodied pulp. *Is he still alive?*

The girl hadn't said two words since she found him in the tunnel, and Logan was certain she knew he wasn't one of them. Why she didn't just kill him and take the book herself he didn't understand other than the possibility that she had something else in mind for him.

They rounded a corner onto a fifty-foot corridor that was thick with fog. Logan saw steps on the left-hand side.

"This way," the girl said, taking the steps. Logan followed dutifully, gripping the book firm against his chest, following as she rounded the corner to the next set of steps.

Logan stopped cold. The buzz was louder here. The fog thicker and the heat was immense. The buzz in his brain went into overdrive, scrambling his neurochemistry.

He saw the girl on the top step, silhouetted by fog.

"Come," she said. "The master is waiting."

Something squirmed in his brain. Felt like brain freeze he could feel behind his eyes. Logan wondered if it was his instincts telling him to run, but he wasn't running. He was walking up the steps as if this woman commanded his feet and he had no choice but to obey.

Logan took the steps up as the girl walked forward.

"My master," she said. "I have a gift for you."

He stepped into the room. The room that buzzed all around him, sending waves of nefarious vibrations coursing through his bones. The fog was so thick he thought he could cut it with a knife. He saw eyes in the fog. Eyes and mouths with fangs bathed in the fog while slithering across the room. He gritted his teeth while taking in the scene. Flashing light like strobe lights flickered wildly from the dark cave on his right. He noticed the fog was coming from the cave.

He stepped closer, the fog parting as if it parted for him when the room came into view. There was a dead body on the floor, minus a head. Logan scanned the clothes, knowing he was looking at Detective Carver.

He saw an unconscious woman on a rock slab. Her breathing labored, her heart hammered in her chest. He could feel her heartbeat like thunder in his bones. A thick fog hung over the woman. Thick streams of fog invaded her nostrils as she gagged on the fog like smoke. John stood beside the slab. His eyes caught in the darkness. He looked possessed, and Logan wondered if he looked the same. In his mind, he called out to John, but he knew his name did not cross his lips.

"Here, boy," said the girl. Logan turned toward her voice but could only see more fog.

He stepped forward with the fog wavering around him, parting to provide a clear line of sight. His escort stood behind what Logan could only assume was the cause of all that's happening in the Hollow. The demon from Sleepy Hollow. His back was turned to Logan. He was looking through the light billowing from the cave, communing with the people on the other side. He wore all black. His shoulders were thick, the same as the back of his head where Logan could see cracked skin along his neck that weaved beneath his hairline with skin beneath those cracks the color of burnt charcoal. It looked like the demon was outgrowing his skin. In his right hand he held a red cane. It was the red cane that Logan locked in on.

The girl leaned into the demon's ear and whispered. Logan noticed she looked at him. The demon nodded before turning to Logan. His eyes immediately scrunched, staring him down.

"I'll leave you to it, my Lord." The girl walked past Logan, eyeing him on her way back to the steps. Logan watched her from over his shoulder, disappearing down the steps.

Logan turned back to the demon that was staring him down. His flesh was cracked in various places across his face. Split like caverns had been opened across his skin. Inside each cavern, he could see dark skin beneath. His horns were ripping out of his cracked skull.

The demon stepped forward, and although Logan's heart jumped like a rabbit, his physical presence did not reciprocate. Instead, he stood like a deer in headlights. The demon studied him, tilting his head from right to left, looking him over.

He took a deep inhale, sniffing Logan's scent. "Human," he whispered. "I would ask how it came to be in your possession, but it is rather apparent the buzz has captured you in its grip." He reached his hand out and took the book from Logan's arms. Like taking spinach from a child, Logan gave it right over without a fight. The demon studied the cover, his fingers gliding across it. He then dropped it into the firepit. Logan watched the flames take hold of the book, licking away at the pages. Devouring its thickness.

"I've searched for this book for what feels like an eternity." He turned to Logan and grinned. "Come, boy, there is always room at our table for another." He gestured to the slab, and Logan followed his command, stepping up to the stone across from John. "The alignment of our constellations has begun."

He tossed two knives onto the slab.

"You may begin bloodletting, gentlemen. In time, Lori will beg Baphomet to release her from her pain."

Logan's hand shook when he took the knife, seeing how John did the same. They shared stares, and Logan wondered if the real John was still somewhere inside his brain like Logan knew he was.

The woman on the slab screamed something awful, her chest rising as if she were suffocating. Logan looked at John. The knife shook in his trembling hand. He turned to the demon whose dark stare of death burned into his soul.

But Logan was fixated on was the cane. It was his primary focus.

Lori woke up with a startle as if her heart had been squeezed and the fear of death burrowed into her mind, waking her to the presence of a threat. Her eyes roamed across the blackened landscape. In the distance she could see the silhouettes of trees, thousands of them, bathed in a dark foreboding. Night draped across the landscape, quiet and cold. The ground was large stones the color of ash. Her breath hitched in her throat, realizing she was tied to a chair, although this wasn't any normal chair. It was huge, fit for a giant. It wasn't made from wood or marble or stone, but some substance Lori couldn't identify, but it was thick and sticky and solid and black to its core.

Lori's arms were secured to the armrests; her ankles tied to the legs. The binding substance was sticky and thick. It looked like long, bony fingers were clamped around her skin. She grunted when she tried to pull her arms free, her heart hammering in her chest, but her skin was glued to the armrests, and her skin refused to leave their comfort, shredding off her bones when she tried to move her arms from the bony shackles.

A bellowing cry erupted in her throat when her flesh tore away from the bone. Lori ceased her endeavor. The pain was too much to bear. Next, she tried her ankles, realizing the same. She attempted to sit forward, but her back was glued to the chair too when the realization ripped into her consciousness. The only way she was getting off this chair was through immense suffering.

Then confusion.

What is this? Where am I? What's going on?

Followed by understanding.

The demon is real.

And finally, acceptance.

Everything Marc wrote about is true.

Which means…

Lori heard something move around her. Sounded like a mountain shifted to a new location. Now, a rickety cluck from a tongue echoed across the trees. Lori couldn't be certain, but she felt a presence surrounding her. She could hear it as if it had awakened and was now shifting position to gaze at its prize.

Now light, red light, glowed from beyond the trees, and Lori's eyes widened.

The light revealed the presence like a ghostly silhouette standing tall. Well over ten feet tall. The red light shone through this thing in front of her as if the presence was translucent. A specter, a ghost with the capability of manipulating the light.

It had long horns extending from its forehead. Its skin was gray like burned charcoal. Its eyes were catlike and yellow. The face was thin and long with a pointy nose. Wings as smooth as raven's claws were attached to its back. Three tails as thick as tree trunks slithered between its massive legs and coiled around its stomach. The ears were pointed and looked like they could pierce her heart.

Black silken hair covered the thing's face and body like fur. Its hands were talons, sharp, long and bony.

It was breathing. Lori could hear the heavy, thick, guttural breath of this beast as if that breath vibrated in her heart.

And then it moved. It seemed to float over to her, craning its neck and bending its head so that she was eye to eye with this beast.

Lori's heart jumped, her body cringed and her breath huffed across her lips. The stink emanating from this thing was foul, like rotting death in a sea of sewage. Unnatural and wrong.

Lori stared into its eyes, watching as it huffed its foul breath. Its head swayed from left to right as if assessing her when it drew in a deep inhale, dipping its nose into her hair while Lori whined in her throat, petrified.

She could have convinced herself this was a waking nightmare, or at the very least, a nightmare. But when the beast inched its talons into her brain, the scorching pain from his fingers was enough to convince her that this was no nightmare.

It was really happening.

Lori felt its thick talons tear into her skin. Two fingers on each side of her head. Her cranium cracked when those digits surged through her skull. Lori's eyes rolled to the back of her head, feeling the fingernails inching into her brain. Blood surged from the wounds. Lori could feel the thick, sticky wetness saturating her shoulders while she shuddered beneath the beast's dark touch. Blood gushed over her lips. Her eyes rolled to the back of her skull, conjuring a scream from the back of her throat when the beast growled before releasing a dark breath that hushed from his throat like smoke. Lori could feel the breath on her tongue, coating her throat, forcing itself into her nose, eyes, and ears. Like a thousand tiny snakes slithering hurriedly into those orifices to her brain, dousing the organ with the beast's burning breath.

Her brain was on fire, rippling anguish from her head to her toes. The beast flexed its fingers, inching them further into her brain.

And Lori's scream erupted off her lips, bellowing from the back of her throat. She could feel the beast inside her, infecting her blood with venom.

Marc felt Lori's scream shudder in his bones. He stood in front of the crypt with the black volcanic rock that Marc now knew belonged to the witch Selena, staring at the stone cherub.

"Before you enter, there are two things you must know." Olga looked at the heavens when another scream wailed across the cemetery, returning her stare to Marc when the scream faded. "Time works differently in the astral plane. Every minute of a human life stretches on for an eternity. Keep your focus on your heart. As long as it continues to beat, you will have time to save Lori."

Marc gave a slight nod. "And the second?"

"Holer's ghost demons should be gone by now." She gestured to the crimson cloud inching closer to the cemetery. "He's taking them through the ether to the Hollow. They cannot cause you trouble." She shook her head. "But Selena will undoubtedly greet you on your journey. When you first came to the cemetery, it was Selena who captured your heart and brought it to Xibalba. That is where you will need to travel if you wish to save Lori and the Hollow."

Jen was on his right. She placed her hand on his shoulder. "Keeps your wits in check. Trust your instincts. It may be the only hope we have."

Marc turned to Olga. "How will I know where he is?"

"The demon exists on both planes. Your heart is how he lives in our world, but in his he will keep the heart safe. Listen to your heart, Marc. It'll lead you to it. You may be here in the ether, but your body is still alive with the same heart that beats inside of you now. Tap into that essence. Feel through your heart and you will find your heart and the demon."

Marc nodded, turning to the crypt. His skin was hot to the touch, burning across his skin. The thunder rumbled across the cemetery, twisting his insides. He could feel Lori's suffering infecting his blood. Lori's possession was ongoing according to Olga, and once the possession is successful, all will be lost.

He leaned into the crypt door, pushing with every ounce of strength he had. The door felt so heavy, opening slowly with a grumble across the ground. His bones felt brittle as if his arms could snap in half, pushing the door wide enough for him to enter.

Sounded like wind inside the crypt, breathing across emptiness, howling to his ears. He couldn't see more than a few inches inside.

Marc pursed his lips. "For Lori," he whispered when another scream belted across the cemetery, echoing blood curdling wretched, whining cries. "I'm coming."

Marc stepped into the crypt, and the darkness swallowed him. Over his shoulder, the door was no longer there. A rising, cackling laugh greeted him. Now he could hear his own breath, huffing between his ears. Marc swallowed with a gasp and stepped forward into eternal darkness. He closed his eyes, following his breath, feeling the breath in his lungs and tapping into his heart, beating like thunder in his chest.

He could hear it pulsing in his chest. Beating between his ears and he opened his eyes.

Now he could see a light in the distance, glowing crimson and beating in unison with the heart in his chest.

Marc stepped forward, waiting for the devils to reveal themselves.

302

On Montgomery's cue, Henry stepped out of the woods into the clearing with his gun drawn, racing through the fog to the house. Montgomery appeared in the clearing on Henry's right, with Cindy directly opposite where Henry was on the other side of the property. He noticed Montgomery raced past the pole holding Carver's head.

He sprinted towards the front porch, his eyes on the second-floor window, his feet crunching through the snow. The house was dark and looked like a beacon of death.

Henry arrived at the porch at the same time as Montgomery and Cindy, huffing his tired breath, his heart hammering against the bone. Montgomery signaled for Henry and Cindy to halt while he took the stairs to the front door, the wood bending beneath his feet when Theo and Tom came around the house from the back, halting once they arrived at the porch.

Montgomery approached cautiously; his gun drawn. He squeezed the doorknob, twisting it when the door floated open. Henry scanned across the property, watching the fog float like specters across the lawn. The buzz in his ear. Now that he was closer to the house, he could feel the vibration beneath the ground. Like the distant roll of thunder, it rumbled in his bones. His legs ached from the run to the house. It was such a short distance, but carrying

284

extra weight was enough to tap his energy, causing him to struggle during the run over. He didn't know how, but he felt heavier, like he had led in his bones. He gasped a silent breath through his lips.

His arms were trembling from fighting through the fog that seemed thicker the closer he came to the house. As if the buzz was solidifying the fog. Henry could sense its dense matter thickening in his cells.

Montgomery buckled up beside the open door. His head craned, looking in, but all Henry could see was thick blackness, aided no doubt by the gray fog slithering into the house that gleamed silver under the crescent moon sitting in the overcast sky. Montgomery entered the house, followed by Theo, then Cindy and Tom.

Henry mounted the porch to the front door and joined the other officers when he stepped into the dark house. It was difficult to see with limited light, but as his eyes adjusted, Henry could see they were in either a living room or ballroom. A fireplace sat off to their right and beside it, a hallway, although Henry could only see a foot into the hall before it was doused in darkness. He noticed the fog drifting into the hall.

Heard a creak upstairs, like a thump as if someone took a step on the second floor. Montgomery signaled for Tom and Theo to take the second floor, then gestured to Henry to explore the area on Henry's left.

"Flashlights on," Montgomery mouthed to the team. Each of them had a flashlight secured to their weapon.

Henry clicked his on; the beam illuminated the back of Theo's head. He was headed to the staircase with Tom on his heels. Henry heard them mounting the steps when he turned to Montgomery, who gestured to Henry's left and then to the hall.

Their plan was simple. No one was allowed to break radio silence until the basement was located. According to Montgomery, Carver knew a basement existed but hadn't been able to locate it when he was here a few days ago. Henry knew, as well as the others, that old places like this were often built with hidden staircases with doors hidden in plain sight. They all agreed that that was exactly what was happening here. The problem was finding the hidden door and finding it before something foul happened to Lori.

Henry nodded, and Montgomery led Cindy down the hall. He heard more footsteps on the second floor, but when he looked back down the hall, Cindy and Montgomery were gone. All he could see was the fog drifting across the beam from his flashlight. Henry swallowed his breath, trolling his flashlight across the room while listening to his own heavy breathing between his ears.

The house looked abandoned. The walls were all cracked. The fireplace stood cold and dusty with cobwebs littered around it. The floor was old wood but with a layer of dust more than a few inches thick. The only furniture in the living room was a high-back red leather chair and a small side table next to it.

Henry heard a screech, like a choked-back squeal, coming from down the hall that quickly dissipated as if folding into the buzz radiating from beneath the ground. He aimed his flashlight at the hall, but once again all he saw was fog. He was certain that if one of the officers was in trouble, they'd send out an alert.

Just the house, he told himself. The foundation settling or the wind shaking the walls.

Henry swept his light across the living room to his left, revealing a kitchen through the fog. He pursed his lips and then swallowed with a gasp, his heart thundering like a rabbit.

Henry stepped into the kitchen, realizing for the first time that he was alone.

The woman on the table was bleeding. Logan ground his teeth while watching the blood drip across the stone where it rose in a metallic-scented smoke to his nostrils.

He and John had successfully made cuts across the woman's body. On her forearms, her temples and her legs just above the knees, and then sliced small cuts across her arms, legs, and torso. He'd never seen so much blood before. It seemed like a river had been set free from the woman's body while she groaned and screamed at the top of her lungs. Crying. Logan watched while the woman cried something awful. He could feel her pain thundering in his heart.

The blood turned black while it sat smoldering on the stone. It looked like clotted motor oil, wet and sticky. Smoke rose from the blackened blood, absorbed by the fog slithering across the body like snakes. Logan craned his head, assessing the woman and her screams filled with torture. His mind was numb, difficult to connect one thought to another. The buzz infected his judgement and the strobe lights flickering around the room brought confusion.

"Yes," said the demon. He was standing in front of the cave. "Consider it done, my Baphomet." His hand was pressed against the flickering light when he turned around. His eyes delighted in the sight of the woman whose restless jerking and shifting across the slab tested her restraints to the limits. When he moved, it seemed like the air moved with him. Seemed like the fog was a part of him, uniquely connected to the demon's shoulders. His cane held firm in his right hand, taking steps to the slab where he reached his hand towards the woman. Logan watched as the shadow from his hand crept across her body, his long fingers clenched into a fist over the woman's heart and she jumped and flailed across the table with a scream bellowing from her throat.

The fog then slithered into the wounds he and John had made and then spiraled into what Logan thought was a funnel. Like watching small tornadoes form across her body, churning effortlessly, solidifying into slimy green leeches attached to the wounds where the blood was draining from.

"Magnificent, isn't it?" The demon stood with his back hunched, devouring the woman with his stare that slowly drifted to Logan. "You can feel her anguish." Logan turned to the woman and his heart dropped into his stomach while watching anguish crawl across her face. "It brings pleasure to my aching heart."

Logan turned to John with his black eyes and his mouth hanging open. He looked lost and demonic. Sweat oozed off his brow. The fog spiraled around him. Over John's shoulder, Logan could see a silhouette. Logan's eyes drifted up, staring over John's shoulder at the specter standing behind him and holding his shoulders.

Logan craned his head. He'd seen a picture of John's mother when he was in John's house, and he was certain he was looking at the ghost of Sheila Hardwood.

John was staring at Logan. Everything seemed like it was happening underwater, as if the world had spiraled into a funnel where sound seemed as distant as the sun. He could feel his heart beating thick in his chest, his breathing heavy in his lungs, his shoulders rising with every inhale. He could hear his breath reverberate between his ears, grinding his jaw with gritted teeth.

He could feel the knife in his hand even though it seemed distant, like a memory of holding the knife. He remembered cutting the woman's skin, drawing blood that dripped to the stone and turned black like ink with smoke rising off the sticky coagulated tar looking blood. Then the demon brought the leeches that were now sucking the blood from her veins. John gazed over their slimy, thick bodies. He could hear them absorbing her blood. Heard her screams from the netherworld.

John raised his head when he felt the demon's stare and looked directly into the demon's eyes.

"The sins of the ancestors will be visited on the son." The demon stood tall, arching his shoulders and staring down at John. "When the time comes, you will make the final incision that will usher Baphomet into this vessel." He unsheathed the knife from his cane. "Only a weapon forged in hell can bring Baphomet to the fold." He trained his eyes on John. "The blood of the ancestor shall shed the blood that seals humanity's doom." He stared at the blade as if marveling at it. "You will pierce her heart so that Baphomet may take full occupancy within this body."

The demon looked up at the heavens. "My Lord," his voice boomed across the room. "I provide this vessel so that you may breathe once again. I honor thee in all your magnificence." His eyes closed. "Together we shall rule."

The woman screamed something awful. A scream John could feel in his bones. He watched her wriggling and pulling on her restraints, screaming bloody murder.

"Soon," said the demon. "So very soon." He sheathed the blade then turned to the cave consumed with light and fog. John looked at Logan, gazing mesmerized into his black eyeballs, and John's heart calmed.

He could see his mother in Logan's eyes, standing over his shoulder.

The journey to hell isn't paved with fire and brimstone, but cold and ash. Ash that fell like snow in the darkness. Falling across Marc's shoulders as he walked, shivering with his eyes on the crimson glow beyond the woods. He could hear his heart beating in the crimson light. The sound was subtle yet profound, a constant drum between his ears.

The laughing cackle bleated continuously across the firmament. Out of the corners of his eyes, he could see movement as if someone was hurrying, bounding over trees and woods with little effort. More of them were on his left. There were eyes watching him. Red eyes engraved inside the dark and the ghostly silhouette of a forest up ahead. Marc wasn't certain, but it seemed like the surrounding forest comprised the dying trees of the western woods.

A screech and rushing feet pounded across the ground. Marc felt the first cut across his back, followed by a wretched, cackling laugh. Pain raced across his back, arching his shoulders, but not deterring his mission. A second cut across his front, across his chest. Marc's assailant rushed past him in a white blur. His hand went to his chest as he trudged forward and came away wet and sticky. The blood the color of black ink across his palm.

Marc stopped for a brief second to collect his wits. The woods were closer now. The crimson beating glow more prominent.

Vapor, like smoke, rose off his wound. The warmth of his blood mixed with the frigid air.

Another cackle. Another flash of white and a cut across his right arm. Marc winced from the pain. His left hand went to the wound. He gritted his teeth.

"Come on!" he hollered into the silence. The cackle answered, and Marc took off, sprinting towards the woods.

A blur and a swipe across his leg, but he kept going. The pain stung like a bee, but still he pressed on.

The ash was falling faster now. Or was he running faster?

A cut across his left forearm.

His stomach.

Marc felt blood at the back of his throat, but he kept moving forward.

The white blur. The cackle and a cut across his left calf caused him to stumble forward, and he dropped into the cold dirt. The cuts across his body were bleeding and stinging. Marc raised himself to his knees when the cackle returned with a slice across the nape of his neck, and Marc winced in pain.

Get up, he told himself. Get…the…fuck…up!

Now!

He climbed to his feet, shaking and shuddering from head to toe, and pressed forward. His limbs were weak and weary. His lungs burned cold and freezing.

The woods were twenty feet away. The ash was falling faster now, as if a volcano had exploded, raining ash across the landscape.

294

Claws across his forehead. Blood rained across his eyes and face. Mad cackling laughter. White blurs across his vision. Another cut across the small of his back, and he went down on one knee, stumbled forward then raised himself up. He took off into the final stretch, his body aching. He could feel blood coat every inch of his flesh as he limped forward to the entrance of the woods, huffing his ragged burning breath and bleeding copiously. His eyes rolled behind his eyelids, and Marc gasped out a breath.

He gazed at the trees. Like redwoods, so tall he couldn't see where the trees stopped. Ash rained over him. His lungs burned, attempting to catch his breath when the trees moved, the limbs and branches too. Moved with a thunderous rumbling that shook the ground beneath him. The limbs and branches formed a canopy; the trees stood like guards. One by one they all moved, forming an aisle for Marc to pass. Beyond the forest, the beating crimson glow called him to it.

Gazing as far as his eyes could see, he focused on a tiny ball of energy floating towards him. It looked like it contained water, flowing inside the opaque ball that grew exponentially, racing towards him and blowing ash as thick as autumn leaves over him.

The ash stung like a bee, like tiny daggers biting into his skin.

But Marc didn't pay too much attention to the pain. He was mesmerized by the flow of ash across his eyes. Mesmerized because the ash contained memories filled with regret that sank his heart.

He could feel the emotion barreling down on his shoulders, filling his cells with concrete, pulling down on his core.

The devils you create will greet you. Olga's assertion burned between his ears.

Beyond the falling ash, beyond the trees, Marc heard a mechanical shift like a giant clock turning its rusty gears, watching as the ground beyond the canopy of trees buckled then fell into the earth, carving a trench wider than the Grand Canyon. His heart dropped into his stomach. On the other side of the trench, there was a mountain. And it was to this mountain that he understood he had to go to. He could hear his heart beating from the top of that mountain. The ground rippled and groaned where the cavern had been carved, creating a mile-wide staircase at the end of the canopy. He noticed the stairs pointed down.

The sight was enthralling yet terrifying. Marc could feel suffering rise from the stairs. "For Lori," he said when a scream erupted across the firmament, and he knew it was Lori's wretched cry for help.

Marc stepped forward when the blur raced past his eyes. Then the cackle. He felt the pain across his throat a second later. Followed by a river of blood that rained from his torn windpipe.

He never saw the witch until she had his throat in her hands.

Lori lifted her weary head. She felt so weak. Every bit of energy had been drained from her body. She was alone now. Alone with her arms wrapped around her legs, her knees against her chest, existing somewhere in the dark with her back against a wall, terrified and trembling.

Sweat covered every inch of her flesh, and she tried to think, but no thoughts entered her mind other than pure terror. Empty. Lori felt empty, as if every heart-wrenching emotion she ever had erupted like a bomb, grinding every pure emotion into oblivion.

She heard footsteps now, outside from where she was, but Lori felt paralyzed, incapable of moving and reserved to trembling, her bones pressed in anguish.

"Lori," she heard her name from the lips of her mother. Lori looked in the direction where the voice came from, staring into the dark depths of blackness overtaking her eyes. Heard rattling, and her heart jumped in her chest. Her entire body jerked at the sound when a door opened in front of her, washing light into the closet she was hiding in. Her mother stood in the doorway. "Oh, there you are. Hiding again, I see."

Now, her father stepped behind Elena. He put his hands on her shoulders. Lori cringed when she saw his eyes were black to the core.

"Come, Lori," her father said. "It is time."

"Baphomet waits for you."

Lori shook her head. "No. I don't want to." Her voice sounded like a child's.

"Enough with this nonsense." Her father stepped around Elena and snatched Lori by the wrist. "You're coming with me." He dragged her out of the closet and into her bedroom.

Lori protested at first. "No, Dad, please," she cried when she caught sight of her bedroom. Her father released her wrist, allowing Lori to stare. She saw herself in the mirror. Her younger self. She couldn't be more than twelve. Elena placed her hands on Lori's shoulders. Beyond the windows was a strange scene. It looked like another world existed outside her window. Dark with a forest that extended for eternity and a beast staring through the window.

Lori's breath caught in her throat, staring confused through the windows and she felt sick, as if venom tainted her blood.

Her mother gasped over her shoulders. "He is here," she said when Lori's father turned around and Lori jumped back with a startle. His features were distorted. The scowl across his face morphed into a wide demonic grin. His brow curled, revealing a monster beneath his skin. Lori looked up to her mother and saw the same. Elena shook her head, said, "It'll only hurt a little," then raised her head to the bedroom door.

Lori followed her gaze to the demon standing in the doorway. He was dressed in a black suit with the thinnest frame Lori had ever seen. His face was thin and long with a goatee and the most menacing eyes that cut her heart in two. Olive skin led to catlike yellow eyes and tiny horns embedded in his forehead. Lori couldn't take her eyes off him. Even when Elena took her by the wrist and laid her down on the bed, she couldn't remove her stare from him.

Her father watched, standing quiet and cold. The demon waited, devouring Lori with his stare.

"The time has come," said Elena. "Baphomet must enter his host." She raised Lori's wrist to the headrest and secured her wrist to the shackle hanging there.

Lori looked at the demon, then at her mother. "I don't want to." She tried to pull on the restraints. "No, Mom, please."

Elena gripped Lori's jaw and squeezed. "Now you listen to me. You take your medicine. You've been a bad, bad girl." She tossed Lori's head back against the headboard and started slapping her repeatedly across the head. Lori could do nothing but take it. Tears welled up in her eyes.

Lori cried to her mother. "I promise I'll be good. Please don't do this to me."

"Enough," her father hollered, stomping over to the bed where he slapped Lori across the face and head, repeatedly whacking the poor child. Lori tasted blood on her tongue. Her father's face rippled with demonic change as he hit her. "I've had just about enough of your antics. You'll do as we say."

The tears came ceaselessly. Lori, huffing and wailing, started squirming across the mattress, trying to break free.

Her mother gripped her arms. "Get her feet! Secure her legs."

Lori's father dug his nails into her legs, stretching the right ankle to the end of the bed and securing the ankle with a shackle. He did the same to the left ankle while Elena secured her right wrist, with Lori wailing the entire time to let her go.

"There you are." Elena gripped her mouth and shook her head. "Time to take your medicine."

Elena stood up from the bed. Her father was on her right side. Lori's eyes flitted from one parent to the next, then to the demon who entered the room. Lori snapped her eyes closed.

Started whispering, "This isn't happening. This isn't happening. I need to wake up. Wake up. Please wake up." She wrestled with her restraints. "Please." Her voice settled when she heard laughter.

Gut busting laughter. Lori opened her eyes to her parents laughing.

Her father said, "You still think those were night terrors?" He laughed and looked at Elena. Lori's eyes followed.

Elena's head was shaking. "Those weren't night terrors, Lori. The demon has had his eye on you for a very long time."

She heard something drop to the floor. Lori looked at the demon, who had undressed. His heavy suit caused the thud. His stare pierced through Lori's soul, standing naked. His skin beaded with sweat, thick with muscle and the longest shaft Lori had ever laid eyes on dangling between his legs.

300

"It'll only hurt at first," said Elena. She was staring at the demon and then trained her eyes on Lori. "Once he is in, there will be no more pain."

The demon breathed across his lips with the sound of thunder and bending steel. Panic set in, as if she weren't panicked already. He stepped towards the bed. His steps landed with a thud. Every step seemed to last a slow century. Lori jumped as if she could untangle her restraints.

"No mom. I don't want to." She shook her head, desperately trying to flee. Her parents laughed. "My God, help me, please."

"Baphomet has arrived," her father said. "Hail Satan!" His hands rose to the heavens.

"Hail Satan!"

The demon stepped closer to the bed.

"Go away," Lori screamed then shut her eyes as tight as he could. "Go down," she told herself. "Shut down. Shut down. Shut down."

She felt the demon's breath, hot and thick across her ankles, slither across her skin. It entered every orifice, every cell, strangling the air from her throat.

Shut down, please!

She felt the bed buckle and Lori snapped her eyes open, staring directly into the demon's eyes. Her breath hitched over her lips in a huffing, ragged panic.

When he spoke, it was as if his voice was garbled, like listening underwater. "Two become one." And then he roared into her face and sank his teeth into her neck.

Logan watched the leeches. Saw how they devoured the woman's blood. He could see their slimy little bodies heaving back and forth, taking long swallows of blood when he felt a wrench in his heart. His stomach twisted, sending pain to his brain.

Heard the demon. "The alignment is halfway completed."

The leeches started screeching. They sounded like baby birds waiting to be fed as they wiggled. Wriggled into the wounds Logan and John had carved into the woman. Logan could see them beneath the skin when the woman belted out the loudest scream he'd ever heard.

The demon laughed. "Baphomet has accepted the offering. The point of no return quickens to meet our fate." He unsheathed his blade and offered it to John. "Take your rightful place. When the alignment has come to fruition, stab at the heart of this woman and allow Baphomet to be released into this world."

John accepted the blade then stepped behind the woman's head. Logan looked for John's mother, but she was no longer there.

The beam from Henry's flashlight trolled across the kitchen. He'd checked all the cabinets and the pantry and even the walls hoping to find a secret entrance to the basement but found none. Nothing but fog and darkness. He stepped into the dining room from the kitchen when an icy breeze flitted through the window. The room was barren; the floor covered in dust and dirt. The walls all cracked like spiderwebs.

Henry looked at the wall behind him-the only one with the capability of hiding a hidden door. Checked the floorboards all the way to the ceiling, but there was nothing that remotely looked like it could be a hidden door. He moved on, back into the ballroom. He scanned across it, seeing nothing but fog and the red leather chair and table, then shined the beam across the walls when he heard a dull roar, followed by warmth across his skin from the fire crackling in the fireplace.

He looked at the fire. His brow furrowed when he saw that someone was sitting in the red leather chair. Someone short with straight black hair. Henry could see the top of their head.

The sudden change in scene was startling, but he approached cautiously. His gun was drawn, circling around the chair.

"Identify yourself," he said, although his voice came out weak. The person never so much as stirred. He tried again. "This is the police, identify yourself." As he inched closer, he noticed the person sitting in the chair looked like Lori. Henry's eyes narrowed, staring, assessing.

"Lori?"

He touched her shoulder, and her head rolled across her shoulders as if her head was dangling off those shoulders.

"My God."

Lori's jaw was hanging wide open. Her skin was all charred as if she'd burned in a funeral pyre.

Henry dropped his gun to his side. *How is this possible?*

Something wasn't adding up. The thought dawned on him that he hadn't heard a word from the other officers. Not a peep. Montgomery had said to maintain radio silence until someone found the basement, but that didn't mean he shouldn't have heard the footsteps upstairs or even Montgomery or Cindy clomping on the floorboards on the first floor.

He was certain he should have heard something from the other officers.

The fire died as quickly as it was lit, dousing Henry with a return to darkness. He looked at the chair. Lori was no longer there. All he saw was an empty chair when the hair on the nape of his neck erected with a shiver that ran down his spine.

A scream from up above. Bloodcurdling and wretched. Henry trained his gun toward the hallway.

Something's going on.

He came to the stairs and aimed his light up to the top where it died inside the blackness existing on the second floor.

A second scream. This one sounded more muffled, as if whoever the scream belonged to was struggling to call for help.

Henry took the stairs up, his feet thumping across the steps to the second floor. He aimed his light into the hall; his breath ragged in his throat. There was a door open on his left that swayed ever so gently in the wind. He could hear a struggle coming from the room. It sounded like people wrestling, with mad grunts filled with rage.

He darted through the door, ready to take out any would-be murdering bastards, but there was no one in the room.

What the fuck?

Henry stepped in. Maybe the trapdoor is in here? Perhaps that's what he heard, and whatever just happened in this room, the people who were struggling went through the trapdoor? Henry aimed his gun and flashlight across the room. There were paintings littered across the room. A mattress lay on the floor beneath shelves that housed candles.

A third scream erupted not two feet from where he stood. Henry snapped around to the sound. Turned to the painting that was set on an easel and his jaw dropped. The painting depicted what looked like the devil himself standing over someone who looked an awful lot like Lori. The devil had his fingers wedged into her skull, and smoke was burrowing into her orifices. Yes, it was a devilish image, but what attracted Henry's attention was that the painting was moving. The smoke flowed into Lori's eyes, ears, and nose, slithering like a funnel that growled like a ravenous animal. The demon's fingers wriggled in her skull while Lori's jaw opened and closed as if she were attempting to swallow that smoke.

And then the devil growled.

Henry raised his head to the devil in the painting, and the devil's eyes widened, glowing red. Henry took a step back, mesmerized by the scene. The devil then laughed, and Henry could see dark clouds racing behind the devil when he turned around.

Turned around to see the ghostliest human he'd ever laid eyes on. He looked like a vampire with his pasty skin and bald head. His eyes gleamed with a silvery glow.

Whatever this thing is, it growled at Henry. He never saw the knife until it came for his throat. He jumped back just in time for the tip of the blade to graze his windpipe. His hand went to his throat instinctively, dropping his gun that rattled across the floor, stepping back as the vampire rushed at him, and his knife found a home in Henry's stomach. Henry snatched the vampire's wrist that held the blade.

The vampire gripped Henry's throat in his free hand, grinding the blade into his stomach, twisting it in his innards when Henry's teeth gritted. Pain raced to his brain, bursting like white-hot supernovas.

Then the vampire spoke. "I need hearts for the master." His breath was rank with the foul stench of sewage and rotting meat when he yanked the blade from Henry's stomach.

The force propelled Henry back into the window that cracked from his weight, and Henry took two steps forward when the vampire hissed then barreled into him, sending Henry flying through the window where he dropped with a thud to the snow-covered ground below.

He felt a twinge in his back as if something exploded.

Before the light went out, he saw the vampire watching him from the window.

Marc woke up in a pile of sludge inside a massive split trunk of a redwood. He could barely move; the sludge wrapped around him like tar. His legs were secured the same as his arms with long tendrils of tar that wrapped around his head, covering his face save for one eye.

He vomited blood over his lips, his stomach rolling with toxicity. He scanned his surroundings. He was still in the woods. A bonfire crackled with burning rage twenty feet from the tree. The heat was a welcome warmth after the bitter cold of the woods.

The witch was on the other side of the bonfire. He could see her-her back at least-driving a knife repeatedly above her head, stabbing something that was beyond Marc's line of sight. He tried to move his shoulders, but they refused to budge. In fact, he noticed the sludge substance tightened its grip. A moment later, the witch started sawing while groaning in her throat. Marc could see her bare back. Her skin was paper thin, clinging to her ribs and bones that were prominently displayed across her back with welts across the skin the size of craters, oozing with green bile. Her hair was black but thin and looked like greasy strands of seaweed stretched across her scalp.

His eye went wide when she lifted the head she had sawed off and added it to the fire. Marc could hear the scream in his own mind before he realized his scream was belting across the woods while staring at the head cooking in the fire.

Marc was staring at his father's head, watching his skin melt like plaster. Rage writhed in his throat, burning his brain. He tried breaking free from his shackles, straining to move his arms, his feet, his head, when the witch turned her attention to him.

"I've been waiting a long time for you, Mr. Saduj." Her voice was rickety and whining. It reminded him of Mrs. Leiter. "Waiting to suck the blood off your bones." She approached him as if she were floating, scraping her toes against the ground with her arms out and her bony talons stretched towards him. Cackling and laughing the entire time as Marc pushed and pulled, doing everything he could to get away.

She slashed at the thick, sludgy tar with those talons. Marc could see her naked body and how those blotches and pus-filled caverns were littered across her flesh. Her teeth were black and rotten. Her breath smelled foul and unnatural. She gripped Marc's throat then hauled him out of the tree trunk with one hand.

"You've been a bad boy," she hollered, stabbing his torso with her razor-sharp nail while Marc wiggled in her clutches. The pain scorched across his skin. His eyes rolled beneath his eyelids while white-hot pain speared into his brain and his blood rained over the witch's hand that she dipped into her mouth before tossing Marc to the ground beside the bonfire.

Marc rolled onto his stomach and immediately clawed to his knees when the witch sliced across his back and his shoulders

310

arched from the searing pain. She then yanked his head back by his hair, her other talon across his throat. Easing back and forth across his windpipe like a knife.

He reached out, his hand clawing for something, anything to strike this bitch with.

She opened her mouth, and black ink dripped across her chin.

"Delectable," she muttered, then cackled a laugh when Marc found purchase with a log of burning wood that he swung against her shoulder with every ounce of strength he had. The bitch released him when she wailed from her throat.

Sparks of fire rained over him, but Marc took the interlude to crawl a few feet away while the bitch kept crying and hollering, and he spun around to his feet to confront her. Her screaming died when the fire died across her skull. Smoke lifted off her charred face and head, moaning and groaning in her throat, her chest heaving with thick breaths.

Marc looked past the witch into the woods to the canopy that waited for him to enter. The witch's mouth gaped open, her hand over her charred head, glaring at Marc.

She jumped at him with a growl, and Marc jumped with a startle, but she never moved. She cackled at him as Marc circled the bonfire, trying to keep a safe distance when she belted out a raging roar from her throat. Her arms and hands stretched in front of her, her knees bent. She approached Marc, following him around the fire in some demonic game of cat and mouse.

He watched through the flames as she approached, the fire dancing across the thick wooden logs.

Another cackle on his left, closer to where he was. Marc did a double take. It was the same witch. *What the fuck?*

Then a third cackle and now there were three of them circling the bonfire. He waved his torch at the one on his left and the bitch went down on all fours and started hissing at him as she backed off, but the one closer to him on the right pounced and he thrust the torch in her direction as the one on his left hissed and swiped at him with her claw only to catch dead air when Marc stepped back.

He backed away from the fire as the three of them slithered around him. He banked to his left with backward steps and the witches hissed at him when the third witch jumped at him with her talons raised and Marc plunged the fire riddled stick into her chest, ripping into her body with a wet splat when the most god-awful evil, wretched howl Marc had ever heard tore from the woman's throat. Blood jumped off the body, dousing Marc in wet, sticky warmth.

She tried to claw at him, but the stick was too long. Marc circled around with the impaled witch then dropped her into the fire with an explosion of noxious gas. She was screaming wretched cries of anguish that echoed across the woods. Her skin melted off the bone.

He watched her burn for no longer than a second, realizing that the other two witches were an illusion. They were no longer there.

Now he could hear his heart again, beating in the distance. He turned to the canopy of trees and raced towards it. Ash washed over him as he traversed across the path to the steps.

Listening to his breath burning between his ears. Listening to his heart rage in his chest when he pulled up and halted in front of the staircase. The staircase that led down. The steps were wide, longer than a hundred yards and made from what looked like tar, smoldering like dry ice. It looked like he was on top of the Empire State Building. The steps continued into the dark depths below where a constant hum echoed with unrelenting agony. The stench that lifted from the bottomless pit was foul, like poisonous gas burning in his lungs.

He gazed over the canyon bathed in red rock and red sand.

How do I get across?

His jaw hung open, his eyes wide, taking in the sheer expanse of what was in front of him. Beyond the canyon were what looked like cities, towns, and forests. Some were burning, and yet others were doused in a gray light. He saw fires scattered across the landscape and mountains that looked like volcanoes in the distance. He heard screams filled with agony rage from every corner he looked at.

He thought about Lori. Thought about his heart when he closed his eyes to feel the beat in his chest.

An explosion erupted like a sonic boom that rattled the ground beneath him. Marc snapped his eyes open. He was right; one of those mountains was a volcano, and it exploded. A thick, menacing cloud erupted from the volcano with raging fires like lightning inside the cloud that mushroomed a second later and came barreling towards him with a force that knocked him on his ass. He hit the ground hard, the back of his head rapped against the forest floor, but he didn't spare one second and clawed to his hands and knees, watching explosion after explosion pop from the volcano. Lava rushed down the volcanic mountain, churning raging screams filled with agony across the landscape that reverberated inside his bones.

Watched as the cloud raced towards him at lightning speed. It sounded like a billion bats were headed his way, screeching and hissing and popping his eardrums. He could feel blood in his ears, watching the cloud dissipate into a trillion pieces of ash that raced towards him.

All he could see was ash as it engulfed him. Like tiny daggers, they cut across his skin. Slice after slice, like diving into an ocean of razor blades. His feet and legs, fingers, hands, arms, and shoulders, across his chest, his throat and face, carving caverns in his skin. He could feel them in his mouth. Slicing inside his windpipe. Feel the blood dripping from his carved flesh as chunks of skin slid off his bones. A scream in the back of his throat. He didn't know if he could take it anymore. They raced right through him like needles shot from an automatic rifle.

He dropped to his knees, gagging on his own blood, holding his throat, burning fear into his brain.

They kept coming, relentless in their desire to cut him to his core. He lifted his eyelids and watched the ash that darted towards his eyes.

Just before they took out his eyesight, Marc saw a memory of his mother stained in the ash.

The same memory that has plagued him all his life.

The memory from when he asked the man in black to end her pain.

Then the world went black, and Marc felt like he was floating, weightless. No longer able to feel his body. Not his hands or arms, nor his feet or legs. Marc was uniquely aware that his body no longer existed. He was consciousness, drifting in open space. Frigid and dark and squeezed with anguish. He would have screamed if he had lips, or a mouth or even a throat. Instead, he screamed inside his head, inside his thoughts, huffing and puffing as if there was air to breathe when he had no lungs but still, he was suffocating. Struggling to bring air into whatever form he had taken.

Kept drifting when he heard his heart take a thick, agonizing beat that burned in his nonexistent brain. Now he can hear the beat of his heart. It turned rhythmic. Beating across the universe.

Now, light up ahead. Bright and white and spiraling like a wormhole. Marc took in the sight, watching as it crushed in on itself, imploding with a rumble that turned anguish into his gut. Saw enormous beams of red light the size of the sun and a larger black hole devouring it. Marc was racing towards the black hole. He himself like a grain of sand staring at the galaxy.

Pure agony erupted in his consciousness when he passed into the black hole. Felt like every bone in his body was crushed in one fell swoop.

Eternal darkness raced past him. Shivering, freezing cold.

Now more light. White and bright.

And he's standing on a staircase in a labyrinth filled with mirrors and windows. But this was no ordinary staircase. It spiraled in multiple directions, both on top of and within itself, with infinite corridors and upside-down steps. The stairs moved and reconfigured with a mechanical crunch. He could see a window far from where he stood, more than a hundred yards away but he could see through the window. See the field beyond it that led to the crimson light with his heart thudding inside the light.

Marc glimpsed the mirrors, and his stomach roiled. Moments of betrayal existed in those mirrors, times when Marc turned away from his own truth. The mirrors cracked then reformed endlessly, shards floating in the stagnant air like razor-edged snowflakes. Each reflected a different lie Marc had told himself. The sight of so many mirrors and the scenes they reflected impeded shame in his heart like a dagger constantly twisting, ripping into the organ when the mechanical shift reconfigured the labyrinth, presenting a staircase with six steps that led to a long and wide mirror the size of a door.

Inside the mirror, Marc could see the scene unfolding, reflecting the point of no return. He saw himself in the mirror, ragged and decaying and covered in blood. Marc looked over his shoulder and became one with the scene. His vision blurred as if a fog drifted over him. Then, the scene became clear.

He was looking at his mother, and she hollered his name.

Theo and Tom were on the third floor when they heard glass shatter.

They both jumped when they heard it, giving up their inquiry into the five dead women draped across a pentagram on the floor.

"Now, what the fuck was that?" Theo swallowed his breath, staring at the door to the staircase that led to the second floor. He could see wisps of fog drifting across the door, illuminated by his flashlight.

Tom turned to Theo. "I'll check it out. Keep looking for a door." He looked over the room. "If any room in this house has a hidden door it would be here."

Theo whispered. "Maybe we should radio Montgomery. See if he found anything."

Tom shook his head. "If he had, he would have told us."

Theo said nothing in response.

"I'll be right back." Tom craned his head to the open door, staring into a pit of black before training his gun and light into the stairwell, cautiously taking the steps down to the second floor.

Theo stepped to the staircase, watching Tom's light fade into the void of the second floor. He waited, listening to his heavy breathing. Theo noticed that the longer he was in the house, the heavier his legs felt, the more difficult it was to piece thoughts together and the harder it was to breathe.

He heard a scrape over his shoulder, as if something was being dragged across the floor. The hair on his neck stood erect. His bones seemed to contract inward, frozen in time.

Heard it again.

Sounded like someone clawed to their feet.

Theo craned his head around slowly. Turned completely around, staring at the dead women on the floor and the fog drifting over the bodies. He stared into the wisps, and his eyes narrowed. It looked like one of those dead bodies was standing up inside the fog.

The door behind him slammed shut. Theo jumped then snapped around to the closed door. Heard the door on the second-floor slam shut too.

Heard footsteps by the door, and his heart cringed in his chest. He tried the doorknob, but it refused to budge.

I'm locked in here with dead people.

He struggled with the doorknob. Theo raised his gun, ready to strike down on the knob when a howling cry erupted over his shoulder, and he snapped around.

"You did this to me."

Theo's eyes were wide open, staring through the mesmerizing fog at the five women standing in the room. Their bodies doused in a gray silvery darkness, Theo's gun and flashlight pointed towards the floor as Theo tried to get a grip on what he was witnessing. Their ashen skin and stringy hair. He couldn't see the whites of their eyes. Instead, dark caverns existed where their eyes should be. Big gaping holes in their chests led to empty cavities that dripped blood across their torsos, and blood as black as ink dripped from their mouths.

They all screamed the same sentence repeatedly. "You did this to me." Their arms raised as they stepped towards him.

"You did this to me."

They ripped and clawed at him, pinning Theo's back against the wall as they reached their talons into his flesh. Their black nails pulled at his skin, tearing off chunks from his cheeks, his arms and throat.

"You did this to me."

His head shook, his eyes wide. "I didn't," was all he managed to squeak across his lips when their claws found his jaw and pulled with such strength his jaw snapped off with a river of blood that rained across his chest. His tongue wriggled in empty air with a scream belting from his bloodied throat. Their nails sank into his face then tore off his skin.

Theo's scream reached a fever pitch when the claws stopped ripping and tearing. His breath caught in his throat; the thick huffs dwindling to slow and steady. The girls lay dead as they did before. Theo stepped away from the wall and shined his light on the dead bodies. He breathed deeply then wiped the sweat off his brow when he heard a thud and looked to his left. His eyes squinted.

There was a door flapping against a door frame. Theo shook the cobwebs from his head with a violent shake, hoping he wasn't seeing another hallucination.

He stepped to the door with his flashlight trained on it.

Can't believe it. I found it.

Theo opened the door when he felt the stab in his throat. It had happened so fast. The fog raced across the doorway, and he glimpsed the person standing in the door. Short and pasty, his pale skin gleamed like a beacon.

Theo didn't see the knife that swiped across his throat before it was too late. His hands went to his throat, dropping the gun and flashlight as he gagged for breath. Blood jettisoned from his throat, and he stepped back as his assailant stepped into the room.

He thought he was looking at a vampire. A vampire with silver eyes holding a knife and walking towards him when Theo collapsed to the floor like a sack of bricks, holding his bleeding throat. Life drained from him in a garble for breath, staring at the beam from his flashlight that shone above him when the vampire crawled over him with his silvery eyes, licking his lips as he stared at the river of blood across Theo's neck.

Theo, unable to move, was dying a slow, painful death.

"They called me a vampire all my life." The assailant craned his head, glaring into Theo's dying eyes. "Ironic, isn't it? That it's the same power the master has granted."

He raised his head with his jaw open, revealing a row of razor-sharp teeth that he snapped around Theo's bleeding throat.

Theo's arms went slack by his sides. Feeling the vampire's jaws swallowing his blood, draining him dry. He could feel his blood passing into the vampire. He followed the blood with his consciousness. His essence spilled into the vampire where he became locked inside its veins, burning in torturous agony.

311

Tom was looking at a broken window when the door to the third floor slammed shut, and he rushed to it.

He tried the knob, but it wouldn't budge. His heart hammered in his chest. Started pounding on the door for Theo to open it when the fire started. He heard the roar first. Felt the heat immediately after, along with the glow from the fire that illuminated the hallway.

Sweat beaded across his forehead from the heat, but it wasn't the fire that caught his attention but the six cobras standing erect above the fire. He froze while looking at them. Tom always froze in the presence of snakes. They scared the shit out of him.

He raised his gun, his hand trembling, aiming at the cobras when the middle snake hissed at him as if assessing his weaponry threat, rising high above the fire. Tom's eyes went wide, his jaw hanging open.

Heard a hiss over his shoulder and snapped his head around. A snake on the wall hissed then snapped at him, biting the top of his nose. Bit him three more times, and Tom dropped to the floor, his flesh stinging with agony from where those fangs ripped into his flesh. Felt more bites on his legs and arms. His face pinched in pain, his eyes squinted, seeing snakes all around him, biting and coiling and hissing.

Felt their venom in his veins. Tom started shaking, foaming from his mouth. Bite after bite. The snakes were all over him. Slithering around his legs and arms, pinning him to the floor. Their bodies tightened around his limbs and one around his throat.

Suffocating, struggling to breathe, his mouth agape when the cobra around his throat hissed in front of his eyes and then entered his mouth, slithering into his throat. Tom started gagging, his lips covered in blood and white foam. His jaw opened to an inhuman size, feeling the cobra slither into his body, biting and hissing and coiling around his organs. Saw the room waver around him like a wave in the ocean. The light went out, returning the hallway to darkness and fog.

The snakes were gone, but Tom hadn't overcome his fear. Not yet. He lay on the floor, frozen. His eyes wide, his breath huffing in his throat when from out of the fog the arm came swinging down, burying a knife in his chest with such brute force it ripped through his armor. He heard the pop of the knife in his chest and his body contracted.

The knife was pulled from his chest, and now Tom could see the person wielding that knife. He looked like a vampire. The knife was jagged and curved. He felt the second stab in his neck. The vampire yanked out the blade with a geyser of blood that rained across the vampire. He seemed to bathe in the blood like a child running across a sprinkler. His mouth opened to take in all the blood he could, and then he stabbed again. Every stab elicited a snarl from the vampire.

He brought the blade down repeatedly. Blood was tossed into the air with every pull of the knife. All Tom could feel was pain, racing to every inch of his body when the vampire stopped, paused with his tongue rolling in his mouth, glaring at Tom.

"So much essence," the vampire clucked over his lips, inching his fingernail across Tom's temple then licking his blood off the tip. "Souls I keep for the master. You will do better not to resist."

The vampire's breath stank like raw sewage and rotten meat. His silvery eyes gleamed as Tom gurgled on his own blood, watching the vampire open his mouth wide and snap his teeth around Tom's mouth. The vampire's fangs ripped into his jaw with a squelch from Tom that bellowed into the vampire's throat. Tom could feel his essence draining into this thing. It lifted its head, and Tom could see light between their two mouths. His light funneled into the vampire.

Then the light went out, and Tom felt himself spiraling, waking up in a pit of anguish with the snakes coiling around him, squeezing him for all eternity.

"YOU'VE BEEN BAAAADDD!"

Lori was running. Running through her house trying to get away and hide. Hide from the monster that was looking for her. Hide from her parents who wanted her with the monster. They were like evil witches, her parents. Lori could feel their evil essence drip off their skin.

They were searching for her, searching for Lori while screaming about how bad she'd been and needing to take her medicine. Lori was frantic, trying to find a place to hide. A place where they could never find her. Every scene outside the window was petrifying. Hell existed outside the windows with a beast close to ten feet tall who kept looking inside, breathing foul and growling, watching everywhere Lori went.

Every mirror reflected a different scene. A scene that the five-year-old Lori refused to see. She kept her head down when she raced past any mirror in the house. The scenes were ghastly. Little Lori didn't know what rape was, but she knew what was happening in the bedroom inside the mirrors was wrong in every sense of the word. She could feel the wretched evil from the mirror scenes, and the essence of fear outside the windows.

She stopped in the living room when a boom rattled the house. Like giant footsteps shaking the foundation.

"Time to take your medicine." Her father raged from the second floor.

"You've been a bad bitch." Her mother appeared at the top of the stairs; her eyes doused in black. "You've always been a nasty little witch."

Her father stepped onto the landing. "Time to take your medicine."

"No," little Lori hollered. "I don't want to."

A growl over her shoulder. Lori craned her head to look outside where the evil yellow cat eyes were staring at her.

"Two become one," it growled, and Lori screamed at the top of her lungs.

"Now, Lori," her father ordered.

"Take your medicine." Her mother was rushing down the steps.

Lori darted towards the kitchen, listening to her parents' footsteps pounding down the steps. Heard screaming hollers, wails and cries coming from every window and mirror along with the growl from outside.

"Two become one."

The ceiling fell as if the beast outside was trying to gain entrance. Lori's breath hitched in her throat.

"You've been a bad girl. A very bag girl."

"Take your fucking medicine."

Her parents were in the living room now. Lori's head was on a swivel, looking up and all around the kitchen for a place to hide when she saw the basement door. The door stretched into the kitchen.

"Come and take your medicine."

Lori snapped her head around. Elena was at the entrance to the kitchen. Lori's heart jumped with a startle, and she took off for the basement door, running as fast as she could, her lungs burning in her chest. She threw the door open, then rushed down the stairs into darkness.

Hoping to find a place to hide.

The house was huge. Cyndi had travelled down the hallway with Montgomery when they arrived at the wall at the end of the hall. The room on their right was where Montgomery went while Cyndi took the hall on the left where a row of bedrooms existed.

Cyndi had checked five of the rooms for a hidden door but had come up empty in every room. She was losing her patience. She didn't even believe there was a basement anymore and felt like a fool for believing Montgomery. Believed they were wasting valuable time on a wild goose chase that would yield zero results, but still she searched, her flashlight cutting across the darkness.

She opened the door to the sixth bedroom when she heard glass breaking on the floor above followed by a loud thump outside the bedroom. Cindy heard it clearly. It sounded like someone had just dropped from a second-floor window. She paused in the doorway and looked over her shoulder, listening for any sound that would tell her Montgomery was headed upstairs. Now she heard footsteps padding back and forth across the ceiling followed by a thump as if someone fell, and her heart raced into overdrive, thumping against her chest.

Cindy swallowed her breath, staring into the hall with her light trained on the far wall. Nothing. Nothing but blackness and floating wisps of fog.

Okay, she thought. Maybe I was wrong.

She pursed her lips, sweeping her gun and flashlight across the bedroom to the window, and went to investigate. She wanted to see if one of her fellow officers was outside, having been dropped from the second-floor. The light from the flashlight glowed in the window as she stepped closer. Stepped closer for a clear view of the outside and the thick fog that raced across the property.

Her eyes were wide. Staring at the fog, she believed her eyes were playing tricks on her. It looked like a horde of ghosts were standing on the property, looking at the house. Looking at her with her light on in the window. Her pulse trembled. Her skin shivered, and she noticed her hand shook as she scanned the property to the body lying in the snow. Her eyes scrunched, staring at Henry, she was certain of it.

Heard thumping on the house outside the room. Sounded like someone was outside climbing across the side of the house.

Now squeaking. Fluttering squeaks like bats echoed across the room, penetrating Cindy's ears. The sound was ear-piercing. Cindy clasped her hands over her ears, but still she could hear that sound, twisting in her brain as she screamed and hollered from the top of her lungs for the sound to stop. Her eyes rolled beneath her eyelids, and she was certain she was about to have an aneurysm. Her head jutted from left to right, shaking uncontrollably, dropping her arms to her sides and feeling blood cascade from her nose and ears. Felt blood pool in the back of her throat and blood ooze from her eyes. She was certain her head was going to explode.

Now she was shaking from head to toe. She took a step forward and collapsed onto her knees. The ringing in her head was relentless. Felt like her skull ballooned to an inhuman size when she hunched over and vomited a river of blood when the ringing amplified, and Cindy gripped her head, wanting to tear her head off when all the sound stopped, and all Cindy could hear was her own ragged screaming.

Her breath huffed over her lips. Her shoulders bobbed back and forth. Her scream faded. Quiet greeted her.

Cindy took a deep breath and put her hand over her racing heart. She gasped out a breath that echoed across the darkened abandoned house. Her eyes flitted from one corner to the other, to the beam of her flashlight against the wall. She shook her head and reached for the gun when a hand reached out from the shadows and pulled it into the corner. Cindy watched it race away from her. Watched as the shadow stretched across the wall, rising above her when two silvery eyes gleamed in her direction.

Cindy reached for the gun holstered on her hip, but it didn't matter. The shadow speared out of the darkness. Cindy hit the ground hard. The back of her head rapped against the floor.

She saw her assailant for only a second before he bit into her face, ripping into her cheek with razor-sharp teeth when the loudest scream belted from Cindy's throat. He ripped a chunk out of her cheek, gnawed on it and swallowed it down his narrow gullet. His body was small, but he had the strength of a giant. His long talons pinned her arms to the floor. Cindy could feel blood rush down her face when the vampire came in for a second helping. His jaw snapped around her nose, and he ripped off the flesh and cartilage. Chewed it in front of her eyes. Blood dripped from his chin, and across his pale skin. Cindy screamed and writhed in agony. She tried wriggling free from his grasp, but he held her tight.

"My God, please don't do this!"

She kept sliding, dragging him with her. He drew her scent into his nostrils with a thick inhale and then waggled his tongue between his lips, raising a knife over his head.

She was frozen, staring at the knife in his hand. "Please, no." She stopped moving, trying to force her hands free as he brought the tip of the blade to her chest and let it sit there.

"Slow deaths are the most intriguing." This thing talked as if reveling in her misery. Bathing in Cindy's agony. "Let's study yours."

"No!"

He inched the blade in, just the tip. Cindy's teeth gritted; the pain seared into her brain. He inched it in further, his mouth gaping a foul stench that added insult to death. Further in the blade went. Cindy could feel the steel inside her chest, cutting skin and cartilage and veins and bone and muscle. Her arms were shaking, her legs jerking in spasms. Felt blood dripping on the inside of her body, soaking her organs.

"I'm gonna eat your heart." This thing hissed, driving the knife down into her heart. She felt it pierce the organ, and her eyes rolled behind her eyelids. Huffing breaths, trying to find air, suffocating and struggling. He opened his mouth with a gaping sigh and brought his lips close to hers. He drew his tongue over her mouth when the knife plunged through her heart.

Cindy died in that moment, but as strange as it was, she could still feel. Feel this vampire slurping the blood from her chest. She could feel herself draining into this thing.

The light went out, and then the pain began.

Loss, confusion twisted with misery. Numbed thoughts, difficult to think, trying to remember as if his thoughts evaporated in real time. As if the need to experience outweighed the need to think.

Experience the devils spawned from past actions. For what worse hell exists beyond the suffering conjured by the self? Who needs a devilish scapegoat when the true devil exists inside the human heart? Hell is simply a display of the truth. Truth that cuts like a knife. Truth that paralyzes the senses, compounding every devious thought and lie, every nefarious action, every regret and moment of shame, of lost hope and moments of self-deprecation, driving them into one single emotion thick with fear, hate, and disgust.

Moments of weakness that continue for eternity. Like a thick pill that gets lodged in the throat, choking on the bone of truth.

Marc took those six steps up to the mirror, seeing his mother in the mirror, sitting on her bed. The essence of the scene crawled across his skin like a thick wave of heat. He stepped onto the landing and craned his head. The mirror wasn't against the wall from where he stood but existed far away. More than a hundred yards down the hall. Another hall on his left and right.

The labyrinth was all stone. And dark. Torches hung every twenty yards down the hall, casting shadows across the stone.

"Marc," his mother called for him from the mirror, and Marc's heart dropped into his stomach.

He knew what was coming. Her wrists were already bleeding. He could see the blood on the sheet and on the pillow on her lap. His younger self came into view with the demon behind him.

"It's all your fault," she told him, raising her bloodied wrists for his child self to see.

Shuffling to his left, like someone running. Marc moved in the same direction, down a long hall when he came to another crossroad and looked in both directions. More halls. More stone and torches casting shadows across the walls but nothing more. No mirrors or windows, just hallways stretching into eternity.

He looked over his shoulder and then turned his eyes up to the upside-down staircase. He could see the window he was looking for at the top of those steps.

How do I get up there?

He looked at the wall in front of him. Looked up to the steps, then back to the wall and put his foot on it, then stepped on with his other foot, climbing the wall to the stairs then up the steps to the landing with the window. He gazed through the window to the field beyond the window that led to his heart beating in the trees beyond the field.

He took the first step to the window when the mechanical crunch reconfigured the labyrinth, dividing steps and hallways, and then stopped with a mirror in front of him.

"Marc!" his mother called. Her eyes were wet with tears. Her hair all nappy, with skin blemished and dry like sandpaper. She sat on the bed cross-legged with the pillow over her legs. A glass pipe on the pillow, all yellow and coated black at the tip. A bottle of whiskey sat half empty between her thighs. The straight razor sat next to the pipe. The bedroom window cast another scene outside it. He watched his father's death happening inside the window.

Marc felt his skin crawl. Noticed he was no longer in the hallway. Now he was in the room with his mother. He turned to the mirror and saw himself as he was on that day. A young one, barely a teenager, looking in on him from the other side of the mirror, but his reflection did not cast Marc in the same light. Instead, he saw himself as the demon.

"It's all your fault." His mother's voice hissed at him.

The razor was in his hand. He took his mother's hand and dragged the blade across her wrists. Marc's lips trembled with the first spring of tears that nipped at his eyes. He grounded his jaw, forced to watch the blood rush from her veins. He couldn't take his eyes off her. "I'm so sorry." His hand over his mouth, clenching his chin. "So sorry."

Heard his dad drop to the ground with a thud and Marc snapped around. His father was surrounded by what looked like gargoyles who were watching him and did nothing while his father's heart ripped pain to every part of his convulsing body. Marc saw life leap from his father's eyes.

"Dad!"

336

Then the gargoyles tore his arms and legs from the body. Marc's body shuddered at the scene when one of the gargoyles stepped through the window, glaring at him when it clambered over to his mother. Her cut wrists were on the pillow. Blood like a river poured from her wrists, saturating the pillow, the bed and his mother as she lay there bleeding. Her head turned in his direction, her eyes black to the core when the gargoyle dipped its talon into the cut across her wrist and his mother screamed.

"You didn't do anything." She coughed blood over her lips, her chest rising and heaving. The gargoyle dipped his finger between his lips. "You didn't do anything," she said again. "You let it happen."

The gargoyle gripped her head and yanked it off her shoulders. It didn't come off easily; he pulled and tugged while his mother rang screams from her throat. Her neck bones splintered and cracked as her flesh tore apart, raining blood across her shoulders.

He bit into her skull. His mother screamed the entire time.

"See what you did to me!"

His father was dismembered. The gargoyles feasted on his innards, slopping them up from the severed body and jamming them between their jaws. Eating. Gnawing bones and cartilage. Blood across their mouths and chins, staring at Marc as they fed.

The gargoyle put her head back on her shoulders and jumped on top of the body then hissed at Marc before dipping its mouth to her wrists and slurping up her blood.

"See what you did to me."

He turned away, finally able to as if he was granted permission to turn. He turned to the mirror he'd come from, and his mother called his name.

"Marc!"

But the scene was different this time. Now Marc was sitting on the bed, but not Marc as he is now but Marc as a child. His mother stood next to the bed, and the demon stood over her shoulder. He was whispering in her ear. It took Marc a second to understand his mother was holding the razor. She closed her eyes and nodded.

"Time to take your medicine, Marc." She lifted young Marc's arm.

"No!" The word hushed out of Marc's throat just before his mother dragged the blade across young Marc's wrist, igniting a river of blood across his arm. He felt the pinch on his wrist, and when he looked at his arm, his wrist was slit and bleeding. The pain stung like a bee sting. He clenched his hand into a fist.

"It was all your fault!" His mother hollered, and the demon over her shoulder laughed.

Marc's head was shaking. His mother stepped closer, and he took a step back. "I'm so sorry. It wasn't me; it was the demon, I swear." Tears flooded down his face. "I wouldn't have hurt you like that. I loved you so much."

His mother laughed in his face and then sliced across his arms, and Marc screamed in agony, holding up his bleeding

338

forearms when his mother slashed across his throat and Marc dropped like an anvil to the ground, bleeding and writhing in anguish.

Then, the mechanical hum reconfigured the labyrinth. Marc watched the same scene unfold, but this time his mother didn't slash his wrists. This time it was his father, and then the labyrinth would shift, and the scene would unfold. Sometimes it was his mother, sometimes his father and often it was Marc.

The same gruesome carnage. The same anguish. He watched the scene continuously loop over a thousand times when he heard the mechanical shift in the labyrinth, and he was presented with a new scene. The time from when he was sixteen and so drunk he couldn't move, waking up to the sound of pleasure. The room was dark around him, but he couldn't move, shivering from head to toe with vomit that coated his chin. Watching through wet, watery eyes as his best friend fucked his girlfriend in front of him. Treated her like a whore, and she loved every minute.

A gargoyle's cock in her mouth. Another fucking his best friend up his ass. They cut their skin with their talons and drank their blood, eating their flesh. Marc was certain he relived that scene for more than a million lifetimes.

The essence of these scenes saturated his skin with poison. He could feel it seeping into his pores, twisting anguish into every organ.

He'd become lost, confusion battering his senses into oblivion. Scene after scene presented itself. Scenes from past lives, but Marc didn't experience these scenes as if they were from another life. Marc saw all his lives, and each moment that conjured shame and guilt, fear, anger, sadness, and hurt turned over into centuries of suffering.

The mechanical shift occurred without prejudice or pattern. Every once in a while, he'd see the window leading to his heart. He could feel the thick beat, painful as it was, rip across his chest as if his heart was going to splinter through the bone, and then the shift would happen, and another mirror was presented. Another hell. So many hells. So many debts to repay for an eternal soul.

Testing his resolve with one single purpose to wipe his intentions clear, but Marc had an ace in the hole. A path that would always lead to Lori. That would allow him to find his heart again.

He kept repeating, "As you wish," with every thick beat of his heart.

As you wish.

As you wish.

It wasn't until the ghosts of the slain arrived that he forgot his mantra.

315

Montgomery ran his hand across the edge of the wall, hoping to find the entrance to the basement when he heard glass breaking on the floor above.

The sound was distant but unmistakable, freezing Montgomery with his hand on the wall as he looked over his shoulder. He saw nothing other than darkness and fog until he trained his gun and flashlight on the hall he'd come through with Cindy. The beam from his flashlight trolled across the hall.

Footsteps now padded down the hall above him.

Something's happening.

His search had yet to yield results. The house seemed as abandoned as it presented except for the buzz he was certain was coming from the basement. The basement he couldn't find, as mysterious as it was lost. He stepped into the hall, his gun drawn, his light bouncing across the wall.

"Cindy?" he whispered, craning his head to the hallway where he knew she went. "Cindy?"

Nothing in return and he thought about breaking radio silence to see if his fellow officers were okay, but he knew something had happened. He could feel it, like the buzz infecting his brain, he knew something had happened to his friends.

Montgomery shuffled cautiously down the hall to the stairs. His heart thundering in his chest, he looked up the stairs but saw nothing but darkness and floating wisps.

Heard a thump in the kitchen and he snapped around to it. His nervous hands trembling the light across the living room to the kitchen.

"Henry?" he whispered but received no response. He stepped into the living room and swept his gun and light across the room. The beam cut through the fog when he swallowed his breath down his gullet.

Another thud down the hall from where he came. He snapped around at it, watching the fog float across the hall.

Montgomery scanned the hall. His eyes scrunched when he noticed the light fixture on the wall across from the stairs and realized it was turned to the side as if someone had moved it.

Now why would that happen? He was certain the light had been upright when he first came down the hall. Montgomery remembered seeing it. For some reason, the fixture stood out to him.

He shuffled over to it, keeping his gun drawn when he pulled on the fixture, and heard a pop down the hall.

"Well, I'll be damned."

He was staring at a door at the end of the hall. Saw fog race out of the door.

"Found it. Son of a bitch, I found it." He took his radio off his hip. Started talking into it. "Montgomery to team. I found it. I found the door. Come to the hallway on the first floor A-SAP."

No response other than static.

Static and cold silence.

Now he heard a scream echo out of the basement and Montgomery acted, racing down the hallway to the door.

Wren watched the detective from the kitchen. He was hiding in the fog. The fog that drenched his cells in everlasting rage.

He could see perfectly. His new eyes turned night into day. Like wearing night goggles to amplify the scene.

The fog enveloped him, hiding him in plain sight so that his victims knew nothing of his presence. Time moved unevenly in the fog, depositing him in two places at once.

The master was right. Xibalba has many gifts.

The detective discovered the door to the basement. He was moving down the hall towards it. Wren followed him, creeping towards the detective. Wren could smell the detective's fear-riddled anxiety. It sent shudders filled with elation coursing through Wren's veins that opened a cavern in his stomach. Needing to fill it with flesh and blood.

The detective threw the door open, his gun drawn and ready to squeeze the trigger. Wren grinned while watching him. The detective's breath huffed over his lips. Wren could feel his heart racing and beating with blood and essence. The light from his flashlight died within inches of the open door.

The essence Wren salivated over with an unrelenting thirst he knew this detective would quench. He read his intentions, knowing the detective sought to kill. The murderous impulse saturated his blood. Wren stepped behind the detective and raised his blade.

Brought it down across the detective's head where it split his head in two, but Wren's strength had grown and the blade kept going, cutting through the neck and chest, slicing down into his stomach and out from his groin. Blood jettisoned from the severed body, bathing Wren in blood. The two halves of the detective stood for a moment longer. Thick and wide with blood, organs, veins and thick gobs of bloodied chunks that dripped down those halves before they fell to their respective sides.

"They always come, Wren." He repeated the master's declaration. "Some men just can't give in."

Wren marveled over his work, staring at the detective's bloodied halves, and crouched down. The heart was severed in half along with the body. Wren dipped his fingers into the carnage, his talons squishing into flesh and veins and arteries, yanking the heart from the body.

He devoured the heart and then went in for seconds when he felt the shift in his bones. Holding the heart in his hands while gnawing on the savory chunk between his teeth, Wren felt the celestial shift take root in the house with a rumble that quaked the foundation.

A wide grin spread across his lips.

"Initium Novum!" He clucked his tongue at the dead detective before tearing off another chunk of heart.

The labyrinth shifted. Marc felt the platform move beneath him. His stomach rolled with anguish, flopping over on his back, lying in wait, his mind infected with venomous vengeance and consequence. He'd caused suffering, centuries of suffering.

His bones ached, his soul thin and fading into nothingness. He felt like nothing, knowing his suffering was just. He brought hell to the Hollow. Hell to everything and everyone he'd ever cared for, across lifetimes and across time. Eventually, those debts had to be repaid, and now was the time.

The platform locked into place. Marc was staring into the mirror. The tall mirror that stood like a beacon of darkness. Beyond its glass prism was the dungeon. His dungeon.

He heard their footsteps before he saw them, standing over him with their thick and large black eyes. The victims of the man in black came for retribution.

They talked as if he were nonexistent.

"I want his skin."

"I'll take his liver."

"Let me cut off his legs."

"Rip his flesh off his bones."

Then giggles.

"I'll take his tongue."

Marc was too weak to fight back. He felt the first incision just below his throat cut into his chest and then dragged across his flesh, opening his belly. His eyes rolled beneath his eyelids. Felt the tug on his skin when they ripped and tore his flesh, ripping it off his bones, gutting him like a pig. His organs were yanked from his body as his skin was peeled off his skeleton. Marc screamed the entire time.

The labyrinth shifted, and he went through the same. This time they didn't use a knife; instead, they clawed his skin off with their fingers. The third time, they cut off his head. Sawed it off while Marc lay awake, his scream continued even after they removed his head and showed him his own body. Another shift. More carnage. More ripping and tearing. More torture and agony, cutting the man down to his bare bones where his soul was on full display.

So much torture. He relived the scene for what seemed like forever. The pain from those moments created a cavern in his heart that would never heal. A stain on his soul that would never wash away. Suffering where there is no redemption, only pain. Pain eternal and pain ingrained.

He tried to remember. To remember his endeavor, his journey and mission, but his thoughts refused him purchase. Numb to the core, he stared at the mirror from the bed he was lying on. An old man looked back at him with the sensation of regret like a ball of thick, shameful energy all twisted in his gut. The old man was lying down, the same as Marc. A mirror above the bed, and in that mirror above the bed, he saw himself, even older than before. Alone with regret. Alone with the shame that he kept in a jar by the bed.

Such precious shame; he'd bring it with him always. Not even the distant screams of torture and carnage could deter him from his jar of shame. The jar where a single withered black rose sat undisturbed. Forever containing the shame of his actions. The shame of living and of dying. It beat thick inside his veins.

Now the whispers came. Incoherent whispers spoken from nefarious tongues, clucking sinister thoughts echoing back into his brain.

Not good.

Not good enough.

Never was.

Not good at all.

Bad. Bad. Bad. Bad. Bad.

You deserve the hell you've created.

It was this last whisper that continued to loop through Marc's brain as he stared at his withered rose.

Deserve. The hell you deserve. Created. The hell you've created.

Marc draped his legs over the bed and stood up slowly, his old bones creaking as he did. He felt so heavy, as if his regrets and shameful thoughts weighed him down.

Heard a scream echo across the room. It sounded familiar. Someone was hurt. Someone who needed his help, but what could this old, beaten-down man do other than offer shame?

Not good.

Not good at all.

Marc looked at his old, withered face in the mirror.

The hell you've created.

You deserve.

You deserve the hell you've created.

Inside the mirror, in the distance that stretched into eternity, he saw the window that led to the field. Saw how the field was filled with acres of black withered roses.

Your thoughts, the whispers said. All your nefarious thoughts clucked off your tongue.

The hell you've created.

So many regrets. So many evils and prejudices.

Beyond the field, he could see the firmament basking the forest in a crimson glow.

He stared at the firmament.

Saw his reflection transform into a withered old man with skin the color of burnt ash.

As you wish.

The red glow. A beat he could feel in his chest.

The field.

As you wish.

He started banging on the mirror. The image wavered as the mirror shook from his pounding hands. Pounding until the glass cracked and Marc stepped back, staring at the crack in the mirror. The thick crack, and inside the crack, he could see the field.

Marc rapped against the mirror one last time, and the glass shattered. Shattered over him.

The glass cut into his skin. He could feel the tiny shards rip into his flesh, drawing blood everywhere they touched. Glass rained into his eyes, and he clamped them shut, feeling tiny pricks of glass in his eyeballs.

When he opened them, he saw through glass prisms. Saw the window with the field behind it and he sprinted towards it, crashing through the window where he fell, plunging into the field then rolling head over heels until he wasn't rolling any longer.

Marc gasped a thick inhale, his lungs on fire, clawing to his feet, frantic and shuddering, when he stood. Stood in the field with all the withered flowers that bellowed cries from their roots in an everlasting buzzing hum of agony.

He heard the hiss before he opened his eyes. Henry's back ached. Felt like his bones were broken and battered. The pain in his abdomen rolled his eyeballs to the back of his skull. He felt sick, weak, depleted, struggling to get up as he rolled over on his side. The cold snow nipped at his face. His hand over his stomach when he heard the hiss above his head.

Henry tried to push himself up but flopped back onto his back. Staring at the house with the fog drifting across the scene and the buzz rumbling beneath him. Gritted teeth, his hand over the wound, staring at the roof and the owl perched on high with its wings outstretched and its head dipped down, hissing at Henry.

It seemed like it wanted him to get up.

Lori was still in the house. He needed to get up. Get up and find her by any means necessary.

The owl hissed again, coaching him to get off the ground. Henry rolled over, his face planted in the snow, forcing himself up with his elbows, gritting his teeth when the pain shot up to his head. He got himself onto his knees when he checked his wound. Blood covered his hand. He lifted his shirt, and a spurt of blood bubbled out of the wound. Henry dipped his hand into the snow and pressed the cold ice to his stomach with a grunt and a cough, staring across the perimeter and the fog-drenched property.

He saw ghosts in the fog. Waiting. He watched while they hid inside the wisps. Henry took a deep, huffing breath then rose to his feet when the owl swooped down from the roof and raced through the fog. The fog that seemed to cower in the owl's presence, parting to make way for the great horned owl.

Henry gasped out a breath. His lungs burned frigid and painful. His head was weary when he took the .38 Special wedged between his belt and his stomach. The owl flew past him, hissing as it floated around the house and disappeared.

Henry watched it go and then followed dutifully.

There's a portal to hell in the basement.

Little Lori raced down the steps into the basement while listening to her parents' footsteps pounding from up above.

"Time to take your medicine."

"You've been a bad, bad girl. You must be punished."

"Time to take your medicine."

The house shook around her. The basement floor rumbled beneath her feet, and Lori fell into the wall, catching herself before falling. She looked up the staircase and saw shadows heading her way.

"You've been a bad girl."

Elena stepped into the doorway. Her eyes the color of black ink. Her facial features distorted and twisted.

Lori looked left and right, hoping for a place to hide when the house quaked with a seismic shift. She saw the ceiling fall around Elena and cracks splinter across the basement walls when a foul gaseous stench burst from those cracks. The odor was foul, stinking of rot and sulfur. Lori hacked on the gas. She could feel it in her lungs, infecting her brain with fear. She could feel it coating her tongue and throat, twisting her stomach to where she needed to puke. Acid in the back of her throat, poisoning her gums and teeth.

Her father stepped next to Elena with the same distorted features as her mother.

"Time to take your medicine," he said, his voice a long drone of nasty.

"No worries," said Elena, her hand on the doorknob. "It'll only hurt at first." She closed the door slowly, locking out the light, bathing Lori in eternal darkness.

Her head was weary from the gas when over her shoulder she could hear the devil's voice. "Two become one."

Lori inched her head around, looking over her shoulder to the wall across from where she was. The wall where a pentagram had been drawn in blood. The blood grew in intensity, glowing crimson with a light like fire that burst through the blood-drawn lines, illuminating the basement in a sick blood-red glow.

The blood moved, slithering like snakes, the lines beaming bright, slithering as if rushing to join itself. She heard moaning from within the pentagram and Lori screamed at the top of her lungs when she saw hands emerging from it.

"Two become one," the demon growled, slithering out of the wall.

Marc was standing in a vast desolate field. As far as his eyes could see, the field continued. Thick dark clouds cast a black glow over the field. Pink lightning speared inside the rumbling clouds, threatening to douse the field and add to the river that churned liquid nitrogen to its shore. The river existed outside of the field, not too far from where he stood but still, it exhausted Marc just to look at it. Beyond the river was Marc's beating heart; he could hear the beat in his chest cascading across the landscape from the woods.

Black roses littered the landscape. Some were smaller than his thumbnail, while others were as tall as redwoods. The stems were thick and gray with a shade of crimson and thorns that looked like crystalized teardrops. The ground was desolate, like sand stained with blood. He could see a tendril of smoke in the distance, listening to a mechanical hum churning like an echo across the field. Torturous screams bellowed from the same direction.

Beyond the mechanical hum existed the trees with the crimson firmament where he knew his heart was kept. He could feel it beating rage against his chest. A buzz like a hum existed. Marc could more than hear it; he could feel it in his bones, in his cells, vibrating, and it turned his stomach nauseous. It took him a moment to realize the hum was coming from the roses, from the roots buried deep within the ground. His head hurt something awful, as if someone had split his skull in two. The stench didn't help. Noxious and ripe with sewage and rot, it weighed him down. Whispers clucked off sinister tongues speared across the field. Like a million digs, a million ridicules and insidious statements all conjoined at the hip, talking over one another and driving his brain into a frenzy.

A scream erupted across the overcast sky. A scream that echoed in his bones, shuddering his heart.

"I'm coming," he whispered, closing his eyes, trying to get a grip and focus, his senses assaulted by the field. He thought his brain was going to explode. His head was so heavy, he thought he was going to puke.

Instead, he took the first step forward. Marc started his journey across the field with the noxious gas, the raging humming buzz and the whispers driving him mad.

He noticed plaques embedded in the ground in front of each withering rose. His legs were like jelly; he could barely walk, but still he pressed on, occasionally dropping to his knees for a rest, but there is no rest for the weary. Not in the field. Not with the buzz and the whispers and the stink invading his nostrils.

One time he dropped to his knees, unable to walk any further. He tried to bring fresh air into his lungs, but there is no fresh air in the field of black roses, only nausea, sickness and withering decay. He could feel the decay inside his bones, infecting his blood with rot.

The rose in front of him was eye level; he studied the rose with the belief that it was alive and aware of his presence. Marc could see the aroma lifting off the rose. It looked like heat lifting off a fire. He studied the teardrop thorns, all crystalized blue and white. The buzz beneath the rose lifted a thought into Marc's head.

I am nothing. The buzz said, and his stomach turned.

Marc couldn't hold it any longer; he vomited blood over his lips. His stomach emptied all its contents onto the sandy crimson ground. His eyes wet with tears, he dragged his arm across his mouth when the ground turned and churned. Marc watched as the sand absorbed his bloody vomit and the rose straightened in front of him, erecting towards the overcast sky and growing an inch higher.

What is this?

He studied the rose from the petals to the stem and down to the roots. The plaque by his knees read, "I am nothing." His stomach rolled with pain across his abdomen, and Marc lifted himself up with a grunt then blindly started back on his path.

He scuttled across the field, taking inventory of the plaques by each rose. Each one had a statement.

The world is a horrible place.

All old people are prejudicial pieces of garbage.

The young don't know shit.

I'm a loser. A disgusting human being.

I can't.

I can't.

I can't. I'm not good enough.

Those religious freaks need to go.

Everyone can just go fuck themselves.

It's a bad, bad world.

There's always something, isn't there?

Why can't things ever go my way?

I'm sick of it. Sick and tired of everyone.

Marc dropped to his knees again. He looked at his hands, all withered and decayed. Dying, but there is no death here, only suffering. His skin was split across his skull, his lips bleeding from the chapped, swollen cracks. Hurt is more than just an emotion here in the field of black roses. It manifests physically. His skin was deteriorating, rotting, splitting, tearing while listening to the whispers' rage in his brain. Thoughts and statements he'd said to himself a hundred times.

Every destructive thought is a seed planted in this endless field where suffering was as thick as steel. It burned hurt into his veins. Saturated his bones with hurt. Hurt caused by his own thoughts. Thoughts that have betrayed him. Thoughts as noxious as the gas he was breathing infected his cells with poison. Marc reached out and plucked a thorn off the stem, and the rose shook with a scream bellowing from the petals. He saw blood drip down the stem from where he had plucked the teardrop. He closed his hand over it and could see through someone else's eyes how the statement affected the stratosphere.

Marc didn't know the person he saw in his vision. In fact, he was certain the effect took hold at a different time than when the thought existed. He could see the thought spiral across a darkened sky, where it sought a similar emotional state to call home. Then it drifted down, infecting the air around a scene where anger erupted.

A family beaten by the husband. Marc could see his black eyes in his mind's eye.

Tears pricked in Marc's eyes. His jaw quivered, but the sonic boom that shook the field caught his attention. Like thunder that refused to relent. He stood up, dropping the tear, looking over his shoulder to the thick crimson cloud with the yellow eyes staring at him.

The cloud funneled down and touched the field then sat there for a second, spinning and spiraling.

Marc could feel it as if it were spiraling in his gut. His face pinched in pain when the cloud lifted off the ground and back into the sky where the yellow eyes continued to stare at him.

He looked across the field to where the cloud had found ground. Another cloud, black to its core, moved like waves in a hostile ocean. Up, down, left, right, the cloud shifted across the field. Marc craned his head when the thought hit him.

That's no cloud.

The swarm raced towards him.

Funny thing about hell. When you come in through the back door, eventually they will find you.

Marc backed up, watching as the swarm turned the field black. There were so many of them, Marc knew he would never outrun them, but he had to try. To try to get to the river, to the path that would take him to his heart.

He turned around and started running, fumbling in his weakened state. He made it to the river when the bats swarmed around him, nipping at his skin and bones and his face and skull. Screeching and hissing, nipping tiny tender pieces of flesh between their fangs.

They dropped him into the river, and he sank to the bottom like a sack of bricks.

"Truth comes at a haunting price."

The demon from Sleepy Hollow talked to the cave. The light flickered across the dungeon, buzzing vibrations unfolding in Logan's skin. John held the blade in his hand, staring at the writhing woman.

"Innocent blood devoured sets the stage for suffering."

Logan saw the leeches slither beneath her skin and the fog suffocating every orifice. Her veins were cracked like spiderwebs across her flesh, their black color inching across skin that turned a darker shade of gray. Her mouth gaped open as if swallowing more fog as her chest and shoulders heaved off the slab. He could see a different face beneath the woman's skin as if she was engrossed in a thick gelatinous film where the face beneath stretched like a fetus groaning in the womb. Sweat oozed from her pores, coating her face all the way to her wide black eyes.

"My father, I yield to your will. Devour the light from this vessel so that you may rise in this world." He turned to the slab. "By the sword born from your bone, and the steel forged from the fire of your blood, we shall strike down on this vessel and release you… with all the power of damnation, we gift to you… *innocence!*"

Logan felt a shift twist in his gut. His hands shook violently, feeling the change in himself. His thoughts grinding in his skull like a knife twisting in his brain. Saw himself reflected in John's black eyes. Saw his skin split like cracks in a mirror. His skin turned the color of burnt ash, and he could feel new teeth, jagged and sharp, tear through his gums. Tasted blood on the bottom of his mouth, seeping across his tongue like acid.

"Initium Novum."

Logan craned his trembling head to the demon. Felt blood drip off his lips and sweat bead across his face.

The demon's eyes gleamed. "You will bear witness to the dawn of a new age." He gritted his teeth, raising his chin high. "Do you feel it? Infecting the Hollow with the essence from Xibalba. All your deeds... all your desires and thoughts... reduced to one simple impulse... to feed, devouring the light until this world is bathed in eternal darkness."

Logan saw the flames of the eternal fire flickering in the waves of light. His breath huffed hoarsely between his ears. He gazed beyond the light to the cave where the fog was coming from, pouring thick into the dungeon. Now he could see deep inside the cave to a black churning sun, and the horde of devils in waiting. They looked like gargoyles, clawing for entry into the Hollow.

"Agios O Baphomet."

The demon's red glaring eyes beamed at him when the woman began shuddering, screaming wretched wails from her throat.

"The alignment is now in its conclusion."

Mrs. Leiter looked up to the heavens, the same as every Hollow citizen who had come to Patriot's Park. It looked like a sea of people swarmed the park. The city burned around them, from the woods to the Hudson River.

One of them howled to the firmament. The wolf's bay reverberated in her bones like ecstasy. She could feel herself changing. Her insides saturated with evil like a demonic baptism. Lightning speared across the overcast sky with a rumble of thunder that quaked the earth beneath her feet. The bonfire shook, as did the burning blocks of buildings, offices, houses and apartments. Felt like a shell had wrapped around the Hollow, carving the Hollow into its own nefarious world.

The groans started low but rose in intensity like a sonic boom ready to strike. The sea of people shook and shuddered with the ghost demons leading the procession. Their arms rose to the heavens, initiating Baphomet into their hearts as the able-bodied citizens contorted into the demonic form reflective of gargoyles.

"Agios O Baphomet." They chanted to the fire, to the heavens when the firmament rumbled and quaked with thunder.

She looked over to Mabel, Mrs. Leiter's lifelong friend who owned the tearoom, and took her hand. "Baphomet comes," she said. "Our ancestors look down on us with pride on this night."

Mabel raised her head. "Such splendid sights shall he show us."

Wind now, funneling from the clouds and overcast sky that spiraled like a tornado to the ground. Mrs. Leiter looked over the Hollow, seeing how the same was happening everywhere she turned. Cloud tornadoes ripped into the earth that rumbled beneath her feet when those clouds raced like a tidal wave across the Hollow, rippling across the ground and opening caverns in the earth as if some demonic earthquake opened grottoes that led towards hell.

The park split in two with a cavern ten yards wide. People dropped into the cavern with screams bellowing from their throats.

Mrs. Leiter took Hal's hand. "He is coming. Our Lord, Baphomet."

"We shall sing his praises and aid him in his endeavor."

Together, all who surrounded the pentagram and bonfire raised their hands.

"Agios O Baphomet. We bend to your will." They drifted to their knees. "We bow in your presence. Unleash your unholy spirit and bathe in the blood of the innocent."

"Agios O Baphomet."

"Come."

"Come."

"Come."

"Come."

"We honor thee with all the darkness in our hearts."

"Come."

"Come."

"Come."

"Come."

"Agios O Baphomet."

323

He was suffocating with emotion. An elicitation of fear invoked through regret.

After Marc was released into the silver river, he dropped like an anvil. Weighed down by destructive emotions as if every instance of those emotions manifested into an anchor and he couldn't lift his arms they were so heavy. He swallowed the silver water, gagging on it and suffocating, but this was no ordinary river or drowning. There will be no light at the end of the darkness but suffering that manifests in the physical realm. In the body.

Marc scuttled across the riverbed, moved by the thunderous current. He passed through scenes and memories, his lungs burning, his throat on fire from the lack of oxygen. Cold. So cold, freezing cold, shivering in the wake of truth.

He saw moments throughout his lifetime. Times when he held back. Times when the fear conjured from the thoughts from the rose field stayed his hand. Even more, he saw what would have happened. What could have occurred had he overcome his fear and made a different choice. He saw beauty and fulfillment, and his heart shattered into a million pieces. What could have been does not contain the beauty of truth, but the taxing toll of regret that ushers suffering to the heart.

Marc witnessed incidents with different outcomes while he shivered and suffocated with fear, regret and shame. Shame that carved a fissure into his soul. He could feel it from the crown of his head to the base of his spine. Then it burned like fire in his blood. As he drifted. Drifting in the cold and the dark, suffocating, his head on fire from the lack of oxygen, swelling his head like a balloon. The current was so strong, he could do nothing but hold on, racing through memories that clung to his soul like moss.

He saw so many instances. A girl he liked, whom he never had the courage to talk to. Saw a good relationship, someone he could confide in who helped steer him on a rightful path. A scene from childhood with Marc in the car waiting for his mother. He wanted to say something to get her to stop. To say something to his father. Someone. Anyone, but the fear that he would lose her took control of his actions. Saw her with the knife in her hand, slicing down the vein. Then another instance of the same scene but inside out, when he said something to his father and the change that occurred from the conversation. The next floating scene was of his mother as an old woman with grandkids by her side.

Marc screamed in his own mind. The pain from the emotion welled in his chest, cracking open like a spiderweb. His heart leaked thick, painful gushes of blood out of his bones.

A time when he was too afraid to take a chance with one of his books. Too ashamed of himself to take a leap of faith. And then the opposing force. Marc was a success.

Floating. Racing. So fast, he thundered through the river.

Lori was in a hospital bed with Marc by her side. Her eyes open, alive and well as Elena rushes out of the room, but he's there with Lori. He has his head pressed to hers, and they're crying. Crying happy tears. He kisses her and says,

"As you wish."

Then, he kisses her again.

Lori.

Lori.

Lori.

The ultimate betrayal. The demon manipulated him, and all Marc had to do was nothing. Lori would have woken up, and none of this would be happening. The demon took more than his life; he took his future. Ripped it away and doused it in fire. The revelation was the most troubling of all he's witnessed.

Nevertheless, Marc floated across the river. His skin deteriorating, tearing away one piece of flesh at a time, suffocating with his brain on fire. His veins swelled across his neck to his eyes. He crashed against the shore, vomiting an ocean of regret. The memories remained. Regret carved into his soul, listening to the water lap against the shore.

Marc didn't know how long he stayed there, so close to victory yet so far away, when he heard Lori's voice whisper in his ear.

"As you wish."

Followed by the beat of his heart and with Lori's eyes tattooed on his mind he clawed to his knees and gagged the last string of phlegm from his throat, half in and half out of the water, staring at the dark and foreboding forest, glowing a darker shade of crimson with every thick beat of his heart. He could see it now. The heart he was looking for was embedded in the top of a tree fifty yards from the river. He could feel it beating in his chest.

The only problem was the devil who was waiting for him.

"It's about time," the devil said, his voice an echoed grovel. "I've been waiting for you."

Henry walked to the front of the house, where the owl was perched on the porch. It was facing the front door.

"What are you? Some kind of protector of the woods." He looked at the house, feeling the buzz beneath his feet. The pain in his stomach twisted his insides. He was so tired. Exhausted and sickly and beaten and bleeding. He took a moment to gather his wits before stepping onto the porch. The wood creaked under his foot, and he paused. Looked down at his feet and then at the house, staring through the cracked-open front door, but there was nothing but darkness in the house.

He approached cautiously, pushing the door open with the butt of his revolver. The owl hooted, and Henry stopped in his tracks.

"Why do I feel like I'm all alone?"

The owl provided no response. Henry shrugged before he stepped through the door into the thick blackness with the thickening fog. He scanned the ballroom and the kitchen then stepped towards the hall, his breathing shallow between his ears. His gun drawn and ready, although he knew his assailant wielded blades. The pain in his stomach was a constant reminder.

He stepped into the hall, scanning the stairs. There was nothing up there. He swung his weapon into the hall when he glimpsed something on the floor. He scanned his surroundings before stepping closer to the severed body lying in a pool of blood. It was Montgomery; Henry could tell by the clothes and body style. He'd been cut in half. Blood spread from the body down the hall. He could hear it dripping from the floorboards. Sounded like those drops of blood were falling far. He could hear the echo of those drops below.

Henry stood in awe of the carnage.

The strength it would have taken to do such a thing.

He scanned across the body and up to the wall Montgomery had been standing in front of when his assailant attacked him from behind. Henry swung his weapon around. More of a startled response, his heart thumping against his chest. Nothing but fog and darkness greeted him, and he swung back around, seeing that the wall at the end of the hall wasn't a wall but a door that stood ajar. It was difficult to see in the darkness, but Henry was certain the fog was racing out of the door.

He found it. Montgomery found the door and paid the ultimate price. The thought of calling the other officers occurred to him, but as quickly as the thought came, Henry dismissed it. After what happened to him and the fact that Montgomery was sliced apart, Henry knew his other officers had met a similar fate. He didn't even know why he was alive and not on his way to fertilizing daffodils.

Henry approached the door where the fog was drifting from, carefully shuffling across the blood-riddled floor. The fog drifted in front of his face. He could see through the fog. Could see how it manifested Lori in the doorway. Lori, with her black eyes and charred skin. Henry craned his head, his eyes scrunched.

Illusion.

Henry snapped around to the silvery-eyed vampire standing in the fog behind him and shot three times. His bullets hit the vampire's chest and shoulder. He winced from the pain but only for a second. Henry went to shoot again, but the vampire swatted the gun from his hand, and Henry stepped back, slipping on the blood and crashing onto the floor, in between the two halves of Montgomery.

He snapped his stare to the vampire with his mouth gaping open, his incisors prominent in the darkness under the glow of his silvery eyes. Henry scuttled backward, slipping in Montgomery's blood and organs and bile. The vampire raised his blade, ready to strike down on Henry when he heard a hiss and his heart froze.

The vampire heard it too. He snapped around to the owl that swooped out of the fog with a shriek and wrapped its talons around the vampire's eyes. The vampire's hands went up in the air with a scream. The owl's wings flapped and batted around the vampire, who shuffled and screamed in agony when the owl lifted off him then swooped back into the fog.

Carrying the vampire's eyes.

The vampire who was screaming and clawing at his face. Henry saw his blade on the floor and snatched it up, then rose to his feet, watching as the vampire took steps forward while swinging his arm around to catch any would-be assailant trying to take advantage of his blindness. Henry followed him into the living room.

There were caverns where his eyes used to be, with blood dripping from the empty sockets. He started laughing and stopped swinging. Laughing a high-pitched cackle. Henry didn't know if the vampire had accepted his fate, reserved to laugh because there was nothing else he could do or if he was aware of something Henry didn't know.

"Humanitatis finis ut novum principium," he clucked off his tongue.

Henry stepped closer.

"Not this time."

He plunged the knife between the vampire's empty eye sockets. The tip tore out of the back of his head, and the vampire fell backwards when the blade punched out of his forehead. Thick, blackened blood oozed out of his skull.

Henry hunched over, holding his injured stomach. Staring at the dead vampire with the blade wedged in his skull, and thought about the owl, wondering,

What did he do with the eyes?

A scream from below. Henry snapped to the hidden door, paused, then looked back at the vampire and yanked the blade from his head.

Henry didn't waste another second; he raced down into the basement.

325

The basement rattled around little Lori. It seemed as if the house was falling around her. The beast was in the basement with her. She could hear him outside the door of the room where she sought refuge.

Another dark closet, but this one was different. When Lori first darted through the door, she never expected a burial ground. Dead bodies littered the room. How many she wasn't certain. Bodies on top of bodies on top of more bodies and Lori had to navigate across them, her feet finding purchase on a head or arm or shoulder or face while she whined over the monster outside the door.

"Two become one," the devil bellowed from beyond the door.

Lori covered her mouth, silencing the whine trying to escape her throat when a shadow passed beneath the bottom of the door.

"Time to take your medicine."

She could still hear her parents on the floor above.

"You've been a bad girl."

The door shook in its frame, and Lori jumped with a start. Red light beamed through the cracks around the door, flickering inside the closet and casting a dull red glow across the dead. Tears streamed down her face.

The door shook again, and Lori jumped off her stomach, scuttling to the back of the closet. The doorknob rattled the door on its hinges.

"Two become one."

That voice did not come from behind the door.

The dead shifted. Lori looked at the dead bodies moving around her. It looked like they were getting up.

She saw the head of a woman in front of her. "Two become one," she said as her body lifted out of the sea of dead bodies, and Lori froze as the woman climbed to her feet, as did another four dead women.

"Two become one," they said in unison, then snatched Lori by her wrists and ankles, dragging her across the rest of the dead.

Lori was screaming, wiggling and twisting and jerking to set herself free, but with little effect. They tore her clothes off when the door burst open, and Lori belted a scream from the top of her lungs.

The beast was all black and stood on two feet. Looked like a boar with its snout and tusks. The yellow eyes gleamed at Lori.

"Two become one." The declaration rattled off its lips as thick green smoke rushed from its orifices towards Lori.

She could feel it enter her, suffocating and painful, like fire erupting in her veins. Lori could feel this monster taking her over, erasing her essence from existence.

The lights went out, dousing Lori in darkness. She looked around, petrified, her heart thundering in her chest. Everywhere she looked was darkness, like an eternal sea of black. All except for the light that beamed red beneath what she assumed was a door.

She wasn't certain, but she believed she could hear a heart beating beyond the door.

"You are a very interesting conundrum."

The devil who greeted Marc by the river stood over him. Marc was on his knees, still half in the water, his lungs on fire, his head felt like it was about to pop.

The devil looked like chiseled marble stone, slick and white like ivory. His eyes were a darker shade of crimson. Silver horns as thick as Marc's legs wrapped around his head from his forehead. His face was thin and distinguished. His teeth were a row of sharpened incisors, and he was tall. Marc assumed he was close to ten feet tall. His clothes were loose fitted white royal garbs imprinted with golden celestial constellations across the lapels.

The essence of pure evil invaded Marc's mind. He didn't know what to expect. Maybe more of those gargoyle things or some pinhead hell-bent on human flesh and all the suffering he could create from it. Hounds ready to chomp into skin and bone, or giant devils that looked like every picture humanity has ever created for Satan, but this devil was something different.

"What is it you seek?"

The devil's voice echoed with a reverberation inside Marc's skull. Marc was huffing over his lips, still trying to catch his breath as he gazed at his heart in the tree over the devil's shoulder. The devil tilted his head, his eyes scrunched, assessing Marc. He rolled his tongue inside his cheek.

"The heart," he said when a grin spread across his lips. He clucked his tongue with a tsk, tsk, tsk. "What to do?" He craned his head as if he could lift Marc's eyes to him. "You've traveled all the way here just to find your heart?" A rickety laugh escaped his throat, and a smile as wide as the Grand Canyon crept across his mouth. "Came all the way here, just to fail now? I find that simply... outstanding."

He looked over his shoulder at the heart, then trained his eyes on Marc. "Speak," he said. "It irritates me when my questions go unanswered. Is it the heart you seek?"

Marc nodded. "Yes," he said. "I need it to get back to a friend."

The devil looked up, thinking, possibly assessing. "Seems the alignment for Baphomet to pass into your world is merely seconds away." He gestured to Marc. "What will you do now, with so little time to save the friend you speak of?"

Marc struggled to his feet, grunting when his stomach rolled with anguish. The devil never took his eyes off him, staring at Marc like he was some mystery this devil wanted to solve. "Time moves differently here." He grunted when gaseous pain billowed in his gut. He wrapped his arms around his stomach. "The... few seconds you speak of can stretch for millennia in this place."

The devil nodded and cupped his hands in front of his solar plexus. "Indeed." He studied Marc, his blood-red stare devouring

378

him. He gestured behind Marc. "As you have undoubtedly discovered during your journey. Tell me, was the labyrinth merciful? Did it rid you of all your nefarious attachments? Or did it leave you in eternal suffering?"

Marc's eyes narrowed, confused. "Isn't that its purpose? To starve those who suffer?"

The devil grinned. "Everything has a purpose. Even here." He looked up and over the forest. "Although perhaps not any purpose you may be privy to. Yet still my question remains unanswered. Was it merciful?"

Marc's eyes fluttered beneath his eyelids, remembering the instances from the labyrinth. Pain, anguish, and suffering. His skin clawed off the bone. His mind raked with talons. Blood. So much blood. Then he saw the demon standing over him.

"Yes," he said. "It was merciful."

The devil gestured to the field. "And in the field, did you see the toll of your tally and the destructive nature of your thoughts?"

"Yes."

"And the river. Did the river show you the true nature of your folly? Did you bathe in the sea of regret? Did it saturate your cells with shame? Leave you washed up and broken and wishing only for redemption?"

"Yes," Marc huffed over his lips.

A branch snapped in the distance, inside the forest. Marc's attention darted to the sound. Now he could see eyes in the forest, watching them. Waiting for a resolution.

"Pay them no mind," said the devil. "They only wish to indulge in your flesh for the next thousand years. They are intrigued by you. As we all are."

Marc shook his head. "Why?"

To this question, the devil seemed appalled. "How could we not be?" He gestured to the woods and the river and the field and the labyrinth. "Those who come here do not consciously choose to, although their souls beg for redemption, which leads them here to us, the harbingers of fear. The keepers of suffering. Our purpose is to indulge our appetites by devouring all your shame. To douse the light into darkness. You, on the other hand, *chose* to enter, and we find this very… very… *intriguing*." He closed his eyes and inhaled deeply. "It saturates your blood with something we have not tasted in an eternity. Strength of heart and a determined will are not common in this realm. To watch such a presence suffer unimaginable anguish is a gift indeed. You have merely glimpsed the eternity of suffering we are capable of. Those who come here do so under the soul's desire, and in doing so they either reach the point of redemption or embody the very evil they sought to extinguish. You, however…" He took a few steps closer, studying Marc. "Came here with a purpose other than the self."

"Mister, are you the devil?"

To this the devil laughed. "The devil is everywhere. We are born from the dark consciousness with the purpose to devour light and usher suffering into the universe. No, I am not the devil you speak of any more than you are the God of your understanding. We are all the same. A shifting wave between darkness and light. As is the nature of our universe." He paused, devouring Marc with his stare, scanning him from his toes to his head. "So, tell me, human. What will you give for me to allow you to reconvene with your precious heart?"

Marc took a step closer, stepping out of the water when a scream belted across the firmament. Thunder rolled inside the clouds.

"Baphomet can be very unforgiving." Marc turned to the devil, who was staring at the clouds before training his stare on Marc. "What sadistic torment do you believe your friend is witnessing at this very moment?"

Marc gritted his teeth. His stare darted from his heart and then back to the devil.

"The question stands. What will you give?"

"I give you nothing," said Marc, stepping closer to the devil. "Nothing. No love. No heartache and no suffering." He balled his hand into a fist that he shook in front of him. "No impurity. No nasty deeds or lies. No joy and certainly no heart. I offer you nothing. If it takes an eternity, no matter what, I'm getting to that heart."

The demon shot his head back then ran his hand over his mouth to his chin, then balled up his fist and gestured as if he was tossing away Marc's declaration. He shook his head. "My, my, you are very interesting. I do hope there are more like you. What splendid sights we can show you all."

Marc said, "We're wasting time."

To which the devil paused, marveling over the human in front of him. "Indeed." He arched his shoulders, standing tall and stately. "You wish for your heart, correct?"

"That is my desire, yes."

"The heart that beats in this realm like the toll of a bell, signaling the coming of hell on earth?"

"Yes!"

The devil punched a hole through Marc's chest, and his body jumped with a start. Felt the devil's hand squeeze around his heart before yanking it from his chest and holding it in front of Marc's eyes.

The heart was still beating inside the devil's grip.

"This heart?" he asked. Marc looked from his bleeding, beating heart to the devil's eyes. "You're a fool, human. See how it beats in my hand?" His head drifted from left to right. "Why would you have to come all this way to find something you already have?"

Marc slumped to his knees and felt drool rush across his lips. He looked down at the gaping hole in his chest, bleeding and hollow, but he could still feel the steady rhythm, his heart beating like thunder between his ears.

"The master needs hearts, human. And I am the master of this realm."

Marc fell flat on his stomach. His arms at his sides. His legs jerked and spasmed with his face buried in the sand.

He saw the devil's legs and feet walk away.

"One final test for our brave intruder."

The devil walked over to the fire and the kettle pot hanging over it.

"Let us see just how deep your love for this woman runs. Can your heart withstand the fires from Xibalba?" He placed Marc's heart in the kettle pot then turned to Marc. "Even more, will you give in to the essence of defeat or shuffle off your mortal coil to realize the error of your ways?"

Marc felt himself drifting, listening to his heavy breath rage between his ears when his blood turned hot like lava in his veins. The burning heat seared his flesh, cooking his skin with a scream in the back of his throat when the fire tore across his body.

And all Marc could tell himself was to focus. Focus on the beating of his heart.

327

"Raise the blade, John."

Logan turned to the demon.

"On my word, strike down into the heart of this woman."

A sound like crunching, grinding steel erupted in the house. Seemed like the dungeon shifted around them. Logan's stomach shifted with it. Felt like he was moving with it. His stomach twisted, sending pain to his brain. His hands shook violently, his head trembling. He looked at John and saw blood drip from his nose as he raised the blade above the heart of the woman wailing and screeching and writhing across the stone.

Logan felt like his heart was about to implode. The raging, beating organ twisted in his chest as if it were being squeezed. He could feel himself changing as if his cells were being transformed, saturated with the essence of evil. He eyeballed the blade in John's hand.

The thought entered. *The blade. The blade from the cane born in hell has the power. Has all the power to send the demon back to hell.*

He sensed that the thought was losing ground as if some dark cloud devoured his thoughts, wiping them clear with a renewed evil lease, consuming all he'd ever known, loved, and witnessed. Changing him into one of hell's minions.

Logan tried to hold on, fighting off the dark cloud erasing his consciousness. He looked around as if he could run away. Run from the dark cloud but he knew there was no method by which he could escape. The cloud was in his head.

Then, a glimpse of light. A tiny sparkle flickered in the corner of John's eyes. Flickered and then remained. Logan looked at the blade.

"Now, John. Drive the blade into her heart."

John raised the blade high above his head. He looked like he jumped to his toes the blade lifted so high.

"Noooooowwwwww!"

The woman wailed the most insidious scream Logan had ever heard.

John brought the blade down, slashing the woman's wrist restraints with a second chop that released her ankles, then drove the blade into the demon's stomach when the wretched fiends waiting in the cave started shrieking and screeching and clawing to get out.

"Not a fucking chance," said John when the demon took a step back.

Logan felt a sudden release, as if whatever spell he was under had suddenly lifted. He gripped the woman and pulled her off the slab, scuttling her away when the demon's arm whipped around and crashed into John, sending him flying across the dungeon, where he landed with a tumble. The woman was still in the throes of the demon's spell, her screams raging from her throat.

Logan draped her arm over his neck and dragged her across the dungeon, limping across the stone.

Marc was burning; the fire thundered around him. His hair seared off his skull. His skin melted like plastic, oozing across the ground into a black sludge-like tar. His nails disintegrated under the heat. His eyeballs boiled in their sockets, popping with a fizzle across his burning cheeks. He felt the fire engulf his bones, his organs raging with fire, eating and devouring his organs, charring his bones that cracked and turned brittle, allowing the melting skin to bubble across the ground.

His body turned into sludge, thick like a puddle of old motor oil. In the center of all that sludge was a charred and blackened heart.

The demon's voice echoed across the woods to his nonexistent ears. "Foolish human. All this way to find something he had all along. It's easy to give your heart to another, although it is a journey to take it back. Feels like it, but it isn't, really. All one must do is know. Know the heart is yours. Mortal coil," he scoffed. "Toss it off with a shrug and be done with it. Celestial beings we are, not the coil of the living. If you want your heart back, all you must do is declare it as so. There is always time to make things right when you have an eternity."

As you wish!

The thought drifted into consciousness, ripe and invigorating.

Heard a thick wallop. The steady drum of his heart.

Lori.

You did this.

Only you can end it.

Heard a bleep like the bleep from a vitals monitor.

Get up!

Bleep.... Bleep.

Heard Lori's scream.

Get up!

Lori.

Bleep... bleep... bleep.

The sludge slithered into the charred heart.

Lori.

Get up!

Make this right.

Bleep.. bleep.. bleep.. bleep.. bleep..

He could feel his heartbeat. Feel himself as the sludge, slither into the heart as his hands emerged from the organ, charred and black.

Bleep. Bleep. Bleep. Bleep. Bleep.

Legs, arms, shoulders, torso, and his head emerged from the blackened heart, and Marc lifted himself to his feet. Charred and blackened, with his heart thundering in his chest, he opened his eyes to the heart beating in the tree's trunk.

The demon said, "Now that was a neat trick. Absolutely marvelous."

The heart, Marc thought, placing his hand over his chest. *Belongs to me.*

Now he's standing in front of the tree and staring at his blackened heart beating in the trunk. The heart was three feet tall and wide. Beating in unison with the thunder in his chest. Heavy screeches tore across the woods. The devils were clawing their way up the tree to the heart. Marc focused on the tree. The heart hung inside the trunk from a thick branch. He studied it, listening to the devils' rickety goading laughs and growls.

Lori's screech erupted across the woods. At the bottom of the heart, a hole existed like a wide mouth with a clapper hanging in the shape of a talon with a thick round end.

What is this? How do I…

The groans and growls were coming closer. Marc could feel the devils clawing their way to him as if some urgency existed Marc was unaware of.

He focused on the heart and how it beat thick and unrelenting. Looked up at the tree and then back at the heart when the thought hit him.

It's a bell.

He felt heat against his back. Felt the ground quake beneath him.

Marc gripped his heart and went to swing the bell.

Heard the demon say, "Oh, I wouldn't do that."

She hollered the most wretched scream and fell to the ground. Logan dropped to his knees when she groaned something awful. Her eyes all black to the core and her skin fluttering with those leeches slithering beneath her skin.

The leeches.

Logan jumped up and took a torch off the wall, then whipped around when he saw the demon pulling the knife from his stomach. Saw John on the floor, unmoving, bleeding from his head.

Lights flickered across the dungeon like some demonic rave party. The buzz reached a fevered pitch, and the demons in waiting all snarled and jumped at the ether. The woman screamed from the floor. The demon growled, removing the blade with a snarl. John watched it inch out of his bleeding flesh.

Now, a second steel crunch grinded across the basement.

The demon raised the blade in front of his eyes. "I guess I have to do it myself," he muttered.

Logan looked at the torch.

The woman screamed, writhing across the floor.

The demon stepped forward.

Four gunshots echoed across the dungeon, and Logan snapped his head around. Someone he'd never seen before had walked into the dungeon. A gun in one hand and a long blade in the other.

The bullets ripped into the demon's chest and shoulders.

"I don't think so, asshole."

He pulled his trigger to the sound of click, click, click.

330

Marc felt a hand wrap around his ankle the moment he pushed the heart with all his strength. Felt the talons from that hand rip into his flesh when the first gong reverberated across the woods.

It sounded like the entire universe screamed in unison. As if every demon in hell was writhing in pain. From where he was standing, he could see across the landscape the destructive force from the gong. Fires ripped across the forest. Places dropped into an unknown black abyss, with bellowing screams following them. Seas boiled and exploded, and volcanoes erupted, spewing golden lava that rushed across the landscape, bathing the planet in a golden molten sea of lava. He saw large devilish heads the size of moons and planets jump out of the golden lava as if they were in anguish, attempting to break free.

He put his hand over his chest and clamped his eyes shut.

"Lori," he whispered.

"I'm coming."

The demon ground his jaw, then looked down at the bullet holes and brushed them off as if they were nothing before training his eyes on the man with the gun. "You can't kill me, human." He stepped forward with the blade in his hand. "The best you can do is die." He belted out a roar that rattled the dungeon.

The guy dropped his gun and braced himself with his blade when the demon snatched the man's throat in his right hand and sank his knife into his stomach. He was so fast, snatching the man's throat in the blink of an eye. The man wriggled in his grasp like a worm on a hook. His face pinched in pain, but he sank his blade into the demon's shoulder when the woman screamed something awful, and Logan's breath hitched in his chest.

The demon tossed the man to the ground. He hit the floor and tumbled over onto his back. With his eyes closed, bleeding.

Bleeding with the blade still in his stomach.

He saw John stir with a groan, but Logan knew he had little time. He needed to get the leeches out of the woman's body. Logan waved the torch across her skin when the most god-awful screech lifted to his ears. The woman was convulsing, shaking, shuddering across the floor.

He could hear the leeches screeching and yipping and clawing beneath her skin. He could see them too, racing beneath her flesh while she cried and wailed, dragging herself across the ground. Logan could hear the demon pulling the blade from his shoulder.

A third crunching sound of steel tore across the room, and the dungeon shifted. Logan felt it beneath his feet. He turned to the demon. The demon, whose head was on a swivel, looked at Lori and Logan with the torch, then at the cave where his demon minions scratched and clawed. The astral plane, where Logan could hear wind like a funnel race into its thick blackness, when a gong erupted in the dungeon and the demon gripped his heart. Stronger than a hurricane, the wind ripped across the dungeon, whistling into the cave. The stone slab cracked in half and fell to the ground. The walls rattled and rocked. Another gong, louder than the first, and the demon cried out in anguish. Torches died and then reignited. The ceiling cracked above them, raining stones into the dungeon when a thick sheet of stone dropped across the steps where Logan had come in from. So much stone, it blocked the entrance.

"No," said the demon, raising his head to the heavens. "Do not forsake me."

Now the yipping and screeching cut across Logan's eardrums with a wince. He looked down and saw the leeches retreating from the woman's open wounds, screeching as they slithered away, wriggling as if they were in pain.

Logan winced when the gong reverberated in the dungeon, and the demon clutched his heart with a groan. Logan felt the gong in his bones. The devils beyond the cave all cringed and clawed at their ears. Screeching and hollering and clawing to gain entrance. Another gong and the demon dropped to his knees. His shoulders arched back, his hand trembled over his chest, groaning, growling and hollering from the back of his throat.

"My brethren," hollered the demon. "Come to me." His voice reached across the Hollow. "Avenge meeeeee." Pain gripped his face when another gong echoed across the dungeon and he dropped onto his back, writhing in agony.

Lori shuddered violently from head to toe when her chest jumped forward, her chin raised to the heavens. Her mouth gaped open to an inhuman size, and the thickest, blackest smoke tore out of her mouth.

She could feel it leave like a fading nightmare.

She fell back down against the stone, her lungs heaving in thick, unrelenting breaths. The smoke billowed into the dungeon, then slithered into itself, coiled around itself and hissed at Lori before the gong echoed across the walls and the smoke screeched as if it too were in pain. She saw yellow eyes in the smoke as Lori choked and coughed. Her throat and lungs were on fire. She heard screeching and snapped her attention to the sound. There were leeches, slimy, nasty leeches covered in blood on the ground, convulsing, wiggling and yipping and screeching, caught in the gong's echo while slithering across the floor until they imploded. Little green splats of blood coated the floor, their bodies fizzling into smoke.

And suddenly, Lori could think again.

333

John rolled over onto his stomach and looked at Logan. His eyes had returned to normal. The demon struggled, attempting to claw himself to his feet, but he was caught in the echoing anguish from the gong. John could feel it reverberate in his bones, and it felt like ecstasy. Calm. Peaceful. Normal was the best word John could use to describe it. Like breathing fresh air.

The woman's screams dwindled to a whining, huffing cry. Her flesh was coated in sweat. Her eyes snapped open as if she'd just awakened. She started looking around when the wind howled into the cave with one final wallop and then went silent. The buzz was gone. No more lights flickering. The fog was gone too. John looked at what had been the cave that now had a wall with doors that were sealed shut.

He could still hear the devils beyond the wall, clawing for entrance.

Henry snapped his eyes open with a groan. Pain tore through his brain from his gut. The blade was still in his flesh. He could feel the tip poking out of his back, and he rolled over onto his side when the gong echoed in his bones. He pushed himself to his knees when the wind tore across the dungeon, followed by silence.

Henry peeled his eyes open. The dungeon was in shambles. It looked like a tornado had barreled through it. He saw a boy with a torch and another boy climbing to his feet. Saw Lori clawing across the floor, trembling with a huffing, whining cry bellowing in her throat.

He looked over his shoulder at the demon clutching his heart. Henry knew this was his chance to put an end to all this carnage. Another gong reverberated in his bones, and the demon screeched from the sound. The boys went to Lori's aid, and Henry inspected the blade in his stomach. He wrapped his trembling hands around the handle and pulled.

The woman belted out a cry. She was leaning against the wall, sitting on her legs with her arms draped across her head. John struggled to his feet, and the man with the knife in his stomach groaned. The demon was in the shadows. Logan could see him writhing on the floor with grunts and choked-back squeals raging in his throat. Sounded like a bull, breathing gutturally and fierce.

"Is it over?" asked John.

Logan eyeballed the blade in the man's stomach. He looked at the demon, clawing to his knees and clearly in pain. Then to Lori. "Not yet," said Logan. He turned to John and pointed to the demon. "She has to kill him. That's the only way we can be certain the demon is gone."

They were interrupted by what sounded like groaning along with a million footsteps thundering towards the dungeon.

And the single word spoken from the demon's lips. "Lori!"

Marc's blood was on fire. He felt weak, like all his strength had been tapped and wrung out dry. His stomach muscles quaked and rolled in his abdomen, fluttering with a burning in his throat. His skin was on fire too. Sweat oozed out of his pores like boiling water, and smoke lifted off his flesh. Every organ seemed to function minimally. He could hardly breathe, his lungs shriveled and dry. Like sucking air through a straw.

The only thing that felt right was his heart, beating effortlessly in his chest.

After the heart-shaped bell captured his bones in its reverberated thickness, Marc slid into a tunnel of eternal darkness. Then he heard breathing and felt rage in his bones when his stomach, followed by his shoulder rifled pain into his brain as if he'd been stabbed multiple times. He heard voices too. Some he didn't recognize, but one that he did. The man in black was speaking, although his words were muffled to Marc's ears.

Then breathing. Thick, guttural breaths saturated with fear erupted between his ears. Then light, and Marc realized he was opening his eyes.

Opening his eyes in the dungeon when the scene became clear. There were two boys in the dungeon, along with some older gentleman, struggling to get to his feet with a knife wedged in his stomach. Marc could see Lori leaning against a wall and crying. His heart went out to her, and he clawed himself to his knees, his body so heavy it felt like he was lifting a thousand pounds of extra weight.

"Lori," he squeezed over his lips when he heard a pounding. Sounded like a parade of wolves running towards them, and he dropped back down on his ass when the most excruciating pain he'd ever experienced gripped his heart.

Felt like the devil squeezed the organ. Marc flopped onto his back, trembling from head to toe when another gong ripped through his bones, and he wailed in agony.

The man in black was attempting to take control, and Marc fought to keep him subdued. He could feel himself changing. Feel the slithering demon's essence crawling frantically across his skin, biting his innards. His skin cracked and splintered, leaving caverns dripping with blood across his body. Marc felt his skin rip open and then reseal only to open another cavern across his face a second after. His forehead would crack when the horns ripped out only to seal over and then crack again.

Marc understood he was on borrowed time, and once the heart-shaped bell finishes its final toll, he will no longer have control. Doomed to live in limbo for eternity.

He rolled over onto his front and pushed himself to his knees, exhausted and boiling from the heat.

The footsteps were getting louder. Marc could feel them reverberating in his bones. Lori was staring at him, leaning against the wall, petrified and lost. The two boys were talking, but he couldn't hear anything they said. The guy with the sword in his stomach pulled the handle, and wet fresh blood rained out of the wound when the blade slipped out of his flesh. His face pinched in pain as he hobbled over to Marc with the blade in hand.

Marc tried to say something. Anything to stop this guy from what he was about to do, when the man's eyes widened, staring at Marc with his jaw hanging open.

"What are you?" he whispered and raised the blade over his head.

"No!" a hard voice called out.

The thunderous footsteps seemed to be on top of them when Marc saw Lori rise to her feet. The boys helped her. She had a stare plastered across her face that Marc wished he never had to see. The man with the blade stepped back, and Marc reached out his arm.

"Please," Marc said. "We don't have much time."

"They're coming," said Logan. "And coming fast."

John and Logan helped the woman to her feet when another gong shook the dungeon, and the demon over his shoulder cried out in anguish. He looked directly into the woman's eyes. She looked lost and sick. Deathly pale, drawn, and covered in sweat. There was a stare in her eyes that revealed a trauma that reached so deep John wondered if she'd ever be able to recover. She trembled from head to toe and looked like she was well past the point of a nervous breakdown.

He couldn't imagine the things this woman had seen nor the places she's been in the last twenty-four hours.

"You have to do this," John said. "It's the only way we can be certain he's gone."

She looked over at the demon, and her lips quivered.

"Give her the blade," said Logan when they heard screeching amid pounding footsteps. He looked at the man with the blade. "If they get in here, we're all fucked."

She hobbled over to the demon. "Lori." The demon raised his hand as if to welcome her into his embrace.

"Why does it have to be her?" asked the man with the blade.

Logan answered. "Because this is all about her. She has to deny him. Only then will the demon be relinquished from the host."

The man nodded. "But she'll kill him too."

"That is the cost of redemption," John answered. "A gift of eternal peace from an eternity of suffering. A gift only love can provide."

338

A searing pain rumbled across Henry's stomach. He'd taken a knife to both sides of his abdomen and had lost so much blood he thought he was going to pass out, but with every toll of the bell in his bones the pain subsided.

The scene he'd walked into was not one he was expecting, but then again Henry didn't know what to expect other than something supernatural and pure evil. He looked at Lori, and his heart sank into his gut. She kneeled beside Marc and took his hand.

He didn't know who these two boys were, but they seemed to know a lot about what was happening in the Hollow, and Henry had no reason not to believe what they said was accurate. Plus, it made sense to him. In some supernatural, mystic way, it felt right, but the thundering sound inching towards them was concerning, to say the least. Henry had seen the townsfolk, and he was certain they were thundering towards them.

He heard Lori belt out a cry. He couldn't imagine being in her place right now. Henry, of all people, knew how much she cared for Marc. He feared she would never recover from the ordeal.

We've got to give her time.

He surveyed the dungeon and all the carnage and demolition. Other than the doors where he came from, the only other entrance or exit he could see was a staircase that led down into what he assumed was a tunnel, and it was blocked off with debris from when the ceiling collapsed. He dashed over to it, just to be certain there was no way anyone could come through it. Henry looked it over, and it wasn't as if the debris couldn't be moved, but it would take some time to get through. He looked up, aware of the door that led down to the basement from the hallway on the first floor. They'll need to secure it to give Lori time.

"I love you," Lori said, and Henry snapped his attention to her.

He looked at the boys, then saw the blade he was holding and paused. Paused briefly before placing the blade beside the body of the demon. The demon who was writhing on the floor. The demon who kept changing. It was like nothing he'd ever seen. The skin cracked open, then sealed closed, and it looked like there was something inside his flesh, crawling around. Looked like a mouth gaping beneath his skin.

Henry locked eyes with Lori. There were tears in her eyes, falling endlessly. She looked so weak and depleted, a shell of her former self. "I'll give you as much time as I can."

It took her a second, but she nodded and then returned to Marc.

Henry looked at the boys. "Our work here is finished." He shook his head. "They can't get through the tunnel, but we have to seal the door from above." He could hear the footsteps and growls and screeches. "We have to give her enough time."

One of the boys stepped up. "It has to be done before the final toll of the bell."

Henry snapped his attention to Lori. She nodded her agreement while Marc struggled, groaning and stretching in agony. His skin was splitting and tearing faster now.

A gong echoed across the dungeon, and the ground quaked beneath their feet. Thunder from above. "Let's go," ordered Henry. "Now."

339

Marc belted out a long, thunderous and painful wail. He was in agony, doing everything in his power to fight the demon from taking control of his heart. His body. His mind and his life.

His endeavor was successful, but he didn't know how long he could fight him off. The pain was excruciating. His skin splitting and tearing, raining blood from every wound only to heal a moment later. So many gashes, he could feel them on every inch of his body, rolling waves of anguish that thundered across his skin. The worst was when his skull cracked, and the horns ripped out of his bone. His mouth was rancid. It felt like acid was dripping across his teeth, rotting his gums with a foul stench like sulfur that coated his tongue. His throat. He could hardly breathe, sucking air with a hoarse gasp that struggled to release. Lori held his hand. He could barely feel her soft skin against his own. She seemed so far away, like she was at the end of a long tunnel that he could never traverse.

His heart went out to her. All he wanted to do was wrap his arms around her and never let go, although he knew that dream was never meant to manifest. Simply seeing her now, alive, knowing her future was ahead of her, brought a sense of peace to his suffering heart. He tried to picture what her life would become. Saw her grow old and content with life and happy. So very happy and the thought brought a sparkle to his eyes.

Marc could see she was struggling, not wanting to do what everyone knew had to be done. He reached his hand out and touched her cheek. Lori closed her eyes and guffawed, her tears stained across her cheeks in thick soot-covered streaks.

"It's okay," he squeezed through his closing throat when the flesh across his face split and tore open. Marc's chest heaved off the floor, his body tense with pain and agony. The man in black, the demon from Sleepy Hollow, Holer himself was slithering beneath Marc's skin. Marc could feel him gaping and clawing his way into Marc's heart when another gong ripped through the dungeon and Marc felt like every bone in his body snapped and shattered. He gasped out a groan that filtered into a sigh when his hand brushed across the sword beside him.

Marc gripped the handle. "It is time." He pulled the blade over his body and rested with it in his hands over his stomach. "Do you hear that sound?" Lori nodded. "That is the sound of death approaching." He gagged and coughed blood over his lips. His head dropped to the ground with a thud. Marc blinked his eyes, traveling between darkness and the light in the dungeon. He inched the sword towards her. "Ta-ta-take it." He took her hand and squeezed the handle into her palm. She looked at him like a lost puppy. His legs jerked when another wave of ripping, tearing flesh rippled across his body, but his eyes never left Lori. "I'm so tired, Lori. So tired of all the pain."

She closed her eyes, and fresh tears dripped from beneath her eyelids. "I don't know if I can."

"You... have to... *release meeeee*." His stare pleaded with her. "Let me find peace."

"Stay here," Henry told the two boys before he took the stairs to the first floor, carrying a torch.

The sound of thunder rained outside the house, and Henry was certain they had already traversed the woods. He could feel their footsteps in his bones and hear the howls as if they were on top of him. He didn't want to think about what would happen once they gained entrance to the house, and he hoped Lori had the courage to do what was necessary. It was the only way they were going to live through this ordeal.

He approached the top step, where Montgomery's severed body was still lying in a pool of blood, and stepped onto the first floor when he looked to his left into the open room on that side of the house. Outside the window, there were dark red eyes staring at him. Behind those eyes were a horde of more eyes, and people scattered around the property, clawing on all fours towards the house when the red eyes in the window hissed at him before charging through the window.

The house sounded as if it had been hit with a thunderbolt. The foundation shook, as did the walls, and Henry could hear them clawing at the walls and windows. He looked to his left, and the demon-looking thing he was certain was Captain Flannery crawled across the windowsill.

Henry bent down and snatched Montgomery's rifle off the blood-soaked floor, then stepped back to the steps, listening to the wolves enter the house. He saw them clawing down the hall when he slammed the door shut and locked it into place with the iron lock above the door.

The door buckled when the horde barreled into it. Their screeching, yipping and howling echoed across the basement. Henry rushed down the stairs to the two boys.

"We're all going to die if she doesn't do what is necessary." One of the boys said.

"She will." Henry gestured behind them. "Get in the shadows. If they come through the door, I'll start shooting. We need to give her as much time as we can."

Henry snapped his head around when he was certain the door was about to burst open.

Come on Lori. I know it's difficult, but you have to.

341

Lori heard the footsteps. Heard the howling and screeching beyond the debris-covered stairs. She felt it when the house shook and heard them clawing across the floor above.

"Release me," Marc groaned when another wave of agony flitted across his skin. The demon was taking over; she could see him beneath Marc's flesh, angry and vengeful. "Before the final toll. That is all the time we have left."

Her breath huffed over her lips. Staring over Marc, she tightened her grip on the knife. Her lips trembled when she looked into his eyes. They weren't the demon's eyes any longer; they were Marc's baby blues. She kissed him, wanting the kiss to last forever. "I love you, my angel," she whispered and then kissed him again when the toll echoed in her bones. She raised the blade over her head. "I'll always love you."

The echo faded. Marc's body jerked twice, his eyes stiff and staring. "It is finished." His voice, a throaty breath of revelation. A whining cry belted from Lori's lips, and Marc looked at her, holding the sword above her head, her arms and hands shaking. "Please," he said. "Releasssse Meeeee."

Lori could feel the reverberation fade, becoming nonexistent. Heard clawing and howls coming through the debris and heard a door crash open from somewhere in the dungeon.

"Give me peace."

She swallowed her cries. Her voice trembled when she said, "As you wish."

Henry stepped back before the door crashed open, taking aim at the stairs.

"They're coming," said one of the boys, and at that moment the door splintered off its hinges and a horde of people fell across the steps. Henry wasted no time and started shooting at anything that moved, but there were so many of them.

Henry popped off round after round, but still they came, funneling down the stairs in a hurried panic.

"This is it."

They were almost down the steps. "Get down!" Henry screamed.

One of the boys screamed, "Now, Lori!"

They crashed through the debris and clawed their way toward Lori. She heard gunfire, rapid gunfire, and saw Marc's eyes turn red and then back to blue.

"I love you."

Lori brought the blade down with every ounce of strength she had. It ripped through his chest, pierced his heart and came out of his back with a steel chink against the stone.

Marc's shoulders jumped with a painful groan. She saw the demon then, in his eyes, and rippling beneath his flesh. The hate and contempt from the demon's stare faded as if the demon funneled back into hell and Marc's eyes returned. Blood gushed from his chest as his body jerked and spasmed.

She took his hand. "I'm here, Marc." Her voice trembled across her lips. "I'm here." She kissed him once again. "Find peace, my angel." She ran her hand across his forehead. "Find peace."

He was staring at her, his chest and shoulders spasming in intermittent jerks. His mouth gaped open as if he wanted to say something. Lori stroked his cheek and dipped her forehead to his.

"Thank you," he whispered when he gasped out his final breath as a bright white light. She watched it, mesmerized, with her jaw hanging open. Watched the light lift to the ceiling then fade before it disappeared.

"Goodbye," she cried when a thunderous boom rocked the house like an earthquake. The ground shook violently, as if a bomb had gone off. As if all the demons in hell suddenly screamed out in wretched agony. The torches flickered on and off. Lori squeezed Marc's hand tight when a hurricane-force wind blew across the dungeon. Lori could feel it sweeping across the Hollow.

And then... silence.

No more howls or screeches. No more thundering footsteps. Everything seemed vacant, hollowed out and empty.

Lori gripped the sword's handle, twisted it and yanked the blade from his heart, tossing it behind her. She took his head in her lap and stroked his hair and face.

And allowed her tears to fall.

Henry had been shooting, squeezing his trigger one after the other when the hounds of hell surrounded him.

He thought he was about to meet his doom when the ground quaked around him and he scuttled back to the wall where the boys were. Then the wind ripped across the basement, and every person clawing their way to him washed away like smoke in the wind. Once the wind dissipated, they were all alone, as if the wind had erased the scene.

Emptiness. Cold and hollow. He looked around and had to blink a few times to make sure he was seeing straight before he stood up.

"She did it," he whispered, then looked at the boys. "Thank fucking God."

The boys both stood up. They too were looking all around.

"That she did." It was the younger boy, Henry was certain, judging by their looks. "You can feel it too. Peace has come to the Hollow."

"But where did everyone go?" Henry asked because this part was puzzling, although he was slowly taking the stance not to question the supernatural.

The older boy answered. "It's part of the reset." Both Henry and the younger boy looked at him. He shrugged. "What? You can find out anything on the dark web."

They were interrupted by Lori's mourning loss.

Lori held him tight, and more than once she thought about turning the blade on herself. The pain was too much to bear. His body lay limp in her embrace; his head rolled to her chest as she cradled his bleeding and broken body.

She knew he was gone, but still she held him, never wanting to let go.

The only thought that stayed her hand was knowing Marc had found the peace he had been searching for. Her heart shattered every time she thought about what he had endured and what he had done for her. What she gave him in return. How he saved her from death's grip and now he was consigned to memory, a phantom from the past that would always live in her thoughts. In her heart. Wherever she goes, he'll be with her. She owed him that much. Owed him so much more.

She owed him a life filled with ecstasy and a heart unfettered by the past. She kissed his stiff lips one last time and then cradled his head against hers.

"I won't waste this gift, Marc. I promise."

She heard footsteps and held breaths. Henry and those two boys were standing in the dungeon. Dire stares traced across their faces; they looked from Marc to Lori.

She arched her shoulders, still holding Marc's head. "What happens now?"

It was the younger one who answered. "Simple," he said. "We burn it all down."

Part IX

One Year Later

346

Excerpt from *The Demon and Sleepy Hollow* by the Original Knickerbocker Dated 1856.

How to Defeat the Demon

When we arrived at the home of Sam J. Curad, we encountered what can only be described as hell and damnation. We became prisoners to our own fears through hallucinations brought by the changing atmosphere the demon was unleashing across Sleepy Hollow. In time, most of us succumbed to those fears. The result was a loss of self, modifying the mind to a lifetime of hallucinatory suffering that ultimately destroyed the mind and expired the body.

Olga was immune to the charms of the demon, and I was saved by an unsuspecting circumstance.

The young man, Horatio Hardwood, had been a prisoner prior to the preceding ritual. Like much of the townsfolk, Horatio was overtaken by possession, although his possession would not hold, and he arrived to help Olga and I, waking me from my hallucinations before complete subjugation overtook my mind. At the time, I believe the demon thought we were dead when we arrived in his dungeon shortly after the botched pairing left the demon in a state of panic, consigned to a life spent in the body of Sam J. Curad and without dominion over humanity.

His anger had struck at the witch, Selena. We found her on the brink of death, but with her last words she provided Olga with an understanding of what had happened. "Only love can slay the demon," she whispered across her lips before the darkness claimed her soul. I often wonder what has befallen her eternal soul, for what punishment can there be for someone who has betrayed their own species other than to walk in eternal damnation? There have been times recently, during my walks around the Hollow, that I can hear her wretched cackle echo from the western woods.

But her declaration was daunting. The love of Sam J. Curad had already been slain, and the demon would forever walk the earth as Sam J. Curad. This is where Olga's quick wit provided us with a reprieve. She cast the demon out of the host body, cursing his essence into the parallel of the cemetery and manifesting Sam J. Curad back into the body, although we were aware such an occurrence may not hold. The demon attempted to regain control of the host, providing us with little time to act. And act we did.

It was the cane. The demon's cane, which Olga had said was forged in the fires of hell. The cane possesses a supernatural charge, with power far beyond human comprehension. Olga used the cane to strike down at the heart of Sam J. Curad and cast the demon into the cemetery's ether. Once completed, Olga placed a hex on the cane. A hex that ultimately led to her death when the power from the cane ripped through her body. I saw this as a type of backlash, as if the cane itself were alive and sought revenge on its assailant.

But should the demon rise once again, it is the cane that can send him back to the hell he came from. Although only love can put an end to the demon's hold on the Hollow, the cane provides a secondary solution if necessary.

After the demon was slain, I brought the cane to the council. It must be passed from generation to generation with a warning about the demon. However, this is also why I am writing this book. The cane is lost, and I fear the most nefarious mind has obtained its power. I write this book to serve as proof of our dealings with the demon of Sleepy Hollow and to provide a warning to those who read it. The cane must be found. I have commissioned multiple organizations to carry out this very task, although to this date no such luck has transpired. Although I know this. Should the demon return, the cane is his weakness and the crux of your salvation.

Only love can slay the demon and end his tirade over humanity, but the cane's blade can doom him back into the ether until such a time that love can have its day.

347

Lori was sitting on a bench, looking over the Hudson River and the Tappan Zee Bridge. The air carried the first hint of spring on its heels, cool yet refreshing across her skin. A reminder that the winter of her life had ended.

John and Logan sat on the bench across from Lori, talking and catching up. They hadn't seen each other in over six months. Lori listened to their conversation.

"It was her, wasn't it?" After the events transpired last year, all parties agreed not to talk about it in detail until this fateful day arrived. They thought it was best so their story wouldn't become crossed with the truth, knowing time was on their side and one day they'll be able to talk freely. "Your mother. She was with us that night. I remember seeing her standing over your shoulder, but then she wasn't. Where did she go?"

John placed his hand over his heart. "In here. It was my mother who released Lori and stabbed the demon. I woke up on the ground after she did it."

Logan nodded. Then silence as they all soaked in what John had said. Lori wondered who would ask the next question, because that's what this meeting was about-a processing session so they could put the past to rest, answering each other's questions and supporting future decisions before parting ways.

It was John who asked the next question. "What I want to know is how you did it? How did you know all that information, and how did you find the dungeon? How did you know what to do?"

"The dark web," he said. "I found the book on the dark web. Or at least a copy of a few chapters, including how to kill it. When the priest and Detective Carver had the book, I knew then it was true. That's also where I discovered all the information about that guy Wren. That's what I was trying to tell you that day at school before… well, before that night. How the information got on the dark web I have no idea, but it was, so I used it to our benefit."

More head nods followed, along with more silence and processing. Lori was grateful to see the boys together. Grateful they were receiving answers to questions they'd been asking for the past year.

John said, "I saw my mother standing over my shoulder when I looked in your eyes." He turned to Logan. "It was the reason I allowed her in. I knew she was safe." He paused, turning his gaze to the river. "If I didn't see her, I don't believe I would have allowed her in." He turned back to Logan. "You saved us, Logan. You saved us all."

Logan thought about that for a moment before shaking his head. "The only reason I was there was because I had the book. The only reason I had the book was because Detective Carver fought his way back to the church." He paused. "With that logic, it was Detective Carver and Father McKenzie who saved us. All of us."

429

Quiet fell over them, the three of them contemplating Logan's statement.

"Yeah," said John. "I like that. Thank you, Detective Carver and Father McKenzie."

They heard a car door close with a thud that drew their attention.

"He's here," John said, jumping off the bench like he was sitting on a spring.

Lori looked over to see Henry walking towards them. The boys went to greet him. He'd become a hero in their eyes, and Lori was grateful for his presence. The boys needed an exemplary role model; someone they could look up to. They greeted him with high fives and half hugs as Lori got up from the bench and joined them. Henry made the trek all the way from the Hamptons to see them off.

"Are there any updates?" Lori asked after embracing Henry with a hug.

"I believe we are clear to move forward." Henry looked around the Hollow. "I don't know what it is, but it's like a reset or something. A new timeline is the best way I can explain it. I mean... look at it." He gestured toward the town. "No fires, no destruction and no one remembers a thing other than us. It's like their memory of the ordeal was completely wiped out and replaced with a completely rational story. Even some of the store's names have changed, like the Hollow jumped on a new timeline." He paused to collect himself. "Marc and that guy Wren took the fall for the murders, including killing Detective Carver, Elena, and John's grandfather. They were able to identify the victims in the basement through dental records after the fire consumed the bodies."

"What will happen to the property?" Logan asked, his eyes squinted from the sun.

"It'll stay in probate for a long time." Henry looked at Lori. "Since Marc had no next of kin, no one's coming to claim it, so there it'll stay."

"What happens if someone buys it?" John, he seemed nervous asking the question.

Henry cocked his head. "Not sure, but I'll monitor it. After we set the house on fire, it burned to the ground and covered up the basement, and since the demon is gone, I'd say that's fair game that the power in the ground has also subsided. I went there before I came here. There's grass and flowers growing all around it, where before the property was dead. I think that's a good sign that the evil is gone."

Lori remembered that night, watching the flames devour the mansion, and all who were in it. After the demon was slain, they all agreed to light the fire. It seemed like the best decision.

Henry continued. "I've got many people I trust looking after the property, and if there is a buyer, we'll know immediately, but I believe we are in the clear."

"I'll keep an eye on it too," said Logan. "I'll be the only one here, so I'll keep tabs on it."

Lori nodded, although in her stomach she felt a slight twist in her gut. She looked at the boys. "Let me and Henry talk a minute." She gestured to the park and to John. "Go and catch up before we leave."

She waited until they were out of earshot before engaging with Henry.

"Are you sure you want to do that?" Henry gestured to John. "Raising a child is a big responsibility."

Over the last year, Lori petitioned the court system to become John's guardian. The boy had no one. No family and no friends and she refused to allow him to become a ward of the foster care system. Not after what he endured.

Lori laughed at Henry's statement. "It's the right thing to do. The boy has no one, and after what we all endured, I feel I owe it to his mother."

Henry paused, looking over at the boys before turning to Lori. "So, California?"

Lori nodded. "We're leaving today. I figured we both need a change. California seems like the right place to start fresh."

"Understood." His stare drifted to Lori's wrist and then back to her eyes. "Is that something you want to take with you?" He was referring to the green rope around her wrist.

Lori pulled her wrist to her stomach, holding it in her other hand as if the mere mention of it could tear it away from her. "It was his," she said. "Somehow, with it on, I feel connected to him.

That's all I have to remember him by." She rolled the rope between her fingers. "That and his book."

Now they both paused and looked at the boys who were laughing and running in the park in a game of tag. Innocent, like children should be, when Henry turned to her.

His stare inquisitive. "What will you do with the notebook?"

"What'd you mean?"

"Well, it's a story, isn't it? And it's my belief that an unfinished story is like a life caught in limbo."

"Are you saying I should finish the story?"

Henry cocked his head with a click of his tongue. "Exactly. Finish his masterpiece for him. You already know how it ends, so you're the best person to do it. Plus, all fiction reveals the truth that hides in plain sight. I believe the story is better off finished and published as an urgent message to the world that we are being stalked by an outside enemy. Maybe then humanity will come together."

"I think you're giving too much credence to the power of a story."

Henry laughed. "Not really. Even a book can change the world."

348

The state psychiatric ward was buzzing with the crazies. Something got into them, some demon, and they were all howling and crying and screeching and clawing at their skin.

It turned the hospital into a literal nut house. Behavioral health technicians scurried frantically around the ward. They already used four-point restraints on four patients and there were no more on the ward. Instead, they insisted on securing every patient while the nurse jabbed their arms with Thorazine. It seemed like something out of a horror novel.

Some patients ran into the walls. Some lashed out, attempting to bloody the poor technicians. Every single one of the sixty patients had lost their minds.

All but Jerry Hardwood.

He was placed in confinement a few days ago after he was found clawing at his skin and tearing off little tendrils of bloodied flesh, then draping them across the windowsill. Now he was in a straitjacket, sitting in the corner of the padded party room, and screaming at the top of his lungs.

"The master waits. The master needs hearts. Hearts in hell." He kept smacking the back of his head against the padded wall in between screaming fits while listening to the commotion outside his room. "The master waits. He is coming to make me a god by his side."

Jerry opened and closed his mouth, snapping his teeth while clenching his jaw, when the door opened and his heart calmed. He could feel her presence even before she opened the door.

The nurse, Jessica, had transferred to the state psychiatric ward a year ago. Jerry immediately took to her and, truth be told, Jerry was a little smitten with the young nurse. She was easy on the eyes, yes, that much was true, but when he discovered her lineage ran all the way back to the Hollow, Jerry knew she was someone he could trust.

She'd even shared some of her family pictures from old Sleepy Hollow. Her great-great grandmother, Selena looked exactly like Jessica. The resemblance was uncanny and undeniable, although the prominent veins in Jessica's cheeks were different from what Jerry expected.

"Have I done well?" Jerry fidgeted beneath his jacket. A guffaw escaped his throat.

"Very well indeed," she responded, holding a syringe in her hand. "But I have to sedate you, Jerry. The master requires it. We must maintain our appearance. The grand façade shall one day fall, and our truth will be revealed."

"Initium Novum," Jerry clucked off his tongue.

To which Jessica repeated, "Initium Novum." She paused, and Jerry took a good long look at the syringe. She gestured toward the center of the room. "Come. Take the necessary position."

Jerry clambered to his knees, shuffling to the center of the room where he dropped his forehead to the floor and crossed his ankles. "As you wish," he said, bracing himself for the needle.

Jessica took a knee beside him. She gazed at the syringe and tapped it twice.

"When will he return?" asked Jerry with his face planted in the floor.

"When he has garnered his strength. There are many methods for him to return. The Hollow was just the first, but he has a plan. A most vile plan. Although it'll take a bit of time, the plan has already been set, and the first phase towards his return is ongoing."

"Truly wonderful to hear," said Jerry. "How does he plan to do it?"

Jessica inched the needle into Jerry's neck. A spot of blood dripped across his neck to the floor.

And Jessica said, "Have you ever heard… of the internet?"

349

Logan opened his bedroom window. His room was stuffy, suffocating, and he required fresh air.

He'd been mostly by himself over the last six months, recounting the events that transpired in Sleepy Hollow and in constant amazement over the reset that had taken place with the Hollow's citizens.

No one remembered anything about what had happened, as if the events had taken place in another time or dimension, leaving no trace of its existence. Sure, everyone knew that the murders had taken place, and a host of police officers lost their lives taking down the murdering duo of Marc Saduj and escaped mental patient and serial killer, Wren Field, but that's where everyone's memory seemed to take a detour. He didn't know whether it was a good thing or a bad thing.

Sure, having no memory of the carnage that took place across the Hollow and how they were seconds away from full possession was probably a good thing, but then again, how could they recognize a similar threat with no recollection of the threat? He believed it would be better to have the knowledge than not.

Which left a new conundrum for the young Logan Reeves. He was alone, walking the earth with knowledge he could never share. Although he was happy that John went to live with Lori, he still wished he could have a friend, someone to hash the past over with. Someone he could trust.

Now, sitting in his room, he felt something he had never felt before: profound loneliness. He thought about his mother, wishing she were with him. Wishing she had come to him like John's mother did for him.

He couldn't help the tears that fell silently, holding his head in his hands with the first sign of spring outside his window. His tears were interrupted by a knock on his front door that was followed by the doorbell echoing through the house.

Logan wiped his eyes and went to answer the door, but the moment he stepped onto the first floor he froze as if he'd stepped into a batch of paralyzing energy that suffocated the air from his lungs. His skin crawled with gooseflesh.

The presence was distinctly familiar. He remembered it outside the church and in the underground tunnels.

The knock came again, followed by the doorbell.

Logan surveyed his house, the kitchen and the backyard outside the kitchen window, but his focus was internal, focusing on his heart and his stomach and the sensation that confirmed he was not alone. Something was in the house with him.

Another knock. Logan gave up his inquiry then stepped from the living room to the front door, thinking of a white lotus when he saw the police cruiser parked in his driveway.

There was an officer at his front door.

Logan could never remember what happened next from his own perspective. It was as if he were watching himself from above. Watching and listening as the cop outside his door told him his father had been found in the trunk of a car off the Taconic Parkway, riddled with bullet holes and clearly tortured.

And just like that, Logan's life took a very unexpected turn.

350

Henry gathered his luggage and walked through his front door. He didn't know where he was going, but he didn't care either.

He required a change. Big change and honestly, he didn't care if he ever saw New York again. It held too many memories.

He locked the front door and took one last look at his house. He'd lived there for the past ten years, and it held a special place for him, but he knew it also held memories he was trying to move forward from.

Henry nodded. "Yeah, let's go." He took a deep breath before turning around and wheeling his luggage to the trunk. "Just drive," he told himself, opening the trunk and dropping his luggage in.

He had no plan or destination. *Just drive* had become his mantra, waiting to see where the road took him. He put in for a six-month leave of absence, citing medical concerns. His absence was granted without a hitch, and his boss had personally thanked him for his time, hoping he would return after his medical concerns were taken care of, but Henry didn't know about that. Over the last year, his passion for the FBI has dwindled.

He was hoping his time off would put things into perspective and if it did, he was confident that his future would not include a career with the FBI. Henry closed the trunk then went to the driver's side door and keyed it open, sitting down quickly, and startled by the bag sitting on the passenger seat along with the red cane.

The demon's red cane. The one Lori had taken with her on that fateful night. He had an immediate aversion to it. The energy beaming from it was both nefarious and addictive. He didn't realize he hadn't breathed since he sat down until his lungs struggled for air and he gasped out his breath.

Henry whipped his head around, looking, scanning the street and his property. Searching to see if he was being watched. When he believed the coast was clear, he took the navy-blue duffel bag and zipped it open.

It was filled with cash, with a folded piece of paper on top. A lot of cash and Henry closed it quickly and took another look around, his breathing shallow and hoarse. He looked back inside the duffel bag and took out the note.

It was from Lori.

Dearest Henry. A Francon always pays their debts. This will probably be the best money I've ever spent. You are worth every penny. Thank you for saving our lives. As you can see, I'm leaving the cane with you. I feel it is safest with you, for you seem to be immune to its power. Your good nature and kind heart are exactly the protection the world needs, and the cane is best kept with you. I hope one day you will use your talents for something larger and more purposeful than the FBI. If you're ever in need of help, or just an old friend to talk to, I am always here for you. And if you ever get an itch to come to California, we will welcome you with open arms. Godspeed, Lori Francon.

Henry stared at the note for longer than was necessary. Stared at the money too, and the cane.

"What to do?" Henry whispered. He put the note back in the bag, zipped it up and dropped it on the passenger seat, then started the car.

California?... Maybe.

He backed out of the driveway and put the car in drive, gazing through the windshield at the long, winding road ahead.

Let's just see where the road takes us.

Lori kneeled in the grass among the wildflowers-the white trilliums-that had grown over the property in the western woods. Her wrist with the green rope rested inside her left hand on her lap. She twirled the rope while thinking.

John stood in the distance, just outside the perimeter, refusing to go any further, but Lori felt she had to.

Had to say goodbye to Marc one final time. After all, his final resting place existed beneath her knees.

Henry was right about one thing: the flowers blooming across the property brought a sense of peace, as if the evil had been vanquished from the Hollow. Vanquished from the western woods. But Lori knew differently. Evil always hides in plain sight, under the cover of beauty and with the promise of love and devotion.

She could feel it beneath the earth, but so far down and so distant it felt like a faded rumble, but still it was there. Lori could feel it pulling on her stomach, and she was grateful. Grateful that they set fire to the house, because what she couldn't feel was Marc. At least not in the ground and not part of the evil existing beneath the earth.

She could feel him in her heart and in the small intervals where clarity and peace existed in the folds of a moment of silence. A conscious memory filled with nostalgia. She could feel him on the heels of spring, carrying the dawn of a new day on his shoulders to offer her a gift for the future. Lori had also gone to the cemetery to pay her respects to Marc's parents, and she felt the same with them, as if they had passed on to a better realm than what they had been exposed to.

"Are you ready?" John called from the woods.

"Just a second," Lori hollered over her shoulder before she gazed over the property and the woods. She didn't know what to say. She had come to speak to Marc, but now that she was here, everything felt different.

Marc was no longer here, which made her question why she had come. "Maybe I just wanted to see it for myself," she whispered. "Maybe I just had to say goodbye, not to Marc, but to the Hollow. To the past. Come to terms with it and take what is necessary and leave the rest." She looked down at her wrist. The green rope was prominent around her wrist. She looked up at the western woods. "No matter what, you're always with me. Thank you…" Her lips trembled, and her jaw quivered with the first tear that fell silently. "Thank you for going through hell to save me. Twice, no doubt." She wiped a tear from her cheek. "Thank you for my life."

She bowed with her fingertips pressed to her forehead, then kissed her fingers and blew the kiss across the landscape to the Hollow. To Marc, when she stood up and walked across the field to John.

"Is it over?" he asked, staring at the clearing before turning to Lori. "Is it really over?"

Lori looked back across the clearing and felt the pull in her stomach. "Only time will tell." She turned to John. "We must always be diligent and keep our wits in check."

John nodded, biting his lip and staring into the clearing. "I have a feeling this is far from over."

They stood in silence for a long while before making the trek back to the car. They drove in silence for even longer. It wasn't until they passed through the Midwest that they felt the energetic hold of the Hollow release from their shoulders.

Marc's blue notebook was in the back seat next to his old typewriter.

Waiting for Lori to finish the story.

352

Excerpt from *The Demon and Sleepy Hollow* by the Original Knickerbocker Dated 1856.

The Great Reset

What transpired after the demon was slain was not to be expected. Young Horatio and I had travelled back to town in the early morning hours where sleep had come willingly and, dare I say, instinctively, but upon our awakening the town had undergone what I refer to now as a reset.

The two of us were enthralled by the discovery that every citizen in Sleepy Hollow had no recollection of the demon and Sam J. Curad was identified as the murderer with no recollection of the demon nor the magical powers that existed in Sleepy Hollow during that time or the fact that they had turned into raving loons, ghosts, specters, and wolves. It was as if their memory of the ordeal had been wiped clean-or reconfigured as I refer to it-where the supernatural aspects of our story were trimmed away, allowing logical minds to conjure a rational explanation that now has become the truth to those who live in Sleepy Hollow. But the truth has an uncanny way to hide the most nefarious parts of itself, spiraling facts into the three-dimensional materialization of logic and the point of view that if you can see it, touch it, and taste it, it is real while scoffing at any twist into the supernatural as if humanity knew everything about the universe.

The most uncanny example of the reset that I can provide, other than the inability for the citizens to recollect the demon, was the change in names and titles. A good friend of mine, Lindsey Von Brom, had maintained an export company for many years before the demon came to Sleepy Hollow, and in the years before the event, I had always referred to his store as Von Brom Exports. However, after the event, I noticed the name had been changed to Von Brom and Sons Exports.

Confused, I asked him when he had changed the name, to which my most trusted friend looked at me with equal confusion, claiming the name had always been the same and that no change had been made. I found this change intriguing.

Since that time, I have indulged myself in research, attempting to understand this very existence in the change in time, events, and its unrelenting toll it has taken on the minds of those in Sleepy Hollow. However, to this day I could not find anything that can account for this strange turn of events.

I will leave that to you, dear reader. Perhaps the time I live in has not provided the answer, although in the future we may have a better understanding of time.

Both Horatio and I are aware of this, and it is another reason I am writing this book. It is my contribution to the future, although Horatio chose a different path, taking up arms to oversee the property of Sam J. Curad from this day forward. He will also provide counsel to his offspring with the single purpose to be prepared should the demon rise once again.

I can only hope that those in the future will be brave enough to confront the demon and the hell he brings with him. I can only pray that humanity will not lose itself to the heart of the evil that exists in the universe. Evil manipulates the divide within humanity. It seeks our morals with the intention to destroy all we hold dear. Do not compromise your values. Do not devolve the human heart to simple pleasures nor take up arms against each other. For when we do evil shall have its day.

353

October 2002

The sun dipped below the horizon, bathing the western woods in a dark twilight when the research team for NewDay Wireless finally arrived at their destination. They weren't expecting there would be no road and had to take the half-mile trek to the clearing in the western woods.

"This is it?" Seth Greenwood nodded while looking over the property. "It's perfect." He looked up to the darkening sky and turned to his supervisor, Mathew Cox, whose attention was on the portable signal meter in his hands. Their third member, Daniel Wilcox, stood behind them, keeping his trap shut. He was new to the team and came along to help with any equipment they needed.

They had been assessing several areas today, and the one in Sleepy Hollow was the last on their list. They wished to be done with their tests and be gone before getting lost in the woods on their way back to the work van.

"How strong is the signal?" Seth was pressing Mathew, wanting to get away from the clearing. He didn't feel right the moment they stepped onto the property, although he had to admit that the clearing was perfect for their needs. As long as the signal was strong, they could chalk the day up to being a success. He didn't care about the strange feeling sitting in his gut. After today, he'll never have to set foot in the western woods again. "Matt?"

Matt's stare was fixed on his machine when a small smile curled in the corner of his mouth, and he cocked his eyebrows. "Better than expected. The signal here is stronger than I've seen anywhere else. Ever." He gazed over the clearing, then to the woods and up to the sky where constellations and stars gleamed in the twilight as if winking to tell him he was spot on right. The signal was very strong in the Hollow.

Seth celebrated with a quick punch of his fist. "Perfect," he said. "Can we go home now?" He looked up at the darkening sky. "I'd like to get out of here." He looked over the clearing. "This place gives me the creeps."

Matt powered down his machine. "Our work is done. Let's go."

"Good. I'm starving. Let's get a slice of pizza." Seth walked back into the woods. Matt and Daniel waited a second longer while Matt placed the reader into its case by his feet and Daniel gazed over the clearing.

"How long does it take?" asked Daniel.

"How long does what take? Setting up the tower?"

"Correct."

Matt looked up at Daniel. "About a year." He gripped the case and stood up, noticing Daniel's stare. He looked concerned. "What is it?"

Daniel cocked his head. "All these internet and cell phone towers. Do you think people will be upset about having one in their backyard? It's kind of an eyesore."

Matt shrugged. "They'll get used to it like everything else. Plus, the signal is so strong here. If we don't put up a tower someone else definitely will." He looked across the Hollow to the Hudson. "With such a powerful signal, we can beam internet across a sizeable area." And with that, he smiled and walked into the woods, leaving Daniel alone.

Daniel took a deep breath when he noticed the owl perched on a tree across the clearing.

It looked like it was watching him.

Watching and waiting.

The Sleepy Hollow Incident represents Book Three in the Dominion of Shadows Series of standalone although interconnected stories. If you enjoyed The Sleepy Hollow Incident, indulge your desires with a little more from PD Alleva.

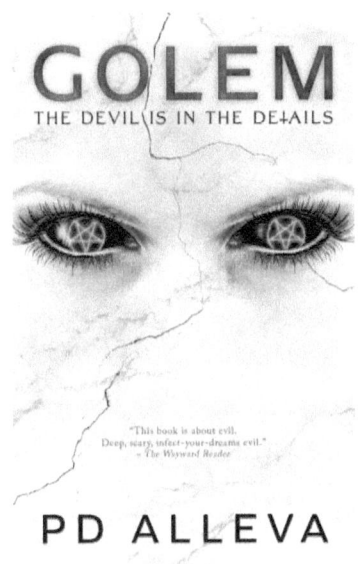

Golem: Book One in the Dominion of Shadows Series

A naïve detective confronts a demonic presence incarnated into a statue created by a high-society socialite and patient at Bellevue's psychiatric hospital.

Grab your copy of *Golem* today at www.pdalleva.com!

Jigglyspot and the Zero Intellect: Book Two in the Dominion of Shadows series.

Wanna go for a ride? Discover Jigglyspot and his cast of clowns, killers, demons, and wretched fiends in a novel like you've never experienced. Horror, mayhem, thrills, chills, fantasy, and spoils are waiting for your reading eyes with an escape into the underworld of mind control and human slavery.

Purchase Jigglyspot and other fine books of horror, scifi, and psychological thrillers from Chamber Door Publishing.

Your Free Book Is Waiting!

PD's Alternative Fiction publishes weekly serialized fiction stories in the horror, scifi, and psychological thriller genres. Subscribe at www.pdalleva.com and receive a FREE digital copy of PD's cosmic horror novella, "Election Retrograde."

About the Author

PD writes books. Horror, scifi, psychological thrillers, fantasy, and sometimes a literary gem. Good ones, crazy ones, fun books, entertaining books, terrifying books that are absolutely insane, and books with depth and thrills that rip out the heart of humanity then tosses it on a slab to be feasted on. Yeah, that's what he does, he writes books. Any questions?

To learn more or join PD's newsletter visit www.pdalleva.com.

www.ingramcontent.com/pod-product-compliance
Lightning Source LLC
Chambersburg PA
CBHW020649110726
47901CB00001B/108

* 9 7 9 8 9 9 3 8 0 3 9 6 8 *